F COP
Copling, Steve.
The shooting season
Colleyville PL

WITHDRAWN

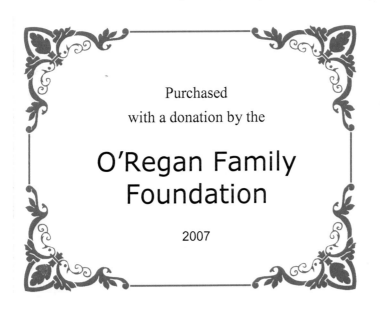

Purchased
with a donation by the

O'Regan Family Foundation

2007

D1071172

The Shooting Season

The Shooting Season

Steve Copling

Five Star • Waterville, Maine

WITHDRAWN

Colleyville Public Library
110 Main Street
Colleyville, TX 76034

Copyright © 2005 by Steve Copling

All rights reserved.

This novel is a work of fiction. Names, characters, places and incidents are either the product of the author's imagination, or, if real, used fictitiously.

No part of this book may be reproduced or transmitted in any form or by any electronic or mechanical means, including photocopying, recording or by any information storage and retrieval system, without the express written permission of the publisher, except where permitted by law.

First Edition
First Printing: October 2005

Published in 2005 in conjunction with Tekno Books and Ed Gorman.

Set in 11 pt. Plantin by Liana M. Walker.

Printed in the United States on permanent paper.

Library of Congress Cataloging-in-Publication Data

Copling, Steve.
    The shooting season / by Steve Copling.—1st ed.
        p. cm.
    ISBN 1-59414-324-2 (hc : alk. paper)
    1. Police—Texas—Plano—Fiction. 2. Serial murders—
Fiction. 3. Plano (Tex.)—Fiction. 4. Snipers—Fiction.
I. Title.
PS3603.O655S56 2005
    813′.6—dc22   2005015989

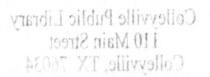

The Shooting Season

To do evil a human being must first of all believe that what he is doing is good.

—Aleksandr Solzhenitsyn

ACKNOWLEDGEMENTS

There are many I want to thank for making this book a reality. First and foremost is my wife, Sonora, whose patience with me while I pursued this dream has been gracious and understanding. My writer's group, *The Every Other Tuesday Group*, Deborah Crombis, Dale Denton, Jim Evans, John Hardie, Viqui Litman, and Gigi Norwood. Thanks so much to John Helfers of Tekno Books, and to Hugh Abramson, the editor who exhibited such enthusiasm, and to the eagle-eye line editors, Lee Howard and Fran Fredricks, who caught all of my mistakes and inconsistencies. I also want to thank my son, Justin, my webmaster, who keeps www.stevecopling.com up and running. My other two sons, Jason and Joel, have always supported me, especially Jason. He and his wife, Payal, both love books and are two of my biggest supporters. And while Sage is too young to have had an impact on my writing, he might just be the most beautiful grandson in the entire state of Texas.

CHAPTER ONE

With a sense of dread working its way from the very depths of his gut, Detective Greg Rush stood just inside the crime scene tape and observed the building mass of humanity.

The crowd of onlookers stood quietly, reverently, as though each of them knew that either Rush or his partner had just been sentenced to death.

And one of them probably had. Although not yet confirmed, there was no doubt in Rush's mind that the body lying forty yards away was that of a doctor. Then, over the next month, a lawyer would be gunned down, followed by a judge, and finally one of the homicide detectives assigned to investigate the first three shootings. Which meant him, probably. Or Rick Chinbroski, who stood beside him, face tight with stress, sweat running in rivulets out of his flattop.

If this was a Billy Ray Jackson shooting.

Billy Ray Jackson. Evil, intelligent enough to elude the entirety of American law enforcement for nearly three years, and without human compassion. Here, Plano, Texas, a Dallas suburb and developer's dreamland, a virtual paradise of shopping malls and suburban excess. Headquarters for a half-dozen world-renowned corporations on the far west side of Interstate 75, and horse farms, rolling prairies, and thick woods covering large chunks of unincorporated land on the far east. The hospital sat on the west side of the interstate, in what was probably the exact east/west center of the city. It had been the primary medical center for the city of 240,000 for close to thirty years, and Rush didn't relish the potential for chaos.

He closed his eyes briefly and shook off his increasing discomfort.

The growing crowd occupied most of the empty parking spaces at the apartment complex across the street and had begun to clog all six lanes of Coit Road, both north and south. People seemed to be rising out of the very cracks in the sidewalk, so swiftly were they gathering against the crime scene tape strung across the physicians' parking lot.

More Dallas area media were arriving every second and the patrol guys were having a tough time keeping them far enough away from what was already a national story.

"Think it's him?" Chinbroski asked Rush. "Jackson?"

Rush tried to swallow the knot in his throat. The date was right. The location. "Let's hope not."

The crowd was silent. Eyes staring. An old woman on crutches, head down, eyes closed, appeared to be in silent prayer.

Chinbroski shifted his large frame, his shoulders stretching the seams of his sports jacket. Chinbroski often reminded Rush of an ancient Viking, minus the beard and flowing locks. His power-lifting frame had been honed by decades of sweat in the gym. So unlike Rush, who more resembled the ninety-eight-pound weakling pictured in so many of the before-and-after bodybuilding photos during the sixties.

But standing here outside the hospital, with the prospect of a Billy Ray Jackson shooting awaiting investigation,

Chinbroski appeared weakened somehow, deflated. "Ain't been here five minutes and I already don't like the looks of this," Chinbroski said. "Everything's pointing to it." His voice fluttered just a little and Rush looked at him. "You know what it means if it is?"

Rush knew. Only a man living in a cave wouldn't. He started to answer when Chinbroski cut him off.

"Means either me or you is in for a shit load of trouble." Chinbroski looked away and rubbed his forehead. Then looked back. He started to say something else but didn't.

At least a dozen police cars had sealed the scene. Fire engines and ambulances ringed the outer edge of the hospital, although they were moving out now, having learned that the only shooting victim was long past saving. Rush pulled a small notepad from his pocket and turned toward the body.

Chinbroski grabbed his arm and whispered. "Listen, you know me. I ain't one to back out of—"

Rush held up a hand, cutting him off. "You're worried about your wedding in three weeks. You think I'd let you take this on?"

Chinbroski dropped his head. "Feel like a coward. Like I'm backing out."

"Don't worry about it." Rush glanced at the crowd again, still staring, several meeting his gaze.

Unnerving.

The body was sprawled across the pavement near the outer edge of the physicians' parking area. With the heat waves rising from the pavement, Rush knew the sun was about to play havoc with the crime scene. The ninety-two-degree temperature, climbing hourly, was expected to top out at 104.

Two nurses stood nearby, huddled together, holding hands, mascara smeared across their cheeks. A patrolman near the body looked ill. A pad and pen dangled in his limp grip. The officer looked like Rush was beginning to feel.

Slapping Chinbroski on the back as he passed, Rush rubbed the sweat off his own forehead and made his way over.

The patrolman stood a few feet from the corpse, looking anywhere but there, tapping a pen against his leg. Sweat soaked his hair, darkened his collar, and invaded his armpits. His face sagged; his drinker's nose glowed.

"Hey, Owen," Rush said.

The officer nodded. "Rush."

"Got anything for us?" Rush jerked his head at Chinbroski and pointed to the nurses standing by Owen's police cruiser. His partner headed that way.

"Got nothing," Owen said, wiping his face. "I mean as far as the shooting goes. Got ID on the victim. The names of the nurses over there." His head was in constant movement, quick jerks from side to side, snatches of looks behind him.

No officer in any of the other cities over the last three years had been shot after responding to the murder of the doctor. It wasn't Jackson's way. He'd always shot the doctor and disappeared. Then he repeated his pattern for the lawyer, judge, and homicide cop. Still, Rush couldn't blame Owen for being nervous. "That's it? Names?"

"No time for much more," Owen said. "Got units across the street trying to find witnesses." He lowered his voice, took a small step toward Rush. His breath smelled like stale beer, residue from a hard night. "Is this that Jackson fella? The guy on the news?"

Rush kept his voice steady. "Don't know yet." He motioned toward the body. "A doctor?"

Owen leaned in closer, misting Rush with his stale Budweiser. "Thayer. That's his name. Gynecologist. Ain't that what the others were?"

The body lay on its belly, ten feet beyond Owen. Splatters of blood dotted the pavement several feet closer. "Yeah," Rush said. "That's what the others were."

Owen wiped the back of his neck and swallowed hard. "In Plano." He started to walk away, making room for Rush to inspect the body. Then he stopped. "You or Chinbroski."

Rush looked at him and said nothing.

Owen backed away. "I mean, you know—"

"Go stand by your car." Rush cursed under his breath and turned away from Owen. He circled the blood splatter, made a wide arc around the doctor. Then he pulled out a phone and called his captain.

"You need to get out here. Bring every detective you can round up. And the media boys. More uniforms. This crowd is growing as we speak."

"I'm trying to arrange things here to prepare for the onslaught," Greer said. "You thinking what everyone's saying?"

The same question three times in three minutes. Rush turned away, glanced across the street, lowered his voice. "Yes."

Greer didn't respond immediately. But when he did, Rush's breath caught in his throat.

"You and Chinbroski have this one. Do it right. Hold on."

The FBI had been chasing Jackson for over two years and they had nothing. The most hunted criminal in the country, and either he or Chinbroski would soon be on his short list.

Rush heard sirens in the background, traffic on Coit Road behind him, Chinbroski in quiet conversation with the nurses. But no crowd noise. He turned and looked at the growing mass once again.

"We're sending out the media team," Greer said. "I've gotta go. And Rush?"

"Yeah?"

13

"Every eye in America is on this."

"Right." Rush pocketed the phone, took a cleansing breath, and approached the body. Doctor Thayer's legs were sprawled, one knee cocked toward his right arm, the other twisted inward. A box of pamphlets, AIDS prevention, lay crumpled beneath him. The blood on the pavement had long since turned black. The coppery smell was faint, overpowered by the human waste released when his sphincter muscles relaxed at death. Blood-matted hair encircled a quarter-inch hole centered in the back of his head.

Rush placed his toes near where Thayer must have been standing before the force of the bullet thrust him forward. He turned and looked behind him, noting the probable origin of the shot.

The apartment complex across the street had close to a hundred people milling about, gawking, taking pictures. He pulled his radio out, tuned it to the west side patrol frequency, and called for the day-shift watch commander, advising him to use as many units as necessary to clear the crowd.

Chinbroski walked up just as Rush slid his radio into a pocket. "What'd the nurses say?"

"Nothing important. He was walking across the lot and just collapsed. No sound, no nothing. Fell in a heap." Chinbroski lowered his voice. "Just like the others. Everybody might as well be deaf and blind."

"I've got patrol clearing the apartments across the street. That has to be where the shot came from." Rush turned and faced his partner head on. "You're in charge of directing the other investigators over there. Greer's sending everybody he can find. I want those nurses gone before the media broadcasts their faces all over the country. Knock on every damn door in that complex. Stay with it until you talk to everybody who was there an hour ago." Rush swiped sweat from his brow and looked up. The sun would bake them yet. "Maybe we'll get lucky. And we're gonna need it because Greer just gave it to us."

Chinbroski nodded and glanced at the body. "Okay, I'll handle across the street." Before he walked away, he gripped Rush's arm. "The media don't gotta know which team has the case," he whispered. "Maybe Jackson won't find out." His expression said otherwise.

"Yeah," Rush said. "Maybe."

His partner gone, Rush scanned the crowd and noticed a hospital employee standing just on the other side of the tape. He walked over. "You work inside?"

The young woman leaned back, appeared surprised that a cop would address her. "Yes, housekeeping."

"Perfect." Rush raised the tape and nodded for her to stoop under. He led her several feet inside the perimeter. "Go grab several sheets. Clean. Bring them to me. And hurry."

The woman trotted off toward the hospital. Rush rubbed the back of his neck; his hand came away soaked.

Then he shivered, despite the heat.

He saw a patrolman lift the tape to admit the Plano PD crime-scene van. Once parked, Randy McBride, Plano's primary forensic expert, wasted no time. He jumped from the driver's seat and onto the ground. Ichabod Crane came to mind every time Rush laid eyes on the ex-FBI crime-lab tech. No chin, wiry arms, and pants that always hung crooked. McBride shaved his head every summer, and the stark, white fuzz was beginning to grow back.

Struggling with his ID kit, McBride made it over to Rush at the same time the young woman returned, carrying five neatly-folded bed sheets.

"Thank you," Rush said, taking them from her. "Would

you mind stepping back under the tape?"

Breathing hard, she nodded. "Did that black man do this?" she asked, eyes eager. "That B.J. guy?"

"We'll have to see. Please, behind the tape."

"Just look at this place," McBride said, glancing around after the woman was gone. "Madhouse in less than an hour. It's on all the radio stations. TV." He looked at the sheets Rush held. "What's with those?"

"To shield the body while you take your close-ups. Then to cover it when you're through."

McBride nodded. "Good thought. It's not like we have to worry about fiber transfer." He reached down and opened his collection kit, grabbed his camera. "How many camcorders you think are pointed at us right now?"

"Another reason for the sheets," Rush said. "Let's get started." He recruited two uniformed officers to hold the sheets while McBride did his work.

Within twenty minutes, several patrol units had cleared the apartment complex across the street, and Chinbroski was leading a team of detectives to knock on doors. A patrol lieutenant told Rush that local television trucks were being held at bay around the corner, but that dozens of newspaper reporters were pushing up against the crime scene tape, demanding some kind of statement. The department PIO was huddled with the chief somewhere inside the hospital, figuring out how vague they could be to the press.

It took McBride twenty more minutes to finish his photos and cover the body. Then he started the task of gathering the shreds of Doctor Thayer's face.

The scene was secure, Rush believed, as he made an appraisal, mentally clicking off what else needed to be done. He needed to send officers around to all the camcorder-wielding citizens and collect their tapes. Since this probably was a

Jackson shooting, they'd need everything they could get their hands on, and it wouldn't surprise him if the shooter were in the crowd somewhere. Rush strolled over to a couple of Burglary detectives and gave them the responsibility of collecting the tapes.

Then his radio crackled. "Rush, you there?"

"Yeah, Chin."

"Ops Two. Got something."

Rush keyed his radio. "Go ahead."

"Apartment number 1065B. Downstairs."

Rush smelled the apartment before he reached the door.

Burning marijuana. Recent. The door stood open, revealing a time capsule straight from the sixties. Beads, flop cushions, black lights, Grateful Dead posters, and Rolling Stones music playing in the background. Chinbroski stood just inside the door, next to a wheelchair-bound hippie wearing a Woodstock tee shirt. His legs were strapped to the chair, his stringy hair pulled back into a ponytail.

"Larry Winston," Chinbroski said, as Rush stopped just inside the door.

The hippie grinned, exposing a row of West Texas, hardwater green teeth. "Ain't had this much attention since a Bouncing Betty shot me in the ass in 'Nam." He rolled his chair forward and stuck out a leather-gloved fist.

Rush shook his hand and nodded. "You see something this morning?"

"Yeah."

Rush waited, fighting the urge to cough in the thick air.

"Motor home. Parked right outside my window."

Chinbroski grinned and Rush figured something good was coming. "Why is this motor home important?"

Winston rolled his chair over to the only window in the room. He pointed. "See right there, that Dumpster?"

17

Rush walked over, took a look. "Yeah."

"It's where I dump my trash every Wednesday. What's today?"

"Wednesday."

"Damn straight, man. Wednesday." The hippie nodded toward the window. "I don't work. Can't. Living off disability. And I got a routine." He rolled his chair back and spun it around, facing Rush. "Every morning I get up and roll me a doobie before breakfast." He held up his hands. "Now I know it's against the law, and I know it was stupid letting you boys in here, but I'm an American, and what that boy's been getting away with every July 24th makes my stomach turn."

Rush backed up toward fresh air, leaned against the front door jamb, and waited patiently for Winston to get to the point.

Winston pointed at Chinbroski. "So when this big cop told me that Jackson might've been in my complex, I had to do my duty."

"And . . . what about the motor home?"

"I seen it. Rolled right by it dumping my trash. I think it was where he shot from."

Rush's pulse quickened. "Why do you think that?"

" 'Cause I think I heard it. A suppressed shot."

Winston rolled his chair into the small dining area, grabbed several magazines from the table: *Guns and Ammo, American Rifleman, American Hunter, Shotgun News*. "Being in 'Nam, getting crippled by a Bouncing Betty, being a gunshow junkie all my life makes me good at one thing: guns and what they sound like. And I'm telling you, boys, that was a silenced shot that came out of that motor home."

"All right," Rush said. "Where were you when you heard it?"

"Just outside my door. I'd just come back from the Dumpster, just opened the door, was about to roll in when I heard it. I looked over but I didn't see anything, you know, like gun smoke or nothing."

Rush stepped deeper into the apartment. He hardly smelled the marijuana anymore. "But you didn't call it in as soon as you heard it?"

Winston shrugged. "Just one of those things. You know, noticed it at the time, but didn't think nothing of it. Till this big cop came knocking. Don't make a lot of difference. I know what I heard."

"Had you seen the motor home before this morning?"

"Hell, yes. Last Friday I saw it. Then on Monday and Tuesday. Now this morning."

Rush glanced at his watch. "The shot was between noon and one. You eat breakfast that late?"

Winston grinned. His green teeth had food crammed in the cracks. "I'm a night owl. Got some great shit on VH-1 after midnight. Get up about noon every day."

Chinbroski pulled a small pad from his pocket. "Mr. Winston says the motor home could have been a Road King. Beige, brown stripes. Didn't look for a tag. But . . ." He held up a finger. "He says the rear window was open a couple inches and that window was facing the hospital."

The media reports from the last couple of years had nothing about a motor home. This might be a major break. "Okay, Chin. Let's have a look. Mr. Winston, come outside, show us where."

The hippie led the way, rolling his chair with powerful pushes, his chest stuck out, his chin raised. "Right here," he said, stopping halfway between his apartment and the Dumpster. "I rolled around the back. It's probably a thirty-five footer, so I was way below the bottom of the window."

Rush looked across the parking lot, across Coit Road, over

to where McBride was hunched near the body more than 200 yards away. It'd be a clear shot, nothing for a rifleman with any level of skill. The only hitch would be timing the shot across six lanes of noon traffic.

Behind him was the back wall of the complex. The motor home must have been parked with its front bumper within inches of that wall.

"This might be it," Rush said to Chinbroski.

His partner nodded, his eyes hinting excitement.

Winston glanced around. "Look, boys," he said, his voice low. "It ain't like I'm a chicken shit or nothing. But I don't want my name getting out. Know what I mean? Not if this is Jackson. I had enough guns aimed at me in 'Nam."

"Don't worry." Rush turned to Chinbroski. "Let's get Mr. Winston to the station. I want a videotaped interview, a notarized statement. If anyone asks, we're arresting him for outstanding warrants."

Winston winked and shot Rush a peace sign, then rolled his chair toward his apartment.

Rush grabbed Chinbroski's arm and waited until the hippie was out of earshot. "Promise me something."

Chinbroski frowned. "Sure."

"Stick by me until you go on vacation. Prop me up." He paused. "I need you to make sure I don't skip town."

The wooden sign dangled from rusty chains and squeaked as the early summer breeze blew in from the south. B.J. set his tattered suitcase at his feet and pulled a rumpled map from the back pocket of his jeans.

Holding the map out in front of him, he carefully located where he was standing, looked up and found a couple of landmarks, then plotted his course. The group of cabins called Apache was on the west side of Camp Indian Hill, just past the dining hall. Thirteen-

year-olds were in Apache, fourteen in Cherokee, and fifteen in Shawnee. He was jostled and bumped by other boys as he memorized the route to cabin 24.

Four long weeks, a whole month of fun. He couldn't believe he was finally here. Archery, swimming, canoeing, hiking, camping in real teepees . . . he'd saved his money for a year to help his mom pay the two hundred dollars.

Stuffing the map back in his pocket, he grabbed his suitcase and hurried along, wanting to get a top bunk with a window that overlooked the rifle range. It was the rifle shooting that he was most excited about. Real rifles. Real bullets. No BB or pellet gun crap like in most camps. Although only .22s, the rifle competition would give him a chance to compete against older boys and actually win something. B.J. knew he wouldn't win anything else: he was too small, too weak, too slow. But he could shoot like no other person on earth.

He had used his shooting skills to convince his mom to let him come. He'd dragged her out behind the barn over a dozen times and forced her to watch him target practice. B.J. explained every shooting point to his mom. Used the same words his dad had used when teaching him. Twice, after B.J. had fired two incredible groups, he'd caught his mom crying quietly. It was the final link to his dad, and B.J. knew his mom understood that rifle shooting had been the strongest thread between father and son, the legacy that he had left for his only child. It had kept him talking during the final weeks of his cancer.

B.J. slowed to wipe his eyes. Mom would've never allowed him to travel all the way to Oklahoma for a month if Dad hadn't made her promise.

Number 24 sat at the edge of the shooting range. He had hardly believed his luck when the camp mailed him his cabin number and map. The information sheet said there were eight boys to a unit, two sets of bunk beds on each side of a single, large room. The pic-

ture in the brochure showed the layout, and B.J. noticed that the windows were high off the ground.

Desperately wanting a window bunk, he broke into a run, the suitcase slapping against his leg. He smiled at the smell, a kind of cedar, pine, wild animal mixture—so different from his grandfather's farmhouse he and his mom had moved into after his father's death. The trees were so tall, towering above the buildings, blocking out the summer sun, creating acres of shade. And the mountains. They had taken his breath away during the final miles in the car. His mom said it reminded her of the Ozarks in Southern Missouri. He'd just nodded and grinned, with her warning him not to hang too far out the window.

He ran past Shawnee with fifteen-year-olds milling about like they owned the place, several of them veterans of Camp Indian Hill, no doubt. Then across a wooden bridge, around home plate on the baseball field, finally circling the expansive dining hall. Stopping to catch his breath, he hadn't realized how big the camp was. The buildings looked kind of rundown, with their faded brown walls and rusty tin roofs. A few were boarded-up. But he didn't care about any of that. He'd live in a tent if he had to.

Studying the small plaques mounted above each cabin door, he headed toward the trees at the end of the dirt lane directly behind the dining hall. Twenty-four was the last one on the right, the closest to the looming mountain woods.

The door was ajar, no boys hanging around outside, no sounds from inside. Hope soaring that he'd have his pick of bunks, he pushed through the door and stopped to examine the layout. Eight bunks, four on each side, like in the picture, but only one window. High off the floor, the window was long and narrow with a small hand crank on one end. The two sets of bunk beds on that side sat end-to-end, meeting in the middle of the only view of the rifle range. And one of the top bunks was taken already. A blonde boy, much bigger than B.J., a boy who looked every bit of fourteen, was sprawled across the bunk on the right, his back to the door, staring out the window. No one else had arrived yet. B.J. scrambled across the room and tossed his suitcase on the top left bunk, sighing. He'd made it.

The boy turned and sat up. He had a plain face, a sort of country-boy look. And he was bigger up close.

B.J. smiled. "This bunk taken yet?"

"Not that I know of. But I've only been here for a few minutes."

"Great!" B.J. rubbed his tired arm.

"My name's Stubs," the boy said.

"B.J.'s mine. I'm from Texas. Where're you from?"

"Dallas." The boy pushed a lock of blond hair off his forehead. He crossed his legs Indian style, leaned his elbows on his knees. "You from Dallas?"

"Naw," B.J. said, climbing the bunk. "Trenton. I've never even been to Dallas."

"Where's Trenton?"

"A long way away. More'n a hundred miles."

Stubs laughed. "A hundred miles ain't far. Dallas is over a hundred and fifty."

Pushing his suitcase toward the head of the bed, B.J. looked out the window. The rifle range was there, right there, with shooting benches and everything! "Well," B.J. said, "I've never been a hundred miles from home before. And it sure seemed far, as slow as my mom was driving."

Stubs laughed again. "My fost—eh, mom drives slow, too. She said gas is too expensive to drive fast. It's almost thirty-five cents a gallon in Dallas."

B.J. nodded and wondered if he should ask about the boy's name. He did. "Stubs ain't your real name, is it?"

"Heck no! Who'd have a nutty name like that? Unless your parents were crazy or something."

"So how come you go by that?"

He sat silent for a moment, turned his face away, stared out the window. B.J. thought he might start crying, but he didn't. He just sat there like he was thinking about his answer. "My real mom started calling me that when I was little," he said finally. "I used to think it was dumb . . . but now I don't." He scooted his body around and grabbed the window crank. "Think I'll open this."

B.J. noticed for the first time how hot it was. In the center of the room a single ceiling fan turned slowly, but didn't move the air much. A slight breeze blew across them once Stubs had the window cranked all the way open. B.J. could fit through, he thought, and walk right over.

The range was fifty yards long, and the target frames loomed like skeletons without the paper targets attached. B.J. nodded toward the window. "You shoot?"

"Oh, man, that's what I do best. That's why I got here early. I wanted to get a bunk with a window."

"Hey, me too!" B.J. said, gathering strength to make his bold prediction to the bigger boy. "I'm going to win the shooting competition. I'm the best shot in Trenton."

Stubs's eyes narrowed. Then he cracked a smile. "Well, you ain't in Trenton anymore. And you're talking to the best shot in Dallas."

CHAPTER TWO

Camp Indian Hill, in the Ouachita National Forest between Cedar Lake and Alimenia Mountain, was closest to Zoe, Oklahoma, a dot of a town off Highway 1. B.J. knew this by the map mailed to him two weeks before camp began. What he didn't know was how he would ever find his way out of the woods if he went too far and got turned around.

During the first week of camp, he and Stubs had spent every minute of their afternoon free-time exploring the sixty acres of camp property and the miles of national forest surrounding it. They'd traveled a maze of deer trails, climbed small cliffs and tall trees, and come close to getting lost more than a few times. The thick forest radiated danger, yet was so unlike anything B.J. had ever experienced, he found himself drawn deeper into the mountains on every outing.

Today they were following bear tracks, had been for close to an hour. "Couldn't be a bear," Stubs had said at the beginning of their trek. "Not nowadays. Fifty years ago, yeah. But not now."

But B.J. was sure of it. He'd seen bear tracks in a picture one time and these looked just like he remembered. Even though Stubs had insisted that he didn't think so, he'd been eager to join B.J. in the hunt.

Feeling sweat run into his eyes, B.J. heard Stubs panting behind him as they hiked farther than ever up the northern slope of the mountain. Finally, they stopped at the mouth of a small cave where B.J. collapsed on a boulder, lungs burning. The breeze ticked B.J.'s forehead, and the smell of evergreen fought through the stench of his own sweat.

Stubs dropped to his knees near B.J.'s boulder and peered up the northern face of the mountain. "We ain't even near the top," he said, practically wheezing the words.

B.J. gazed up, rubbing the sweat from his eyes. It looked like a jungle. Through a thicket to the right, he heard a squirrel jumping in the branches of a tree. Still panting, he lay back on the boulder and closed his eyes.

"We've been going up and down so much, I don't know if we're even very high. We might be in a valley or something."

"Naw," Stubs said. "We're like halfway up."

"What about the big hill we just came down?"

"Well, sometimes when you're going down, you're still going up."

Opening one eye, B.J. looked over at Stubs. "That don't even make sense."

"Sure it does. See, in mountain ranges like this, you go up a long hill, then down a little, then up a bunch more, down a little, then up. And the whole time you're going up." Stubs dried his face with his shirt.

"Who are you, Fess Parker?"

"I know my way around, that's all. We ain't got lost all week, have we?"

" 'Cause you always have me lead the way back." B.J. gave him an I'm-better-than-you chuckle.

"You're nuts. If it wasn't for me, you wouldn't even come out in the woods."

"You think so?"

The Shooting Season

" 'Cause you're scared." Stubs jumped up and did a chicken dance. "Bawk, bawk."

B.J. shook his head and laughed. He closed his eyes again and wiped his forehead. The rest felt good. This had been the longest and hardest hike yet. He tried to imagine what it would have been like to hike with his dad. Hiking was always something his dad had promised they'd do, but had never done. The cancer had been hard and long, zapping his strength for nearly two years before finally killing him.

As B.J. lay there on the flat rock with his eyes closed, he tried to picture his father in full health, but just couldn't come up with an image. B.J. had just turned ten when his dad started getting sick, and the memories of his frail, cancer-ridden body were so vivid, so absolutely dominating, that no other recollections could break through. Not having memories of a healthy dad had been the root of several of B.J.'s crying spells this past year.

"I'll go in if you will," Stubs said.

B.J. opened his eyes and sat up. Stubs stood pointing to the small cave, grinning, sandy hair plastered to his sweaty forehead.

The dark opening, a jagged triangle three feet wide and two feet high, was big enough for a bear. B.J. let his eyes drift to the tracks, now more scuff marks than animal prints. He didn't know how old they were, which meant they could be only hours old. Maybe minutes. His chest tightened when he imagined himself venturing inside.

"Wish I had one of the .22s," B.J. said, thinking of the rifles they'd been shooting all week.

Stubs laughed. "For a bear?"

B.J. looked at him and pointed to the opening. "Better than nothing. And if I shot it in the eye, the bullet might bounce around in its brain for awhile."

"If you could hit him in the eye," Stubs teased.

They both knew B.J. could hit a bear in the eye with one of

those Stevens .22 bolt-actions. Stubs could, too. They were clearly the best shots at Camp Indian Hill, and from the looks of things, it was going to be a real showdown for the championship in three weeks. None of the other thirteen-year-olds would even sniff first place.

Sliding off the rock, B.J. took a tentative step toward the opening, peering into the darkness.

"I still say these tracks aren't from a bear," Stubs said. "I'm thinking maybe mountain lion."

B.J. stopped and turned toward his friend. "Mountain lion?" His voice cracked and he swallowed hard, embarrassed.

Stubs wore a serious expression. He stepped past B.J. and squatted near the cave's mouth. "See," he said, pointing to a spot four feet inside, just at the edge of the darkness. "There's a real good track. Looks like my foster mom's tomcat. He don't never come in the house, but I see his tracks in the flower garden all the time. Looks just like that, except a lot smaller."

"Don't a bear track look the same?" B.J. asked, stepping a little closer.

"No way. A bear's got a wide foot. That ain't wide at all."

B.J. stared at his friend for a moment, trying to figure out if the bigger boy was pulling his leg. The dirt rings on Stubs's neck were starting to run from his sweat, but his face was as serious as B.J. had ever seen it. Stubs dropped to all fours and moved a foot inside the opening. Then he glanced back. "You coming?"

"Yeah, wait a minute." B.J. searched around for a big stick and finally settled on a fist-sized rock. He didn't drop to his hands and knees like Stubs, as he was small enough to squat and make it through. Good thing because he wanted to stay on his feet, stay mobile. This was one time he was glad he was a runt.

"Don't it feel great in here?" Stubs asked when B.J. stopped beside him several feet inside the cave. "So cool."

A refreshing breeze drifted from the darkness in front of him.

"Yeah," B.J. whispered. He put a hand against the wet wall of the cave and wiped his face with the moisture. The ceiling of the cave was much higher than the mouth of the cave, and B.J. was nearly able to stand. "Wish I had a flashlight."

Stubs nudged him forward. "You take the lead. Since you got a weapon."

The rock felt so light against the heavy darkness.

B.J. gripped it harder, unwilling to show fear in front of his friend. He took several steps and hit his head on the slowly declining ceiling. "Ouch."

"Shh," Stubs said. "If there's something in here, we don't want it to know we're coming."

No sounds came from deeper inside the cave, no smells. B.J. had never been in a cave before and he half-expected to bump a hanging bat with his face. He shivered, and was suddenly glad it was too dark for Stubs to see him. No little kid's stuff allowed. At least for the next three weeks.

In the weeks leading up to camp, he'd sworn to himself that he'd act like a grownup the entire time he was here. It was a silent pact he'd made with himself, something he didn't think his mom would ever talk about with him. Then she'd reminded him of the fact that he was a young man now, just before giving him a goodbye kiss under the Camp Indian Hill sign. It was her way of saying, "Don't be a baby."

With the darkness so thick it seemed a solid wall, he was forced to feel his way along. And when the ceiling finally dropped too low, he was forced to drop to his hands and knees. His breath echoed in the small cavern and the breeze felt stronger the deeper he went. He sensed that the small cavern opened up into something bigger, but the darkness was absolute and offered no hint of what might lie ahead. He caught a glimpse of something deep into the cave, maybe a prickle of light, but then it was gone. B.J. moved his head around and *tried to find what he was sure he had seen, but came up with nothing.*

He was about to move forward again when he realized that the only sound he heard was his own movements. He looked back, expecting Stubs to be right there.

But he wasn't. He was gone. Frantic, B.J. spun around and knocked his head against the wall. He cried out in pain as white dots sparkled in his eyes. He blinked and rubbed his head, then noticed that the cave opening was half the size it had been just a minute before. Someone had rolled a rock against the mouth of the cave!

Dropping his rock, B.J. scrambled toward daylight. Then he saw Stubs roll a second rock into place and the opening shrank even more.

"Hey!" B.J. yelled, his voice echoing off the walls around him. "What are you doing?" As he got closer, he stood under the higher ceiling. He dashed forward and wriggled through the remaining triangle.

Stubs was on his back, holding his stomach, convulsed with laughter. B.J. stood, gasping, sweat dripping into his eyes, anger choking his throat.

"I . . . got . . . you," Stubs screamed between gulps of air. "I . . . got you good."

B.J. said nothing. He looked at himself, dirt from head to toe. He swallowed hard and fought to hide his fear.

"You . . . should have seen . . . the look on your face!" Stubs bulged his eyes, dropped his jaw, and jutted his neck forward, mimicking B.J. "You thought that bear was gonna eat you for supper!" He fell back again, rolling over in the dirt, gasping for breath.

B.J. strutted over to the rock he'd sat on earlier, brushing himself off, wearing his courage as proudly as he could. When he looked back at Stubs, the bigger boy's face was streaked with dirty tear stains as he struggled to stand while holding his side, laughing harder than anyone B.J. had ever seen.

"At least I had the guts to go in!" B.J. shouted. "At least I didn't turn tail and run like some chicken!"

Stubs just kept laughing, did a chicken impression again until finally, B.J. saw the humor. Now back in the sunlight, out of the claustrophobic confines of the cave, B.J. knew how funny he must have looked racing out of the cave, bug-eyed. Then he started giggling, too. Stubs staggered over and slapped him on the back, tears sliding down his face. B.J. laughed, called Stubs a butthead, and then laughed even harder. Stubs fell on him, knocking him off the rock, and they rolled around on the ground, holding their sides as though they might actually burst.

At 5:00 P.M., Rush and Chinbroski walked into the chief's law library to await a meeting with FBI Agent Zeke Bunning, the bureau's lead man on the Jackson serial sniper case. Chinbroski wore a haggard look: his mouth drooped at the corners, worry lines creased his forehead, and Rush had seen more active eyes on a corpse.

Chinbroski's flattop was half flat. Sweat beaded his forehead and ran down the slope of his nose. He had shed his tie on the way back to the station, as had Rush, and both of them were sipping one-liter bottles of Dr Pepper purchased on the way to the station.

Rush felt like his partner looked. They had spent the balance of the afternoon directing activities, compiling information, and interviewing anybody even remotely connected to any aspect of the case.

Doctor Thayer's body was being autopsied at that very moment. Rush had given specific instructions to handle any bullet remains with the utmost care, with Hanson from Forgery attending, ready to courier any evidence straight to him.

They never found the core of the bullet, which was probably lost in the hospital landscaping. Two Auto Theft detectives were escorting Larry Winston around to various motor home dealers and RV campgrounds to try and identify which model he had seen outside his apartment.

The lobby of the police department was under siege, with media having appeared from every corner of the country in only five hours. Probably had their bags packed, Rush thought, while they sat at the airport and watched CNN. They knew Jackson's pattern, knew they'd be flying somewhere to the Midwest. And now they were clamoring for some kind of statement. But no statement had been made. Plano's chief was hesitant to comment publicly until he had spoken with Agent Bunning, which he was doing now behind closed doors.

Although Captain Greer had assigned Rush and Chinbroski the case over the phone several hours before, the case had been unquestionably assigned to them just an hour ago by the chief himself. It was the FBI connection: Rush and Bunning, FBI task force members nine years earlier. Chief Powell's procedure was to team people familiar with each other. The problem, though Rush hadn't mentioned it, was that he *did* know Zeke Bunning, and wanted no part of working a case with him. Could Rush tell the truth without sounding cowardly, without sounding as if he were trying to remove himself from the case? It had been a long time since his and Zeke's task force days. So he had to assume Zeke was different now. He had to hope.

"What are we gonna do?" Chinbroski asked, his face a mixture of bafflement and worry.

Rush wiped the sweat from under his eyes and glanced at his watch. Agent Bunning was late.

"Tell me, Rush, what are we gonna do?"

He'd never seen Chinbroski like this. Not in the fifteen years they'd worked together.

"Two years of hunting and the FBI ain't got jack. What are we gonna do?" Chinbroski asked for the third time.

"Work the case, Chin. What else you want me to say?"

Three years ago in Everett, Washington, a Seattle suburb, the police thought the first murder was random, maybe a drive-by. The chief got an envelope with a spent .308 rifle casing. Not the actual casing from the shooting, but one suspected of being fired and ejected from the same rifle. The return address on the envelope said: *1234 Dead St., Everett, Washington.* They found a perfect print on the casing. Ran it on AFIS. Billy Ray Jackson's right thumb.

Six days later, after the first shooting in Everett, a lawyer was shot as he stepped out his front door for the morning paper. That afternoon the chief received a second envelope with a second casing.

Eight days after the lawyer, a judge got it while fishing on a private pond behind his house. The chief got a third casing in the mail. By then the shootings were getting heavy press coverage in the Seattle area. That's when Everett police released everything they had on Billy Ray Jackson, including his Nashville PD arrest photo. The one everyone had used since.

Seven days after the judge, the lead detective was shot through the front windshield of his car as he backed out of his driveway.

"What about us?" Chinbroski asked. "They really think we're gonna be able to work this with a clear head?" He pushed away from the table and faced away from Rush. "They've been searching for Jackson with everything the government's got, and they want us to work it?"

Rush rubbed away the sweat on his forehead and let Chinbroski vent. Chinbroski wouldn't be safe in his own home. Nor would he. He'd have to get Mallory out.

Billy Ray Jackson disappeared from the map until July 24th of the next year. That was Tempe, Arizona. The doctor was shot in the back of the head as he walked into a side door of his office; the lawyer while fishing on a private pond behind his house; the judge as he stepped from his car at the courthouse; the cop watching his kid play soccer.

"The shots," Chinbroski said. "You know about the shots?"

Rush looked up at his partner and said nothing.

"You ever do any rifle shooting?" Chinbroski asked, leaning against the table.

Chinbroski had always claimed a distant interest in long-range shooting, though Rush had never known him to pick up a rifle.

"Have you?" Chinbroski asked again, his voice tight.

"As a kid," Rush said. "Long, long ago. Why?"

" 'Cause I've followed this Jackson thing pretty close. Curious about the degree of difficulty. Wondering if the guy had any exceptional skills. Last year in Colorado, the doctor got it while eating breakfast at his kitchen table. The shot came from a wooded area four hundred and thirteen yards away. What remained of his face ended up in his cereal bowl. And that ain't the longest one. The cop in Tempe watching his son play soccer was over five hundred."

The skill that must take, Rush thought. The training.

Although all of this repulsed him, he couldn't help feel a sliver of admiration for the degree of difficulty involved in pulling off this entire shooting spree. All headshots that hadn't left the cops one hint of how to catch him.

"Last year the judge got it from behind, between five other heads. Two hundred and fifty yards."

Rush just looked at him, the room quiet as a tomb.

"So I'm getting married in three weeks, you got a wife who ain't in a mental hospital only because you're the most stubborn man in Texas, and your only kid is a lawyer, which puts him and every other Plano lawyer at risk." Chinbroski stopped his tirade, took a quick breath, and looked away, his eyes coated with a film of moisture.

Mallory. Rush's heart quickened. Yes, he knew his wife should be institutionalized, and the thought of her being left alone if he were killed had been weighing on his mind from the very moment he'd been notified of the shooting. Daniel could take care of himself. His expanding law firm had made him financially solvent, and Rush suspected that Daniel had years before prepared himself emotionally to handle the death of his father. Families of police officers understood the risk of death in the line of duty, and Daniel was no different. It was Mallory who concerned Rush. She no longer had the capacity to understand, to fear, or to grieve.

"You want more history?" Chinbroski asked, pulling Rush's attention back to the present.

"The whole country has the history, Chin. It's all we've heard about for the last month. This damn national countdown is all we hear about on the news. I have the history."

"Three cities. Twelve people. Thirteen, including ours. No witnesses. No evidence. No suspects. No direction. And one of us is next." Chinbroski sat down and stared at Rush. "Me or you. That's what we're looking at."

Chinbroski wiped away a full tear that had slipped from his left eye. The tops of his ears were red and his bottom lip refused to hold still.

Rush had nothing to say. What could he say?

"I'm scared," Chinbroski said, the words barely audible. "I'll only say that once. You probably knew already, but I just wanted to say it."

"It's a given, Chin. Come on. And so am I." Rush looked away from his partner and thought about Mallory again.

He met her after her first husband had nearly beaten her to death. Like many abused women, Mallory had suffered the beatings in silence. But the difference between Mallory and other abused women was that her abuser accelerated his violence faster than any other wife beater Rush had ever investigated. Only eleven months passed between slapping her for the first time and stomping her with his steel-toed boots, then pounding her with a baseball bat to within an inch of her life, leaving her for dead on the floor of the entryway, just inside their front door.

Her physical rehab lasted through Rush's investigation, through her husband's trial for attempted murder, through his being shipped off to prison. And, except for her inability to ever have children, her body had healed.

Rush began falling in love with her shortly after the trial, beginning with a short visit at her home to tell her of a beating her husband had suffered in the county jail just before being shipped off to Huntsville.

He watched her recover, helped her with rehab, encouraged her at every turn. Nearly a year after the trial, they married in front of a Justice of the Peace, with Chinbroski and Daniel present as witnesses.

Rush understood violent crime victims, understood the long-term effects of Post Traumatic Stress Syndrome. After a couple of years she seemed fine, slowly weaning herself from the psychologist that had been her anchor through it all. She went back to college, busied herself in redecorating Rush's bland twenty-five-year-old house.

Then last summer, during one of Rush's particularly brutal murder investigations, she started slipping. He'd find her crying for no reason, talking to herself when she thought she was alone. She became obsessed with watching surgery shows on The Learning Channel and scrubbing away a blood stain only she could see from the entryway tile just inside the front door of their home.

After the brutal murder investigation ended, Rush had taken her back to the psychologist; he'd taken leave from work, spent every waking hour with her for nearly two months. But she continued slipping, spiraling ever downward into a dark area of her mind where no one could reach her.

She'd dropped out of college with three hours left toward her degree. She'd suffered through three four-week stays in a mental hospital, and was on more medication than should be legally allowed. Chinbroski was right, he hadn't institutionalized her. He just couldn't abandon her after what she had been through. She was a sweet, loving woman whose ability to bear children had been ripped from her womb by the pounding of steel-toed boots. Her body, patched back together by a team of incredible surgeons, was a living testament to the wonders of medical science. And the three stays at the mental hospital was all Rush could stomach. He could never commit her to such a prison, regardless of the inconvenience of caring for her himself.

"Hey," Chinbroski said. "You with me?"

Rush looked up at his partner. "I'm sorry."

"I asked about Daniel."

"What about him?"

Chinbroski sighed in frustration. "Pull your head out of your ass. You need to get both of them out of town."

He's got a law practice, Rush thought but didn't say, though clearly understanding Chinbroski's point. "That's his call," he said instead. "I'll talk to him. But you know what he'll say."

"What?"

"That he's one of probably a couple of thousand lawyers that either work or live in Plano. The odds would be astronomical. And he'd be right."

"Then you tell—"

The library door opened suddenly, and FBI Agent Zeke Bunning stepped into the room. He stood there a moment, slowly taking in both of them. Rush thought Zeke looked even worse than he had on his most recent television appearance. He'd lost so much weight, his suit hung on him like a jacket on a broken hanger. His face matched his white shirt in tone, with cheeks sunken enough to make Rush think of a war refugee. Rush wondered how gray Zeke's hair would be, if he had any.

Zeke's gaze landed on Rush and he blew out a breath.

"I was afraid of this," he said. "I worried about it all the way from D.C. I only just heard the news from your chief." He made his way over and clasped Rush's hand, shaking it hard. "When I heard Plano, I could hardly believe it. How are you?"

"I was fine," Rush said, giving Zeke a pat on the forearm. "Until this morning."

Zeke's probing eyes seemed to take in every inch of Rush's face.

Rush introduced Chinbroski and then pulled out a chair and waved Zeke into it. Zeke's life had been profiled over the last month every bit as much as the killer he was chasing. At the top of his FBI Academy class academically. A cop before joining the FBI. And a Ph.D. in psychology with a full-time practice before that. Born with a silver spoon. Earned his Ph.D. and opened a practice by the time he was twenty-three. But his clients bored him. Distressed housewives, spoiled teenagers, eating disorders. He saw himself fat and bald at thirty-five, ready to commit suicide.

He wanted to study the criminal mind. Figuring the best exposure was the street, he became a police officer. He tried to keep it secret, but his practice slowly died when his clients discovered they were telling their secrets to a cop.

And now he's chasing the biggest criminal of all, Rush thought. And I get to help him. He felt his jaws clench at the thought of working with Zeke.

Zeke studied them both for a moment before speaking straight to their concerns. "We're going to make it through this. Together. All of us."

Rush made eye contact with Chinbroski, who lifted an eyebrow. Rush smiled. It was forced, felt like it might actually burn calories.

"You wonder how," Zeke said. "We have nothing, you're thinking. They've made no progress, you've probably told yourselves within the past fifteen minutes. And you know what? All of that is true." Zeke swallowed and cleared his throat. "The director told me just before I left to come out here—well . . . let's just say the director is insistent this shooter be caught. And sooner rather than later." He rubbed his neck and frowned. "It's about the media this year. About what I feed them."

Rush said nothing.

Zeke's voice softened. "I've struck an agreement with your chief. He's allowed me to assume control of all of the press briefings."

"Okay," Rush said. "And?"

"Direction. Every year, after every shooting, we've allowed him to sit out there and marvel at the media feeding frenzy. That frenzy is partly what drives him. You know what else drives him? That after every shooting, we stand up and admit we don't have any leads. In essence, that we're too stupid to catch him." He locked eyes with Rush.

39

"That changes. Starting now."

"What do you mean?" Chinbroski asked.

"This year *I'm* going to use the press to *our* advantage," he said softly, "to drive him into the open, or at least into a mistake. The director is tired of our agency being blamed for not catching this guy. He's decided that if we're going to be blamed, we're going to deserve it."

Zeke stood and paced the room, silent for several moments. "Taking the media will save your chief from being inundated with interview requests, from being followed with cameras, from being asked to explain every move, defend every mistake. From being second-guessed by experts, screamed at by victims' families. But for my plan to work, no information can be released by anyone from this agency."

He's going to lie, Rush suddenly understood. He's going to fill the airways and newspapers full of bullshit. He's attacking Jackson's profile, attacking Jackson's ego. He's going to try and piss him off, drive him into a mistake.

A cold chill stabbed Rush at the base of his skull and worked its way south. He rubbed the side of his face in disbelief and his expression must have caught Zeke's attention.

The FBI agent focused on Rush and raised an eyebrow.

"It will work," he said, reading Rush's mind.

"What will work?" Chinbroski asked.

Zeke ignored him. "I don't think it's him. Jackson. It doesn't fit." Zeke watched Rush's reaction, but Rush gave him nothing.

"The real Jackson was born and raised in a bad part of Nashville," Zeke said. "Reform schools, high school dropout, drugs, robbery, assault, weapons, rape, and finally homicide. Arrested for a rape/murder of a twenty-year-old Vanderbilt coed. During the investigation the homicide cop beat him, put him in the hospital for three weeks; a jury with eight blacks acquitted him of all charges. A month after his trial three years ago—on July 4th, as close as we can tell—he disappeared. This was three weeks before the first shooting.

"Jackson had an extensive drug history. No firearms training that we can find, no evidence of organizational skills or planning ability. It doesn't fit. It's not him. The picture the media has shown for the last two years is of a dead man. I'm convinced of it."

"What does your profile say?" Rush asked. "What are we looking for?"

"White male, mid-thirties to mid-fifties, ex-military or ex-police, single, either no kids or grown kids from whom he's estranged, a loner, neat, organized, above-average IQ, able to control unnecessary impulses." Zeke shifted his weight, cocked his head. "And very patient."

"Yet you can drive him into a mistake," Rush said, unconvinced.

"He's a killing machine," Zeke said. "The best I've ever seen. It's about ego. It's about showing everybody that he's the best. It's about not being thought of as a sloppy, careless amateur. He doesn't want to be lumped into the same class as losers like John Malvo. My plan will work."

Rush stared at Zeke through several moments of silence.

"There is one thing the two of you should know. Something I haven't given the media about his profile."

Rush couldn't ask. He glanced at Chinbroski, who wore a frown of confusion.

"What?" Chinbroski finally asked.

"Whoever this is doesn't profile as a serial killer."

"Everything I've ever read about this case," Chinbroski said, "says—"

"Says he's a serial killer, I know. But it's worse than that."

Zeke took a deep breath and stood, buttoned his suit coat,

and locked eyes with Rush. "It's the worst possible news, Greg. This shooter will die for his cause. Whatever the hell that is. Which is the strongest argument for what I'm about to try."

The agent's eyes were bloodshot, Rush noticed for the first time. And as Zeke opened his mouth to continue, Rush found himself holding his breath.

Zeke leaned forward slightly, his words sounding distant, as if they came from the end of a cold tunnel.

"He profiles as an assassin."

CHAPTER THREE

They were trapped in a thunderstorm of biblical proportions at least a full mile from camp, ten minutes before the dinner bell was set to ring. Steve, one of the college-age counselors, had warned them just the day before not to be late for dinner again.

It had been Stubs's idea to follow Nicksaw Creek all the way north past the twin towers, the pointed, ragged peaks that appeared to have fallen from the sky and stabbed the earth dead center of a lush, bowl-shaped valley in the northern section of the national forest. Stubs had told B.J. that he'd overheard a couple of counselors talking about it, and despite B.J.'s concern over the impending thunderstorm, had insisted they make the twin towers their objective for the afternoon. They never made it.

Now, they sat hunched under a rock overhang watching the Nicksaw Creek slowly mature to river status.

B.J.'s feet were soaked and his pants were wet to mid-thigh from the frantic dash across the creek when the rain had come. His back was starting to ache from being hunched over for nearly an hour. Next to him, Stubs had stopped his mindless chatter a half-hour before. B.J. was mad and wasn't in much of a chatting mood. He should never have let Stubs talk him into going today. Not with the storm coming.

"Ain't my fault," Stubs said suddenly, for the fifth time, and the only words he had spoken in the last thirty minutes.

B.J. had ignored him the first four times, but he wouldn't ignore him again. "Then whose fault is it? Mine?" B.J. snorted and shook his head, edging away from Stubs a little more. There was barely enough room for both of them under the big rock. B.J. could smell Stubs's body odor and it wasn't pleasant.

"I'm just saying it ain't my fault it rained. Sometimes the sky gets dark and it don't even rain at all. Nobody can predict it right."

"Well, the counselors were telling us all day yesterday and this morning that a big storm was coming." B.J. rolled his eyes at his friend's stupidity. "What if we get kicked out of the camp? What then? Huh?" The force of his own voice surprised B.J. He was literally shaking.

"Come on, B.J. We ain't getting kicked out. It ain't our fault we're gonna be late. It's an act of God."

"Did God magically transport us a mile from camp? Did God make us so stupid that we went out before a storm? They told us not to be late for dinner anymore. They told us that yesterday."

"I'll handle it."

"How?"

"I'll tell them we had two choices. Either hide under this rock or get struck by lightning. They won't kick us out."

B.J. closed his eyes and took several deep breaths. He needed to calm down. Stubs was probably right. They would've made it back to camp easily if they hadn't had to wait out the storm. "What if they do a head count?" he said suddenly, as soon as the horrible thought popped into his head. "And they send out a search party? And get the sheriff out using dogs and everything? They'll kick us out for sure, then."

Stubs laughed, which really made B.J. mad. "What's so funny!" he shouted. "This is all your fault! Stop laughing at me!"

"I ain't laughing at you. I'm laughing at the thought of old Koo Koo Kramer leading a search party." Stubs laughed harder and pretty soon B.J. was giggling, too.

Gerald Kramer, the owner of the camp, was probably five hundred pounds, had glasses as thick as the bottom of a vinegar bottle, and couldn't hear any better than Helen Keller. Everybody called him Koo Koo because he looked as crazy as Red Skelton doing one of his skits.

Stubs fell forward laughing and landed face-down in the mud, which made him laugh even harder. With Stubs out from under the rock overhang, B.J. leaned over onto his side and stretched his back. The rain was coming down sideways and Stubs was soaked to the bone within seconds. He stood up, faced himself into the rain, and let the mud wash away.

"Look, I'm Koo Koo." Stubs put his hands out in front of him, closed his eyes, and started moving around like a blind man, yelling, *"B.J., where are you? I'm searching for you. Can't you see me? Koo Koo's got the whole sheriff's department with him. Koo Koo's gonna save you."*

The noise from the storm was so loud that B.J. barely heard Stubs's rant, but he heard enough to laugh out loud for the first time in over an hour. Stubs continued to stumble around in the driving rain.

"Oh, Stubs," Stubs hollered, mocking Gerald Kramer, his eyes still closed. *"Koo Koo fixed you some supper. You're late for the supper bell. I know you like supper best of all. And if you don't hurry, Koo Koo's gonna eat it all."*

B.J. saw it coming a few seconds before it happened, but was laughing too hard to warn him.

With his arms flailing out to the sides and his eyes closed, Stubs walked straight into a tree and whacked his forehead hard enough to knock him flat on his butt.

That made B.J. laugh even harder. He grabbed his side and

45

rolled onto his back, tears flooding his eyes.

Stubs lay in the rain for several minutes before finally sitting up and looking back at B.J., who was winding down and sitting up again, wiping his eyes.

After another few moments Stubs stood and opened his arms wide. "Let's just walk back. It's only water."

The rain continued to hammer down, thunder rumbled some-where over the mountains, and lightning flashed periodically in the distance. Though it was only 5:00 P.M., dusk had come early with the storm.

"Think we'd get lost?" B.J. asked. "I think we should wait until the rain lets up."

"We'll just follow the creek," Stubs said. "What's the big deal?"

B.J. looked at the rising creek and worried about a flash flood. He'd read about flash floods at school, and knew he wasn't a strong enough swimmer to save himself if he got pulled into the water. "Maybe if we just kept the creek in sight, we'd find our way back."

"What?" Stubs yelled. "I didn't hear you."

The rain was so loud against the trees, and the rushing water in the creek, B.J. had hardly heard himself. His fear had stolen the power from his voice.

"What?" Stubs asked again, louder this time. "Let's just follow the creek. We need to head back. This rain might last for hours."

B.J. looked at the creek again, then at Stubs, who still stood defiantly in the downpour, until he finally agreed. "Okay," he shouted. "We'll follow the creek." B.J. crawled out from under the rock overhang, and, like his friend, was drenched within seconds. He walked over to Stubs and put his mouth close to his ear. "Let's just stay way off the bank. I can't swim very good."

Stubs grinned and nodded. "Okay. Good idea. You want to lead?"

Like always? B.J. didn't ask. He just nodded and turned back toward camp.

They'd been trudging through the Oklahoma mountain swamp for nearly thirty minutes before the rain finally slowed to the point of just being a normal thunderstorm. They were lower now, where the trees were thicker, and the branches blocked much of the direct impact of the large raindrops. They were also in familiar territory again, on ground they'd traveled dozens of times since arriving at camp.

B.J. felt better, knowing they would make it back without falling into the creek or getting lost. Stubs was also better, evident by the chatter he'd started a few minutes before. The bigger boy had a habit of talking to nobody in particular and sometimes even answered himself. B.J. wondered if he wasn't plain crazy.

B.J. was daydreaming about the rifle competition, about how it would feel when he walked up to accept the first place trophy, when a question from Stubs yanked him back to reality.

"What?" B.J. asked. He stopped and looked back at Stubs. "I didn't hear you."

Stubs stopped. "I asked where your dad learned to shoot. You keep saying he was a champion."

"Oh." B.J. turned and started walking again. "He was in the Marines. He was on their rifle team. An expert."

"Was he in the war?"

"Yeah."

"The one going on now?"

B.J. grabbed a branch and pushed it out of the way, then held it so it wouldn't hit Stubs. "Naw. He was already out before Vietnam started. He was in Korea."

"Oh. I don't know much about that one."

"Me either. He didn't talk about it much."

Stubs moved up next to B.J. and slapped him on the back. "I'll take over the lead now." Stubs took a couple of giant steps forward and B.J. fell in behind him.

"Did he kill people?" Stubs asked.

That was the question that had always haunted B.J. because though he was never meant to know the answer, he did. B.J. just didn't know if he wanted to share that answer with Stubs. He'd only asked his dad once if he had killed anyone in the war, and his response still made goose bumps break out on his arms.

They'd been shooting, his dad sitting in his lawn chair coaching, and B.J. lying on his shooting mat, having just fired a five-shot group the size of a nickel at 100 yards, when he asked. His father, sick with cancer, his eyes as hollow and pale as those of a corpse, patted his knee and told B.J. to come sit. B.J. put a rag over the barrel of his rifle to keep the heat off, and climbed onto his father's bony leg.

"Whether I did or didn't, would you think less of me?"

B.J. didn't really understand the question, but he knew there was nothing his dad could say that would make B.J. love him less.

"Would you think of me as a monster if I told you that I killed dozens of people with my rifle?"

"No, sir."

"Would you think of me as a coward if I told you that I killed nobody?"

"No, sir. I know you ain't no coward."

His dad nodded and smiled, his gaunt face strained under the pressure of the disease. "Then it doesn't matter much if I did or didn't." He gazed off into the distance for several moments before he spoke again. "Do you understand why a good man, a just and honest man, would kill another human being?"

"You mean like in a war?"

"Like in a war, yes, but other times too. I'm not talking about *police officers doing their duty. I'm not talking about a man protecting his home against an intruder. I'm talking about a law-abiding citizen who just might have to kill another man, even if he doesn't really want to."*

B.J. considered an appropriate answer for several seconds, but just couldn't think of one. "Well, in a war, a soldier has to do his job."

"That's right, son. America fights wars because of an injustice. Soldiers do their job. But even in ordinary life, good men sometimes kill other men to set something right. Always understand that some injustices are worth killing for. Always respect life, but never forget that some principles are more important than the life of a bad and unjust man."

"Hey," Stubs said, yanking B.J. from his memory. "You gonna answer me or not? Did he kill people?"

"No," B.J. lied. "He was just a rifle shooter."

Just before 9:00 P.M., with darkness driving the sunlight over the horizon, B.J. pedaled his bicycle slowly along the west side of the hospital, checking for television crews still at the shooting scene. Nothing. He traveled south on the sidewalk along Coit Road, inspecting each car for police surveillance teams, then over to the apartment complex with the same goal. For thirty minutes he slowly circled, looped, and backtracked, unable to spot anything even remotely resembling cops. He finally crossed 15th Street, coasted into a business park, and leaned the bicycle against a tree.

Dressed in jeans, a Dallas Cowboys tee shirt, and running shoes, he strode through the front door of the hospital, across the lobby and through several hallways, following signs to the emergency room waiting area.

Plastic chairs lined three walls in the empty room, magazines littered a glass table, and a television hung in the corner.

The room smelled of disinfectant and the floors were clean enough to eat Thanksgiving dinner on. The television, tuned to CNN, showed a news anchor standing outside the front door of Plano PD announcing a press conference at 10:00 P.M., starring Zeke Bunning, the famous FBI agent who, B.J. thought, wasn't smart enough to investigate his own hemorrhoids.

B.J. grabbed a magazine and stuck his head in the hall, looking both ways. After a nurse disappeared around the corner to his right, he slipped out of the room and headed left toward the parking lot.

His rental car was near the edge, parked facing the physicians' lot, carefully positioned that morning, hours before he had rearranged Doctor Thayer's face.

The absence of people, even on a Wednesday night, seemed unnatural, as though the stain of death had driven everyone indoors.

As he maneuvered his way through the other cars, he rested one hand against the small automatic in his waistband. He slapped the magazine against his leg with his other hand, just casually strolling while scanning for watchers.

He approached the rental from the front. An Escort radar detector sat squarely in the center of the dash, staring straight ahead, covertly pointed toward the spot where Doctor Thayer had always parked his SUV, but never would again.

The lens of the color camera inside the radar detector was wide-angle, low light . . . miniature technology at its best.

Digging out a key, B.J. climbed into the car, drove it to the business park and retrieved the bike. Tomorrow he'd swap the rental for his pickup, that was parked near the car rental agency across town. Tonight the farmhouse sat sixty miles away, with a little more than an hour until the FBI news conference.

As he drove, he listened to a Dallas all-news radio station. The shooting dominated the airwaves. Plano PD was silent, unsure, waiting for the FBI to lead them, or so the announcer reported. Nine hours since the news broke. It seemed odd that the police department hadn't yet held a news conference to report at least *something*. But even more amazing was that the FBI hadn't spoken yet. Frustrated from a lack of evidence, he figured. Or shying away from standing in front of the country for a third consecutive year to admit defeat, of having to confess that he was smarter than them all.

B.J. stifled a small urge to drive by the police station and sneak a glance at the commotion. Must be an army of media by now. But a smart department would have detectives in unmarked cars positioned around the building, undercover officers in the crowd, maybe even video cameras pointed at the crowd.

The traffic heading north out of Plano was light, and he had no problem keeping his speedometer pegged right at 70 miles per hour. But he went no faster, wouldn't risk being stopped and given a ticket. The last thing he needed was to leave a paper trail in Texas.

It'd be kind of exciting, though. To come face-to-face with a police officer and see his reaction once he realized that he'd just stopped the most wanted man in America. It'd add some spice to an otherwise boring out-of-town trip.

These annual shooting seasons had become routine: shoot, wait a couple of days, shoot again, wait some more; same old, same old. The feeling he used to get, like the rush of bringing down a trophy buck, had faded two years before in Tempe. He thought it might come back in Colorado last year, but it hadn't. The thrill of long-range killing had grown stale, something he never thought would happen.

He remembered his first human target, and the dizzying

high that had snatched his breath away. It was an old vagrant in Nashville, a nobody, a nameless, faceless scourge of society he had killed from 100 yards away.

The old drunk wasn't a doctor, a lawyer, or a judge. Wasn't a cop or anybody important enough for the police to spend any time investigating, yet his death had been the best, the most emotionally fulfilling.

B.J. figured that he wasn't much different than a coke addict who tried to recreate the rush of his very first bump. Impossible. A cokehead could slowly increase the amount every day, but the only way to match that first high was to change dope.

So B.J. was changing his dope. It wasn't the shooting he'd looked forward to this year. It was the chess game, the effort to stay a step ahead of the FBI. As of yet the FBI hadn't come close to catching him because it was nearly impossible to stop a long-range precision shooter, especially somebody trained in police tactics, someone who knew his adversary as well as he knew himself.

This year he'd give them something, let them sniff his presence, let them get just a little closer, to see what they could do with it. He wanted to see just how good Zeke Bunning really was.

It was the last chance for Bunning because this year was the end game, the last of the shooting seasons. Everything he had done to this point was to make this year special. He'd saved the best for last. Stubs. That alone should recreate the excitement of the first kill. Stubs, the little bastard from summer camp, had grown up to become a fine homicide detective. Time to pay him back for all the shit he'd caused when they were both thirteen. Hell, the only reason he was killing cops at all was to make that son-of-a-bitch sweat for a few weeks. Could've killed him anytime, B.J. knew, years ago, even. Could've picked Plano the first year. But how much fun would it have been to just shoot him without his knowing that little B.J. was still pissed off?

By coming to Plano in year four, after three other homicide cops were killed, B.J. had assured that Stubs would clearly see the Grim Reaper in his rearview mirror, around every corner, in every shadow. Stubs would assume that every distant glimmer, every sparkle of chrome or reflection of sunlight, was the eye of a riflescope aimed in his direction. He'd stink with the sweat of a coward before venturing outdoors, regardless of where he was or what he needed to accomplish. He'd avoid windows, become obsessed with using binoculars to scan the horizon in all directions. He'd disrupt his own patterns and schedule; become so cautious with even the most simple of chores that the stress of pumping gas would eat the lining of his stomach. He wouldn't eat, lose weight, wouldn't sleep. He'd be irritable and unpredictable and useless to the investigation; the other detectives wouldn't get near him for fear of being shot. Simply put, Stubs would be the most miserable human on the face of the planet, for a short while, at least, a wonderful penance for his sins before he died.

But would Stubs be the lead detective? It could be any number of cops. B.J. knew that. Not that it would matter much: Stubs was a dead man walking. But it would be nice if his old friend ended up being the lead. Be nice to see him stare death in the face.

An hour later, B.J. pulled down the gravel driveway and parked behind the house next to the kitchen door.

Normally he spent most of three months choosing the city, researching the police department, identifying which doctor, lawyer, and judge to shoot, finding a place to live, mapping out escape routes, conducting surveillances, taking photographs, familiarizing himself with city streets, and ironing out all the small side issues.

But not this year. The farmhouse had been in his family for the last sixty years. The house on ten acres was a two-bedroom, one-bath junker that now tilted. Buckled wood floors, cracked walls, rusty tin roof that leaked in three places. Overgrown, red-tipped photinias hid the front door. Waist-high weeds. The whole setup just had a marvelously abandoned look. And secluded: five miles down a dead-end gravel road, ten miles from the 500 people calling Trenton, Texas, home.

B.J. hurried from the car, his stomach churning as he unloaded the video equipment from the trunk. The ratty kitchen table was just sturdy enough to carry the weight of the video system, a self-contained Pelican case with a compact VHS recorder, power supply, and battery.

Retrieving the videotape, he went into his bedroom and put it into the VCR, then ran it forward to the point where Doctor Thayer pulled his SUV into the parking space.

Thayer stepped from his car, opened the rear gate and grabbed the box, closed the door, and started his walk toward the hospital . . . until his face exploded. The nurses scrambled, cars screeched to a halt, and a crowd started gathering.

B.J. fast-forwarded the tape to the detectives' arrival. Two detectives: one big and muscular, a forehead that shrouds his eyes; the other smaller, narrow-shouldered, wispy blonde hair. The small guy was giving orders, motioned to the big guy to pull the nurses off to the side.

B.J. rubbed the nub of his left pinkie finger and leaned close to the screen. Stubs. There. In living color. B.J. sighed and clenched his fist. Same walk, same way he cocked his head when he spoke, same round face and wide forehead.

B.J. paused the tape, stared at the television, and burned

into his memory the face he'd avoided for twenty-seven years.

At straight-up 10:00, B.J. shut off the VCR, put in a clean tape, turned the television to the Dallas CBS affiliate, and pressed *Record.*

If he were home in Tennessee, he'd watch two stations at once, using the picture-in-picture on his big-screen TV just to ensure that he got all of the information the media had dug up. But if he were home, there wouldn't be anything to watch. He wished he were able to get more than one Dallas station this far north. After the local news, he'd walk out to the barn and watch Fox News from the eighteen-inch dish mounted on the roof of his motor home.

He grabbed a beer and a bag of potato chips from the kitchen, then flopped down on the bed in front of the TV. A reporter was repeating the same information carried by the 6:00 P.M. broadcast. They showed tape of the hospital parking lot, the yellow crime-scene banner, the crowd. B.J. looked closely at the parking lot in the background, studied the cars parked along the street, saw his rental. He laughed. Simply genius.

Then they flashed a picture of the dead doctor and his family taken a year before. Thayer looked a lot different with his face all put together.

He cranked the volume when the scene switched to the press conference inside the building.

Agent Zeke Bunning positioned himself behind a podium in what appeared to be a municipal courtroom. Every year the agent looked worse. Two years ago, when B.J. had first seen him, Zeke's large frame had a commanding presence. His height carried his thick build with grace. The shaved head, round spectacles, and square jaw all combined to give him a dominant air, a kiss-my-ass-I'm-the-FBI look.

But tonight he looked like a bug had crawled up his ass and feasted on his innards. Pale face, sagging jowls, limp suit, sunken eyes. Beaten. B.J. chuckled.

Bunning adjusted a small stack of note cards and peered into the cameras, cleared his throat, began. "Ladies and gentlemen, I'm FBI Agent Zeke Bunning." He paused and blew through his nose. Twitched his glasses. "Another tragic shooting took place this morning. Like past victims, Doctor Charles Thayer was struck in the head and killed instantly. And like past shootings, no one heard or saw anything. We have to assume this is the work of the same shooter everyone has referred to as Billy Ray Jackson."

"No shit, Sherlock." B.J. adjusted himself on the bed and slumped back on his pillow. He reached over and flipped on a lamp. A roach scampered across the floor and disappeared into a crack in the wall.

"At this point, however, no .308 rifle casing has been received by Plano PD. As everyone knows, in past years the shooter has mailed a casing to the local chief. In addition, fragments recovered from the victim indicate the bullet may have come from a different gun than that used in earlier shootings."

A low mumble moved through the crowd.

B.J. frowned and stared at the TV, puzzled. What in the hell was he talking about? A different gun? He sat up on the bed.

"The remains from today's bullet," Zeke went on, "will be sent to the FBI crime lab for extensive testing. Despite the inconsistencies, we are working under the assumption that this shooting is a continuation of the series that began on this date three years ago. At least until we discover evidence to prove otherwise. The Plano Police Department is assisting the FBI in the investigation of today's shooting. But this is now the

FBI's case." He paused. "I'll take questions now."

B.J. nodded and considered the casing. It was too early to worry. It probably hadn't made it yet.

"Are you saying today's shooting might not be related to the previous twelve? That you may be dealing with a copycat?" The reporter was from CNN, one B.J. recognized.

"It's too early to make that assumption," Zeke said. "The fact that we haven't yet received the casing is not unusual. In four of the previous twelve shootings, the casing wasn't received until the next day. And the different rifling marks on the recovered bullet fragments aren't confirmed yet."

"But it *could* be a copycat," the reporter pressed, "if the rifling marks are different."

"Again, I couldn't say that. Maybe the shooter bought a better rifle."

That amused B.J. "Right."

"Why is the FBI taking over the case?" someone shouted from the back of the room.

The camera cut to a close-up of Zeke's face. The lines around his eyes deepened as he squinted. "Due to resources and manpower capabilities, we felt this would be the most productive move. Plano PD will be—"

"Is it to protect Plano's detectives?" the same voice interrupted. "Is it to confuse Jackson?"

"Tell us," B.J. said. " 'Cause I'm confused as hell."

"It's an investigative decision," Zeke said patiently. "Plano PD has assigned a number of detectives to the case. The Bureau will simply coordinate the direction."

"What about the witness brought in this afternoon?"

B.J. leaned forward. Witness?

"While canvassing the apartment complex this morning," Zeke said, "Plano detectives came across a man they knew had warrants. They arrested him. He had nothing to offer this case."

B.J. thought about that for a moment. Last year the FBI claimed to have a witness and then tried to set a trap, hoping he would just stroll into it. Of course, that meant they really didn't have a witness. Now Zeke denied having one, which probably meant they did. And if they did, it was probably from the apartment complex. And that meant they probably knew about the motor home.

Not good. But the excitement of the FBI having a real lead was undeniable.

"What about the legal community?" a reporter probed. "What advice do you have for them?"

"The same advice as last year. Take precautions. Close all blinds and curtains in your house and office, take different routes to work, call the police if you see anything suspicious, work out of your house if you feel it would help, keep indoors as much as possible. In short, make yourself a difficult target. We realize people must live their lives, and that we can't put the legal system on hold in Plano, but be careful and alert. Until the shooter is caught, it's important to assume it could happen to you."

"That advice didn't work last year, Agent Bunning," the same voice pressed.

"If you wish to state the obvious, yes. That's true. Would you like to offer up something else?" Zeke squinted to his left, his face hard.

"How many agents are being assigned?" a voice yelled out.

"The exact number is unknown at this time. Several dozen. Some are arriving as we speak. Most tomorrow."

B.J. grew tired of the mundane questions and flipped off the TV. He finished his beer and crumpled the can against his leg.

He strolled to the back door and looked at the barn twenty yards away. A single bulb positioned over the barn door cast a weak circle of yellow light on the ground. The first leg of the tunnel ran from the shower stall in the hall bath to the barn. But since he'd dug that leg four years before, the wild grass and weeds had long-since covered the slight ridge that had once protruded like a serpent across the flat farmland.

He'd finished the second leg two years ago, which led from the center of the barn to the neighbor's property line eighty yards to the north. The third leg was also completed, with only a couple of rusty hinges on one trapdoor needing to be replaced. Tomorrow.

Tonight he'd spend the next ten minutes checking the barn, locking down the house, and activating all of the surveillance cameras and video motion detectors. Once he was confident that everything was in order, he would lock himself in his bedroom and cut the lights.

Once in bed, he stared at the ceiling and recalled what little information Agent Bunning had revealed in the press conference. So he was taking the lead in the case.

Interesting. But it wouldn't work. The FBI couldn't protect Stubs. Nobody could. They just didn't know it yet. He hadn't shot thirteen people in four cities to stop now. He hadn't laid false leads all over the country just to stop because the FBI decided they'd take over the case.

B.J. laughed out loud, his voice vibrating through the thin walls of the farmhouse. Just as sure as he could hit a quarter at 400 yards, the little asshole from summer camp all those years ago was a dead man walking.

CHAPTER FOUR

The key to accuracy with rifle shooting is having everything happen exactly the same way every time. That's what B.J.'s dad had always told him. There were the things you could control: the position of your body, bone support, eye relief, cheek weld, trigger pull, sight picture, and breathing. And things you couldn't: the wind and temperature and humidity, and the target itself. The mechanical stuff, like the rifle, the bullet, and the scope were equally important. And, depending on how much money a person had to spend or how much skill he had in building his own gun and loading his own ammo, and how much time a person was willing to devote to training, the art of placing bullet after bullet through the same hole was absolutely doable.

Shooting the Stevens bolt-action .22s at Camp Indian Hill had proven to be a challenge for B.J. He had the skills of course, for he had put in more training time than anyone else and had been taught by the best rifleman the Marine Corps had ever produced. Nor were the elements a problem. He could figure wind drifts, calculate minute angle adjustments in his head, read mirages off the hard, hot ground, and understood what humidity did to bullet drag. He could angle shoot, hit moving targets by leading, tracking, or ambushing, knew the difference between a half and quarter value wind, could figure distances using the mil dots on a scope, and could read the light well enough to adjust the impact of the shot.

No, none of what his dad had taught him was causing him problems shooting the Stevens .22s. The problem was the gun itself. And the ammo: the cheap .22 longs the camp had probably bought by the thousands from some guy in a dark alley. B.J. noticed the rifles the first day the boys had been allowed to shoot. Most had rust spots dotting the faded bluing, some had cracks in the stock, and some of the bolts were gummed up, making the gun hard to cycle.

B.J. hadn't mentioned his concerns to any of the other boys, opting instead to keep quiet and carefully sift through the rifles to find the best one for himself. The very first morning the boys from his age group were allowed to enter the shooting shack one at a time to carefully choose a rifle that would be assigned to them for the remainder of camp, B.J. had spent longer than anyone in the cramped, musty shed. He'd chosen what many of the boys considered the ugliest rifle of all. The stock was a plain walnut, with a chunk of wood missing where the stock met the butt plate. The wood was streaked with some kind of black oil that emitted a strange odor. The fore stock was cracked from end to end and had been hastily repaired with duct tape.

But what the other boys didn't know about B.J.'s selection was that the bolt and action were tightly milled, the bore was unpitted and smooth, and the rear sights appeared new, with positive adjustment clicks that were easy to feel. Many of the other boys had laughed at B.J.'s choice, but he knew that a pretty stock made no difference.

Stubs had made a pretty nice choice, and his performance had verified that he had some knowledge of basic rifle marksmanship. But he would never beat B.J. and both boys knew it.

It was a few minutes before lunch on Friday of week two and

B.J. had just shot his fifteen rounds. Stubs was prone, settling in for his first shot. He was last today and the rest of the boys were itching to get to the dining hall. The others had no interest in how Stubs was about to do, because he and B.J. were so far ahead in total points none of the other boys had a chance at first or second place.

But B.J. was very interested. B.J. had dropped three points when one round took a fly and landed in the seven-ring. If Stubs hit all fifteen ten-ring shots, his 150 points would put him within twenty points of first place. Though Stubs hadn't yet shot a perfect score on any of his strings, he'd come close three times.

From his position directly behind Stubs, B.J. watched as the big boy settled down behind his rifle. His legs were spread wide, the insides of his feet flat against the ground. His loop sling was tight around his left bicep, and the rifle rested comfortably in the palm of his left hand. His head was positioned correctly, with just a slight cant to the right, allowing for near-perfect eye relief. His problem, B.J. knew, was the lack of bone support under the rifle. He should have shortened his sling, forcing his support arm into more of a ninety-degree angle, that would have allowed the rifle to rest on solid bone. Stubs was counting on the sling to support the rifle, which would be fine for the first few shots. But then his left arm would begin to fatigue and he'd start muscling the gun. And because the key to accuracy is doing the same thing every single time, Stubs was sunk before he ever started.

The judge yelled out the result of Stubs's first shot: ten-ring. The next four shots, the same. B.J. watched Stubs wiggle the fingers of his support hand and exhale loudly. Shot number six was a ten-ring, but was only called so after the judge studied the hole for several seconds, which meant the bullet had torn the line of the nine-ring.

Four shots to go. B.J. studied the muzzle of Stubs's rifle and noticed a slight quiver. His support arm was wearing down.

Stubs shifted position, edged a little closer to the rifle, pulled it tighter into his shoulder. B.J. knew what was happening. Stubs was trying to support the rifle by pulling it tighter into his shoulder, allowing him to take some of the pressure off his support arm.

Mistake.

Shot seven hit high into the top of the eight-ring. B.J. could have predicted it. Stubs had changed his sight radius, moved his eye relief, and had muscled the rifle down into his shoulder, causing the muzzle to point more skyward.

Shot eight hit high into the top of the eight-ring, also.

Stubs would over-compensate on the next shot. B.J. knew it just as surely as he knew the last two shots would fly high.

"Bottom of the nine-ring," the judge shouted. "Last shot coming up."

Shot number ten took awhile. Stubs lay there for what seemed five minutes before the report of the .22 rang out. As soon as the recoil had worked its way through the rifle, Stubs rolled onto his left side and slipped the loop sling off of his left bicep. The big boy sat up on his knees as the judge announced that the last shot had hit the ten-ring.

He dropped five points, B.J. quickly calculated. That meant Stubs had fallen two more points overall behind him. A weak clap worked its way through the group of impatient boys, and only then did the judge release everyone to the dining hall.

Within seconds B.J. found himself alone with Stubs, who was packing his rifle onto the cart that would be pushed into the old shed.

"Good job," B.J. said, walking over. "I thought you had me when you started off with six straight ten-rings."

"What'd I do wrong?" Stubs asked as he swiped his sweaty forehead. "Was it my support arm?"

B.J. liked Stubs. He was turning into maybe his best friend. But he wasn't about to give him any shooting tips. "Your sling *looked tight to me," B.J. said. "Did your arm get tired?"*

"Major. I think I should have had my support hand up under the rifle more. I need to shorten my sling." He shrugged and slapped B.J. on the back. "Don't matter now, though. The shots are down range. Let's go eat."

That's what made B.J. nervous about this competition. Stubs was smart, a fast learner. Maybe Stubs hadn't gotten the kind of instruction B.J. had received from his own father, but the big boy could figure stuff out. B.J. wasn't far enough ahead to think he had the trophy in the bag. And he knew that Stubs wanted it as badly as he did. So there would be no shooting tips given. No way. B.J. still had a long way to go. There was a lot of shooting left to do. And Stubs would never give up trying to catch him. Never.

The meeting was impromptu, but required. Rush had peeled away every shred of politeness when he had called Chinbroski at nearly 11:00 P.M. and practically ordered him to bring Nanci over to his house that very minute. It was nearly midnight before Chinbroski and his fiancée snuck into Rush's kitchen through the back door.

Daniel, Rush's twenty-seven-year-old son, was sipping a lite beer on the sofa when Chinbroski escorted Nanci into the living room. Rush watched Daniel raise his beer in Chinbroski's direction, and watched Chinbroski snort at him before flopping down on the loveseat next to Nanci.

"What in the holy hell is going on?" Chinbroski asked. He glared at Rush, scowled at Daniel, then softened his expression before glancing at Mallory, who sat in her rocking chair next to Daniel's end of the sofa.

Rush studied his wife as she sat in her chair, slowly rocking and nodding, keeping beat to a song playing inside her head. She ignored the group around her, tightly clutching the stuffed rabbit that had lately rarely left her hands. Her face and neck, a patchwork of scars, seemed to sag in places not normal for a woman in her late thirties. Over the last eighteen months, while her mental condition steadily deteriorated, her physical presence had declined just as noticeably. She used to light up a room with her smile, purposefully work a crowd, making her way to each and every person and leaving them with a heartfelt squeeze of affection or a genuine compliment.

But that was before.

"We're about to have a meeting of the minds," Daniel told Chinbroski. "We'll make sure and speak two-syllable words, so you can keep up." He smiled and tipped his beer bottle.

Daniel was a near spitting-image of Rush, something that Rush had always been proud of, but never mentioned. He was a crack attorney with a thriving little defense firm in McKinney, the Collin County seat.

"I've met your mind, you pencil-neck. So I won't have to be disappointed again. So already, it's a positive meeting."

Nanci gave Chinbroski an elbow jab in the ribs.

Like Mallory, Nanci was a violent crime victim, but unlike Mallory, had fought through the Post Traumatic Stress Syndrome. Nanci wore her black, shoulder-length hair parted in the middle. It fell lightly against her oversized glasses and framed her lean face, softening her features. Her 100-pound frame was an athletic version of Mallory's. She had fallen for Chinbroski within minutes of meeting him the previous summer. That was fortunate for Chinbroski, who had fallen for her within the first five seconds.

"We're here to talk about the shootings," Rush said, probably not surprising anyone in the room. "We need to discuss the evacuation."

Three of the four faces stared at him in silence.

Mallory nodded to the song in her head.

"Chin and I have to work the case," Rush said. "There's

no getting around that. But there's no reason why the three of you should hang around here."

Daniel chuckled. His hollow laugh, one that Rush had long ago recognized always preceded a serious disagreement, was the only sound in the room.

"You don't have to convince me," Nanci said. "I talked to Rick about it this afternoon. I'm heading to Kansas City tomorrow morning. Mother has offered my old room back for as long as I need it."

"Good." Rush nodded. "Good. What about the wedding?"

Nanci shook her head and glanced at Chinbroski. "We're postponing. I made several calls today. I'll make the rest before I head out tomorrow. Since Rick cancelled his vacation, we see no need to risk anything."

Chinbroski's face flashed red when Rush looked over in surprise. "You cancelled your vacation? When?"

"Today. I pulled it before our meeting with Zeke."

"And you didn't tell me?"

"I would've. No big deal."

Rush leaned forward. "But I already told the captain that you were gone in two weeks. He's only counting on you for two weeks. Don't cancel your vacation, Chin. Get the hell out of Dodge."

"And leave you hanging? Right. What a great partner I'd be."

"Listen," Rush said with more hardness than he intended. "You don't have to prove yourself to me. Get the hell out of here. Meet Nanci in Kansas City in two weeks. Get to know her mother."

"Bad move, Pop," Daniel said. "More than a few hours with Chin would be enough to make Nanci's mom poison his tea to save her daughter from a lifetime of misery."

"I've already told the captain I'm staying," Chinbroski said, ignoring Daniel. "Drop it. I ain't leaving you here to fight this on your own."

Rush stood and shook his head. He walked over and stood behind Mallory, who had begun singing quietly. She rocked the stuffed rabbit and stroked its furry ears.

"And I'm not leaving, either," Daniel said. "Because contrary to common belief, I actually work for a living. People depend on me. And besides, I have court most of next week."

"What about this week?" Rush asked.

"This week? You ask because this Jackson character shoots the lawyer next?"

"Can you take this seriously?" Chinbroski said. "Yes, he shoots the lawyer next."

"And I work in McKinney," Daniel said. "He'll be shooting someone in Plano, if I've correctly read the newspaper accounts of his history."

"But you're living here," Rush said.

"Temporarily," Daniel reminded him. "Something I could fix, starting in about ten minutes. My house in McKinney would surely put me out of harm's way. Am I correct?"

"While sounding like a little snot," Chinbroski said.

Nanci gave him another elbow jab and added a wifely look of warning. Chinbroski fell silent.

"This is going to sound crass," Rush said, after giving Mallory's shoulders a squeeze. "But I want you out of here until Jackson shoots the lawyer." He walked around and leaned against the entertainment center, facing Daniel squarely.

"I take that comment to mean that you have given up on catching him before that time. Sounds defeatist, if you ask me." Daniel drained his bottle and placed it carefully on the coffee table. "Not that I'm criticizing. By the way, it did sound crass."

"The FBI hasn't got a clue," Rush said. "And all indications are that Jackson plots every shooting—except the detective—weeks, probably months, in advance. Will you be the target? The odds are impossibly remote. But we can't know that. So I want you out of here."

"And what about Mallory?" Daniel asked, all traces of humor and sarcasm gone. "The nanny has made it clear that she just won't stay past eight o'clock. Not without double-time, which you can't afford. And I have no doubt you'll be burning both ends of the candle working this case."

He was right, Rush knew. His unpredictable work schedule was exactly why Daniel had been living with them the last two months. "Can you take her with you?"

"You mean in the evenings?"

"Right. After the nanny leaves." Rush knew it was a lot to ask. Daniel worked fifteen miles away. He'd have to drive down to get her after work every day, then drive back to McKinney. Rush would pick her up at night, of course, but Daniel's part would be very time-consuming. "Just until Jackson shoots the lawyer," Rush reminded him shamefully.

"That does sound crass," Nanci said. "Fatalistic."

"Inevitable," Chinbroski added. "Rush is being a realist. Ain't no way we can prevent Jackson's next shooting."

Rush sighed heavily and sat down again. He couldn't get comfortable. Nerves, he knew. Stand, sit, pace, he just could not stay still.

"Whatever it takes," Daniel said. "It's not like I have a social life, anyway."

He has given so freely of his time, Rush thought.

This was why it had been so hard to ask. He and Daniel had discussed at length the pros and cons of sending Mallory to a permanent home, and though he knew Daniel was right to strongly recommend that Rush do so, Rush just wouldn't do that to her.

"Thank you," Rush told Daniel. He wiped a tear away as he watched Mallory play with her stuffed rabbit.

He couldn't look at her without remembering her scrubbing the imaginary stain on the entryway floor, the manifestation of her near-death experience. She scrubbed as though she could somehow remove the horror of her past. He remembered her conversations with specters seen only by her, and then the slow withdrawal into the recesses of her own broken mind.

No medications had worked, no amount of group sessions with similarly afflicted victims helped. Hypnosis had been a waste of time. Besides her long-term doctor, Rush had spent more money than he really had on one-on-one visits to leading psychologists in the Dallas area. He was at his wits end, with nothing left but a state-run hospital as an option. Or in-home care, which he and Daniel had been trying of late.

"So, listen, Pop," Daniel said, standing. "You have anything else?"

"Just to remind you to take this seriously. You have an annoying habit of ignoring most every suggestion I make."

Chinbroski snorted a hearty amen.

"Not since you warned me of the dangers of syphilis have I taken you as seriously," Daniel said. "But it's late. So if there's nothing else, I'll swing by here tomorrow evening to pick Mallory up." Daniel gave Mallory a peck on the forehead, smiled sweetly at Nanci, and blew Chinbroski a kiss before heading toward his bedroom at the back of the house.

Chinbroski waited a beat before turning to Rush. "You're really not worried are you? About Daniel?"

"No. But there's no reason not to play it safe. Jackson has

been fairly consistent with his timetable, prior to last year, at least. So if I can get Daniel to stay out of Plano for a couple of weeks, everything should be fine."

Nanci stood and pulled on Chinbroski's arm. "We need to go. It's late. And I've got a long drive tomorrow." She walked over to Mallory and gave her a squeeze. "Sweet thing," she whispered. Then Nanci gave Rush a hug. "Take care of her. I still believe."

That she'll eventually be okay, she didn't finish. Rush had heard Nanci's prediction of Mallory's eventual recovery for a year now. But she had only gotten worse.

"I'll keep her out of harm's way," Rush assured her. "You have a safe drive to Kansas City and try not to worry about us. Thanks for going."

Nanci nodded and wiped her eyes. She turned quickly to Chinbroski. "Let's go. It's late."

Chinbroski followed her to the door and waved at Rush. "Tomorrow at the diner," he said. "After I see Nanci off."

"Okay."

When the front door closed behind them, Rush turned to his wife and felt a sudden wave of exhaustion. It would take him thirty minutes to get her showered, dressed, and tucked into bed. Then he would report to the guest room, where he'd been sleeping the last six months.

She was still a beautiful woman: soft brown hair, high cheekbones, full lips that exposed a wonderful, girlish smile. Her body, though soft from inactivity and crisscrossed with scars, was full and round in the right places. Rush ached with a constant loneliness that seemed to hover just beneath the surface of his skin.

He gently led her into the master bathroom. She clutched the rabbit with a childlike fervor and smiled at Rush, humming a made-up tune. Though he'd never place her in a mental hospital, a nursing home might not be too far in her future. He just hoped that once there, if she ever did recover, she would forgive him for giving up on her.

Rush woke the next morning, having gotten little sleep.

Rubbing his eyes, he had a fleeting thought that he'd just awakened from a nightmare: that Billy Ray Jackson wasn't really in Plano, that he wasn't the lead investigator, and that the clock wasn't ticking on his life.

Then reality returned. He stared at the ceiling, wondering how in the hell they were going to catch Jackson. Zeke had offered nothing after the press conference the night before. But Zeke was tired, or looked it anyway, and probably hadn't wanted to get into everything right then. Rush would get the plan this morning.

He was in and out of the shower by 6:30. Pulling on his suit from the day before, he holstered his .45, clipped on his badge, and shoved handcuffs into the small of his back. He walked into the master bedroom and kissed Mallory lightly on the top of the head. She didn't stir. After the nanny arrived at a few minutes past 7:00, he left the house with a knot in his stomach.

He pulled into the parking lot of Paul's Diner right behind Chinbroski. Their usual breakfast spot, Paul's was a no-at-mosphere cafe on the east side, four blocks from the police station. Chinbroski was dressed in a tee shirt, jeans, and running shoes. His flattop stood erect, his freshly-shaved face as pink as a baby's bottom.

"Yo, Rush," he said, holding the café door open. "How's it hanging?"

"Bends to the left. Checked this morning." Rush waved at the waitress to bring coffee and two blueberry muffins. A creature of habit.

Chinbroski waved also, and in minutes was sitting behind five eggs, four strips of bacon, three biscuits, and a thick slice of ham. He shoved a fork full of eggs into his mouth and nodded at Rush's muffins. "Need to eat more than that. How many times I gotta tell you?"

Rush ignored him and his table manners.

"I assume you got Nanci off okay?" Rush asked, watching him sop up egg yoke with a piece of biscuit.

He nodded between bites. "She was happy to get the hell away from here."

The breakfast crowd was filling the café. Rush shifted in his chair, adjusted his holster. "What do you think about the lie? Zeke's I mean. The press conference last night."

"The lie?" Chinbroski said. "You mean lies. Not getting the envelope *and* the shit about the rifling marks being different." Chinbroski brushed crumbs off the front of his shirt and checked for eavesdroppers before continuing. "What's he up to?"

Rush waited for a construction worker to pass before answering. "He's not saying."

"Why?"

"He said he couldn't discuss it right then. I caught up to him just after the press conference." Rush shrugged. "Believe me, the conversation is far from over. But he told us as much in the meeting yesterday. About feeding the press. Force Jackson into a mistake. My gut says it's going to get a lot worse before it gets better." He lowered his voice. "You know me, Chin. I don't worry about many things. But I'm worried about working with Zeke. It's not that I don't like him. He's a friendly guy, I'm just not crazy about working with him."

Chinbroski stuck a piece of ham into his mouth, stared at him while he chewed.

"He can't make decisions under pressure," Rush continued. "And he has to be under more pressure than anything we can imagine. Again, I like the guy. I just don't trust him."

His partner just chewed.

"He'll get a person killed in the heat of battle. And what scares the shit out of me is that he might piss off this shooter."

Chinbroski frowned. "If he's not any good, why would the FBI put him in charge?"

Rush took a bite of muffin, shrugged. "Who knows? It's the FBI way. They think they have all the answers. You think they'd admit that putting Zeke on this was a mistake?"

"Assuming it was. You're the only one who seems to have that opinion."

The waitress filled Chinbroski's coffee cup. Rush covered his cup with his hand and shook his head. She shuffled off.

Chinbroski ran a hand over his flattop and leaned back in his chair, his expression still skeptical.

"Think I'm nuts?" Rush asked. "Maybe stress-related hallucinations?"

"What I've read about him is pretty amazing," Chinbroski said. "Didn't he figure out who was murdering all those old farmers in Minnesota a few years back? And catch the two guys robbing and killing the fishermen down in New Orleans? And then the guy in Philly who thought he was the next Son of Sam? Sounds like he works under stress pretty well."

Rush waved him off. "I know all that. That doesn't change the fact that I *know* him. That I've seen him clam up under pressure. Freeze, unable to think. I've seen it, Chin. More than once."

His partner didn't look convinced.

"Want examples?" Rush scooted his chair closer to the table, propped a fist near his mouth. "During our FBI violent crimes task force days together we, Zeke and me, were teamed up, partners, during several training sessions.

"We're doing an investigative detention exercise. Zeke and I walk into a bar scene, supposed to question a bank robbery suspect we know is inside. Zeke sees him across the bar and starts heading that way. I'm on his heels. Halfway across, some guy steps out from the bar screaming he can smell a Fed a mile away. Blocks Zeke's path. Gets right up in his face, screaming, spraying spit all over him."

Rush paused and lowered his voice, which had climbed with the memory. "I'm ready to drop the guy," he continued, "but I'm a few feet back and I'm watching the bank robbery suspect, who's starting to move around to the far wall with his hand stuck inside his coat like he's armed. I glance at Zeke, thinking he needs to either drop the guy in his face or walk around him. But he's just standing there, frozen, looking at the *floor!* I'm still watching the bank robbery suspect, who's now almost behind us, still heading for the door. The other guy bumps Zeke's chest, shoves him. Well, we're supposed to be a team. I figure the robbery suspect is the most important thing, so I head in his direction and cut him off before he hits the door. I order his hands out of his pockets, face down on the floor, all that jazz. Handcuff him. I look back at Zeke, and the other guy's shoving him all over the room. I run over and slam the guy from behind. Handcuff him for assaulting a federal agent. Zeke did nothing. Nothing."

Chinbroski shook his head. "Guess he failed that part, huh?"

"There was no pass/fail, but the instructor wasn't happy."

"Okay, so the guy's a pencil-neck who couldn't fight his way out of a girls' locker room. What difference does that make? We ain't looking for him to kick Jackson's ass."

Rush shook his head. "You're not listening. Had a bank robbery exercise. Zeke grabbed a note the suspect gave the teller and ruined the only latent print. Brain-lock. Kidnapping exercise. Zeke forgot to start the tape recorder to record the suspect's demands, then wrote the directions down wrong. Brain-lock."

"Almost ten years ago, Rush. Who cares?"

"I do."

Chinbroski chuckled. "You're a perfectionist and always have been. So Bunning did crappy when he had to perform with an instructor breathing down his neck. He doesn't have that kind of pressure now. He has time to think things out. And he's done a hell of a job, or they wouldn't have him chasing Jackson."

Rush was silent for a moment and considered that. "What if Zeke pisses this killer off? I mean really pisses him off? If he brain-locks again, it'll mean people's lives. Real lives, not another agent's in a training exercise."

Chinbroski just stared at him. "Well, I guess Zeke's pretty damn lucky," he said finally, "that you're on the case to bail his ass out. Again."

The investigative briefing was held at the Tri-City Police Training Academy on the far east side of Plano. The room resembled those commonly found on college campuses: a podium in front and theater-style elevated rows. It easily held the sixty-plus investigators.

Rush and Chinbroski sat in the back row. Zeke stood behind the podium, staring at the ceiling. He wore a wrinkled blue suit and scuffed loafers. The bags under his eyes reminded Rush of burnt marshmallows. Rush had decided to catch him after the briefing. He wanted in on whatever plan Zeke had hatched last night, convinced it was some kind of psycho-babble, some concoction where Zeke would try to outsmart the killer instead of just trying to catch him.

"I want to thank everyone for being on time," Zeke said

after everyone found a seat. "For those Plano detectives who don't know me, my name is Zeke Bunning. I'm a profiler assigned to the FBI's Criminal Behavioral Analysis Unit. I've been assigned to the Jackson shootings for the last two years."

He walked out from behind the podium, leaned against the edge of a table. "Let's talk about some of the things we need to accomplish over the next few days. We'll check registration records for every hotel, motel, RV park, apartment complex, and condominium and townhouse project within a fifty-mile radius. We'll visit every newspaper office in the Dallas area and check six months of back issues for house rentals and private apartments. Why six months? The research and planning necessary to do these shootings would take at least two or three months to organize, and we want to make sure we've covered all the bases. After we have these names—thousands, I'm sure—we'll set out eliminating them, one by one."

Rush heard a low rumbling in the crowd. Most of it from the Plano detectives, unaccustomed to tackling an investigation of this magnitude.

"The gathering of this information will fall to all of you," Zeke continued. "However, hundreds of FBI agents will be supporting the effort to eliminate these names. The bureau will act as a clearinghouse by utilizing agents in offices all over the country to exonerate these people."

He stepped back behind the podium. "I have an assignment for each of you. They're up here on the table in front of me. We have a huge task ahead of us. Let's keep things organized and confidential. The command post for the investigation will be here at the academy building.

"The special 800 number given to the public will be answered here. The phone company is working on that now. The phones will be monitored twenty-four hours a day, and agents will enter all tips directly into our special computer program. We don't have any concrete information to work with, so don't get frustrated when you come up dry. It's happened before and will again. If we can run an organized investigation, we might get him this year."

Chinbroski glanced at Rush and raised an eyebrow.

"Each of you will be assigned to a specific response team," Zeke said. "Each team—Red, Blue, Green and Gold—will have a different responsibility when the shooter strikes again. You will be issued a special radio and beeper that must be kept with you at all times. You'll find the list of names of each team here on the table. Memorize your respective instructions and leave the sheets in the room."

Zeke stepped away from the podium, but then stopped.

"Oh, one last thing. We'll get several dozen police protection requests from lawyers. I have a special team of agents to deal with those. It's mainly a public relations offering. Okay, that's about it. Questions?" People looked at each other, but no one asked anything. "Great, let's do it."

Rush grabbed Chinbroski's arm as his partner started to stand. "Hang on."

Chinbroski nodded and slumped back into his chair. As the crowd thinned, Rush leaned over and spoke quietly. "Let's find out what's going on."

Chinbroski turned in his chair and faced Rush, whispered, "Remember, the stuff you told me? Ten years ago. Ancient history."

From the front of the room Zeke glanced at Rush. He broke away from his conversation with another agent, slowly strode to the back of the room, and pulled out a chair.

"Good morning, Greg. Sleep well?" He glanced at Chinbroski and nodded.

"Last night's press conference," Rush said. "What the—"

Zeke held up his hands, cutting him off. "I know what you're going to say. I'm just throwing him a little curve ball."

Rush nodded. "A curve ball. We didn't get the envelope? He might have bought a better gun? The rifling marks might be different? Any idiot would know we haven't had time to run the ballistics."

Zeke folded his hands on his lap and smiled. "I'm counting on the idiots this year."

Leaning back in his chair, Rush crossed his arms and set his jaw. He silently counted to three before he spoke. "What's going on, Zeke? What are you doing?"

Chinbroski shifted in his chair. Rush could hear him breathing, like little shots from an air compressor. Getting pissed.

Zeke held eye contact with Rush for several seconds before finally looking away. He reached into his jacket and pulled out a photo. The picture was a four-by-six snapshot, color, worn at the edges. He laid it face-up on the table and slid it toward Rush. "I'm trying to prevent this from happening to you."

Rush didn't look at it. Sweat trickled down his back.

"It's last year's lead detective. Susan Mandling. Mother of two-year-old twins." Zeke leaned forward in his chair, rested his chin on top of his interlocked fingers, his eyes locked on the photo. "All the victims up to that point had been male. You know what I told Susan and her husband?"

Rush said nothing.

"I told them I really didn't think this guy would shoot a woman." Zeke looked up. "Can you believe it?"

Wrong again, Rush thought. Yes, he believed it.

"I told them that because I was short-sighted with my profile. We worked our asses off to protect her, I told you that yesterday. But I really didn't think he'd shoot a woman."

Zeke rubbed the side of his smooth head and frowned. "Know what's ironic? It helped Susan, helped get her through everything. And her husband. Until . . ."

Rush snatched a look at the photo, but cut his eyes away when he saw a ragged hole in the center of the woman's forehead, the blood seeping from her vacant eyes, and the single fly feasting on raw, exposed flesh. Flipping it over, he pushed it back toward Zeke, feeling as though he might choke from the knot in his throat.

"So what I'm doing, Greg, is trying to do whatever the hell I have to. And what you heard last night was . . . well, it was a curve ball. And that's all I can say."

Rush couldn't get his mouth to work. Faceless Susan had clamped his jaws shut.

Zeke picked up the photo, hid it away, and stood. "Every time I start to doubt what I'm about to do, I look at Susan's picture to remind me that this assassin doesn't give a shit about us. And now . . ." He paused and looked at Chinbroski. "Greg is the first . . . he's a friend. And I feel as though . . ." He turned away and lowered his voice. "I just can't let this son-of-a-bitch win this year."

CHAPTER FIVE

"Do you have a girlfriend?" Stubs asked B.J. as they lay on the gravel bank nearest a deep part of the mountain creek. It had been several days since the big storm, and the creek had returned to normal size.

They'd found the perfect swimming hole. Nearly seven feet deep, the section of creek curled around a series of small cliffs that jutted out of the bottom of the mountain like the toes of a giant foot. The jump from the rocks to the water was no more than six feet, and Stubs and B.J. had worn themselves out the last two hours climbing in and out of the water.

Resting before they headed back to camp, the question about having a girlfriend had taken B.J. by surprise.

"Naw," he said. "I don't do girls."

"I got three girlfriends," Stubs said, not at all shocking B.J. with another brag. Or another lie.

"I heard Dallas has a big school for blind girls," B.J. said. "But I didn't know you knew any of them."

"What?" Stubs frowned for a second, then got the joke. "Funny. Don't believe me. But it's the truth. Their names are Sandy, Doris, and Gretchen. They're all friends, but none of them know that I'm going steady with any of the others."

"Huh?" B.J. said. "Are they like retarded or something? Do they have BO?"

"Keep making jokes. But you should see them. Sandy and Doris already outgrew their training bras. What's that tell you?"

"It tells me you're a peeping Tom, because there ain't no girl who's gonna tell you that."

"How do you know? Maybe the girls are different in Dallas."

"And maybe you wouldn't know a training bra from a jock strap." B.J. sat up and brushed a couple of small rocks from his back. Then he grabbed his shirt and stood. "You ready?"

Stubs climbed up and swiped at the seat of his swimming trunks. "I know more than you think I do," he said, pulling his shirt over his head. "Like periods. You know about that?"

B.J. knew. His dad had told him. And it sounded like Stubs was fishing for information. "Like at the end of a sentence? Instead of a question mark?"

"You're a retard," Stubs said. "You don't know nothing."

B.J. laughed and shook his head as he started wading across a shallow section of the creek.

"Have you ever French kissed?"

This time B.J. really didn't know what Stubs was talking about. "Sure."

"With who?"

"None of your business." French kiss? He'd seen kissing on TV, he'd seen his mom and dad kiss. A lot of times people closed their eyes. Is that what he meant?

"Your mom, right?" Stubs asked. "You French kissed your mom? Most boys do. I do. I mean my foster mom said boys are supposed to."

B.J. had absolutely no experience with girls. He'd never kissed one, never held one's hand, never had a girlfriend, and he just didn't care.

"I tried it with Doris, but she slapped me," Stubs said.

At the other side of the creek B.J. shook the water off his feet and walked over to their shoes. He dried his feet with his socks before pulling them on.

"So you never heard about French kissing your mom?" Stubs asked. " 'Cause I'm getting a weird feeling about it."

"I don't even know what it is," B.J. finally admitted. "I'm an ignoramus. You caught me. Okay? I'm girl stupid."

"It's using your tongue."

B.J. stopped tying his shoes. "What?"

"You know, sticking your tongue in each other's mouths."

"That's gross. I just kiss my mom on the cheek. Lips are off-limits. I've never heard of that."

"I hadn't either until a few months ago." Stubs quickly tied both shoes and picked up the big stick he'd carried all the way from camp. He'd used that stick to hammer at least two hundred tree branches on the hike up.

"Sounds weird to me," B.J. said. "I sure ain't sticking my tongue in no girl's mouth. Especially my mom. Does she squeeze your butt while y'all are French kissing?"

Stubs made a face. "Get real. She said that was the way all boys kissed their moms. What's the big deal?"

"You're the one who brought it up. Don't ask me." B.J. started the hike back to camp, then he stopped and looked back at his big friend. "How long have you lived with this foster family?"

"Since my real mom died. Four years."

"Did you ask your foster dad about it? About the tongue thing?"

"Naw, she said that a mother's affection is a private thing between mother and son." Stubs swung his stick and whacked a low-hanging tree branch, sending leaves flying.

"Maybe you should ask him," B.J. said. " 'Cause it sounds weird."

Stubs nodded. "Maybe I will."

*B.J. noticed how red his face had turned. "What?" he asked
Stubs.*

*He swung the stick again, sent more leaves flying, then grinned
with half of his mouth. "It kind of—I don't know, kind of, you
know, makes me—" He didn't finish the sentence.*

*He didn't have to. B.J. knew what he meant. He pointed a
finger at Stubs and gave his friend his most commanding voice.
"You better tell your foster dad."*

"Right. Yeah."

*"I mean it. That's serious stuff. She's a grown woman." B.J.
stared at him, but got the impression that Stubs didn't think it was
that serious. "Whatever," he said, spinning around back toward
camp. "But I'll tell you one thing," he said over his shoulder. "If
you turn into a pervert, don't say I didn't warn you."*

B.J. pored over his hand-drawn maps and traced the exact
route that would lead him both into and out of the neighborhood. The paths were different because he couldn't risk
being seen twice by any one person. But both routes were
long, circular journeys through alleys, across yards and open
spaces, and down streets where the houses sat tight against
each other. He'd be forced to negotiate around streetlights,
avoid houses with any signs of activity, and, if possible, avoid
the dogs. He couldn't be sure how many dogs he would encounter skirting the edges of the dozens of backyard fences,
so the possibility existed that his arrival and departure would
be telegraphed.

But risk or not, this year was the end game. This year was
what it was all about. In addition to the danger increasing the
fun of the chase, this shooting would disable Stubs's mental
capacity to work the case.

It would be his most important statement to date, because
of the lawyer's relationship with Stubs. Cops always worked

harder avenging the death of one of their own, and Stubs would consider the young lawyer one of his own.

B.J. leaned back in his chair and, rubbing his eyes, considered a short nap. He was tired from spending the morning in the tunnel replacing the hinges on the trapdoors, which had rusted from the damp earth during the last year. Changing them was really a two-man job, one he considered skipping, but couldn't. He hadn't come this far to be undone by something as trivial as rusty hinges.

The combined drone of the television and air conditioning was hypnotic as B.J. sat in front of a window unit, letting cold air blow down the back of his neck. Then the noon news started.

"I'm Jeanie Kemper reporting from the Tri-City Police Training Academy, which now serves as the Billy Ray Jackson investigation headquarters. FBI Agent Zeke Bunning is directing a task force of sixty who have assembled in Plano over the last twenty-four hours. Agent Bunning made a short statement minutes ago, with nothing new to report. His report reconfirmed that Plano's police chief has not yet received a bullet casing similar to the ones mailed to the police chiefs in every other Jackson shooting.

"Agent Bunning said that Plano PD has relinquished all investigative aspects of this case to the FBI, an unusual move, and one not fully explained by either agency. Agent Bunning reiterated his full control of the case . . ."

B.J. flipped off the TV, concerned about the casing. Rubbing the stub of his left pinkie, he considered another possibility: they had it and were lying. He closed his eyes to contemplate their advantage with that strategy. Bunning held a Ph.D. in psychology and now controlled the press releases. Was the FBI man trying to confuse him, to draw him out?

That thought amused him, because he wasn't a nut who

would lose control. It could be that Bunning simply wanted to control the press. Having been in law enforcement, B.J. understood how the media hindered high-profile cases. But the casing was evidence, and cops usually didn't lie about evidence.

Then again, Stubs had. All those years ago, Stubs had lied. Although they were only thirteen then, he'd broken his vow of silence and lied his ass off, leaving B.J. alone to be punished, taunted, ridiculed, and tormented. After the camp ended, B.J. had returned home. The lies followed. He found himself an outcast among people who'd known him all of his life.

His face grew hot with the memory.

Taking a deep breath, he shifted in his chair, not sure if Zeke Bunning was lying. Then he jolted straight up in his chair. What if Bunning was lying to *Stubs?* What if the FBI had *truly* taken over the case and was in the process of convincing Stubs of these lies? What if Stubs wasn't worried because Bunning had convinced him that he, the FBI agent, would be Jackson's target? Now *that* would piss B.J. off.

B.J. rubbed his eyes. It was just too early, he thought as he stretched out on the sofa for a nap. And he didn't have time to occupy his mind with trivial matters. He had final details to work out before tonight. The young lawyer would be tricky.

Rush and Chinbroski sat in the training sergeant's office across the desk from Zeke, who looked haggard as he spoke quietly into the phone, staring off at a spot somewhere over Rush's left shoulder. Zeke's pallid skin and sunken cheeks contrasted sharply against his blackened, baggy eyes. His voice sounded tired and empty. Might the Jackson case eventually kill him, Rush wondered?

Zeke had commandeered the windowless office an hour before. From there Rush had watched him make his short, terse statement to the press during a telephone interview. Rush just shook his head as Zeke reaffirmed his lies from the night before.

"I feel as though I should explain a couple of things," Zeke said after hanging up. "I agree with what Detective Chinbroski said this morning, that you deserve to know what's going on because it's your ass on the line."

Rush nodded and glanced at his partner, who sat with his arms folded across his chest, his eyes fixed on Zeke.

"But . . . as much as I agree, I simply can't discuss my plan." Zeke leaned forward. "Before I explain why, let me tell you a little more history about the case."

The muscles in Rush's jaws ached as he fought to keep his mouth shut. He nodded again and tipped his head forward, encouraging Zeke to continue.

Zeke picked up a pencil, twirled it between two fingers. "Do you know about the fires?"

Rush could feel his blank expression. He looked at Chinbroski, who shook his head. "Fires?"

"We think it was the first thing the shooter did to cover his tracks," Zeke said. "Remember back five or six years ago all of the black churches that burned in the South? Several dozen? What got lost in the commotion were the fires inside four rural Tennessee courthouses: four different courthouses over an eight-month period. Each arson was set in the district clerk's office and each suffered heavy damage."

Chinbroski shifted in his chair, leaned forward. "Covering up birth records, maybe?"

"Maybe. Mixed in with those fires were six lawyers' offices. Same result, massive damage."

Rush quickly thought through the possibilities. They were endless.

"Covering up a criminal record?" Chinbroski guessed again.

"No, Chin," Rush said suddenly. "The killer was covering up a lawsuit he'd filed at one time." He looked at Zeke. "And with doctors, lawyers, and judges being shot, you think everything ties to some medical malpractice suit."

Zeke nodded.

"But the problem," Rush continued, "is because he set fires in four courthouses, you don't know which one to focus on. Same thing with the six lawyers."

"Right. And of the six lawyers whose offices were burned, three of them were murdered less than a month after their respective fires."

"Covering his tracks," Chinbroski said.

"What about the judges at the courthouses?" Rush asked. "Maybe one of them threw a malpractice case out of court."

"One judge from each courthouse died within three months of each fire. But none of those looked like murder cases. The remaining judges can't offer anything important."

"Seems like someone could've linked something together at the time all of this happened," Chinbroski said. "That's a lot of fires. A lot of dead people."

Zeke drummed his leg with the pencil. "Remember, all of this occurred over the course of a year, *before* he started these annual shooting sprees. And all of it happened in different parts of Tennessee. The local FBI wasn't involved in any of it. They were busy helping with the churches. Not that it would have made a difference, but now the trail is cold."

Zeke paused and Rush waited.

"To your point, Detective Chinbroski. Don't think the FBI hasn't given every effort in combing through the ashes trying to reconstruct all of the destroyed records. But you have to understand that these were very rural courthouses where records were oftentimes not backed up with downloaded computer files. We've spent months recreating the losses."

"And you're sure all of this has to do with these shootings?" Rush asked.

"Can't prove it. But I think our assumptions about the malpractice are on the money. If so, the fires are connected."

"What about hospital records?" Rush asked. "If someone filed a malpractice suit, maybe a hospital was named in the suit. There may be a copy, some records."

Zeke laughed, a hollow, uncommitted sound. "Hospitals won't open their records so the FBI can go fishing. If we had a name, we could subpoena records for that name. Otherwise, forget it."

"But you've tried?"

"At several places."

A silence fell over the room. Rush glanced at Chinbroski. His partner sat quietly, his arms still folded, his unblinking eyes still studying Zeke.

Rush set his jaw and took a deep breath. "What's with the lies, Zeke? What are you doing?"

The room grew silent again. Rush could hear the voices of other FBI agents outside the closed door. Zeke stood and paced behind the desk. "All I can tell you is that it centers around the shooter's assassin profile," he said finally, sitting on the edge of the desk. "Last year we tried a couple of things. We claimed we had a witness to the first shooting, even had a name leaked to the press. The shooter never bit. We ran surveillance on the alleged witness for two months, well after the shooting season ended. And while we were protecting Susan, the detective whose picture I showed you earlier, we set up a shooting corridor around her house and hotel, a shooting lane. We put her on a stage, tried to woo the guy in. Didn't work. He just wasn't falling for the traps we'd set."

Rush tried to swallow. Couldn't. *He* sure didn't want to be put on a stage. And couldn't imagine what he'd think about it if they tried. "What about this year?"

"Nothing that drastic. This year it's mind games." He sighed, pausing as he moved back around behind the desk. "I've made a deal with my director, Greg. He's told me to use whatever means necessary to catch this guy with the understanding that I'll be protected if I fail." He shrugged, his baggy jacket slipping lower on his shoulders. "So I'm doing what I think is necessary. But I simply can't discuss details. I know it's your ass. And I understand all the arguments. But how can I know . . . if somehow . . ." He held up his hands, gathered his thoughts. "Last year, with Susan, the shooter may have discovered our traps by some small comment made by one of the cops, some unintentional sentence spoken by someone who should have kept his mouth shut."

Rush glanced at Chinbroski, then turned back to Zeke. "But you don't know that."

"No. I don't know that." Zeke interlocked his fingers and rested them under his chin as though he couldn't keep his head up. "I believe this shooter's weakness may be what makes him so thorough: pride. I don't believe he suffers from the emotional cycling and cooling-off periods that affect serial killers. I think something tragic happened in his life, made him snap. Some triggering stressor, probably dealing with his family or a loved one. That's usually what it is. Some trauma drove him over the edge, possibly to the point of suicide. But then he decides to get some revenge before he dies. He develops a plan that covers every possible scenario of being captured." Zeke paused and stared hard at Rush. "Pride. Ego. Intelligence. This shooter has an ego as wide as Tennessee, and that's what I'm going to work on."

He sounded so confident, Rush thought, so sure. But then, Zeke sounded that way back in their violent crimes task force days. Even when he was right in the middle of being dead wrong.

It was late evening when B.J. cruised by the Tri-City Police Training Academy on his way to the east Plano neighborhood where he would soon kill the young lawyer. The huge academy parking lot was sectioned off into two distinct camps: media and police. The media contingent rivaled what B.J. remembered seeing on the news during the FBI/Waco siege in 1993. Satellite trucks by the dozens, motor homes, vans, rental cars, the entire back half of the lot overflowed with the thrill seekers carrying press passes. The front half was cordoned off by barricades, big signs prohibiting all non-police vehicles. At the rear of the building, near the gun range, sat a Dallas PD helicopter. B.J. nodded to himself and drove on.

Young Daniel Rush currently stayed in the middle house of a five-house cul-de-sac. To shoot him right under Stubs's nose would be B.J.'s crowning achievement thus far. At 8:30, as darkness began settling across north Texas, with a large tree blocking most of the light from the street lamp at the curb, the illumination across the front yard was slowly dissolving into a black haze.

B.J. had watched the house every night for six weeks. The pattern he'd observed wasn't concrete, except for Daniel Rush's arrival each evening from his office in McKinney, and his habit of sitting at the same end of the sofa between 8:00 and 10:00 P.M. each night, working on cases he'd brought home from his office. Last night at nearly midnight, Stubs had sat around with his detective partner, the young lawyer, the retarded woman, and a second woman obviously discussing the infamous Jackson shootings and how their lives might be affected. B.J. saw the worried faces, the frightened hand-wringing, the occasional tear. The midnight meeting was the strongest indicator that Agent Bunning had lied only to the press and not to Stubs. From the look on Stubs's face last night, he was plenty worried. And shooting young Daniel right under his nose would make him useless.

The biggest surprise during the six weeks of surveillance was the retarded lady, Mallory Rush. B.J. had learned her name through county marriage license records.

Most nights she just sat in the chair at the end of the sofa near the lawyer, playing with a stuffed animal. She sang songs to herself or to the toy, B.J. wasn't sure. But one thing was for certain, the lady was hot. Crazy, but hot. He wondered if Stubs was getting any off her. Taking advantage of a crazy woman. That'd be Stubs's style. Maybe French kiss her.

B.J. drove his escape route through the adjoining subdivision. He had one detail to work out, the biggest detail, the only concern about this particular shooting: getting in and out of the neighborhood without being seen. He didn't feel safe taking the shot from his truck in the middle of a residential area, because of how often people called the police about strange vehicles. And his rule was to only use the motor home once in each series of shootings. So he'd be on foot.

He'd determined his shooting perch weeks ago. Straight across from the living room where young Daniel Rush conducted his nightly file review was Dale Drive. Two hundred yards due west, Dale Drive turned to the north. The first house into that turn looked straight through the living room window, although from a distance of 280 yards. His shooting perch was beside a row of untrimmed boxwood shrubs on the south side of the house. By lying prone as close to the bushes as possible, his body and rifle would be totally hidden.

But where should he park his truck? He'd considered parking one street over. But if someone heard the pop from the silencer, the truck might be discovered before he could escape.

So distance was best. A mile and a half from the cul-de-sac stood an old nursing home. Better than a shopping center because of the late hour of the shooting, it was farther than he'd planned, but the best of a group of poor choices.

He'd hidden the cameras for the shooting five nights before, at 3:00 A.M. at the house next door. Large wooden planters, one on each side of the sidewalk, sported healthy geraniums eighteen inches tall with purple and white blossoms, and large green leaves thick enough to hide almost anything.

In one planter he'd placed a small CCD black-and-white camera equipped with a third-generation, 18mm night vision lens. The camera's video cable fed into a 1.3 gigahertz video transmitter the size of a pack of cigarettes. He buried the transmitter and the battery under the dirt and placed the camera lens just over the lip of the planter.

The range of the video transmitter was a solid 1,000 feet. Because he'd planned this shooting on a night before trash pick-up day for the neighborhood, the video receiver would be inside a box, in a trash bag, two alleys and five houses away. A video cable would connect the digital phase-locked loop receiver with a Sony battery-powered compact 8mm video recorder. The recorder was attached to a timer that would begin the recording at 10:00 P.M. sharp. B.J. would put the receiver in place an hour before the shooting. The planter cameras would capture the shooting clearly. Each was pointed directly at the large picture window that no one had ever felt the urge to cover.

B.J. would allow the video recorder in the trash bag to run for several hours after the shooting to film the police response.

The planter on the other side of the sidewalk was identical

to the first. It served as a backup. It would transmit to a second receiver, on a different frequency, to a second trash bag. B.J. didn't want to miss this one. He simply wouldn't allow anything to interfere with seeing Stubs's reaction.

The biggest risk in the elaborate recording system was discovery. It hadn't happened with the first thirteen shootings, but if any of the equipment were found now, he'd never be able to record the one he wanted most.

At 9:30 P.M., B.J. placed the two video receivers in the alley. At 9:45, he dropped his rifle under the row of boxwoods, and drove to the nursing home to park his truck. Wearing green army fatigues and a matching ball cap, he carried nothing, jogging sidewalks to within a block of his shooting perch. Then he cut between two houses and hit the alley behind Dale Drive. It was 10:10 when he peered through his riflescope and looked into the living room.

The room was empty, the house dark. He dialed his scope to full magnification and checked the sight picture, resting the cross-hairs on a lampshade. Then he relaxed, closed his eyes, and silently counted to five. When he opened them, he saw the cross-hairs had moved three inches to the left of the lampshade. Shifting his entire body to the left, he closed his eyes and repeated the drill. Perfect, natural point of aim.

He remained under the bushes totally relaxed. The house remained dark, the neighborhood quiet. Daniel Rush's car wasn't in the driveway like every other night, and the other two cars were always parked in the garage, so B.J. didn't worry that the driveway sat empty. Nor did he worry that the house was dark. He couldn't expect every single aspect of his plan to work out in his favor, couldn't expect the young lawyer to sit around his father's house every night. If B.J. couldn't do it tonight, he'd come back tomorrow night. Then the next. Every night until the shot was there.

At 11:45, an unmarked detective car pulled into the driveway. As it slowed to wait for the garage door to open, B.J. could make out the back of the retarded woman's head in the passenger's seat.

B.J. felt a joy unlike any other he'd ever experienced when he thought of the look on Stubs's face once this shooting happened. It was all he could do to not laugh out loud.

Once the car had pulled safely into the garage, but before the door started its descent, B.J. watched the great detective open the driver's door and step out. His wife made no effort to open her door. He was making his way around the other side of the car to open her door when the garage door closed.

A couple of minutes later, lights began flicking on around the house. Through the picture window B.J. could see a small part of the kitchen, the doorway leading into what he believed to be the dining room, and the doorway leading to the back of the house toward the bedrooms.

Up to this very point, B.J. had been determined to follow the pattern he'd spent three years building. Everyone—the FBI, the local cops, the media, and Stubs—expected him to shoot a lawyer next. But was it necessary to accomplish the goal of getting Stubs's head out of the game?

So as he watched the woman shuffle over to her favorite chair and sit down, and as he saw the great detective moving around in the kitchen, B.J. knew that he didn't have to shoot the lawyer to mentally devastate Stubs. Shooting the retard would work just as well.

Through his scope he watched the lady's head move up and down as she stroked the stuffed toy as though it were a child. Her head was a foot to the left of the lamp and slightly lower.

He could take the shot now, but he'd have to muscle the

rifle to place the round that high. So B.J. scooted his body an inch to the right and pushed the butt stock of his rifle a tad higher into his shoulder. Perfect.

"Patience," B.J. whispered to himself. If he shot her now, the great detective wouldn't get to see her head explode. And though her murder would be on B.J.'s video, the detective's reaction wouldn't.

The great one continued to piddle around in the kitchen. B.J. caught glimpses of him each time he moved near the refrigerator. It appeared as though he was emptying the dishwasher.

"Come on," B.J. coaxed. "Stick your head around the corner to check on the missus."

Finally, as if receiving mental messages, the great detective took a full step out of the kitchen and looked at his wife. B.J. could see his lips moving as he asked her a question.

"Take one last look," B.J. said as he squeezed the trigger.

CHAPTER SIX

The images, the sounds, and the reality of what had just happened didn't register until after Rush found himself on the floor with his .45 clutched tightly in his hand. From behind the sofa he saw the blood splatter on the wall behind Mallory, he saw the bone fragments, the jelly-like substance he knew were bits of Mallory's brain. From that angle, he could see her deflated head slumped back, her lifeless face staring at the ceiling.

As the event forcefully replayed itself, Rush recalled hearing the tinkle of broken glass as the bullet pushed through the front window, the slap of the round hitting Mallory's head, the crack of skull bones splintering. He remembered the pink puff of brain matter mixed with blood, and the gasp of air escaping through her lifeless lips. And as the scene seared itself into Rush's memory, a rage so completely consuming, so utterly overwhelming, enveloped him, that he found himself out the front door, pistol in hand, searching the darkness before he even considered that a second shot might blow through *his* forehead next.

Fighting through the urge to sprint into the night in search of Mallory's murderer, Rush ran back into the house and hit

9-1-1 as fast as his fingers could stab the numbers. He didn't wait for the operator to finish her greeting.

"This is Detective Greg Rush," he shouted into the phone. "My wife's just been shot by a sniper. Send units to Dale Drive west of my house. Seal off the neighborhood from all directions. Call FBI Agent Zeke Bunning at Tri-City. This is a Jackson shooting!"

Rush started to throw the phone back onto its cradle when the 9-1-1 operator asked if his wife needed an ambulance.

"She's dead! Just send cops. As many cops as we've got on duty!"

He slammed the phone down, ran to his bedroom, and grabbed a flashlight, an extra magazine for his .45, his police radio, then pulled on his ballistic vest. He took his cell phone as he sprinted out the front door, his rage driving him like nothing manmade ever could.

He had to hurry. B.J. knew the great detective would call 9-1-1 as soon as he wiped the retarded woman's blood out of his eyes. B.J. estimated he'd make the panicked call within three minutes, maybe sooner. The moment the cops suspected it was a Jackson shooting, they'd call out the troops, set up an outer perimeter, and seal off the area. But the perimeter would be thin until the FBI task force arrived. That'd give B.J. at least twenty more minutes, and he'd be out by then. Even with a mile and a half to run, he'd be at his truck in fifteen, max.

The helicopter he'd seen at the Tri-City Academy earlier in the day would probably be in the air within minutes. The pilot no doubt bunked out in the building, ready to roll. B.J. had avoided helicopters the last three years and he could do it again.

The difference now was the darkness, the cooler ground.

Even as hot as the day had been, his body was warmer than the ground and he'd be easy to spot with their thermal imaging system. They'd also use dogs as soon as they located his shooting perch, but at their very best, they'd be thirty minutes behind.

No screams followed him as he turned south into the alley, though he hadn't expected the great detective to scream like a woman. South for a half mile, he then cut east and crossed Ridgemont Drive. A siren shrilled ahead of him, moving fast. He checked his watch. Four minutes since the shooting. Right on time.

Cutting between houses, he turned south on Rockwood, staying in the shadows. A police cruiser screeched around the corner and turned toward him. The squad's lights splashed red and blue off windows in the neighborhood. B.J. hugged a tree as it sped by.

Taking a moment to catch his breath, he searched both directions before stepping out to continue.

"Hey! You there!" came a shout from behind him. "What are you doing?"

B.J. froze. Then snatched a look at an enormous man standing on a porch, not quite ten yards away. Without hesitation, he ran straight north toward the shooting, away from his truck. But once out of the fat man's sight, he turned east and finally circled south again, moving slower than before, watching, listening for signs of pursuit. Eight minutes had passed since the shooting. Still making good time; even with the diversion, he should have at least twelve minutes until things became too crowded.

He almost laughed out loud at the adrenaline racing through his veins. It was back! The incredible high that had snatched his breath away when he'd shot the old drunk in Nashville all those years ago.

Then he heard the helicopter and the smile died on his lips. It came from the east, from the direction of the academy. A mile off, at least. He ran south down an alley, staying to the edge, near the six-foot stockade fences. Dogs began barking, a chorus of alarm penetrating the still, night air all around him. Picking up his pace to a full sprint, he held it for two minutes and covered another quarter-mile before he stopped and hid under a driveway overhang. The helicopter swung past him, heading northwest. It hovered in the vicinity of the house where the fat guy had seen him.

Even with sweat soaking his shirt and running into his eyes, he couldn't spare the time to catch his breath, so he headed south again, still in the alley, now a mile, ten minutes, from the shooting. He counted almost two dozen cars as they headed toward the center of activity.

The alley came to a dead end. He crossed between two houses, stopped, looked, then sprinted across Briarwood Drive, exposed no more than ten seconds. Looking behind him, he heard nothing except the helicopter in the distance. One more street to cross and he'd be safe.

Rush had delivered the news of death dozens of times in his career. He had stood by and watched hard men collapse into weeping bundles of nerves; observed timid women rise up to become pieces of granite onto which their entire families leaned; witnessed children suffer silently, showing nothing more than a single tear as evidence of their pain. He had held mothers and fathers, sons and daughters, grandparents and grandchildren; he had been grabbed and held himself, as though he could somehow reverse the news if they squeezed him tightly enough. He had cried with them, laughed at impromptu stories uttered in the middle of incoherent grief, and watched in stunned silence at those who had had no reaction at all.

There was no pattern to human suffering, no formula to predict individual response. Grief, he'd learned long ago, often took time, took reflection. But sometimes it was immediate, overwhelming, debilitating. Rush had often wondered about himself, how he would feel, whether he would be stricken into inaction.

Now he knew. As he raced due west from his house, into a darkness where death might await him, he knew.

He felt cold. Despite the summer heat, despite the thick sweat already coating his skin, a bitter coldness had frozen his heart.

Mallory was dead.

Dead.

Shot by a man FBI Agent Zeke Bunning had failed to stop.

Rush's rage heated his face, battled the cold that had seized him; it drove him, pressed him forward, away from the murder that Zeke had failed to prevent. As he penetrated the darkness, as he searched for the spot he knew he must find, Rush vowed to not forget what he felt at that moment.

He found Jackson's perch near where he knew it should be. It was the only spot from which to take the shot without lying in full view of anyone who happened to drive by. Rush closed his eyes, took a deep breath. He heard sirens coming in from every direction, but mostly from the west.

There was nothing he could do except wait for the dogs. He didn't want to move now that he'd found Jackson's shooting perch, because his own scent might ruin the track for the dogs. Kneeling, he pulled out his cell phone and called dispatch and told them exactly where he was, to send the canine guys to his location. He told dispatch to have one officer go to his house and protect the crime scene. They asked where he would be; he told them he'd be with the dogs. What he didn't say was that he didn't know if he could ever again step foot into his house.

The wait seemed eternal, though the first officers arrived within minutes. It was a rookie Rush had seen in the hallways at the station. Rush gave him orders rapid fire, explained exactly where to place other officers, told the rookie to keep away from the shooting perch, that they couldn't afford to contaminate the scene.

The first dog team arrived soon after. Probably the fourth cop to get there. The young officers were setting up a good perimeter. Rush heard a sergeant and lieutenant check en route.

Rush stayed off the radio, preferred to use a cell phone if he had to. He didn't want the press alerted any sooner than necessary.

As the dog man got his German Shepard ready to track, Rush realized that he was thinking about anything other than what had just happened to Mallory. He couldn't think about that. Despite the rage driving him, he suspected that a complete breakdown loomed just behind the thin film of tears covering both of his eyes. If he stopped, even for a second, the flood would come and he'd be useless.

"Ready," the canine officer told Rush. "The row of bushes?"

Rush nodded and stepped back, his pistol and flashlight ready.

The dog man let the Shepard's leash out. Within seconds of the canine sniffing the grass under the row of boxwoods, the officer was nearly yanked off his feet as the dog shot south into the alley.

The dog man announced into his radio the direction of the track and that Rush was serving as his cover officer. At that point, Rush knew, every officer in the city would stay clear of the direction the dog was heading.

As Rush followed the dog south through the alley, he glanced back and saw a team of three officers clearing areas behind them. They were additional backup, there in case the dog overran the scent and missed a spot where Jackson might be hiding. They gave Rush comfort.

B.J. was 100 yards from his truck. Trapped.

The traffic was unnaturally heavy for this time of night. He'd been huddled in the dark for almost three minutes, waiting for the road to clear before he made the dash across. But it wouldn't clear. Several cars were making U-turns, driving back and forth on 14th Street in front of him. They blocked access to Rigsbee Drive, the street in front of the nursing home. Had to be cops.

Sixteen minutes since the shooting. He should have been in his truck by now. Being seen by the fat man, and now sitting like a duck on a pond, had cost him at least five minutes.

The rifle was still strapped to his back. He couldn't cross the street with all the traffic, and he could hear the helicopter approaching as it made sweeping circles, searching in slow, ever-increasing spirals. The police dogs would be on his trail soon, if not already. He'd wanted excitement, but . . .

Remembering his numerous scouting trips, he looked west and knew nothing in that direction would help. To the east, three-quarters of a mile away, a railroad track crossed 14th Street. A half-mile farther, Rowlett Creek ran under the road. If he crossed at that point, he could skirt a tree line along the large field to the south and circle west, approach the nursing home from the rear. The problem was time. That trip would take another twenty-five minutes, and he didn't know how successful he'd be eluding dogs and the helicopter.

His truck was safe for the moment. But if he didn't drive it away before dawn, someone would notice it. Wiping sweat off his face, he considered the cops patrolling back and forth in front of him. Even if he reached his truck within the next several hours, it wasn't safe to drive it out until the cops finished looking.

Damn it.

The cops had arrived and set up an outer perimeter ten minutes ahead of B.J.'s most generous calculation. And he hadn't expected an outer perimeter set so far from the shooting site. He'd expected the cops to improve over last year, but not by such a drastic leap. Zeke was getting better.

Each second brought the helicopter closer, and he'd just wasted another minute. He had to do something. He briefly considered finding a place to hide, but he'd never fool the dogs. Cursing under his breath again, he was forced to go the long way around. So he headed east at a half-speed run, still in the alleys, still in the shadows.

At this pace, he'd reach the creek in nine minutes.

Rush had heard the 9-1-1 call dispatched, because the dog man had his radio volume turned up so loud. So there was a witness. Rush had slipped his flashlight into his back pocket and was on the phone now. At this moment, he knew Zeke and Chinbroski were leaning over the hood of a squad car back at the scene, studying a Plano map. Chinbroski had arrived within minutes of Rush leaving with the dog. He'd called Rush's cell phone, tried to express his condolences before Rush had cut him off. While Chinbroski stuttered through something supportive to say, Zeke had arrived and taken the phone from Chinbroski's hand. Rush had also stopped him from extending any well-wishes. There just wasn't time.

So they were busy plotting on the map, while Rush gave

Zeke updates about where the dog was leading him.

"So he was headed south," Zeke confirmed with Rush, "then east, and south again when he was spotted in the yard. He immediately turned north. I'm betting the dog moves east and then south again. I think his vehicle's south."

"He turned north because he knew the homeowner who saw him would call the police," Rush said. "Wanted to throw us off."

The dog was working hard, nose on the ground, panting, an occasional low growl. The dog man talked to his dog the entire way, soft commands, gentle coaxing, enthusiastic encouragement.

The dull ache from the memory of Mallory's head thrown back, the gaping hole, the streaming blood, sat right behind Rush's eyes, pushing, trying to explode into a stream of raw emotion. But Rush held on, occupied his mind with the raw hatred for the man he and this dog would give their lives to find.

The neighborhood was still quiet, considering the number of sirens that had passed through only minutes before. Zeke told Rush over the phone that he had sent a patrol officer to the witness's house for safeguarding. Rush didn't want to hear about that right then. He told Zeke to focus on the chase.

So Zeke did. "He was a half-mile from the shooting site when he was spotted," he said.

"How far does the perimeter run to the south?" Rush asked.

"We have units patrolling 14th Street to the south and Shiloh Road to the east. If he's made it south of 14th, he'll be home free."

"That's a mile and a half from my house," Rush said. "He'd park that far?"

"I wouldn't, but this is the first time we've had a dog pick up a trail. Who knows what he's done in the past?"

"We just turned east on Ridgeway," Rush said.

"Okay. I say we pull the blue team from the north and extend the south perimeter another half mile in all directions. Have some patrol units move into the area, too."

"Do it," Rush said. "Do it fast."

It was a major blunder parking his truck so far away, B.J. admitted. He'd also failed to think through the consequences of heading east toward the creek. He recognized his error after he crossed Shiloh Road behind a 7-11 store. Once the dog had a solid scent, they'd flood the area with cops and hem him in. They'd also figure his truck was somewhere south and close every street in the area. They'd run the license plate of every vehicle parked within a two-mile radius. The TV said they had sixty investigators assigned to the investigation. If he didn't get to his truck soon . . .

So he changed his plan, inspired by the police car he saw parked behind GEO-MAP Corporation, on the south side of 14th Street between Shiloh Road and Los Rios Boulevard. The business provided a prime location for the officer to observe the large field to the south. The cruiser was out of sight of anyone driving by, and B.J. saw it only after he passed to the east of the building.

Across 14th Street from GEO-MAP, an eight-foot brick wall guarded a new housing development. The homes under construction were two stories, several almost finished. Skirting through an alley, he chose the house closest to the brick wall, kicked in the back door, climbed the stairs, and ran to a window that looked across and over 14th Street. Positioned much higher and 100 yards behind the cruiser, he placed his rifle on a windowsill, and saw the officer looking through a pair of binoculars into the field to his south. His back was to B.J.'s rifle.

After a quick mental calculation on the impact of the bullet at that distance, B.J. aimed at the base of the officer's head. If the impact point were the center of the spine, it really wouldn't matter where the bullet went, just as long as it hit the spine. A neck shot would be just as deadly as a head shot. Even a hit just below the neck would be fine, as long as it was above the officer's shoulders, which would cripple his arms, preventing him from using his radio to call for help.

He ejected the spent shell from the earlier shooting and placed it in his pocket. Sliding a new round into the chamber, he took aim.

"It'll be three or four more minutes before Blue team is in place," Zeke told Rush. "The southern perimeter will extend to the south city limits. The eastern perimeter to the Tri-City Academy building and west to Avenue K. As the helicopter searches ahead of the dog, the shooter will be driven from the north and into our net."

"The dog's heading south again," Rush said.

Zeke acknowledged, excitement in his voice. "This is the closest we've ever been."

Rush said a silent prayer.

"The dog is heading straight south. What's there?" Zeke asked Rush.

"A nursery, an automotive shop, an apartment complex, a nursing home, a beer store, and a convenience store," Rush said. "All within a block."

"It's got to be the apartment complex," Zeke said.

Rush considered that. "Or the nursing home."

"How big is the nursing home?"

"Small. Couldn't be more than twenty cars at any given time."

"Too small. Has to be the apartments. I'll put the rest of Green team there. Half on foot, half in cars. We need to shut it off and not let anyone in or out. Also start writing tag numbers."

Rush began to tire as the adrenaline of the chase subsided. The night was hot, muggy. Sweat covered every inch of exposed skin, and soaked his shirt and ballistic vest. He had wiped his palms dry several times, not wanting to risk dropping his pistol when he needed it most.

The dog man was working his dog with amazing efficiency. The scent was strong, or appeared to be, as the dog never wavered in his track. They were approaching 14th Street, where Rush saw nearly a half-dozen cars cruising back and forth along what was just a few minutes ago the most southern perimeter.

"We're turning east through the alley running parallel to 14th Street," Rush told Zeke over the phone, attempting to keep the fatigue out of his voice. "The dog's picking up speed. We're almost at a full run now. Get the northern units heading south on Shiloh Road."

Over the next five minutes, Rush followed the dog down the alley, through unfenced backyards, between houses, behind a church, and then the far side of an open field that sat east of Ridgewood Drive.

Once they had made it through the Windsor Place apartment complex, Rush could see several marked units blocking the intersection of 14th Street and Shiloh Road. The dog was still strong, his pace fast. The dog man kept stride, gently pushing his canine to an even faster pace.

They had traveled well over one mile, probably closer to two. Rush couldn't believe that a man running with a rifle hadn't been seen by a passing car or some insomniac gazing out a window.

Rush wondered what was happening back at his house, wondered if Chinbroski had called Daniel. Rush knew he wanted no part of standing around while the crime scene people completed their work. He wanted to be miles away when the ME arrived to take away Mallory's body. He'd want someone else to complete the cleanup.

As he ran, as he followed the dog that seemed just as eager to catch the shooter as Rush, he made the decision about Mallory's burial. It struck him as odd that such a decision would come at a time when every fiber of his being wanted to catch the man responsible for her death. Then he realized that the harder he tried not to think about Mallory, the harder it was to keep her from his mind.

Tears slipped from both eyes as he ran. With both hands occupied, he let them slide down his face. His ache of loneliness, that ever-present being that had resided just under his skin for the last six months, was gone. Squeezed aside by rage, Rush hoped that the loneliness was gone for good, though he knew the chances were slim.

At Shiloh Road, the dog led them behind the 7-11 store and a small shopping center. Just ahead was another apartment complex, then a housing project. Across the street was GEO-MAP, a free-standing building and the only structure on that side of the street.

They pressed on.

Blood soaked the dash and seat. The dead officer was slumped over the steering wheel. B.J. didn't have time to waste. He slipped on a pair of leather gloves, unbuckled the officer, took his pistol and extra ammo, pulled him out of the car, and laid him on the ground, stripping him of his blood-soaked shirt. Then he took off the dead man's boots, stripped off his Sam Browne and pants, laying them over the seat. B.J. leaned his rifle, barrel up, inside the car, grabbed the dead officer's portable radio, and climbed in.

Blood splatter surrounded a small hole in the windshield directly in front of B.J.'s face. He considered wiping the blood away, but knew it would smear, creating a worse problem. So, wearing the uniform shirt, he headed east out of the GEO-MAP parking lot and saw a group of officers following a canine unit a couple of hundred yards to the west, heading his way. B.J. drove past the Tri-City Academy building, and turned north on Brand Road. After a mile, he stopped to hide his rifle in a drainage pipe under the road.

He then drove straight to his truck, passing several marked police units on the way and counting two dozen other slow-moving cars. As he passed the house under construction from which he'd shot the policeman, he noticed the flicker of flashlights in the upstairs window from the very room he had used.

They'd find the dead officer within minutes. He had to hurry.

Once at the nursing home, he was out of the main traffic flow. After turning on the cruiser's overhead lights, he stripped off the uniform shirt, climbed into his truck, and headed out. Just as he pulled onto 14th Street, he picked up the dead officer's walkie-talkie, and screamed, "Two-Four-teen needs assistance behind the nursing home on Rigsbee! I got the suspect running south in the field! I'm in foot pursuit!"

The dispatcher sent everybody. "Standby Two-Fourteen, I'm relaying to the task force at this time." After a moment, "Location, Fourteen."

"A hundred yards south . . . of the nursing home . . . in the middle of the field." B.J. had to work at sounding out of breath. He headed west on 14th Street approaching Jupiter Road, cars racing past him on the way to the nursing home. "Still got him in sight . . . he's got a rifle . . . strapped to his back . . . running hard."

"Two-Fourteen, the task force is en route. There should be several officers entering the field at this time."

B.J. laughed.

"Location, Fourteen," the dispatcher's voice strained.

"Two-Fourteen, this is Air-One, we're over the field at this time. Location."

"Two-Fourteen . . . I've crossed the railroad tracks . . . I still see him. Heading southeast." B.J. hoped he wouldn't hyperventilate.

"Fourteen, this is Air-One. We don't see you. Stand by."

B.J. continued west, keeping his speed well under the limit.

"Fourteen, can you give us a more exact location?"

"Can you see . . . my squad car . . . in front of the nursing home?"

"Ten-four, Fourteen."

B.J. took great gasps of air, still screaming into the radio. "I'm south . . . of my car. I can still see . . . the suspect."

"We can't find you, Fourteen," Air-One said, the helicopter blades beating in the background.

B.J. continued west on 14th Street, stopped at the red light at Avenue K, clear of the perimeter. He laughed and turned off the radio, knowing they would figure it out soon, if they hadn't already.

"He bled out in the car," Rush said, bending over the body. Finding little blood on the pavement, he stood, feeling sick, enraged, terrified. The dead officer had been a lifelong Plano kid. Wiping his eyes, Rush turned and walked away, his back to Zeke, who stood quietly off to one side.

Dread enveloped Rush. He blew out a breath and faced the body, forced an attempt at police work.

"Assuming he was dragged out of the car and dumped," Rush said, "the car was facing south, toward the field. And the shot came from the house we just searched." He turned to Zeke. "He has one of our radios now."

Zeke nodded. "He's got a patrol radio, Greg. Not one of our task force units. We're still okay." He approached Rush and put a hand on his shoulder. "Chinbroski and I need to go see our witness. The 9-1-1 call."

"Let's go." Rush practically staggered to Zeke's car.

"Not you, Rush."

Rush looked at Zeke, then at Chinbroski, who stood off to the side wearing an expression Rush couldn't read.

"Like hell."

"You're in no condition. We need your statement about what happened to Mallory."

"That doesn't help anything right now."

"I say you're in no condition." Zeke's voice didn't match the look of determination on his face.

"This whole thing's your fault, Zeke. He's loose because of you." Rush stepped forward, his rage having overwhelmed his cold grief. "I'm in this case. Now more than ever. You'll have to lock me up to stop me."

Zeke turned to Chinbroski, as though looking for support. Chinbroski said nothing.

"I'm not jeopardizing my case by having the husband of a victim involved in the investigation," Zeke said. "You want this case thrown out? Have his lawyer defend on bias?"

"Are you really prepared to deny me this? Deny me my closure?" Rush checked his anger, knowing he needed Zeke at that moment. He took a hesitant step forward and swallowed hard, softened his tone. "Zeke, this . . . I need this. The worst thing would be for me to stop now, to never have a chance to do what Mallory would have insisted of me. What would you do if you were in my place?"

Chinbroski moved over and stood next to Rush. The other officers remained silent, all eyes on Zeke.

"I can give you a day. I'll need to check with legal tomorrow, speak with your chief. I just can't have the case contaminated. You can understand that."

Rush nodded. "I'll take a minor role, Zeke. Tell your legal people that. I need this for me. And you need my passion."

The address was 9701 Rockwood. Harold Blane, a massive 300 pounds, was sweating rivers. He wore shorts, a food-stained tee shirt, and a dirty Dallas Cowboys ball cap. Rush stood by the door, Chinbroski next to him. Zeke sat on the sofa across from the fat man.

"I was sitting here in my chair," Blane said, "watching some TV, when I heard sirens. So I went to the window. All my lights were off in the room here, so I was hid pretty good. I seen some movement over by the tree out there, so I took a closer look. I thought I seen some guy peeking out toward the street, so I walked out on my porch real quiet-like. The guy was dressed in jungle fatigues and had a rifle strapped across his back. After he ran off, a couple more cars drove by, and I seen one of them was a detective car. I ain't stupid. I've been following all the stories 'bout that Jackson fella being in Plano, so I thought I better call."

"Was he black?" Zeke asked.

Harold Blane scrunched his face and scratched his nose. "Well, I don't know. He had a hat, long-sleeve shirt, maybe some gloves. And it was awful dark."

"Did you see his face?"

"Never looked right at me. Just a glance. But he seemed white."

"How can he seem whi—" Zeke cut himself off. "In court, Harold, could you say he was white?"

Swiping a hand across his sweaty face, he thought about it. "Couldn't swear to it. But he was built like a white man. Narrow shoulders, small butt and legs. Not much muscle tone. Know what I mean?"

Zeke glanced around the house, almost an inspection.

"Are you single?" he asked.

"Got fat. Wife left me. Been single for twenty-five years."

"Kids?"

"Nope."

"You said you've been following this story. Then you know how serious it is that we catch him?"

Nodding, he set his jaw and glanced at Rush and Chinbroski. "Gotta catch him."

"I'm going to need your help." Zeke stood and paced the room. "I'm going to tell you a couple of things, Harold, between us. You've got to be a player, though. You a player?"

"I'm a player."

Zeke sat down and explained what he needed.

CHAPTER SEVEN

B.J. lay atop his covers, staring at the dark ceiling, afraid to move. His sunburn ran from the nape of his neck, down his back and legs, ending at the soles of his feet. And that didn't include the front of his body. He and Stubs, along with several other boys from their cabin, had arranged a dunking contest at the camp swimming pool to end all dunking contests. From mid-morning to late afternoon, with only a short hamburger time in between, they had dunked and dived and dared each other into the worst sunburn known to man. Or the worst sunburn B.J. had ever had, at least. Stubs didn't look too bad, nor did a few of the other boys. But it was all B.J. could do to lie perfectly still atop his bunk and let the breeze from the midnight sky wash over him.

Steve, one of the camp counselors, had coated his body with some kind of stinky lotion, but it hadn't done much good. It was nearly 1:00 A.M. now. B.J. listened to the other boys' sleep sounds: heavy breathing, a soft snore, the squeaky beds, an occasional snort. The whippoorwills were out in the mountains, the crickets in the woods. B.J. heard a couple of squirrels playing in the trees an hour ago. They were everywhere, the squirrels. The entire mountain range seemed to be a squirrel sanctuary. And rabbits were plentiful, too.

B.J. needed to pee. He'd been holding it for at least an hour and didn't know how much longer he could last. It was going to hurt climbing down from the bunk, which was why he hadn't gone yet. The sheets on the bunk were rough, and the blanket, an old Army surplus item probably, was even worse. B.J. really hated that he had to move.

But when he could stand it no longer, he finally inched his way to the edge of the bed, trying mostly to slide on his butt, the only area not burned. Once he had both feet on the bunk bed ladder, he sighed with relief and lowered himself to the floor. The concrete floor felt cool to his feet and he wondered if maybe he should just sleep on the floor tonight.

He crept across the bunkhouse past the other sleeping boys. Most of them were wearing the stinky lotion and the smell was strong enough to make B.J.'s stomach rumble. He envied the other boys because they were sleeping through their sunburns and they didn't have to deal with the odor.

After relieving himself, B.J. crept back into the bunkroom and started the climb up the ladder.

Stubs stuck his head over the edge of his bed and grinned in the darkness. "Whacking off?" he whispered.

B.J. rolled his eyes and ignored him.

"We kicked butt today," Stubs said. "But I'm hurting now."

"Not so loud," B.J. said, as he turned around on the ladder, sat down on his unburned butt, and scooted to the middle of the bed. He placed the palms of his hands out behind him and slowly lowered himself flat onto his back.

"You're as stiff as that alien robot on 'Lost in Space,' " Stubs said. " 'Danger, Will Robinson, danger.' " Stubs laughed softly at his joke. "In a week, you're gonna peel like a snake."

"So will you." B.J. sighed as he closed his eyes and tried to relax. He might as well be sleeping in an oven, he thought, as his skin generated enough heat to fry an egg on his chest.

"I've been meaning to tell you a secret," Stubs said, his voice close to B.J.'s head.

B.J. hadn't heard Stubs scoot to the far end of his bunk. "What secret?"

Stubs hung his head over the side of the bed and looked around the dark bunkroom before answering. "I'm gonna run away when I get back to Dallas. I ain't living with that foster family no more."

"Why?"

" 'Cause stuff's been happening there."

"What kind of stuff?"

"Stuff I don't want to talk about."

B.J. couldn't tell from Stubs's voice if he was upset, maybe on the verge of tears. But the bigger boy's voice sounded deeper than normal. And a couple of the words sounded shaky.

"Where will you go?" B.J. asked. "You said you didn't have any other family."

The sound of a different whippoorwill, closer than the others, cried from the woods outside their cabin. Stubs didn't answer for a while, but he finally admitted what B.J. thought he might say.

"I don't know where I'll go. Just somewhere." His bunk squeaked as Stubs scooted closer toward B.J. "I was thinking maybe I could come live with you. With your mom and granddad."

B.J. immediately liked the idea of having his best friend living with him. And Stubs was that, his best friend. B.J. didn't have many other friends. His granddad's farmhouse was so far out in the sticks that B.J. saw his school friends only on the bus or at school.

"I don't know," B.J. said. "We're pretty poor. My mom said granddad barely made enough money to feed himself. And that was before me and my mom moved in."

Which was the truth. His mom didn't have to talk about money or the lack of it; he knew how poor they were by the clothes he wore, by the food he ate, by the car they drove. It was why he had been so lucky to come to this camp.

"Doesn't your mom make money?" Stubs asked.

"She makes some, cleaning businesses at night. But Trenton is pretty small, so she doesn't make much. My granddad just planted a huge garden, but he won't make any money on that until later this summer."

"Okay."

B.J. could hear the disappointment in his friend's voice, but he didn't want to get his hopes up. There was no way his mom would let Stubs come live with them. "What's so bad at your foster home? Does it have to do with the French kissing?"

The blades of the ceiling fan turned slowly enough that B.J. could keep his eyes on a single blade as it made its endless rotations. He turned his head toward the window and gazed out across the rifle range as he waited for Stubs to answer. The big boy's breathing was heavy, but not like he was crying or anything.

"I just can't talk about it," Stubs finally said. "And it's not too bad yet. I just have to get away before it gets any worse."

It had to do with the French kissing, B.J. knew. There was something worse going on. Maybe Stubs couldn't tell his foster dad. Maybe his foster dad was the kind of pervert who liked to watch his wife do nasty stuff with other men. Just the thought of that made B.J.'s sunburned skin tingle.

"I tried to look Trenton up on the map in the camp office," Stubs said. "I couldn't find it."

" 'Cause it's so little," B.J. said. "All I know is that Highway 121 runs through there." B.J. didn't pay attention to road signs while on the school bus. Or when he was riding around with his mom or granddad.

"What would happen if I just showed up one day?"

"I don't know," B.J. said.

"Maybe I could live in your barn. You said there's a hayloft. You could sneak food to me."

"I would, too."

Stubs started giggling.

"What?"

"I could like . . . be your pet." He laughed louder.

"Shh. You're gonna wake up everybody." But then B.J. started giggling, too, his body shaking against the rough bed sheet. "Ouch," he whispered. "Stop laughing. You're gonna kill me."

Stubs reached across and tousled B.J.'s hair before sliding back over to his own bunk. "Goodnight, you walking French fry."

B.J. smiled in the darkness, thankful to have such a good friend. "Goodnight, butthead."

Rush and Chinbroski sat low on the sofa in Chinbroski's darkened den, each nursing his third Coors. At a few minutes past 3:00 A.M., Chinbroski had driven Rush home and practically demanded that he drink away the memories of his murdered wife.

Insisting on the darkness, Rush didn't want his partner to see his own glistening eyes. They were silent now; only their breathing and an occasional clink of a bottle penetrated the darkness. Chinbroski's massive silhouette blended into the sofa, his face softly illuminated by the faint glow of a VCR's digital clock.

Rush had always faced danger with an air of invincibility, with the stolid, emotionless demeanor of a hard-nosed cop. What was that phrase: *nine feet tall and bulletproof?* But this case had opened something within him: raw fear and vulnerability.

For the last three years the most thorough, far-reaching law-enforcement agency in the world hadn't stopped a lone gunman. Knowing he was condemned to join the list of victims was unlike any feeling Rush had ever experienced. But now, with Mallory dead, his survival simply didn't matter as much anymore. And though he would never stop hunting Jackson, never allow his rage to diminish, none of that washed away his fear.

Daniel had responded to the call Chinbroski had made to him while Rush was running with the canine unit. Daniel was waiting outside Rush's house when Rush returned with Chinbroski from Harold Blane's. After accepting his only son's hug and tear-gathering words of comfort, Rush recorded his statement into a patrol officer's micro-cassette recorder to be typed later by a CID secretary.

Then he waited in Chinbroski's truck while the medical examiner's van carried away Mallory's body. Daniel was allowed in to pack a couple of suitcases for Rush's extended stay away from the house, and then offered Rush the spare bedroom in his apartment for as long as needed.

But Rush declined, opting instead to stay in Chinbroski's house. There were no photos of Mallory in Chinbroski's house, no pieces of memorabilia chosen especially by Mallory for Daniel prior to his law school graduation. Daniel's apartment would rip Rush's fragile mental state to shreds.

No. He needed to stay with Chinbroski. Needed to be close to the case. Needed to be ready to respond when Jackson hit again.

Nanci's scent was present throughout Chinbroski's living room. It was the one thing that forged a direct link from Rush's grief to Mallory's imagined presence. Nanci and Mallory shared the same love for Chanel No.5.

Rush closed his eyes in the darkened room and took in the faint scent of his lovely wife. But he didn't keep them closed for long. If he let down his guard for even a fraction of a second, the image of her lifeless face staring up at the ceiling came crashing in, planting itself front and center.

"Run," Chinbroski said through the darkness, his voice deep and even.

It had been the first word spoken in several minutes, and one that Rush had contemplated, even considering what had happened. It was a word Rush would give specific and direct attention to, one he would consciously battle back.

"Only a coward would run, Chin," Rush said after some length. "One side of my brain feels like hiding, like finding a house in the middle of the mountains, changing my name. The other side knows that cops can't do that. They can't hide. They can't run. They don't wake up in the middle of the night, shaking, sweating, unable to think of anything else."

"But what—"

"Let me finish," Rush cut in again, keeping his voice barely above a whisper. "My head is so crammed with shit I can't think. This Jackson makes me feel . . . weak—like a kid being tormented by the playground bully. I want—"

"Oh come, Rush." Chinbroski leaned forward. "The most hunted man in America and you're comparing him to a playground bully? I say you get the hell out of here. Ain't no one in the department who'd blame you."

Rush laughed, a squeaky, croaking sound that died as soon as it passed his lips. "Right. Leave, run. And sentence someone else to die in my place. I could really live with myself, then. That'd earn the eternal admiration of the entire department."

"Who's to—"

"What makes me a coward, Chin, is that I actually considered it." Rush let the sentence hang in the darkness for a moment. "Even before tonight, even with Mallory's condition, I thought, hey, nobody knows I'm lead, right? We've kept it quiet. Sure, all the Plano officers know I'm out there working with the bureau, but so is every other available detective. I could just slip out of town, take Mallory, go find some run-down, off-the-beaten-path motel, and stick my head under the pillow for a month."

Chinbroski paused before sighing. "That's what I considered, too."

"You're getting married. It wouldn't have been hiding. You would've started vacation in another two weeks, regardless. In fact, you're the one who needs to hide, just in case Jackson gets us confused."

"What do you mean? Get us confused?"

The fear in Chin's voice cut Rush to the bone. He immediately regretted saying it. He regretted it because it provided a reprieve—the most despicable, pathetic, and cowardly of all his thoughts. He hated himself for admitting that a part of him wanted the possibility to exist.

"Forget it," Rush said, sipping from his bottle.

His partner scooted closer, the first time he'd moved in what seemed an hour. "Forget what?"

Rush silently cursed himself. "That's not what I meant."

"No, Rush. We're in this together. And if you see something I haven't—"

"I haven't seen anything, Chin. It was just stupid speculation. And with Mallory tonight, it's clear who the target is. Forget I said it."

"But you did."

He nodded. "Yeah."

A small popping noise in the ceiling, the house settling, made Rush think of a silenced rifle shot, the shootings. Even without a silencer, he knew that none of Billy Ray Jackson's fifteen victims had heard the shot that killed them. With the bullet traveling faster than the speed of sound, death came an instant before the explosion reached their ears. The silencer simply provided protection—a comfort zone—for the shooter. And frustration for the cops.

"I know what you meant," Chinbroski said, after draining his bottle. "It just hit me. And what's scary is that before just this minute I hadn't considered it."

Rush said nothing, afraid of his response.

"You and me have been to both shootings," Chinbroski said. "Together the whole time, together with Zeke in meetings. So Jackson might think it's me—not you."

The silence became thicker when Rush didn't immediately respond.

"You should go on vacation," Rush said finally. "Go to Nanci."

"And leave you out there alone?" Chinbroski leaned his head back, stared at the ceiling. "If things were reversed, if I was officially the lead like you are, would you leave me out there alone?"

If I had a wife to protect? Rush didn't say. To answer that honestly wouldn't help Rush's situation. And it wouldn't change what Chinbroski would eventually decide to do. "Go, Chin. There's no reason for both of us to be targets. I'm the lead. I drew the short straw. Mallory's gone. It doesn't matter now."

Chinbroski was silent as he placed his empty bottle with the others. "I hadn't considered any of this," he said. "That I might be the guy on the hot seat. I've been showing up at these killings almost with the attitude of a spectator. Watching you, mainly, seeing how you were reacting to it all, glad as hell I wasn't in your spot."

His voice trailed off. Rush closed his eyes.

"But now," Chinbroski continued. "Now, I can see how narrow my focus has been. I mean, sure, I want to catch the son-of-a-bitch. And after tonight . . ."

He didn't finish the thought.

"How?" Rush asked, turning to his partner. "How did he know it was me? How did he know so fast?"

"Are you sure it's you? Absolutely sure?"

"He shot Mallory, Chin. He could have shot me, but he didn't. Can you think of a bigger message?"

Chinbroski put a hand on his arm. "What if he shot Mallory to drive you out of the investigation? To make sure I was lead?"

Which was the point Rush had nearly blurted out a minute ago. He drew in a deep breath of Chanel No.5.

"It changes everything, doesn't it?" Chinbroski asked.

Rush looked at him. The glow from the digital clock flickered in Chinbroski's eyes. Rush shook his head. "I'm not sure—"

"I can't get married until this is over. And I can't tell Nanci. It's how Jackson decided which detective he'll kill. By knocking one of us out." Chinbroski's whisper made Rush's skin prickle. "How did Jackson figure out we were on the case? An FBI leak? From Zeke?"

The words struck Rush. He rubbed his forehead, unable to utter a response. Could he accuse Zeke of such a devastating betrayal?

"Didn't Zeke say they had done everything in their power last year to conceal the name of the lead detective?" Chinbroski asked. "They protected that woman cop around the clock. And—"

"Which may be what gave it away," Rush interjected. "I thought of that when Zeke mentioned it. It's exactly the kind of error he would make. But to accuse him of anything but stupidity . . ."

Rush couldn't stop the swell of hatred that suddenly heated his face. Zeke *was* stupid, always had been. It was the point he had tried to make to Chinbroski not even twenty-four hours before.

"I'm holding Zeke responsible for Mallory's murder." Rush uttered the words out loud, even though he hadn't intended to. His voice, without emotion, was no more than a whisper, his words vibrating with anger.

Chinbroski said nothing, but Rush could feel his presence as the big man scooted closer toward him.

"This should never have happened." Tears filled Rush's eyes and slid onto his cheeks. "Mallory didn't deserve— Her whole life . . . the pain . . . she never had a chance for . . ."

The first sob was sudden and powerful, an explosion of emotion that came from his core, squeezing his chest like a vise. His throat seized and grew hot, and his body shook as he hid his face from his partner.

His wails echoed through Chinbroski's living room, as great, heaving sobs racked his body. He felt himself being pulled into Chinbroski's chest, his partner's powerful arms locking him into an embrace. Rush tried to pull away, but Chinbroski held him strong, pulling him forward and backward, rocking him as though he were a child. After another moment of futile resistance, Rush gave in to his emotion, the waves of grief blotting out all thought, washing and cooling the burning hatred that had sparked inside his frozen heart.

He didn't know how much time passed, didn't try to cut short the flood he so much needed to release. He only knew that after the living room grew quiet, after Chinbroski slackened his arms and released him, after his partner had moved across the living room to give him space, Rush pulled his hands away from his face, spent.

After rubbing his cheeks with the heels of his hands, he sniffed away his final tears and sat quietly, ashamed of his display, though knowing Chinbroski would never speak of it.

Neither spoke nor moved, until at length Rush looked over at his partner. "Thank you."

Through the darkness, Chinbroski nodded, but said nothing.

"I think I need some fresh air," Rush said, climbing to his feet. He padded softly to the back door.

On the porch, Rush pulled the door shut after Chinbroski stepped through. The night was hot, a muggy eighty degrees. The other houses on the street were dark, silent. Chinbroski's backyard was well kept, neatly trimmed. Rush looked in both directions before sitting down on the porch steps.

"He could be out there now," Chinbroski said, having looked both directions himself. "Watching us."

The same thought had struck Rush only a second before. "It's not our turn," he said. "Or I'd be dead." He shivered despite the hot, humid air. "I had a thought tonight while I was running with the canine. That Zeke is probably right about the shooter not being a black guy. But it'd sure be convenient for Jackson if we all thought that."

Chinbroski looked at him through the darkness.

"We assume," Rush continued, "that a man would be nuts to mail bullet casings to the cops stamped with his own thumbprint. Knowing a guy wouldn't be that stupid, knowing Jackson's past doesn't match the intelligence aspect of Zeke's profile, knowing blacks generally don't commit these types of crimes, we start looking in other directions. Meanwhile, Jackson has changed his looks just enough to pass for someone else, while we search for a white guy."

Chinbroski stared at him. "You think it *is* Jackson?"

Shrugging, Rush crossed one ankle over another. "Just mental calisthenics. I don't know what to think. And to answer your earlier question, I don't know how he figured out we were on the case."

"Zeke thinks he's a rogue cop, don't he? This shooter."

"I don't know, Chin. He's not confiding in me."

Chinbroski sighed and surveyed the dark neighborhood again. The night sounds were remote: traffic out on Park Boulevard, an occasional cricket, a teenager's car stereo. Rush thought about how peaceful his neighborhood must have seemed just before the shot.

"If he's not a cop, he has to be military," Chinbroski said. "This guy is too good."

Rush said nothing.

"You see the latest spread on Billy Ray Jackson in today's newspaper? All the family photos they dug out from somewhere?" The sarcasm in Chinbroski's voice told Rush all he needed to know about his partner's opinion of the notorious black man.

Nodding, Rush looked at him.

"Ain't never seen a man who looked more stupid. It's almost like this shooter drove around Nashville and said, 'Now who can I get to blame all this on, while at the same time making the cops shake their head in amazement?' "

Chinbroski was right. Every photograph of Billy Ray Jackson appeared as though the cameraman had caught him at the peak of apathy. Dull eyes, sagging facial features, mouth partially open, exposing a lazy tongue resting behind his lower lip. Zeke had told them Jackson's high school IQ tests barely broke 85, nowhere near the capacity needed to execute this monstrous shooting spree.

The most incredible thing was that many in the media actually believed it could be him. Rush referred to the shooter as Jackson only because he didn't know what else to call him.

"Jackson has to be dead somewhere," Rush said, "buried where no one could possibly find him."

The neighbor's cat stalked across the yard, freezing for a

moment to stare at them, its eyes reflecting light from the street lamp, glowing like a demon's in a B-grade horror flick.

"Remember the newspaper article from a year ago?" Rush asked. "About us from *The Listener* case? The big feature?"

"The one in the weekly rag, yeah."

"What if that's how he's picking his victims? Zeke didn't mention if they'd ever checked that angle." Rush looked at his partner. "It wouldn't be a reach to assume we'd grab lead on this, if you'd read that article. The story made both of us look like Dick Tracy. Newspaper stories. It'd make it easy for him. And if that's how he's researching, we might be able to predict which judge he'll shoot."

"And if we can postpone the judge . . ."

"It gives me more time," Rush finished for him.

"Or me."

"No, Chin."

"What makes you so sure all of a sudden? 'Cause you weren't ten minutes ago."

Rush drew in a breath, suddenly confident. "Somehow the shooter studies the response to the first shooting. That was the most natural crime scene. Only local cops were there. They didn't know what they had. At the first shooting, the true lead detective took charge."

Chinbroski's brow shrouded his eyes as he considered Rush's theory.

"Look at it this way," Rush continued. "Every year this thing has gotten bigger. For us, only the hospital shooting was handled like an ordinary murder. You and I showed up and did what we would ordinarily do. But tonight's was totally different. The FBI was in town. We had over sixty cops ready to jump at a moment's notice. You see?"

"But why are you so sure it's you and not me?"

"Because at the hospital I took the lead. I gave commands.

I directed McBride. I shouted orders. Anyone watching could have seen that."

Chinbroski digested it all. Then his face relaxed as his mind jumped to the next logical assumption. "To know all of that, the killer would've had to see you take the lead."

"It's me, Chin. Bank on it. Tonight was about distracting me."

"But he would have to *see* you take the lead, Rush. You're not getting my point. It would mean he was in the crowd."

"Maybe not," Rush said. "I think he took the shot from that motor home. And if he did that, he couldn't have been there."

"A partner?"

"Maybe."

Chinbroski stared at him. "Zeke sure as hell never threw down that theory."

"Think of the media frenzy if the FBI reported they were chasing a modern day Bonnie and Clyde."

"You think there's a woman involved?"

"I don't know."

Rubbing his eyes, Chinbroski glanced in both directions and sighed. "This is such a nightmare."

The words caught in his throat, so Rush never managed to tell his partner that he wished it *were* just a nightmare. At least then he could wake up.

CHAPTER EIGHT

Late the next morning, with the sun beating through the windshield of his pickup, B.J. cruised the fringes of the great detective's neighborhood. He had no reason to believe the cops would still be patrolling the area, but it would be foolish to go in without taking the necessary precautions. His rifle was still where he'd left it the night before, in the drainage pipe covered with weeds. He'd retrieve it before heading back to the farmhouse.

On his one pass by the cul-de-sac he saw one or two people milling around outside. Maybe off-duty cops, well-wishers, sympathizers? He couldn't be sure. He drove out of the area, in a wide arc, circling back toward the alley where his trash bags of video equipment were in danger of being hauled off if he didn't pick them up.

He examined every car he passed, ignoring those with children, teenage drivers, and old men or women. He disregarded motorcycles, flatbed trucks, classic or luxury cars. Only young-to-middle-aged men or women alone in late-model cars caught his full inspection: FBI agents in rental cars. The two-year-old Chevrolet Luminas and three-year-old Ford Tauruses driven by Plano detectives were easy to spot. His goal, as he maneuvered his way through the neighborhood, was to travel every street only once.

Coming in from the west, he circled to the north, putting the great detective's house a quarter mile behind him. Stopping along a curb, he consulted his map, wanting to avoid approaching the alley from either the west or south.

If he approached from the north and cut east two streets from the cul-de-sac, he could enter the alley with no fear of being seen by anyone coming or going from the murder scene.

Leaving, though, could hook him. If he traveled out the other end of the alley, he'd have to turn onto Briarwood Drive, only seventy yards from the entrance of the cul-de-sac street.

At 11:55, B.J. tuned his radio to catch the FBI news conference scheduled for noon. Double-checking his route again, he dropped his truck into gear and pulled away from the curb.

Wiping the sweat from his forehead, he drove slowly as FBI Agent Zeke Bunning's voice filled the cab of his truck. ". . . a housewife was killed as she sat in the living room of her east Plano home. Our investigative team tracked the suspect, but he was able to slip through our perimeter and escape."

B.J. pulled his pickup into the alley where his video equipment sat waiting. Slowing, he saw an old man, bent with age, tramp down his driveway and make a beeline toward the trash bags.

As B.J. passed, the old man stopped at the end of the driveway, put his hands on his hips, and stared at the bags.

"Speculation and assumptions would lead a person to theorize," Zeke's voice droned on, "that the two shootings over the last two days are a continuation of the three-year series allegedly involving Billy Ray Jackson. But is it? We haven't received any .308 casings. Does this mean we're dealing with a copycat shooter who has no casings to send? The bullet remains recovered from the first shooting, and then again last night, positively prove a different gun is being used than in previous years. Last night's shooting, chase, and then murder of a police officer, was the work of a man out of control, one unable to adequately plan his escape route. Last night's shooter parked his escape vehicle a full mile-and-a-half from the shooting site. Clearly the move of an amateur."

B.J. wanted to laugh, but he was worried about his recording equipment. He stopped two houses past the bags and watched in his mirrors.

The old man had just opened one of the bags.

B.J. rubbed the stump of his left pinkie against the steering wheel. The alley was deserted ahead, no cars, no people, no witnesses. And behind him, except for the old man, now reaching into the open bag, the alley was clear. Inside each bag was a cardboard box sealed tightly with duct tape. The old man lifted the box out of the first bag and sat it at his feet. It would take him a minute to pull off the thick tape and open the box, so B.J. dropped his truck into reverse, slowly backing toward the nosy old geezer.

Stopping less than ten feet from the man, B.J. grabbed his hunting knife and slipped the blade up into his right shirtsleeve, holding the handle in his palm. He opened the driver's door and stepped out. Still clear in both directions.

"Who are you?" the man asked as B.J. walked around the back of the truck. Mid-eighties, B.J. thought. Thick glasses magnified piercing brown eyes. His wrinkles had wrinkles. Age spots peppered the fair skin of his face and dotted his bald scalp. Although his slightly stooped, bony frame wasn't more than 120 pounds, his voice boomed with authority. "What do you want?"

B.J. smiled at the old man, who looked remarkably like his long-deceased grandfather. "Just doin' a public service. I collect trash just before the big city trucks come through. Find lots of valuables that way."

The old man raised a crooked finger. "Well, you can't have my trash."

Casually looking both ways, B.J. didn't want to kill the old guy. He even sounded like his grandfather. But he couldn't allow him to open the box. "It ain't your trash," B.J. said. "I was drivin' by here earlier and these bags fell out of my overloaded truck. Just come back to collect them."

The geezer's face relaxed, but quickly went hard again. He stepped back and looked B.J. over. Then he stepped around him and looked at the truck. "Tennessee plates," he mumbled under his breath as he looked through the glass in the door of the camper. "How come your truck's empty?" He frowned and stepped away. "You live around here? What's your name?"

Although the Tennessee tags were registered to a rental truck currently sitting in his barn back home in Duck River, and although the truck was rented under a fake name, B.J. couldn't afford to have the number reported to the police. Grandpa look-alike or not, the old geezer had, for the last time, stuck his nose into somebody else's business.

After a second glance in both directions, B.J. swung his left fist and hit the man in the middle of the forehead. He staggered backward and collapsed. B.J. caught him and carried him into the garage, laying him on the floor next to a rusty sedan. Scanning the garage, he ran to a shelf along the front wall and grabbed a claw hammer.

Then the door leading into the house rattled. "Don't forget to run to the store for me," said an old woman from just inside the house. "This old door," she mumbled, finally popping it open.

B.J. ducked behind the car, quietly set the hammer down, and ran from the garage.

He was in his truck with his equipment and moving within seconds. Not wanting to exit onto the street in front of him, he stopped, backed his truck into a driveway, and turned around. As he passed the geezer's garage, he saw the old woman cradling the man's head in her lap. Zeke was still talking on the radio. B.J. glanced at his watch. He'd been out of his truck less than two minutes.

"A single, new piece of evidence was delivered to the Plano police chief in this morning's mail," Zeke was saying.

Last night, during his escape, B.J. had figured out what Zeke was up to. This confirmed his theory.

"It's a short letter addressed to me and signed Billy Ray Jackson."

B.J., actually laughing out loud, could hear the crowd erupt over the radio.

"The letter is typed," Zeke continued. "Although I will not read the entire contents, I will divulge the two most interesting sentences: '*Who you believe is, is not important. Who you believe was, is.*' We're studying possible meanings. Since we've just received the letter, interpretations will be withheld until a full evaluation can be completed. However, several aspects of the letter clearly indicate the work of a copycat."

B.J. just shook his head. The futile attempt by Zeke to enrage him to the point of losing control was pointless. He wasn't some animal who couldn't control his impulses.

He drove west until he reached Preston Road, where he turned north and stopped in front of a TGI Friday's. Backing into a parking spot in front of the restaurant, he gazed out the back window. A *Barnes & Noble* bookstore was 250 yards away, due west across Preston Road. The judge would be shot there, tomorrow evening, as he walked in the front door to attend the weekly meeting of the Lesser North Texas Writers.

Let someone write about that, he thought.

After spending the morning considering his options, Rush drove to the academy with one goal: survival. Last night had been a sleepless replay of Mallory's lifeless face, the smell of death, and visions of blood-splattered walls.

He noticed little as he drove, eyes straight ahead, jaw set. His surroundings held no importance, except to remind him that the world would continue after Jackson moved to the next city. That realization, in the early morning darkness of Chinbroski's spare bedroom, eyes fixed on the ceiling, had galvanized his determination to win this fight.

The late-night session with Chinbroski had done him good. He'd needed to admit his fear, his desire to run and hide.

But it was more than that. Baring his soul had not caused this morning's determination to control his own destiny. That moment came last night when Chinbroski's voice had grown weak with fear . . . when Chin faced the realization that *he* might be quartered in Jackson's cross-hairs.

Having heard that naked panic, Rush simply couldn't hand this case off. He had to fight. And he couldn't allow anyone else to take the responsibility for that fight.

The death of another police detective would mean little to the public following this case. Just a name. *Greg Rush, poor guy, could you pass the sugar, dear?* The media would almost cheer for Jackson to survive, to prevail for one more shooting season. Jackson's an enigma, Rush thought, a conundrum, a human puzzle who murders without malice: bigger than life, water fountain fodder, entertainment for people with dismembered priorities.

Who would remember a detective who happened to be at the wrong place at the wrong time? The fascination with this case, the chess game, far outweighed one man's life, one man's attempt to survive.

Rush had followed the national attention during the weeks leading up to July 24th: the fervor, the zeal. The media held a certain passion for stories of this magnitude, regardless of content. They celebrated the attention they themselves generated, fed off the tragedy they glorified. Throughout the annals of crime, who ever remembered those who died?

Rush knew that he was as guilty as everyone else. Ask him to name any of John Gacy's victims, and he'd draw a blank. How about Jeffrey Dahmer's? Ted Bundy's? The Hillside Strangler's? Jack the Ripper's? No one cared about them. The savagely murdered linger as obscure footnotes, serving only as answers to trivia questions for the most avid criminology enthusiast.

Unless somebody got serious about catching this son-of-a-bitch, Rush would be just another footnote, the sixteenth notch in the stock of Jackson's rifle. To depend on someone else to stop this lunacy was the real definition of cowardice. At least for Rush. He couldn't run. That was clear. He could never handle someone being shot in his place. So he had only one choice: do it himself.

He arrived at the training academy at 12:30 P.M., went straight to the office Zeke had commandeered. The FBI agent held the phone between his cheek and shoulder, baggy suit already wrinkled, sagging face freshly shaved. He looked across the desk at Rush and nodded, waved at him to be seated.

Zeke's laptop computer sat on the credenza behind him, its screen filled with some kind of spreadsheet. Rush couldn't make out the details.

After Zeke grunted a couple of acknowledgements, he said good-bye and hung up.

He stared at Rush for several moments as though trying to read words written across his forehead. "I spoke to your chief this morning. And my legal people."

As Rush had expected.

"Everyone's concerned. Your chief considered ordering you off. He has the power."

Rush wouldn't argue the obvious point.

"Like me, he's concerned about last night."

"I'm not letting Jackson win," Rush said. "He killed her to drive me off the case. He wins if I get taken off. I'll work it on duty or on bereavement leave. I need this."

Zeke nodded and gazed at the ceiling, considering his next words. "The chief relayed that very point after talking with you early this morning. He told me it was my decision. My legal people can live with it. Since I'm running the case, since we'll be filing federal charges on Jackson, they can skate the bias issue if you have a minor role."

Rush nodded, relived that he wouldn't be forced to fight to stay on.

"What about Mallory?"

"She's dead and I can't bring her back."

"You know what I mean. What about a service?"

"I'm her family. My son is handling cremation arrangements. It's what she wanted. I'll grieve when this is over. The service will be me and Mallory's remains in a closed room after I kill the son-of-a-bitch." Rush sniffed and held his jaws tightly closed. He could feel the thin layer of moisture that had begun coating his eyes.

"We talked about this briefly last night, but I want to ask you again. Do you think he was there for Daniel?"

Rush believed so. He'd mentioned it to Zeke in passing last night, but now he was convinced of it. Daniel was a creature of habit, more so than anyone Rush knew. He'd probably sat at his end of the sofa next to Mallory's chair every single night for the last three months. He'd work until midnight, always within full view of the neighborhood. It would have been nothing for Jackson to research the homicide detectives at Plano PD, all seven of them, and discover one of them had an attorney son. It was perfect.

"He was set up," Rush said. "Mallory was a target of opportunity. If Daniel had been sitting there, I'd be burying my only child instead of cremating my wife."

"Why not leave?" Zeke said. "Who would blame you?"

"Drop it."

"I just want to—"

"Either on duty or off, I'm in this."

"So, that's it."

Rush nodded and said nothing. His face was hot. He unclenched his fists and took a deep breath. He'd spoken his last words on the subject.

Zeke must have sensed that, because he glanced over at his laptop and pointed to the screen. "I'm not convinced that Daniel was the targeted lawyer, but we have to move forward as though he were. I'm adding twenty more agents. Ten from Houston, five from New Orleans, and five from Kansas City."

Could have used them last night, Rush thought. He doubted Jackson would make such a blunder again. Rush let Zeke direct the conversation. No sense alienating him before he had the latest information. Crossing an ankle over a knee, he waited.

Zeke dug in his briefcase and pulled out a single sheet of paper. "List of judges," he said waving it in the air. "Did the fine-tuning on it this morning, unbelievable cooperation."

"I can imagine."

"They're completing their schedules now. We should have them all by this afternoon. As terrified as they are, they want it over with." Zeke sighed and cupped his chin in a palm. "We had a judge call the 800 number early this morning, after the news from last night. Asked if it was time for the judge. We told him yeah, maybe, and he starts screaming. Said he had a life to live, said he wished Jackson would hurry up so he could play golf again."

"Any judge but him, right?"

"Right. I figure he'll be one who cancels his entire docket and sneaks away in the middle of the night until all of this is over."

"You get his name?"

"Yeah. And I'm betting he doesn't fill out a schedule. Probably doesn't trust us. Of course, his family will sue, if he's the one."

Rush nodded, fighting the urge to jump into the reason for his visit. "So the protection starts today?"

"Every judge working or living in Plano is being surrounded as we speak. The men got their assignments early this morning as soon as the list was finalized."

"How many?"

"Nine. Six investigators to each one. It's not enough, but as soon as the other twenty get here, we'll have eight per judge. Hard to do all the legwork with everybody playing bodyguard." He shook his head and rubbed his face as though washing it without water.

"Any word from your team in Tennessee?"

Zeke shrugged. "It's slow-going. They've talked with over

three hundred motor home owners. They have thousands to go. A daunting task, personally interviewing every person who owns one of those things. Since the crippled guy couldn't identify the exact size or model, we're starting with the biggest ones first, those thirty feet or longer. Very time-consuming. I'm about to request that headquarters up the number of agents out there. Tennessee may be the key to this whole investigation."

Rush frowned. "Too bad you can't go public with that. Have the RV owners call in, submit to a spot inspection."

"Yeah," Zeke said. "Too bad. But think of this: I'm the shooter and I hear on the radio the FBI is looking for a motor home. Well, I'm not in Tennessee because I'm in Texas killing people. The FBI wants me to call in to a special 800 number and tell them I'm okay, that I'm not the shooter, and the reason I'm not home is that I'm on vacation. Now before I make that call, I'm thinking several things. First, there's a witness who's seen my RV, and if he saw my RV, he might have seen me, and I might want to find and kill that witness. Second, the FBI has the name and address of every RV owner in Tennessee, and if I don't call the 800 number, they drive out to my place and ask why. And I sure don't want them at my place. But if I do call the 800 number, they're going to ask me where I am. So I'd have two choices: call or not call."

"So what you'd do," Rush said, finishing the thought, "is drive to some other state, make the call, allow the FBI to come inspect your RV, which would be polished and clean of evidence. At that point you look like a law-abiding citizen. Which means it does us no good."

"Or," Zeke said, "I drive the twelve hours from Dallas to Nashville, clean my house free of evidence, call the FBI, and have them come out and look. Either way, it does nothing for us."

"You're right to keep it quiet." Rush had known all this, but Zeke probably felt better showing him how he'd thought of everything.

"What about me?" Rush asked. "I'm assuming you're preparing something—"

Zeke waved his hands, cutting Rush off. "I have a technical team arriving this morning from the FBI office in Houston. They're installing microwave camera systems in covert electrical transformers at each end of your street.

"The leader of Green Team found a vacant house four blocks from your place. We're working a deal with the landlord to rent it for the next month. We'll use it as a secondary command center, a covert location to set up our monitoring station. We'll also set cameras in stationary vehicles to cover the dead spots."

Rush nodded. "So you're thinking he'll hit me at the house? Why? He's been there once already. If he were that stupid, you'd have caught him already."

"That's not the only location we'll have covered."

This surprised him. "Really? Where else?"

Zeke reached across the desk and picked up a blank form, handing it to him. "The same information the judges are giving us. Your normal routine. I want every single thing you regularly do, every activity."

Rush rubbed his forehead. "I don't see the point—"

"We don't know how long he'll watch you. Maybe only a day, in which case he'll hit at a place he knows you'll be."

"Like Susan, the detective from last year, at the police station," Rush said.

Zeke swallowed hard. "Right. Hit the next . . ." He cleared his throat. "We were setting up over a dozen microwave systems when . . ." His sentence trailed off.

Rush glanced at the form and folded it, slipping it into a pocket.

"We have enough cameras to cover half this city," Zeke said. "If he gives us time, we'll have him covered somewhere with surveillance." He shifted in his chair, straightened, his voice rising. "If you don't have much of a routine, we'll script you one. It'll be to places where taking a shot would be difficult at best. And we'll wire those places with more cameras than you can count. The beauty of all of this is the fact this shooter doesn't know you. He won't know your routine is scripted."

He's been watching my house long enough to know Daniel was staying there, Rush thought, but didn't say. Zeke was putting him on a stage. In the middle of a shooting lane. The plan sounded solid. But he didn't buy that it would be so easy. Zeke had just admitted they'd tried it last year in Colorado.

And Rush's theory about the old newspaper articles nagged him. With the Internet, Jackson could search from the security of his hideout. After last night, Rush didn't think Jackson would run any surveillance on him. He'd find something in Rush's past, some nugget of information out of the stream of normal routine, and strike then. He might have it already.

"Okay," Rush said. "I'll give you a schedule. But I want to scout some locations first."

Zeke nodded. "Fine. In the meantime, I need you to keep a low profile. And I need to get that list of locations to the tech guys as soon as possible."

Rush paused, rubbed his eyes. "What about the fat guy?" Rush asked. "Harold Blane?"

"I suggested protecting him. After you and Chinbroski

left. He doesn't want to go anywhere. Said he doesn't feel comfortable anywhere but there."

"You don't think Jackson will make a move on him?"

"Hasn't the last two years. Remember I told you we leaked witness names to the press, set a couple of traps? A big zero. This guy doesn't bite."

"There's a difference," Rush said. "Jackson knows Blane saw him, because he yelled at him. Jackson knows there's a real witness."

"True. If I'm the shooter, I'd have to ask myself if killing Blane is worth the risk. The shooter knows Blane didn't see his face. And it was dark on top of that. There's no equity in it for him." Zeke twirled a pencil between two fingers.

"So you're not running any protection on him?"

"Can't afford the manpower." Zeke waved a hand in front of his face. "Let me back up. I'm not running full protection on him. But I'm not hanging him out to dry, either. I'm having a couple of off-duty patrol guys baby-sit him. Set it up with your CID captain this morning." He shrugged. "It's the least I could do, after I offered him protection last night."

Rush nodded again, waited for Zeke to continue, to steer the conversation in another direction. When he didn't, Rush got to the point of his visit.

"So tell me about this letter," he said, staring straight at Zeke, trying to keep the anger from his tone. "This incredibly-timed note from the most hunted criminal of our era. A criminal with an 85 IQ and an amazing knack of writing in symbolism." He raised an eyebrow. " *'Who you believe is, is not important. Who you believe was, is.'* You're shitting me."

Zeke paused for a split-second before smiling and leaning back in his chair. "Earlier this year I predicted Jackson might try and contact me. Imagine how shocked I was when it actually happened."

Rush couldn't stop his anger seeping through. "You know, Zeke, I almost get the feeling that, despite all of the stuff you just told me about putting cameras all around my house, this thing is a big game with you."

Zeke's smiled died. "How dare you!" He slammed a hand on the desk and came out of his chair.

"It took me a couple of days to figure out what you were doing," Rush continued. "This news of the letter sealed it for me."

"I've spent over two years chasing him. It's no game."

Rush stood. "You're trying to piss this guy off. With all of your degrees in psychology, you're trying some decades-old cop trick. No wonder you wouldn't tell me what you were up to."

Zeke couldn't hold Rush's glare. He broke eye contact, peered over Rush's shoulder as though hoping someone would barge through the door and interrupt them.

Wasn't up for a fight, Rush knew immediately. The agent's eyes were bloodshot, his voice weak, his hands quivered.

"I'll give you the list you want, but I'm not hiding behind you or your games," Rush said. "If Jackson's going to hunt me like I'm some trophy, then he *will* have to work his ass off."

"What are you talking about?" Zeke leaned on the desk. "What are you going to do?"

"I'm taking control of my destiny, Zeke. What have I been doing the last three days? I'll tell you. Jack shit. This isn't an intellectual exercise, some chapter out of a textbook. It's my life." Rush caught his breath. "The problem with this whole setup is that you don't have a stake in this. You sit behind your desk, pull your strings, tell your lies, and then shrug if Jackson doesn't take the bait. I'm not standing around while

143

your lies drive this guy into doing something crazy.' "

"I've already started the process, Rush. I can't just step up to the podium now and say, 'Excuse me, ladies and gentlemen, I've fed you several falsifications. Stand by for the truth.' "

Rush laughed, a single burst, sudden, like a rifle shot. "I don't give a *damn* whether or not you look bad. I don't give a *damn* how you explain it to the Jackson subculture. My role in your investigation *will* be minor because I'm not following you around anymore. That's what I came here to tell you this morning. I'm going out there to catch that son-of-a-bitch. That should make your legal people ecstatic."

Zeke closed his eyes momentarily and then sat heavily into his chair. "Greg," he said softly. "We have to give my strategy time to work. I admit Jackson isn't cooperating because of how quickly he advanced on the lawyer. On Daniel. I initially assumed, well . . ." he paused, flipping his hand in the air as though struggling for the proper terminology. "I had planned on having more time with the press, to parcel the . . . the misdirection with a greater degree of sincerity. I wouldn't—"

"Listen to yourself," Rush interrupted. " 'How quickly he advanced on the lawyer, the misdirection, a greater degree of sincerity.' You sound like you're conducting some classroom psychology experiment." Rush sat and leaned forward, hands on his knees. "Let's assume you're right about Jackson's ego, that he couldn't bear for the public to believe that a copycat had continued his work. And let's assume it *really is* pissing him off. What kind of mistake do you believe he'll make?"

"Like the one last night."

"That had nothing to do with him getting careless. It was a fluke the fat guy saw him. You think he'll be so pissed he'll show up at some news conference to set the record straight? That he'll call *Sixty Minutes* for a phone interview? What,

Zeke? He has his system down pat. And it's obvious he has chosen his victims well in advance." Rush threw up his hands, exasperated.

"What are you afraid of?" Zeke asked, his words hanging in the air like a rancid odor.

Rush jumped up, charged around the desk. He caught Zeke as the agent was attempting to rise from his chair. Grabbing the lapels of his coat, Rush shoved Zeke backward, the chair slamming into the wall. "I'll tell you what I'm afraid of, you bastard! I'm afraid of more people dying! I'm afraid that your bullshit plan will make him kill out of his normal cycle just to teach you a lesson! And I'm afraid that if you hide me, he'll kill some other Plano cop instead!"

His face ashen, Zeke swallowed hard and cut his eyes away. Rush gave him a final shove and released him, stepping back. His hands shook from rage, sweat ran into his eyes.

Zeke said nothing as he recovered, righting himself in his chair, shrugging his jacket into place.

Rush walked to the door, put his hand on the knob, and turned back. "The chief assigned me to this case, Zeke. But I don't have to sit around and do nothing while you make a fool of yourself."

"This is a federal investigation," Zeke said with as much strength as possible. "If you say anything publicly to harm what I've already started, I'll have you arrested."

Rush would have laughed out loud had the entire situation not been so serious. He just stared at Zeke and shook his head.

"I'll have you arrested," Zeke said again, the conviction in his voice more prevalent the second time. "I believe he'll make a mistake. And it will be his ego that causes it."

"You're pathetic," Rush said, taking a half-step toward Zeke's desk, "if you think I'll run to the press and expose your lies. I'm distancing myself from everything you say. *You're* the father of *this* abortion. And I'll make that point clear if I have to."

"Fine." Zeke averted his eyes, started moving papers around on his desk, suddenly too busy to continue the conversation.

CHAPTER NINE

B.J. concentrated on the front sight of the rifle, his focus as narrow as a laser beam. The sun was directly to the west, causing the left side of the sight to wash out. His dad had always told him to aim toward the light source when that happened, because the shadow created by the edge of the sight made an optical illusion. Not much, he'd always said, but in a competition every fraction of an inch might make the difference between winning and wishing you had won.

He'd been at Camp Indian Hill for three weeks now, and the battle for the top two places in marksmanship was all but decided. Starting the day, B.J. was ahead of Stubs by eleven points. No one else in camp, even the fifteen-year-old braggarts, could possibly catch them.

On this final day of shooting before the championship match next week, the sun was scorching. Stubs had already shot his final string and dropped two points, both off to the right. B.J. figured the shadow got him. B.J. had thrown a point early in the match when he fired during a breath. He'd hit low, directly below the X-ring. But he'd hit everything since, and if he hit this next one, the last of the day, he'd go up by another point overall.

Ignoring a drop of sweat that hung off the tip of his nose, he worked the bolt of the Stevens .22 and gently seated his last round. He was at the farthest distance, fifty yards, and the NRA target appeared smaller than it had five minutes before. His mental clock told him he still had over a minute left to fire. He liked the slow-fire stage best, because he had time to think about all the things his dad taught him, like fighting through this shadow.

The crowd of boys watching was lined up behind him. B.J. heard some mumbling, a giggle or two. But mostly they were respectful, having just been prone themselves, fighting the heat, battling the shadow. Stubs was somewhere off to the side. Probably praying he didn't lose another point to the leader.

Cutting his eyes away from the target, B.J. breathed deeply and pulled the stock a little tighter into his shoulder. Then he focused again on the front post, held a hair left of center, and pulled straight back on the trigger. The rifle jerked backward, and he fought to hold his target through the recoil. That was one advantage Stubs had over him. B.J. was at least forty pounds lighter than Stubs, and B.J.'s bony shoulder didn't offer much resistance against the recoil.

He smiled after the shot, feeling good about where his front sight had been when the trigger broke. Rolling over to his side, he loosened the loop sling, slid his arm out, and left the rifle lying on the shooting mat, bolt open for the range master to check before walking downrange to check the target.

Stubs strolled over and squatted down beside him. "What'd you think?" he asked, shielding his eyes from the sun as he watched the range master head toward the target.

B.J. shrugged, sitting up. "I think I hit them all."

"Which means you'll be another point ahead. Twelve total." Stubs stood and wiped a bead of sweat off his neck. "You're gonna have to really screw up bad for me to beat you."

"Best shot in Trenton, Texas," B.J. said with a chuckle. He brushed off the front of his pants and glanced back at the crowd of

other boys. Most were waiting for the range master to shout out any misses. Some had wandered away.

"We going hiking to the cliff today?" Stubs asked.

"Heck, yeah!" B.J. turned back toward the range master, who was bent over examining the target. Stubs watched too, waiting for the word.

When "No misses!" was shouted out from down range, B.J. closed his eyes and sighed. Stubs slapped his back.

"I'm gonna have to do something desperate," Stubs said. "Maybe like take you back up to that cave and lock you in for good."

B.J. laughed. "Yeah, right." Then he turned serious. "My dad always said it ain't over till it's over. I might drop a bunch next time."

"Naw, won't ever happen," Stubs said. "I been watching you. You look like you get inside some kind of bubble or something. I don't think you'd notice even if I jumped on your back while you were shooting. Maybe I'll just bend your front sight." He slapped B.J. on the back again. "Come on, daylight is wasting and it's a long way up to the cliff."

They hiked in silence, using their mouths to breathe rather than talk. B.J. followed Stubs, as always, constantly dodging the tree branches the bigger boy grabbed, held, and released at the last possible moment.

He'd been hit twice so far, both times across the chest. Stubs said he thought it was funny that B.J. chose to dodge rather than hang far enough back to avoid being a target. But dodging was fun. B.J. pretended he was in a street fight, jumping low kicks, ducking high punches, blocking karate chops. Might as well pretend, he thought. Since he'd never win many street fights.

The cliff overhang was great. High atop the northern mountain, it was another twenty-minute hike past the cave where they'd tracked the bear. From the large, flat rock that jutted out across the top of the trees they could view all of Camp Indian Hill. And not only the camp but also the road approaching and the valley surrounding. B.J. didn't know how far it was from up there, but it looked like at least a mile.

Stubs stopped at his usual spot to rest, sweat poring from his face. They were getting close to the toughest part of the climb, a narrow, steep path with loose rocks and sand that made it impossible to get any traction. The Slide to Hell. The first time up, Stubs had made B.J. go first, in case he lost his footing.

Stubs said B.J. was so light that he could stop him from sliding. And he did. Stubs had saved him three times already, the last one being the scariest. B.J. had been a handhold from the top when he lost his footing and came crashing down. Stubs dug in, planted his shoulder against a boulder, and caught him with one arm. Said it was like catching a feather. B.J. had told him he bragged more than the fifteen-year-olds.

"You ready?" Stubs asked after they took a breather.

"Yeah." B.J. stepped around him, planted his right foot against an exposed tree root, and grabbed a low hanging branch, pulling himself up the path.

"You been noticing all of the squirrels out here?" Stubs asked, waiting for B.J. to climb higher before starting his ascent.

"Squirrel city. I saw one right before your last branch hit me in the face. I think that's why it hit me. I was looking at the squirrel."

"There must be a million of them out here. Wonder why nobody ever comes here to hunt?"

B.J. grabbed another tree root and dug his toes in. "My dad always said you ain't supposed to hunt squirrels in the summer. That they have worms or something."

"I never heard that. Wish we could hunt them. Man, we'd fill up a whole gunny sack in no time."

Stubs had started his climb; B.J. could hear the strain in his voice, the small rocks sliding down the path. "*I go hunting some-times,*" B.J. said. "*But since my dad died, I've only been once. It was when my uncle came to visit. My mom's new boyfriend hates hunting. Watches football all the time.*"

"*I like football,*" Stubs said. "*But I like hunting more. I bet I'm a better shot than you out in the woods.*"

B.J. *stopped and looked back. The top of Stubs's head was dark with sweat, his blond hair wet clumps.* "*Why would you bet that?*"

Stubs looked up, grinning. "*I just think so. See, you're a good shot when you get to lay on the ground all pretty-like. But I bet if you had to carry the rifle all over the place, your arms would get tired and start shaking. Probably couldn't hit a bear from fifteen feet.*" *He laughed.*

"*Yeah, right!*" B.J. *started climbing again, being especially careful. He didn't want to end up in the braggart's arms today. Not after just being told he was too weak to carry a rifle.*

"*We ought to do it,*" *Stubs said from below.*

"*Do what?*" B.J. *was halfway up.*

"*Go squirrel hunting.*"

B.J. *lunged for a jutting rock and grabbed it with the tips of his fingers. He strained as he pulled his knees up under his belly. Then he lunged again and grabbed another rock. Kicking his feet wildly, he fought for traction, knocking sand and rocks down on top of Stubs.*

"*Hey, watch it!*"

"*Sorry,*" B.J. *said, finally pulling himself past The Slide to Hell. He was almost at the top. He relaxed some.* "*How can we go squirrel hunting? We don't have any guns.*"

Stubs spit dirt out of his mouth before answering. "*We have a whole shed full of guns.*"

That stopped B.J. *again. He had his foot anchored against a rock and both hands on the ledge above. Turning, he saw that Stubs* had stopped also, right in the middle of The Slide to Hell, looking up, grinning from ear to ear.

"You heard me right," Stubs said. "A whole shed full. We could sneak in there, get one, then come up here and shoot us some squirrels."

"You're crazy. We can't steal a gun."

"Not steal. Use. We'd put it back."

B.J. looked up, peered over the ledge. The big rock that overlooked the valley was off to his right. "We'd get arrested, too. If we got caught."

Stubs grinned, his face streaked with the dirt B.J. had kicked on him. "We wouldn't get arrested for shooting a couple of squirrels. You're the one who's crazy."

"Your face looks like somebody wiped his butt across it," B.J. told him.

That made Stubs laugh. He swiped a hand across his face, letting go of the small rock he'd been gripping with his fingertips. His feet slipped, kicking sand down the slide. "Whoa!" he yelled, grabbing the rock again. He lost his other handhold and kicked wildly with his feet.

"Grab that root!" B.J. shouted. "Over on the right!"

Stubs groped to his right, hanging on desperately, feet digging into the soft sand. He was out of reach of the root because his body had shifted to the center of the slide. His fingers were bone white.

"Hang on!" B.J. screamed. "I'm coming!"

Six feet above his friend, he carefully lowered himself, legs spread wide across the path, toes ripping gashes into the soft earth. He looked past Stubs to the flat area below. They'd been safe there only moments before. The twenty-foot fall wouldn't be that bad, as long as they didn't land on any of the sharp boulders that rose from the ground like giant teeth.

Stubs was trying to swing now, feet still scrambling for purchase.

Lower, only three feet. B.J.'s right foot was securely planted just above The Slide. "I'm going to lower my foot," he yelled to Stubs. "Grab it like a rope and I'll try and pull you up."

The lower he dropped his foot, the deeper he had to bend his right leg. When he could lower it no more, he looked down. Stubs's fingers had slipped. Only his middle finger still gripped the rock. His other fingers were bleeding. With a desperate lurch, Stubs grabbed for B.J.'s dangling foot just as his last finger gave out.

B.J. screamed out in pain as all of Stubs's weight clamped onto his foot, pushing his right knee almost through his chest. His kneecap felt like it was about to snap.

"Pull me up!" Stubs screamed.

"You're too heavy!"

Stubs grabbed B.J.'s left knee and pulled himself toward the top.

"You're pulling my pants down," B.J. said, straining to hang on. He felt his right foot slipping. "Hurry!"

"I'm trying!" Stubs reached over and took hold of the small root with his right hand. Then he grabbed the small rock with his fingertips again, releasing B.J.'s knee.

B.J. pushed himself up as fast as he could, and within seconds had both hands wrapped around the top of the ledge. They were both in the same position as before.

"That was close," Stubs said from below. B.J. heard fear in the bigger boy's words. And he grinned to himself. He'd saved Stubs this time.

"I can see the crack of your butt," Stubs said, laughing. "Hurry up and get over the top before a big old turd slips out of your pants."

B.J. pulled himself over and looked down at Stubs, watched him quickly climb to the top.

"That was your fault," Stubs said after he'd flopped down on the ground beside B.J. "If you hadn't made that joke, I

153

wouldn't have started laughing."

B.J. gave him a shove and limped to the large rock overhang, his right knee aching. He felt on top of the world, almost like God inspecting His creation. The valley stretched out below him. The northern mountain was the highest of the three in that area of the national forest. In a field a quarter-mile east of the camp was the tepee village where every boy in camp got to spend two nights in real Indian tepees. B.J. and Stubs's cabin would be there tonight and tomorrow night. He couldn't wait.

"I'd hate to face someone who had a gun up here," Stubs said, walking up behind him.

B.J. nodded. "Yeah, nobody could sneak up on you."

They both took in the view, quiet for several moments.

"Thanks for saving me," Stubs said quietly.

Shrugging, B.J. felt his chest swell. "I'm glad I finally got to save you for once."

"Did you hurt your knee or something? I saw you limping."

B.J. shrugged it off. "It's okay." He didn't dare mention something so minor after doing something so brave.

"So do you want to do it?" Stubs asked. He'd wiped most of his face clean with his shirt, leaving one wide brown streak across his forehead.

"Do what?"

"Go hunting. What we've been talking about."

B.J. shook his head. "You mean what you've been talking about. I'm not gonna steal no gun."

"Like I said, it ain't stealing." Stubs licked the ends of his bloody fingers. "And I just had another idea. We can come out here at night. Squirrels come out big time at night."

"Did some of that dirt fall into your ears and get inside your brain or something?" B.J. turned away and gazed out over the valley. The camp swimming pool looked no bigger than a postage stamp. He could see some boys playing a football game in the field

next to the tepees. They looked like ants.

"Why do you say that?"

"How are we going to hunt at night? There's no noise at night. You could hear the gun a mile away." B.J. shook his head in disbelief.

"So what?" Stubs said. "So someone hears a few shots from way far off. Nobody would think it's us. From the camp it'll sound like it could've come from anywhere. Who's gonna know?"

The breeze tickled the sweat under B.J.'s hairline. He ran a hand through his hair and sighed. "Why do you wanna do it?"

" 'Cause, camp's almost over. What's the big deal? It'd be fun." Stubs strolled to the edge of the rock and peered over. Then he turned back and faced B.J., serious, challenging. "I think you're afraid for me to show you I'm a better shot than you in the woods."

"I ain't afraid of nothing! And I'm the best shot in this camp!"

"Laying down all nice and pretty."

B.J. huffed. "Laying down, sitting down, or kneeling down. I've been proving it for three weeks." B.J. surprised himself by jumping so boldly to his own defense. His words had sounded tough, spoken with a harshness he never knew he had. "I don't have to prove nothing to you!"

Stubs raised his eyebrows, an amused look on his face. "You got that right. 'Cause I know I'm the best shot in the woods. I'm the best shot when you have to kill something. I've got hunter's blood."

B.J. could feel the heat rising in his face, his throat squeezing tight with anger.

"I'll bet your dad wasn't a good hunter, either."

"You leave my dad out of it!" B.J. yelled. "Don't you say nothing about him! He was the best hunter in Trenton. And the best shot. He won medals in the Marines. He won the Wimbledon Cup! Twice!"

"Who cares about tennis?"

"You're so stupid! I ain't talking about tennis! I'm talking about the hardest shooting match in the country! He beat the best shooters in the military! And he taught me everything!" B.J. took a step closer and put a finger in Stubs's face. "I could beat you anywhere, anytime!"

Stubs shrugged. "So, prove it. Go hunting with me. We can sneak in there and get a .22. We'll wait until after midnight. We come way out here, and whoever sees the first squirrel gets one shot at it. If it's a miss, then the other guy gets to try."

B.J. waved his hands at the bigger boy. "As soon as you shoot, the squirrel will run away." He didn't want to do it, sneak out. It was breaking the rules. But he had to admit it sounded like fun.

"So then we'd find another squirrel," Stubs said, hiking his shoulders. "Come on. We won't get caught. It'll be something we'll remember for the rest of our lives."

"What if somebody sees us sneaking out?"

"I told you, we wait until after midnight." Stubs turned away, looked over the edge again. "Tell you what," he said suddenly, spinning around. He hurried over and raised one of his bloody fingers. "We can be blood brothers. And blood brothers can never betray each other. They can never tell on each other. They'll protect each other till death! If we do that, then if we get caught, we can take the blame together."

"How would that help?"

"Because they'll go easier on two people than just one. But we don't even have to worry about that, because there's no way we'll get caught. No way!"

B.J. stared at Stubs, his eager face, the dirty sweat mark running down his forehead. Then he looked at his bloody finger. He'd never had a blood brother before. Never had such a good friend. Not since his dad died. And it would be fun. Especially proving that he was the best hunter. That he could win two *shooting competitions. Just like his dad.*

"When?" B.J. asked, still not quite sold.

"Thursday night. The night after we get back from the tepees. That way, if we do get caught, they can't send us home early 'cause we'll be going home on Saturday, anyway. So really, there's nothing to lose." He grinned.

B.J. was quiet for a moment. Then he nodded. "Okay. But first we have to become blood brothers. Just in case something happens."

The *Plano Weekly News* anchored an old strip center on Plano's east side. Sandwiched between a do-it-yourself pest control shop and a small French bakery, Rush wondered if the *Weekly News* employees ever suspected the owners of the two businesses of getting together to create a diazinon-filled pastry. Such a conflict of smells, he thought as he strode to the front door, fighting the urge to hold his nose.

The newspaper staff numbered less than six; including the receptionist and editor-in-chief. They didn't report on national or statewide events, leaving that up to the *Dallas Morning News.* Their focus was strictly Plano citizens, Plano businesses, and Plano happenings. With a circulation of only a few thousand copies per week, Rush wondered how many new residents on the booming west side of town even knew of its existence.

Peering up at the dingy sign mounted above the front door, he remembered thinking that Jackson might be researching old stories over the Internet. But surely this newspaper wouldn't have spent the money necessary to archive their old stories online. Hoping for archaic technology, he lipped a silent prayer as he swung the front door open.

A grandmotherly type smiled as he approached the receptionist's desk. Her skin appeared plastic, stretched, with a shine that reflected the sun filtering through the front door. Her glasses, secured with a gold chain that looped around the back of her neck, covered half of her face. The small waiting area, spotless, yet faded, was a monument to early-seventies vinyl. Two avocado greens, two burnt orange and brown, and five vinyl-covered chairs stood at attention along one wall. A red vinyl-covered sofa lined another. Nothing else. Nothing modern, nothing pretty. Rush had known the editor of the *Weekly News* for fifteen years, but this was the first time he'd paid the old gentleman a visit.

"Help you?" asked the grandma.

Rush smiled. "Sure. Cliff Dolan. He's not expecting me. Greg Rush, Plano PD."

"From that horrible murder case several months back, right?" she said, smiling, her plastic skin stretching even tighter.

"Right." Rush's photograph had been on their front page as recently as seven months before, after solving the brutal strangulation of a homemaker. The murder, dubbed *The Listener Case* by cops within the PD, had dominated most of the space the small paper usually allocated for Christmas stories.

She picked up the phone and punched in three numbers.

Cliff Dolan, the editor, did nearly everything else, too. Not a close friend of Rush's, but someone who'd help and not ask too many questions.

When grandma replaced the receiver, Rush went straight to Dolan's office. The newsroom, if one could really call it that, was as quiet as a library. One lone employee, college-age, sat hunched over a drafting table, copyediting an article. He wore headphones and didn't look up. The rest of the room was organized chaos. Stacks of old issues crowded three desks along one wall. The desks, army green with heavy wooden tops, were each adorned with desktop computers that belonged in a computer museum. He saw nothing in the way of modern office equipment, unless one counted a printwheel printer spitting out the AP wires.

Trash cans overflowed, boxes of paper blocked access to the men's restroom, and leftover pizza stiffened on paper plates. Rush could see the pressroom through a door on the left. The presses were quiet, the room dark.

Guarding Dolan's office was a pair of pink flamingos, heads held high, defying anyone to enter. Someone had painted human eyes on each, and fitted both with menacing grins, wolf-like teeth, and rabid-dog foaming mouths.

Through the glass, Dolan waved at Rush to enter. Rush cracked the door and stuck his head in, not wanting to interrupt Dolan's phone call. Dolan shook his head and waved him in again.

"So you have nothing for me?" Dolan said into the phone, wrapping the cord around his wrist. "Right. Okay. I'll call you in a couple of days." He untangled the cord and practically tossed the receiver into its cradle. "Greg Rush." He stood. "Haven't seen you in a month of Thursdays."

Rush shook his hand. "Hey, Cliff, thanks for seeing me." Dolan was a runner. Marathons. He towered above Rush's six-foot frame, had a head full of bushy, blond hair cut short because of the kinky curls, and a voice that rattled one's eardrums.

"No problem," he said, waving to a chair opposite his desk. "You bringing me something?" He lowered his voice, leaned forward. "Something on the Jackson case? Maybe giving the hometown small fry his fifteen minutes of glory?" He grinned and folded his hands behind his head.

Neither the police department nor FBI had released Mallory's name as the victim of last night's shooting. And Rush had no interest in sharing that piece of information. He felt a churning in his gut as he tried to hide his emotion. "You're assuming I'm on the Jackson case."

Dolan laughed. "Everybody's on the Jackson case." He raised his eyebrows, waiting for confirmation.

Rush shrugged. "Not a bad assumption. You run anything on it?" He hadn't even thought to check. Only a few of the oldest convenience and grocery stores carried the *Weekly News*. Rush had never seen it west of Central Expressway.

"Our first big spread was yesterday." He leaned over and grabbed a copy from the corner of his desk, tossed it in Rush's lap. "Of course, this proves you're on the case."

Not Just a Plan-o Shooting, the headline screamed. A photograph of the hospital parking lot was centered above the fold. Rush cringed when he saw himself standing over the body, huddled with Chinbroski, pointing toward the apartment complex across the street. The caption took his breath away. *Detectives Greg Rush and Rick Chinbroski, Plano's top investigative team, speculate on the origin of the shot most of America had been waiting for.*

"A little dramatic," Dolan said, chuckling. "But you know what? I'm getting old. And this is the biggest Plano happening of my *lifetime*."

Rush rubbed the back of his neck and scanned the story, which sported Dolan's byline. It chronicled the Jackson case, listed the victims. Then it speculated how successful the Rush/Chinbroski investigative team would be when assisted by the wide-reaching resources of the FBI.

"So you're still writing," Rush said, tapping the byline.

Dolan nodded. "It's my first love. And probably my last big story. It took me hours to write that little piece." He picked up a pen and stuck it behind an ear. "That headline has sold some copies, though. Gotta give myself credit for that. Up five hundred Thursday and seven hundred this morning."

Rush couldn't be angry with Dolan for putting his name and face out there. Not at someone just doing his job. But he wanted to kick himself for not calling Dolan Wednesday night, before Zeke announced to the national media that he was taking over the lead in the case. Dolan would have pulled that photograph and rewritten his story, leaving his and Chinbroski's names out.

"I'm running an exposé next week," Dolan went on. "I think you'll like it." He raised an eyebrow.

"An exposé," Rush said. "And just who are you exposing?"

Dolan grabbed the pen from behind his ear and pointed it at Rush. "You."

His face must have paled because Dolan suddenly looked uncomfortable. "Something wrong?"

"You trying to get me killed?" Rush asked, his words snapping more than he intended. "Didn't you hear that the FBI has taken over the case?"

The newspaper man waved the question off. "I don't believe a word of that crap. This is about the local cops. For some reason Jackson has a hard-on for the locals."

"I don't . . ." Rush spread his hands wide. "So knowing that, you're putting me out front? You're making sure Jackson knows which detective to shoot? What's the matter with you?"

Dolan's jaw went slack for a moment. He stared off into space. "I never even *considered* that. I mean, well, what . . ." He slumped forward and pressed his temples with the heels of his hands.

Rush remained silent. He still hadn't mentioned the reason for his visit. He didn't want the exposé, but his plan to fight back needed something right along those lines. If Rush could make Dolan sweat a little, get a good guilt trip brewing, the guy would fall over backwards trying to help.

"I really didn't mean to put you in danger," Dolan said, his voice suddenly sounding his age. "I guess I just figured . . . well, actually, I didn't figure at all. I'm sorry. I'll pull it." He shook his head and sighed. "I suddenly feel like the excited copy boy who screwed up his first reporting job."

Rush let the silence grow thick, staring at a spot over Dolan's left shoulder. Dolan nodded and rubbed his forehead, slumped back in his chair, stuck his pen behind his ear.

"Let's drop that for a moment," Rush said, looking at Dolan solidly. "I actually dropped in for a reason. A little research project."

Dolan remained motionless except for his eyes. They moved off of Rush's face and locked onto a blank notepad in front of him.

"You did a story on Daniel, my son, a couple of months ago. Remember?"

The newspaper man nodded, sat up in his chair. "Sure, after the big piece on *The Listener* case. Edited it myself. Melissa wrote the piece."

"Melissa?"

"College intern I had last summer. Journalism major who grew up in Plano. Went to school with Daniel. Kind of has a crush on him. Anyway, her prose was a little weak, so I cleaned it up."

Rush nodded. "I wonder if maybe your paper might have done something on Charles Thayer, the doctor killed at the hospital."

Dolan's eyebrows raised.

Rush turned and glanced over his shoulder. The newsroom was still empty, save for the line editor in the corner.

"We need to have a conversation," he said, lowering his voice. "But I need your absolute confidence."

Grabbing the pen from behind his ear, Dolan prepared to write. Ever the reporter. "Pertaining to?"

Rush smiled. "What do you think?"

Dolan whistled. Then a smile cracked his suddenly serious features. "Absolute confidence, huh? On the hottest thing in the last forty years? Hell, the hottest thing to *ever* hit Plano. You don't ask for much."

"There are certain questions I won't be able to answer. Most, in fact. But first, I need to know if you ever ran a piece on Thayer."

Dolan spun around in his chair and faced the computer on the credenza behind him. "This baby's only a couple of years old," he said, clicking his way into Microsoft Word. "Keep all the stories I write or edit in here." He spent the next minute searching for Thayer. He finally shook his head and looked at Rush. "Nothing."

Rush blew out a breath.

"But," Dolan said, holding up a finger, "like I said, I've only had this thing a couple of years. Anything older than that I kept indexed on three-by-five cards." He practically jumped from his chair. "Follow me."

Rush followed him into the newsroom. Along the wall nearest the men's restroom stood a row of filing cabinets the same shade of army green as the desks. Dolan marched over to the one on the far left and opened the bottom drawer. "Thayer *would* be on the bottom. If he's in here, we'll dig through back issues over there." He jerked his thumb behind him, toward the dozens of stacks piled against the front wall. Rush hoped all of those stacks were arranged in some kind of system, because he didn't have hours to go through everything.

"Here!" Dolan practically shouted, holding up a single card. "Issue fifty, page two, three years ago." He stood and turned. "Going to be in the fifth stack this side of the front door. Should be near the bottom."

Rush looked at the hundreds of issues and shook his head.

"Issue fifty means mid-December." The excitement in Dolan's voice was contagious. He trotted to the correct stack.

The young paste-up artist, hunched over the drafting table, pulled the headphones off his ears and watched Dolan remove the top of the stack and thumb the remaining issues until he had the right one.

"Can we take it to your office?" Rush asked.

"You bet." Dolan glanced at the kid. "You going to have that ready by two, Randy?"

"Yes, sir," the young man said with a curious expression, following Dolan's march across the room.

Rush held Dolan's door open, then closed it after Dolan passed through. "Let me see it."

Dolan handed the paper over.

Flipping it to page two, Rush had to search for a moment before he found the small article on the left side of the page. He quickly read the piece and nodded. It would be enough, he thought, for Jackson to choose Thayer as a target.

"Read it," Dolan said, his words sharp and high-pitched.

"Dr. Charles Thayer, a Plano gynecologist for fifteen years, has started a new Christmas tradition: free pap smears for low income, single mothers. Dr. Thayer announced his program at the annual Plano General Hospital Christmas banquet last night. Thayer will set aside Christmas Eve each year and expects to perform as many as two dozen exams from 8:00 A.M. until 6:00 P.M. Appointments can be made by calling his office number listed in the ad below. Thayer cited the Christmas spirit as his reason for the free exams. 'I want to give back to the community,' he said.

'Catching a problem early might be the best gift I could ever give someone.' ''

Rush looked up at Dolan. "Could there be any other articles about him?"

His answer was quick. "It would have been noted on the card. And I got this computer a few months after that issue. So, no. That's it."

And now the most important question. "How would Jackson have found this article?" Rush asked. "Surely he wouldn't have walked in here to do his research. Maybe the Internet?"

Dolan laughed. "I don't think so." He leaned back in his chair. "When do you think he might have researched? How long ago?"

Rush shrugged. "I would guess within the last three or four months. Maybe as long as six."

"Then the only place is here."

"You sure? What about the library?"

"They keep them one year. That's it. This issue is over three years old."

"You sure about that?" Rush asked. "One year?"

"They have a yearly sale, *Friends of the Public Library*; you've probably heard of it. Seems like every year someone from the library calls to ask if I want my old copies back. They used to microfiche them, but stopped that . . . oh, I don't know, several years back. Before that article was written."

Rush thought about that. Could Jackson have chosen Plano that far in advance? Certainly. For all anyone knew, he might have every city mapped out for years to come. But then the article about Daniel was more recent, not even a year. So that meant he was still searching as recently as seven or eight months ago. Maybe. He might have selected a different lawyer at the same time he chose Thayer, only to have something happen, forcing him to choose Daniel.

He sighed heavily. He couldn't forget that having both Thayer and Daniel appear in the same small-time, weekly newspaper was really nothing more than a coincidence. A person couldn't establish a real pattern until the judge was shot. But then that was wrong, too. The number of judges in each victim city was infinitely smaller than the number of doctors and lawyers. Jackson wouldn't have as big a choice. In Colorado last year, he hit the only judge available.

No, the only way to determine if Jackson was researching his victims through old articles from small, insignificant newspapers was to go back to the first three victim cities. And the FBI was most capable of doing that.

"Greg," Dolan said. "Did you hear me?"

"Oh, no, I didn't. Sorry."

"I asked if you wanted me to go back and check for any old articles on judges?"

Rush knew that would have to be done. Eventually. "What I want you to do is pull everything you've done on me in the last year. Anything that might still be in the library."

Dolan stared at him a moment, as though figuring out Rush's angle. "Right. Now that I can do from here." He spun around and started a computer search. "We did several articles late last December, the beginning of January. Back when you and Chinbroski solved that McElroy murder."

"Right, *The Listener Case*," Rush said. "You made me and Chinbroski look better than we are."

Dolan laughed.

"There was one article where you mentioned how I visit my birth mother's grave every year on her birthday. Remember?"

"Sure. Here it is." Dolan clicked, the printer started humming. He turned and faced Rush. "You think Jackson might have read that?"

"I don't know. We're still not sure how he knows which detectives to target. But once he discovers their names, he has to do something to gain a little insight."

Rush tapped the newspaper. "Why not look in here?"

Dolan reached over and lifted the printed sheets out of the tray. His eyes were bright with excitement. "I guess you couldn't offer me an exclusive once all of this is over, could you? Throw me a bone?"

"If I survive it? You bet." Rush took the printout from Dolan and scanned it. The piece of the article Rush wanted to confirm was near the end. It told how he still visited his birth mother's grave every July 31st. Told how his mother had died when he was nine, forcing Rush to spend the rest of his boyhood years jumping from foster home to foster home. July 31st was only five days away, the cemetery in the center of east Plano. Maybe this was why Jackson was in such a hurry, trying a hit on Daniel only one day after Thayer. That meant the judge would also be soon.

They didn't have much time. *He* didn't have much time.

"Let me tell you what I'm going to do," Rush said. "I'm going to call FBI Agent Zeke Bunning and have him send a team of agents in here to read every back issue you have. It's going to disrupt your office, and even though Jackson may not have found his judge in your paper, we still have to look."

Dolan nodded. "Fine." He started to say something, then stopped.

"What?" Rush said. "Go ahead. Say what's on your mind."

"What about you? What about the cemetery? You going to lay a trap?"

"I have something in mind." He scooted to the edge of his

chair. "This is important, Cliff. And I swear if I make it through this, you'll get the only interview I'll ever do. You can videotape it in a studio and sell it for a lot of money. You can write a book about it, make even more money. But you have to keep the cemetery business to yourself. That's all I ask."

Cliff cupped his hand in his chin, tapped his fingers on the desk. "Are you talking about keeping it from the FBI or from non-law enforcement?"

"I'm talking about not breathing a word of it to anyone. Including the FBI, any other Plano cop, or your wife. If they're breathing, they're included."

"And you give me an exclusive? Me, the editor of a once-a-week rag?"

"Your fifteen minutes of fame."

"You'd turn down the national publications?"

"They never cared about Plano before Jackson," Rush said, stroking Dolan's ego. "And since you're the only one still interested enough in this city to do what you do, who would be better?"

Dolan chuckled. "Deal. One question, though. What about after July 31st? What if you don't get him?"

Rush stood and folded the printed article, slipping it into his jacket pocket. "If he kills me, I won't care much what you write. But until I'm dead or Jackson's caught, you have to sit on it."

"I can live with that. And I'll cancel the exposé."

"Good move." Rush turned toward the door, then stopped. "Expect your office to be crawling with FBI agents within the hour. I hope there'll be three other small papers with the same problem."

"But I can't write about that, either."

Rush shook his head. "This can't get out. It's as simple as

that. But when you do write about it, you'll still be first."

"That's the goal," Dolan said, standing. "Come on, I'll see you out."

"One other thing before I forget," Rush said. "Between now and when the FBI comes knocking, copy me a list of all your out-of-town subscribers. There's always the chance you're mailing him what he wants to know."

Dolan chuckled. "We have seventy-two. Sit tight and I'll print it out." He clicked his mouse to a new program, then the printer started humming. "What if the FBI wants this list? Should I give it to them?"

"Sure. I just want a copy for myself. You know how the bureau can be." Rush winked.

With the list stuffed into his shirt pocket, Rush led the way as they strolled out of Dolan's office, through the newsroom and receptionist's office, stopping just outside the front door. The heat felt like an oven.

"You be careful," Dolan said, shaking Rush's hand. "And keep your head down."

The old cliché made Rush flinch. Right, keep his head down. He'd be sure to remember that.

CHAPTER TEN

The afternoon passed uneventfully; the evening, without any news from Zeke's team of FBI agents searching the back issues of *The Plano Weekly News*. Rush had relayed the information to Zeke by way of a quick telephone call, avoiding the topic of their earlier conversation. And he didn't tell Zeke of the article mentioning him visiting his mother's grave every July 31st. That information would be his and Chinbroski's to consider. He wondered if the FBI would find it anyway.

After sitting in his dark car outside his house for nearly an hour, staring at the large picture window with the bullet hole so clearly visible, after crying silently for nearly the entire time, Rush wondered when he would next step foot into the living room. It was irrational to avoid going in, but he somehow felt he'd be letting Mallory down if he did so without first avenging her murder.

Daniel had taken care of everything, once Rush had agreed to sign power of attorney over to him. Mallory's remains had been delivered to the crematorium, the house had been released by the FBI and professionally cleaned, a window company was due tomorrow morning for glass replacement, and Daniel had moved enough of Rush's personal belongings into Chinbroski's spare bedroom to last at least a month.

The memory of Mallory's murder, seared forever onto Rush's mind's eye, had caused a shift in his willingness to play by the rules expected of him. He wondered if maybe a single man, focused by tragedy, might have better luck tracking Jackson than what was going on now. Zeke's plan to enrage Jackson was marginal at best, criminally negligent at worst.

Luck. Most of the time it came down to that. Or an incredibly stupid act on the criminal's part. And even though Rush knew that the resources the FBI had already committed to this case couldn't be duplicated anywhere else, he also knew that no one involved in the search would be as passionate to kill Jackson as he.

The chief had come close to pulling him off the case this morning. And for the first time in his career, Rush actually begged to remain on. For nearly fifteen minutes Rush insisted that his mind was in the game, promised he would hold up, assured the chief of his continued professionalism. After finally relenting, the chief gave Rush his blessing, told him to go wherever the case took him, and promised support for anything he needed.

But Rush knew the chief's support had its limits. Rush had to hit it hard now. For the next month. He'd told Daniel earlier in the day that a service for Mallory would not happen until Jackson was either dead or in jail. Hopefully in that order.

So, while staring through the darkness at the hole in his front window, Rush decided he would step foot into his house only after he put a bullet in Jackson's brain.

It was nearly 11:00 P.M. when Rush sat down at his regular table just inside the front door of a Bennigan's on Central Expressway.

After his meeting with Zeke and the newspaperman, Rush had spent the afternoon cruising Plano, evaluating the best surveillance spots at both the cemetery and the areas around his house. He'd spotted FBI agents mounting fake electrical transformers on telephone poles at both ends of his street. According to Zeke, the transformers concealed both a high-resolution color camera and a low-light black and white CCD camera, each with powerful electronic zoom lenses mounted on pan and tilt units. Beginning tomorrow morning, the cameras would transmit microwave signals to a monitoring house a couple of streets over. Agents would watch for suspicious activity around the clock. They'd have a vast array of electronic equipment at their disposal with agents itching to use them. Typical FBI overkill, Rush thought, except this time he hoped their efforts would lead to overkilling Jackson.

Rush drafted a schedule of his normal activities, including his fitness center, church, grocery store, video rental locations, and the weekly poker game at Chinbroski's house. Zeke would order cameras installed to cover every one of those spots. Zeke had mentioned a new technology that transmitted video signals over regular telephone lines. He planned on having everything sent to the observation house in Rush's neighborhood. But to believe such a tactic would produce positive results was foolhardy. Jackson simply would not attempt his shot during Rush's normal routine. Of that Rush was certain, although the other three detectives were killed during *their* normal routines. But Rush had a hunch, a gut feeling. Jackson had tripped up—for the first time—and almost gotten caught. He *had* to be feeling increased pressure from an ever-growing number of hunters.

Jackson's reputation as a near-mythical figure, capable of

appearing and disappearing at will, was expanding exponentially with each killing and each escape. There would come a point, Rush suspected, when Jackson would start believing his own press clippings, when he would underestimate his opponent.

The thin restaurant crowd provided little distraction as Rush studied his neatly organized notes, written in a code only he could understand. He was on his second Diet Coke, having sworn off alcohol until this ordeal was over.

At 11:15 his partner strutted in with a small towel draped over one shoulder, his biceps bulging, neck arteries pulsing. "Yo, Rush," he said, flopping into the chair across the table. "Sorry I'm late. Had some pencil-neck hogging the squat rack. Put me behind on my workout."

Rush hadn't seen Chinbroski all day, hadn't spoken to him since that morning. He assumed his partner had been busy on the Jackson case in some capacity. "Have you been around much today?" Rush asked, waving at his waitress. "Any scuttlebutt?"

Chinbroski ordered a beer and waited for the waitress to leave before answering. "Zeke called a press conference for tomorrow morning. Early. Something about that letter he says he got, you know, the one from this morning?"

"Right." Rush sipped his Coke. "Anything else?"

"Heard you dropped out," Chinbroski said, his eyebrows raised. "I didn't get pissed. I mean, without hearing it from you first. But I figured if it was true, you needed some space. So I just waited you out."

"Is that the rumor? That I dropped out?"

"Since nobody's seen you all day, it wasn't hard to believe. Wanna tell me what's happening?"

"I'm not dropping out," Rush said as Chinbroski's beer

was delivered, after which he filled his partner in on everything.

During Rush's five-minute update, Chinbroski sat patiently, his eyes finally settling on the notepad in front of Rush. "This have something to do with your mom's graveyard?" he asked, tapping the pad.

"Something."

Chinbroski sat quietly for another moment, his chin cupped in his hand. "We gonna bait the guy?"

"It's like a blind guy shooting at ducks at the county fair," Rush said. "But it is exactly the kind of setting Jackson would use."

"And what makes you think he'll even know about that?"

A high-school-aged couple sat down at the next table. Rush scooted his chair closer and leaned forward. "Like I said a minute ago, the FBI is checking the previous victim cities for the same M.O. I'd be willing to bet there's a weekly paper in all three cities. Should know something tomorrow." He leaned forward even more, shielding his mouth from the high school kids. "This is important. If the other detectives never had any publicity, Jackson would have been *forced* to shoot them during their normal routines."

"But he wouldn't be forced with you, because we'll know he used the *Weekly Rag*, and an article about you has been in the *Weekly Rag*."

"Exactly."

"But you don't know if he's still reading the *Weekly Rag*, right?" Chinbroski glanced at the kids at the next table, rolled his eyes.

"Of course not. But if that's his method, why would he change? He can't know we've discovered it." Rush glanced over at the kids. The boy's hand had disappeared under the girl's miniskirt. Chinbroski's face was heating up.

"Look," Rush went on, "every year the FBI will devote more resources to this case. It's going to get harder for Jackson to keep all of this up. I think that's why he went for Daniel so early."

"To stretch our resources," Chinbroski said, throwing a hard look at the zit-faced teenager next to him. The kid wasn't accepting looks right then. Chinbroski glared at Rush and frowned.

"You paying attention?" Rush asked.

"Yeah. You're saying to stretch our manpower. Shoot early before the FBI gets all its agents in place."

"Right. And I'll bet that Zeke's task force is protecting a list of judges Jackson won't come within two miles of."

Chinbroski tapped his glass of beer and slowly nodded. "Somebody obscure, you're thinking. A judge to stretch the resources."

"Yeah, somebody retired or disbarred, or maybe a visiting judge we don't know is in town."

Chinbroski nodded and shrugged.

Rush looked at his watch. "I want us to scout the cemetery tonight."

"Now?"

"We'll be there by midnight, finished by one. Promise. I don't want to do this during business hours."

"Who would want you to?" Chinbroski asked. "Except maybe Jackson." He glanced at his watch, then his empty glass. "We got time for one more?"

"We need to hit the road."

"Fine." Chinbroski stood and leaned over the teenager's table. "Your daddy know that an ugly, zit-faced kid has a hand up your dress?" he asked the girl.

Both kids straightened in their chairs and said nothing.

Rush dragged his partner away before he got himself in trouble.

B.J. battled the idea of visiting the fat man most of the afternoon and evening. He blamed Zeke's lies. The media had latched onto Zeke's claim that this year's shootings were a copycat's. B.J. understood the FBI, understood how they controlled investigations, took information from every source available and then kept it to themselves, even from the local cops. No one would ever counter Zeke's lies.

B.J. wasn't mad about Zeke's attempt to piss him off. But he *did* care about Stubs's mental state, his level of fear, whether terror gripped him every time he took a shit in front of the small window in his master bathroom. If the FBI convinced Stubs that the shooter *was* a copycat, then Stubs might feel no fear at all. And B.J. couldn't allow that.

Tonight, B.J. would make sure Stubs knew.

Five blocks from the street where the fat man had seen him the night before, B.J. coasted to a stop between two darkened houses. At 12:15, the street was quiet and dark, void of life.

He sat for a moment, the engine popping as it settled, a sliver of apprehension in the center of his chest. Then he recalled his purpose: crush Stubs in a vise of fear. Then, just before Stubs died, let him know who had signed his death warrant.

So B.J. would force Zeke to tell the truth. And the fat man would be the perfect messenger.

He'd driven by the house just before sunset and noticed the first line of defense: an unmarked police car occupied by two plainclothes officers, munching potato chips. They'd parked down the street, six houses from the fat man's. Far enough to fool a fool, but close enough to protect their witness and react within seconds.

The second layer of defense was a cop in the house next door. A *For Sale* sign planted in the middle of the yard, weeds tall enough to hide a Great Dane, and no curtains in the windows—all said vacant. When B.J. saw the glow of a cigarette in the window facing the fat man's front porch, he didn't have to read a detective novel to understand what was going on.

The fat man was the first real witness to any of the shootings. Last year in Colorado, Zeke had tried to convince the media there was a witness. B.J. even sniffed around a little to verify. It'd been a setup. But this year he *knew* he'd been seen because he'd heard the fat man yell at him.

But why such a halfhearted attempt to guard him? They might have a room full of agents inside the house, but B.J. didn't think so. He'd spent over an hour today trying to predict how Zeke must have read last night's circumstances.

It was dark when the fat man had seen him, and even darker in the shadow of a tree, where B.J. stood. A squad car had raced past, bouncing red and blue light off everything, its siren blasting the quiet evening. B.J., dressed in camo, his ball cap throwing an extra shadow across his face, his gloves concealing what little skin had been exposed, hadn't been identifiable.

If Zeke had arranged an ambush tonight, the house would look like an easy target. Why risk scaring B.J. away with two sweaty detectives munching potato chips? This was a Cover-Your-Ass assignment. Zeke was posting guards to make the witness feel nice and safe.

At 1:30 A.M., after more than an hour crawling on the ground, ducking, hiding, and searching, B.J. was convinced that the cops were only in the two places he'd determined earlier. The best spot to penetrate the fat man's property was a darkened corner just outside a six-foot stockade fence surrounding the backyard, well out of view from the cigarette smoker.

Balancing onto one of the fence rails, B.J. studied the yard. A single-bulb fixture above the back door cast a dim circle of light over the cluttered patio. No doghouse, chew toys, or doggie dishes.

He dropped quietly into the yard, crouching in the shadows. A sagging clothesline hung between a fence post and a large oak. The yard hadn't seen a lawnmower in at least two months, and a rotting picnic table had collapsed on one side of the patio next to a hollowed-out gas grill. Through the neglect, he noticed an absence of children's toys.

The inside was dark. B.J. dodged the obstacles to the back door and pressed his ear to the glass. Silence except for the hum of an air-conditioning unit. He unscrewed the light bulb.

He didn't expect an alarm system. Still, he checked for sensor tape, then aimed a small flashlight into the corners, looking for a motion detector. Through a window several feet from the door he looked for a magnetic-break sensor. Nothing.

Creeping back to the door, he inspected the lock, pulled his hunting knife from its sheath, and slid it between the door and the jamb. Seconds later, the door popped open.

He closed the door quietly and stepped directly into the living room. The streetlight through the grease-coated windows on the other side of the room was enough to allow him to make his way without using his flashlight. He smelled the trash, the human sweat, the mold. The room held one couch, an overstuffed recliner, a coffee table, and a big-screen TV. Next to the recliner stood a large garbage can stuffed with frozen dinner trays, beer cans, Taco Bell bags, and Twinkie wrappers. Scattered around the chair on the floor were more beer cans, McDonald's cups, potato chip bags, and candy wrappers. The smell of sweat hung heaviest there.

The kitchen was worse than the den. The smell of spoiled food nauseated him.

From there, he checked the first and second bedrooms. Empty. That left the master bedroom on the other side of a closed door at the end of the hall.

Outside the door, B.J. heard ragged snoring. He popped the door open an inch and waited a beat. The room was as dark as the inside of a wood stove. B.J. stood at the doorway, his heart pounding. This was only the second time for him, getting this close to prey. The first time, though successful, had been unforgettably messy and violent.

As his eyes adjusted to the darkness, he fought to control his breathing, then timed it with the snores coming from the center of the room.

The rush from last night's chase was different than what he was feeling now. He'd always been a long-distance man, and had never tried to scare the shit out of someone close up.

After a moment his eyes adjusted to the deeper darkness and he made out the king-sized bed. He eased his way to the window and slid the drapes open a couple of inches, allowing all the light he needed to seep through. He peeked out onto the street in front of the house to spot the detectives, but couldn't see the potato chip twins from that angle.

He turned and sized up the bloated mound in the middle of the bed. The man was huge, bigger than any human B.J. had ever seen. On his back, breathing through his mouth, his snores punched the silence of the house.

B.J. crept through the room, searching for weapons. A .38 revolver sat in the open drawer of the nightstand beside the bed.

Tucking the gun into his waistband, B.J. explored the garage, searching for some rope. He settled on a thin extension cord and cut four six-foot pieces.

Back in the bedroom, he took a sock from the fat man's dresser and closed the door, just in case the fat man decided not to cooperate.

Moving like a shadow, B.J. tied the extension cord to each of the four bedposts, fashioning slipknots on the loose ends. The mound hadn't stirred. He remained on his back with a sheet pulled midway up his chest, flabby arms at his sides.

B.J. paused, took a deep breath to steady himself, and slid two of the slipknots around the man's hands, pulling them snug before the fat man stirred. Then he slipped over near the corner of the bed and quickly secured one ankle.

The bed rocked as the big man jerked awake.

"Wh . . . wh . . . what's this? What—hey!"

He pulled hard against the restraints. The knots tightened. B.J. wrestled the man's other ankle into the final loop and jerked it tight.

"What . . . who?"

B.J. jammed the sock into the man's open mouth. Then he jumped off the bed, and hurried to close the drapes, throwing the room into darkness thick enough to feel. He whispered, "I'll cut your throat if you yell out again."

Thrashing wildly, the fat man tried to scream through the gag, pulling at the restraints.

"You ain't careful you're gonna have a heart attack," B.J. whispered. "All I wanna do is talk. If you promise not to yell, I'll take that sock outta your mouth. If you promise, nod your head."

B.J. felt the bed move with the man's frantic agreement.

"Good, good, good. You're a smart man." B.J. tugged the sock out, but remained within inches of the man's face, smelling his sour breath. "What's your name?"

The man gasped, unable to speak.

"Remember, big boy," B.J. whispered, "quiet. Name?"

"Blane." He swallowed hard. "Harold Blane. I don't have any money."

B.J. pulled out his hunting knife and pressed the blade against Blane's neck. "You know what this is?"

"I . . . Yes."

"Razor-sharp." B.J. backed off the bed and slid his knife back into its sheath. "Do you know who I am?"

"I don't. I can't see. Do you want money?"

"Do you know who I am?"

"No." Blane's voice was soft and raspy.

"You been talkin' to that FBI agent about what you saw in your yard last night?"

After a pause, "Oh, my God!"

The entire bed quivered. B.J. smiled in the darkness.

"Now you know who I am, Fat Man?"

"I think—I mean—I don't know your name. I don't want to know your name."

"What'd you tell the FBI man?"

"I didn't see nothing. I didn't tell him nothing."

"Let me tell you somethin', Mr. Five-by-Five, I'll kill you if you lie to me. And I ain't sittin' here for very long. What'd you tell 'em?"

"I—I told him I saw somebody out by my tree. Said he looked like a white man, but I wasn't sure. I couldn't see his face. Your face. That's all, I swear, that's all I said."

"FBI said you called 9-1-1 because you heard a prowler in your backyard. How come?"

Blane swallowed, sucked a gasping breath. "Agent Bunning warned me that he was gonna say that. Asked me if I was a player. Told me to keep my mouth shut. I don't know why he lied. I swear. Maybe so the press would leave me alone."

B.J. leaned in close. "What else?"

"The agent said he didn't want the press to know they had a witness." He blurted the words out. "But I ain't a witness, because I didn't really see you."

B.J. stood and walked to the window. No movements outside. "You tell him you saw the rifle strapped to my back?"

Blane remained silent for a moment. "Yeah, yeah, I forgot about that. I told him about the rifle."

"What about the detectives who showed up. How many?"

"I don't know. My yard was full of cops."

"How many detectives came in the house? I'm losin' patience."

"Uh . . . just a couple."

"Were they here with the FBI man?"

"Yeah. Sure. They were all together. Got here together."

"Describe them."

Harold's breathing sounded like a horse recovering from a race. "One was a big guy. Weightlifter. Had a flattop. The other was smaller . . . about six feet, with kind of sandy hair, thinning."

B.J. closed his eyes and leaned his head back. Stubs had been here, had heard the fat man's story. So the FBI couldn't pretend the witness didn't exist. Zeke had lied to the media, but Stubs knew the truth.

"How'd the cops act? Scared shitless?"

"I wasn't paying much attention. They didn't say much. Agent Bunning did most of the talking."

B.J. considered that. Probably true. But Stubs had to be feeling it. Death stalking him. "What're those detectives' names?"

"Uh . . . Detective Rush was one. I seen his picture in the paper a bunch of times. He's the smaller one. The muscle man was Chabroski or Chillbriski or something. Something Polish-sounding. I can't remember."

B.J. almost laughed out loud. Stubs knew the truth. Maybe after shooting the judge, B.J. would telephone Stubs to tell him he was next.

"Listen to me," B.J. whispered. "Here's what you're gonna do. You're gonna tell the FBI man a few things. You're gonna tell him exactly what I want, or I'll come back and gut you like a hog. Understand?"

"Yes, sir."

"You believe that?"

"Yes, sir."

"I've been killin' people for years. Never been caught, right?"

"No."

"Ain't gonna get caught. Cops can't protect you. Maybe for a few months, then they'll get tired of it. Get relaxed like they did tonight. Then I'll look you up. One day you'll wake up in the middle of the night, and I'll be standin' over your bed, just like I am now, and I'll gut you. Understand?"

"Yes," Blane said. "I'll say what you want."

"Tell him that I know what he's doin'." B.J. paused for emphasis. "He's lyin' to the press because he thinks I'm gonna screw up. It ain't workin'. I ain't some out-of-control psychopath. I got a plan and nothin' he does is gonna change it. If he don't tell the truth, I'm gonna shoot him, too."

The bed moaned with Blane's nodding. "Okay, I got it, I got it."

"He made up the bullshit letter he said I sent. Ain't no letter. You hear me, Fat Man? It don't exist. I didn't write it. All a lie. That FBI man better tell everybody he made it up. Can you remember all this?"

Blane nodded again.

"Say it, Fat Man. Can you remember all this?"

"Yes. I can. I can. Everything. I won't forget. I'm smart, real smart."

"Tell him he better confess his lies."

"Okay. Yes. I'll tell him."

"I'm gonna shoot a judge soon. Before next week. Then I'm coming for one of those cops. Zeke ain't the lead on this case. But I know who is."

"I got it, sir. You can count on me." Blane's voice climbed.

"Quiet! When those two cops come back, you look both of them in the eye and tell 'em to make funeral arrangements."

B.J. backed his way to the door and opened it.

"Wait," Harold said, his voice rising again, sounding as if his windpipe had been pinched shut. "What about these ropes?"

"You just worry about what you're gonna tell the cops."

It took B.J. half an hour to sneak back to his truck, fifteen minutes to reach the north city limits, and five more to find a pay phone. He dialed 9-1-1.

"Plano police emergency." The voice sounded white, female, serious.

He whispered with a rasp. "Yeah, I wanna report a man tied up in his house."

"Sir, I can hardly hear you. Can I have your name?"

A stalling tactic. B.J. envisioned the Caller ID on the dispatcher's phone, a squad car being sent to his location. He'd have none of that. "Shut up and listen to me."

A pause. "Yes?"

"There's a fat man tied to his bed." B.J. gave the address. "Go untie the fat man."

He heard the clicking of a keyboard. "Untie Fat Man?"

"And listen to his message." B.J. dropped the receiver and let it dangle.

Jumping in his truck, he circled east, and then south. Next stop: the great detective's neighborhood.

CHAPTER ELEVEN

The humid air drifted into the open window and did little to dry the sweat that covered B.J.'s face. Although warm, the heat wasn't the cause of his perspiration.

Hunting night. And B.J. wasn't sure he could do it.

Stubs lay on the bunk at B.J.'s feet, snoring like an old man he'd once seen at the Trenton bus station. Stubs had set his little alarm clock for 1:00 A.M., put it under his pillow, and promptly passed out.

B.J. wasn't a coward. He'd told himself that at least fifty times during the last hour. He could kill squirrels, had dozens of times. It was breaking the rules that worried him. A Marine, his dad had always been strict with rules, always said, "Son, society without rules is a society in chaos. A brave man follows rules, a coward breaks them."

B.J. wasn't a coward. If his dad were here, B.J.'d tell him that sometimes a man had to prove himself, had to step outside the rules to show others that size and strength doesn't matter. He'd tell his dad that the only things that matter are the size of your heart and what's between your ears.

"Follow your heart," his dad had said moments before dying. "Follow your heart. Think things through and then follow your

heart. *If you'll always remember that, you'll never have to apologize for anything."*

Crying silently, B.J. wished his dad were here now, right in this
room. B.J. would ask him if he should go hunting tonight, whether
he should sneak out, go with Stubs, and retrieve the rifle Stubs had
hidden earlier that day.

It came down to two rules: curfew and borrowing the gun.
Maybe three if they wandered into the national forest when they
shot the squirrels. Two rules didn't seem that bad. And B.J. was
convinced they wouldn't get caught. Two rules to prove to Stubs
that he was the best rifle shot anytime, anywhere seemed like a fair
trade.

The championship rifle match was tomorrow. If B.J. beat
Stubs tonight, he would have two titles, just like his dad.

But what if they got caught?

His dad had told him to face problems with your brain. Always
ask yourself, "What's the worst possible thing that could happen?"
His dad had taught him a lot of things in those last months. A lifetime of lessons.

When B.J. asked him what the worst thing was about the
cancer, he'd replied, "Dying."

So what was the worst thing that could happen now? They
couldn't get kicked out of camp, because camp was only three more
days. They could stop him and Stubs from shooting in the championship, except that he and Stubs were the championship match. If
they weren't allowed to shoot, the whole thing would be a joke.

Then again, the camp director might get so mad that he'd tor-
ture them both by making them sit in the stands and watch somebody else win the big trophy.

Really though, the chances of that happening were slim. Stubs
was right when he said that no one would see them running from
their cabin into the woods. The only outside light was right over the
front door. All they'd have to do was slide out the window and be

gone. Stubs had hidden the rifle somewhere just inside the trees near a path that ran straight north. They'd be exposed no more than fifteen seconds.

And it would be fun! And Stubs was his best friend ever.

The alarm clock went off.

B.J. heard the muffled buzz and held his breath. Maybe Stubs wouldn't wake up. The buzz continued, like a giant, angry yellow jacket. The sound vibrated around the quiet room, growing louder, it seemed, the longer it went unattended.

Finally Stubs stirred and the buzzing stopped. B.J. blew out a breath. Maybe Stubs would go back to sleep or realize how comfortable the bed felt.

"You ready?" came Stubs's whisper, thick with sleep.

B.J. said nothing, lying there with his eyes closed, taking deep, even breaths. Maybe Stubs would feel bad about waking up his friend.

Then he grabbed B.J.'s foot. "Hey, B.J., you ready?"

They made it across the clearing between their cabin and the woods without making any sound at all. The night sounds surrounded them: an owl in the distance, crickets all around, a whippoorwill somewhere to the north. The moon was just a sliver, though the stars seemed brighter than normal. B.J. saw the Big Dipper directly overhead.

He waited on the narrow path while Stubs crashed around in the bushes looking for the rifle. B.J. wanted to tell him to be quiet, but he'd have to yell even louder to be heard over the racket.

After a minute, Stubs pushed his way onto the path, holding the rifle over his head in victory. "Got it."

"Could you be a little quieter?" B.J. whispered. "What if one of the counselors is standing outside taking a smoke?"

"Why would somebody smoke outside?" Stubs said. "That'd be stupid."

"I saw one smoking outside right before lights out tonight. He was standing behind cabin 23, right next to us."

Stubs stepped around B.J. and headed north on the path. "It's one o'clock in the morning. He ain't gonna be smoking at this time of night."

He quickly disappeared in the darkness. B.J. followed him with a knot in his throat. As they moved up the slope of the mountain, the trees would be thinner, the underbrush less dense. Good thing, because they'd never see a squirrel in this gloom.

"Hey, slow down," B.J. whispered as Stubs hurried along the path. "We ain't in no race." B.J. was tempted to play the cave trick on him. Just stop and let him trudge along by himself. But Stubs slowed and B.J. bumped into him.

"You scared or something?" Stubs asked. "Afraid of the dark?"

"Just don't walk so fast. Maybe you wouldn't sound like a water buffalo running from a wolf."

Stubs laughed. "You're a retard. There ain't no wolves where there's water buffaloes, except in the zoo."

"I'm just saying you need to walk quieter. You sound like your shoes are two feet long."

B.J. glanced behind him and could no longer see any lights from the camp. The crickets were everywhere, the hoot owl directly north, like a foghorn guiding them.

"What are we gonna do if we get a squirrel?" B.J. asked. He hadn't even thought of that until now.

Stubs let a branch go and it hit B.J. in the chest.

"Hey!" B.J. yelled, then immediately lowered his voice. "If you do that again, I'm going back! I ain't playing around!"

"Okay, okay. I was just kidding."

They walked for another five minutes, the grade slowly rising. B.J.'s eyes finally adjusted to the dark.

Stubs suddenly turned left, onto a small path that B.J. believed ran around toward the back side of the camp.

"Where you going?" B.J. asked. "I thought we were going up?"

"I saw a better place. Yesterday I went looking around right after lunch, while you were canoeing. Great place, too. Saw more than a dozen squirrels. There's about five big pecan trees real close together."

B.J. pushed underbrush aside as they slowly traveled west. "You sure about this?" He wanted to put as much distance from the camp as he could. Gunshots would really carry.

"Yeah, I'm sure. I paced it off from the edge of the camp. It's almost a half-mile. The squirrels were jumping around like rabbits."

"Do you know for sure that this path leads there? 'Cause I don't think it does."

"Just call me Tonto," Stubs said.

They walked on, Stubs carrying the rifle over his shoulder like an infantryman in the Civil War. B.J. hung back a few feet because Stubs had continued to flip branches. The stars were bright overhead, peeking through the trees like diamonds. A lightning bug landed on Stubs's back, flashed once, then flew away.

B.J. wiped the sweat off his forehead. "Seems like we're heading toward the teepees."

Stubs laughed. "Man, you're all turned around. The teepees are back thataway." He pointed off to the left, south. "Don't even worry about that."

So they walked some more. Stubs started humming a tune B.J. didn't recognize. The night sounds enveloped them, the darkness swallowed them. They were less than a half-mile from camp, B.J. calculated, much too close to do any shooting.

"Hey, I don't like this," he finally told Stubs.

The bigger boy stopped and looked back. B.J. imagined him frowning, although the darkness hid his features.

"When you said we were going hunting, you said it'd be up in the mountains. I ain't shooting nothing this close to camp."

Stubs made sounds like a chicken.

"It must be you who's chicken," B.J. snapped. "Are you afraid to hike up the mountain? Afraid of some mountain lion or something?"

"Yeah, right!"

B.J. stood his ground, crossed his arms, and said nothing.

"What's the big deal?" Stubs said finally. "You're two feet away and I can barely see you. You think somebody's gonna see us when we're this far from camp?"

A trickle of sweat slid down B.J.'s nose. He swiped it away and shook his head. "That ain't the point. If a gunshot wakes somebody up, we'll get caught sneaking back to our cabin. Is your skull three inches thick or something?"

"You're just trying to find an excuse so I won't show you up. Go ahead and go back if you want. That is if you're not afraid to walk back alone." Stubs's tone made B.J. want to choke him.

Maybe he should go back. But knowing B.J.'s luck, Stubs's shooting would cause one of the counselors to run out of a cabin just as he was running across the clearing near his cabin. He sighed. Why had he ever agreed to this?

"Look," Stubs pleaded. "All we gotta do is go up this path a little farther and you'll see all the pecan trees I'm talking about. Then if we sit real quiet, we'll see the squirrels everywhere. Come on, it's gonna be a blast."

An owl hooted somewhere behind them and B.J. jumped. He didn't like being this close to camp. Then he thought of a solution. "Here's the deal. Since you're so sure of yourself, you can shoot at a squirrel down here. Miss or not, it'll be my turn. And I'm taking my turn up in the mountains." He paused while Stubs shuffled his feet, thinking. "Take it or leave it," B.J. said.

"What if I hit a squirrel, then you hit one too, both on our

first shot? Who's the winner?"

They should have discussed this already, but hadn't.

"Whoever hits closest to the head," B.J. said. "And if you hit one in the eye, you're the automatic winner."

Stubs laughed. "Hit one in the eye? You're nuts! In this dark?"

B.J. shrugged. "If you think you're so good, it shouldn't be a problem."

"Deal." Stubs spun around and stalked off, his feet once again sounding as if they belonged to a giant.

Stubs stopped after another five minutes of walking. B.J. bumped into him. Then the bigger boy crouched and pointed straight ahead. "Look," he whispered. "That's where I saw all the squirrels. Up in those trees right there."

B.J. could see Stubs's arm raised toward the tops of trees in front of them, but couldn't begin to tell if they were pecan trees. He didn't know how Stubs could, either.

"Don't move," Stubs whispered, "and we'll be able to hear the squirrels moving around."

Above the crickets, whippoorwills, and hoot owl? B.J. wanted to ask. But he stayed quiet. This was Stubs's game this close to camp. He squatted next to Stubs and leaned against a tree. A mosquito landed on his arm and he brushed it away.

Stubs inched forward, moving as quietly as he could.

He held the .22 in his left hand. B.J. didn't hear any squirrels. He wondered if squirrels could smell. If they could, neither he nor Stubs would get within fifty yards of one, because they both smelled like B.J.'s dad had one time after he dug potatoes all day.

After more than ten minutes of sitting, B.J. rubbed his eyes and yawned. Stubs was still scooting himself closer to the pecan trees. He was just a shape now, a shifting black spot in the darkness. B.J. yawned again and closed his eyes. This was stupid. All to prove that he was a better shot or a better hunter or not a coward or whatever reason he thought was so important.

"B.J.," Stubs whispered. *"Hey, B.J."*

"What?" B.J. *tried to find Stubs in the darkness but saw nothing.*

"I think I hear them. Over to the left. I need you to scare them my way."

Scare them his way? *"What are you talking about?"* B.J. *leaned forward and stared hard into the darkness.*

"Go over to the left, kind of directly beside me. Rattle some branches or something. They'll come toward me and I can shoot one."

Now I'm a sheep dog, B.J. *thought.* *"Can you see any?"*

"I think I did. Way up high, over to the left. I almost shot, but it was too far away."

B.J. *looked up and saw a canopy of tree branches. This was really stupid.*

"Come on," Stubs pleaded. *"I'll help you when we get up to the mountain."*

He rolled his eyes and stood. *"Just don't shoot me."* B.J. *went straight south, slowly, trying not to make too much noise. But he did anyway. He couldn't see anything and probably crunched a thousand small sticks.*

After twenty yards or so, B.J. *went west again, trying to calculate where Stubs was, hoping he didn't get down range from him. Ten yards. That's it, he'd go no farther.*

"Okay," he said, *"I'm in position. I'm gonna rattle some branches, so don't think I'm a squirrel."*

"I'm not that stupid."

B.J. *shook branches until his arm ached. No gunshot. He grabbed a branch with his other arm and shook some more. Still nothing.* *"Come on,"* he said under his breath. *"Either shoot or get off the pot."* *That made him giggle, coming so close to the cuss word his dad used to say when he was mad.*

"I'm moving forward," Stubs said after another minute. *"I see*

one. *It's sitting on a stump about ten yards in front of you."*

In front of me? B.J. frowned and stopped making noise. Stubs sounded like he was on his hands and knees, moving slowly but making a lot of racket. B.J. strained to see the stump Stubs was talking about. He moved his head left then right, forward then back. There was nothing that looked like a stump.

Stubs finally stopped. He was probably fifteen feet away, but definitely down range. B.J. sighed and wiped his forehead.

"It's still there," Stubs whispered.

Must be a deaf squirrel, B.J. thought. He stuck a finger in each ear, closed his eyes, and waited for the shot. It came a few seconds later.

The blast echoed through the woods and the whippoorwills went silent. The crickets didn't, but big wings started flapping directly overhead. Maybe the owl flying off.

"I think I missed," Stubs said, moving forward again. "And the squirrel's still there."

"What? That's impossible!" B.J. crept forward. "Don't shoot, I'm coming."

After about ten feet, B.J. saw Stubs standing directly in front of him. Then he saw the stump.

"It was just a chunk of wood," Stubs said. "I can't believe it."

From a tree struck by lightning years before, an oddly shaped piece of wood protruded directly from the center of the stump. B.J. started to laugh but quickly clamped his mouth shut when an agonizing cry drifted through the trees. "What's that?" he asked Stubs.

"I don't know. Shhh."

The cry came from the south, the direction Stubs's bullet had traveled. And it was getting louder. A numbing chill worked its way up from the bottom of B.J.'s spine. Goosebumps prickled his skin.

A light flicked on through the trees from the direction of the crying. Then voices. A lot of voices. Voices of other boys. And close.

"Oh, shit," Stubs said, dropping the rifle and stepping back.

B.J. tried to remember the layout of the camp from the map he had in his suitcase. The teepees.

Two flashlight beams cut through the darkness like a sickle. Growing bigger.

"Oh, shit," Stubs said again. "We better get out of here." He turned and ran into a tree. "Ouch," he said much too loudly.

"Who's out there?" a man's voice blasted from the darkness. The flashlight beams came closer. Fast.

Stubs got up and crashed through the trees. B.J. stood frozen, not sure what to do. He didn't want to get caught, but running away wasn't right, either.

A sliver of light lit up the tree next to B.J.'s head. Stubs had disappeared, moving fast. B.J. heard him fall and then curse again. Then he must have found the path because the sounds of his escape quickly faded heading east.

As the searchlights came ever closer, B.J. made a decision.

Run. He could make it back to the cabin.

Ducking down behind the stump, he searched the ground with his hands and found the rifle. Then he spun around and hit the same tree Stubs had run into. He fell backwards, slammed his shoulder against the stump, and dropped the rifle.

The lights seemed everywhere. He could hear panting from the two pursuers. He picked up the rifle and climbed back to his feet.

He didn't take another step before a strong pair of hands clamped down on his shoulders.

Rush and Chinbroski arrived at the cemetery a few minutes past midnight in separate cars. Chinbroski parked at the funeral home across the street, Rush parked behind him.

The cemetery was gated, enclosed by an eight-foot iron fence.

Since his mother's funeral when he was eight years old, this graveyard had given Rush the creeps. It was the shadows, he'd decided almost thirty years ago, a few years before joining the police department. Although he'd made a point of visiting her grave every year at the time of the car crash that had taken her life, he'd never gotten used to the midnight shadows.

Rush wanted to conduct his reconnaissance in the dark because he figured Jackson would be here, somewhere in these shadows, at midnight on the last night in July, assuming he had read the *Plano Weekly*.

Chinbroski exited his car first. He arched his neck and popped his back.

Rush pocketed his cell phone and locked the doors. The humidity was high, making the temperature seem higher. Sweat quickly gathered along his forehead and started a slide toward his eyes. He'd changed into his running shoes before going to Bennigan's, but still wore his suit pants.

"Where's your mother's grave?" Chinbroski asked.

"On the far side, the eastern edge." Rush opened his trunk and grabbed a small flashlight. "Jackson will be on foot; there's no way you can see her marker from the road."

"Unless he shoots you when you park your car." Chinbroski said it with humor in his voice.

Rush shook his head and grinned. "Assuming he shoots me and not you."

Chinbroski's smile died.

"But assuming he lets me get to the grave," Rush continued, "to shoot me, he'll have to be on foot."

"Right."

They walked in silence crossing 18th Street. "I don't ever

195

visit my mother's grave," Chinbroski said when they reached the iron gate.

Rush knew Chinbroski was young when his mother died.

It was something they shared in common. But Rush had never known the circumstances. "Why?" he asked.

With a shrug, he wiped a bead of sweat off his forehead. "Never had a way down there at first. Mom was all I had, no other family. By the time I could drive, had my own car, it was almost like her death was part of a different life."

"Car crash, right?" Rush asked, pulling on the heavy chain draped between the gate and fence.

"I thought they kept this gate unlocked," Chinbroski said.

"Used to. Vandals changed all of that. I've had to jump over the last few years." Rush wiped his neck and put a foot up on one of the cross bars when his beeper went off. He stepped down and pulled it from his belt. "Dispatch," he told Chinbroski. "With a 9-1-1."

"So your mom died in an auto accident, too?" Rush asked Chinbroski again, pulling out his phone.

"Well," he said, hesitating, "I used to think so."

"What do you mean?" Rush punched in the numbers to call dispatch, but didn't push *Send*. This was the first time Chinbroski had ever discussed his mother, besides once a few years back, when he'd mentioned a car wreck. Even through the darkness Rush could tell something was bothering him. "What do you mean, you used to think so?"

Chinbroski looked away, into the darkness of the grave-yard. "A couple of years after I hired on here, I drove down to Dallas and located a copy of the accident report. But it wasn't an accident." He looked at Rush. "It's why I don't visit her grave," he said quietly. "I don't like quitters."

Rush stared at the ground in silence and said nothing.

Chinbroski put both hands on the iron fence and gazed

into the cemetery. "I ain't wasting my time on a quitter."

And he'd had no family to see him through it, Rush thought. At least Rush had had an older cousin he could call on the phone after his mother died.

When it became apparent that Chinbroski was finished with the subject, Rush completed the call to dispatch.

"A patrol officer wants assistance at Plano General," the dispatcher said.

"What's he have?"

"Said an old guy was attacked in his alley yesterday. He came to about an hour ago. Insists on talking to a detective."

"I'm tied up right now."

"The officer said he doesn't know much, but what he does know will interest you, because the attack happened two blocks from your house."

"Who's the officer?"

"Kirk."

Good sign. "He say any more?"

"The suspect was driving a truck with Tennessee tags."

Rush looked at Chinbroski, who was still gazing out over the cemetery, and snapped his fingers, getting his attention. "Is that all?"

"That's it."

"Am I the first one you've called?"

The dispatcher hesitated. "Yeah. Who else—"

"Forget it. Call Kirk back and tell him I'm on the way." Rush pushed *End* and told Chinbroski.

"Jackson?" Chinbroski asked.

"We'll know in fifteen minutes."

Clarence Kirk, a career deep-nights cop who loved working the street more than anything in the world, was a fifteen-year veteran who seemed to know everything going on all over town. As soon as Rush knew Kirk had called, he knew enough to take seriously what the victim was about to say.

Rush shook Kirk's hand just outside Room 419. Kirk's hair was always too long, his beard a day old, and the faded tattoos of naked females on each forearm were always in view. Ex-Marine. Tough. Rush's kind of cop.

"Sorry to drag you way out here at this hour," Kirk said. "But I think this cranky old bastard might have something."

"You've heard it all? Dispatch said he hadn't told you much," Rush said.

"As soon as I hung up the phone and told him a detective was coming, the old guy opened up a little."

Chinbroski leaned next to the door, listened for any noises in the room. "What's his name?" he asked.

"Elwood Drain. Eighty-one. Feisty old fart." Kirk chuckled. "Before I agreed to call a detective, he threatened to whip my ass if I didn't."

"You think this has something to do with Jackson?" Rush asked.

Kirk frowned. "Don't know. Drain's story is odd. But it happened two blocks from your house. It may be nothing. See what you think."

Rush slapped him on the arm. "Yeah. Thanks." He nodded at Chinbroski, and his partner pushed through the door.

The old man had a bruised knot on his forehead the size of a golf ball. An I.V. snaked from his right arm to a clear baggie dangling from a bedside rack. His eyes were clear, magnified by thick lenses, brightening a face set in a deep scowl. Clearly bent with age, his frail body appeared childlike under the thin hospital blanket. His strong voice surprised Rush during the introductions.

"About damn time I get to see a detective," Drain almost

shouted. He studied Rush and Chinbroski before speaking again. "Ain't all your fault, though. Would've called earlier, except my wife wouldn't go home. Didn't want her to know what really happened. She still thinks a gallon can of paint fell on me."

Chinbroski strolled over to the only chair in the room and sat down. Kirk leaned against the bathroom door. Rush approached the bed, bending over slightly to inspect Drain's injury. "I understand you were assaulted," Rush said. "Is that where he hit you? In the forehead?"

"Sucker-punched me. Caught me looking off. Might've taken him, otherwise."

Rush kept a straight face.

"Boxed in the Navy," Drain said. "Ship champion."

"World War Two?"

"Damn right, the big one. Still got some moves left, too."

"What ship were you on?" Rush asked.

"The *Missouri*. Fine vessel."

Rush nodded and smiled. "Okay, so what happened?"

Drain told Rush about the two trash bags, of opening one to find a box sealed tightly with duct tape. Then he explained about the pickup with Tennessee tags, of the man lying about the bags falling out of his truck earlier that morning.

"Why do you think he was lying?" Rush asked.

"Because of how them bags were sitting. They were heavy, at least fifty pounds each. And they were right next to each other like somebody set them there nice and neat. Besides that, if they would've fallen off the back of his pickup, they'd have been in the alley. Right?"

It made sense. Rush glanced at Chinbroski, who raised an eyebrow.

"So this was a white guy?" Rush asked. "You haven't described him yet."

"Yeah, he was white. Southern accent. Matched his license plate."

"Right. How big?"

"Small guy, really. Maybe five-seven. Had narrow shoulders and sandy-colored hair. Looked about your age. Early forties."

Chinbroski took out a pad and wrote it down.

That Rush was in his early fifties didn't matter, at least they had an approximate height. "What'd he weigh?"

"Maybe one-sixty." Drain shifted in his bed, fingered his I.V. "You ain't asked me the most important question yet," he said, his voice as raspy as a file across a board.

Rush considered that, quietly thought it through. "Okay. I think I know what that would be. Why did you want to talk to a detective?"

"Bingo!" Drain shouted. "Because of something he did after he put me on the garage floor."

"What's that?"

"He drove by again. I saw him 'cause I'd recovered by then. He drove by slowly and looked at me."

Rush wasn't sure why the old man thought that was important, so he asked him.

"Because, dammit. A man wouldn't take that kind of risk, unless he was afraid of getting caught for something bigger." Drain glared at Rush, he eyes intense.

The old man's logic escaped him. Rush scratched his head and glanced at his partner. Chinbroski shrugged and shook his head.

"How about this?" Rush said. "Why don't you tell me what you think is going on. That may crystallize things for me."

"Okay, I'm gonna tell it to you real slow. And if I can figure it out at my age, well . . ." Drain didn't finish the sentence.

Rush understood the insult.

"Now," Drain said, pushing himself up in the bed. "I come out of my garage and I see these two bags sitting there near the alley. I head that way, but I also notice this guy's truck coming. Didn't pay no attention to it then, but I know it's there. Driving real slow, too. Now I ain't set my trash out yet, but if I did, it'd be the big green can the city provides. Nobody just sets bags on the ground like that anymore." He paused and glanced at Chinbroski, then back at Rush. "You following this?"

"Trying to."

"Well, I don't see you writing anything down."

Rush nodded toward Chinbroski. "He's my secretary tonight."

Chinbroski held up his pad and pen and nodded.

Drain sniffed. "Well, anyway, I don't know if the truck was stopped when I first saw it, but if not, it was moving awful slow. But like I said, I ain't really paying attention to it right then. It drives by me, goes down the alley a ways, then stops. All this time I'm looking into one of the bags. By the time I pull the box out of the first bag, this guy has backed up next to me and stopped." He paused again. "What do you make of that?"

"I'm still not sure why you think this man was involved in something bigger."

"Because a man don't nearly kill someone with a sucker punch to the head, drag 'em into the garage to make it look like an accident—unless he's involved in something bigger!" The veins in Drain's neck protruded against his onion-thin skin. "Do you see what I mean? If those were his bags, he should've stopped the first time. Not backed up after I opened one."

Rush had to admit the suspect's actions were odd. "Go ahead. Finish your theory."

"It ain't a damn theory! I'm just telling you!"

Rush held up his hands. "Okay, Mr. Drain. Just go on."

"I will!" The old man took a deep breath. "So then this guy gets out of his truck and comes around. Tells me he dropped the bags earlier. Said he goes around picking up bags before the big city truck comes. But it's like I said. Nobody even uses trash bags like that anymore. Course that made me suspicious, so I looked in the back of his truck. Had a topper, by the way. Guess what was in the bed?"

"What?" Rush asked.

"Nothing, that's what! Nothing! See, he said he'd been picking up trash bags and these two fell out because his truck got so full. Then where were all the other bags? Huh?"

Rush shrugged and glanced at Chinbroski, who wore a blank expression. Rush looked back at Kirk, who had covered his mouth with his hand. He shrugged, too.

"Maybe he lives in the area," Rush said, turning back to the old man. "Took all the other bags home."

Drain snorted and pointed at Officer Kirk. "That's what he said." He shook his head and fingered his I.V. again. "You know what those trash bags were tied closed with?"

"No."

"Baling twine. Know what kind of knot was used?"

"No."

"A bowline knot. Know what that's used for?"

Rush remembered something about knots. "Is that when you want to make a loop that won't slip? Used in rescue work?"

"Well, I'll be damned. I got a Boy Scout on my hands. That's exactly right." Drain looked around the room. "I think he tied that kind of knot so he could use the loop for a handle because the bags were so heavy." The old man's chest swelled. "Why does somebody go to the trouble of tying knots like that if they're gonna throw the bags away? Why does somebody use five pounds of damn duct tape on a box they're gonna throw away? Why does somebody sucker-punch somebody else just to get those boxes back? And why does somebody try to make that sucker-punch look like an accident?"

Rush had no answers. Chinbroski had slipped his notepad into a pocket.

"What'd you do for a living before you retired, Mr. Drain?" Rush asked.

"Park Ranger. Yellowstone. Moved down here because my wife couldn't stand the cold any longer." He pulled his blanket up on his chest and leaned back on his pillow. "I don't know what that guy was up to, but I've been around crazies like that all my life. And I'm telling you those eyes of his had no life. He was up to something."

And if it was Jackson, Rush thought, he had an idea. He turned to Officer Kirk. "I want you to take an assault report. Make it the most detailed report you've ever done. Have Records expedite it. Send it to me."

Kirk nodded.

"Call McBride, get him out here to take photos. When McBride gets here, have him call his artist friend at ATF. I want a sketch of the suspect while it's fresh in Mr. Drain's mind."

Kirk wrote it down.

"Chin, you ready?"

Chinbroski stood, headed for the door.

"Mr. Drain," Rush said, "I hope I have half of what you have upstairs when I'm eighty-one. You have a fine eye for detail. Thanks for demanding to see me."

The old man nodded. He looked tired. "Just don't tell the missus. Don't want her worrying none."

"Don't worry about that. Could you pick this guy out of a lineup?"

"You're damn right I could."

"Fine. Let's hope we get that chance."

Rush met Chinbroski in the hallway and glanced at his watch. Almost 1:15. But he'd never be able to sleep with his heart racing like it was. "Somewhere near my house is the rest of Jackson's equipment."

"What are you talking about?"

Rush was halfway down the hall, Chinbroski practically running to keep up. "I think I've figured out how Jackson knows which detectives to shoot."

"How? And would you slow down?"

Rush slowed and looked hard at his partner. "He videotapes them. I think his receiving equipment might have been in those boxes."

"Shit."

"Before, I told you that Jackson might have had a partner hanging around in the crowd after the first shooting. So he'd know which detective was the true lead. But videotape would work, too."

Chinbroski walked in silence beside him. Then they stepped on the elevator and Rush pushed the ground floor button.

"So why we heading back out to your house?"

"Because if I'm right, he hasn't picked up his cameras yet. They're hidden somewhere close."

"You figured all this out listening to that kooky old bird?"

"That kooky old bird might be the first real mistake Jackson has made."

"Not killing him, you mean?"

"Right."

204

The elevator doors slid open and Rush led the way out to the parking lot.

"Tell me one other thing," Chinbroski said, as he was about to climb into the car.

"What?"

"How the hell did you know what a bowline knot was?"

"Because I tied about a thousand of them when I was at summer camp as a kid."

"I went to camp, too," Chinbroski said. "But I didn't learn nothing about tying knots. You must have *been* a Boy Scout."

Rush cranked the car, dropped it into gear, and looked at his partner through the darkness. "No. My camp was a place for boys who'd lost a parent. And I sure as hell wasn't a Boy Scout."

CHAPTER TWELVE

Rush and Chinbroski climbed out of their car in front of Harold Blane's house a few minutes before 2:00 A.M. They'd been detoured on the way to Rush's neighborhood after an urgent call from the same dispatcher who'd sent them to the hospital.

Two uniformed officers stood just outside the open front door. Rush nodded and pushed his way through, Chinbroski on his heels. Dispatch had told him that the detectives conducting the surveillance of Blane's house had heard the call and rushed in before patrol arrived.

Rush was in no mood for chitchat. The possibility that Jackson had waltzed in under the noses of three veteran detectives made him crazy.

"We didn't see nothing," one of the plainclothes said as soon as Rush walked into the house. It was Baker from Auto Theft. He wore a black tee shirt dotted with crumbs and grease stains. Potato chips. Next to Baker was Wilson from Juvenile, a burly weightlifter who hated Chinbroski.

Harold Blane sat in a recliner, sweating rivers. Rush could smell him from across the room. Johnny Marshall from Burglary, sucking on an unlit cigarette, was propped against the doorjamb leading to the kitchen.

"Nothing," Baker said again. "The guy must have spotted us." He looked from Rush to Chinbroski, then back to Rush. "We weren't sleeping. We were—"

"Stop," Rush said, holding up a hand. "No excuses. In fact, get the hell out of here. All of you. Outside."

The three ambled out the door in silence. Rush fought the urge to kick their collective asses as they made their way out.

Blane was wearing a pair of cotton gym shorts and a tee shirt. "We got some talking to do," he said after Rush closed the door. His skin glistened. Moisture darkened his armpits and his hair was plastered to his scalp in the front, and stuck straight out in the back.

Chinbroski positioned himself by the front door; Rush walked over and leaned against the sofa.

"First," Blane continued, breathing hard, "I don't *ever* wanna meet Jackson again. Ever." He spoke in a near-whisper, mopping his blotchy, meaty face with a dishtowel.

"Are you okay?" Rush asked.

"The guy scared the bejeebers out of me. Almost had a heart attack."

Rush didn't have time for small talk. "Dispatch said something about a message."

"That's right. That FBI fella, Zeke something, is in a heap of trouble." Blane hesitated. "And one of you boys, too."

A cold chill passed down the back of Rush's neck. "Why?"

Blane leaned forward in the recliner, the chair creaking. He looked past Rush toward the front door, lowered his voice. "I gotta tell this in the order he said it or I'll forget. Okay?" He wiped his face and took a deep breath. "Said he knows what Zeke is up to, lying to the press and all that. Trying to piss him off. Force him into mistakes. And that he ain't some psychopath who can't control himself."

Rush glanced at Chinbroski, who had moved over near Blane's recliner.

"Is that all?" Rush asked.

"Said if Zeke don't come clean with the press—start telling the truth—he was gonna shoot him. And he's gonna shoot a judge within a week."

Rush nodded, wondered if that might satisfy Jackson, killing Zeke instead of the lead detective.

Blane said quickly, "Talked about that letter Zeke claimed he got. Said the letter's a lie. Said he didn't send it and that Zeke better tell the press he made it up. If not, he's a dead man. That's all." He sighed heavily and collapsed back in his chair, like a huge weight had been lifted. "There," he blurted out suddenly, "delivered the message." He mopped his face again. "Except the part about one of you two."

Chinbroski looked at Rush, then to Blane. "What?"

"He said he knows Zeke ain't really the lead investigator. Said he'd get one of you, no matter how long it took."

Zeke's plan, such a roaring success, Rush thought. He stepped close to Chinbroski, leaned over, and whispered in his ear. "Go out to the car, have dispatch get hold of Zeke. He'll need to hear this for himself. Keep the car running, I'll be out in a minute."

Chinbroski tore his eyes away from Blane. He clenched his jaw and nodded, hurrying out the door.

"I want protection," Blane said suddenly, leaning forward. "Good protection, I mean. Should've had some already." He wagged a stubby finger at Rush. "Would've caught the guy if there'd been somebody in here."

Rush agreed. But he couldn't second-guess Zeke in front of a civilian. "Look, there was no way to predict this. And we can't put an officer—"

"I ain't buying that," Blane interrupted. He wiped the

towel across his face and cocked his head toward his bedroom. "Had a lot of time to think while I was tied up. I'm a witness. And Jackson is the most wanted man in America." He shook his head, his face set with determination. "Like you told those other cops, no excuses."

"Mr. Blane," Rush said, hoping he wouldn't choke on the words he was about to speak. "The FBI is committed to protecting any citizen who is in substantial risk of—"

"No!" Blane shouted. He struggled out of his chair and stood, pointing at Rush, his hand shaking. "If you don't think—if you don't think being a witness to Billy Ray Jackson is substantial, just what *is?*"

Blane glared for a moment, then shook his head. He turned and waddled into the kitchen, disappearing around the corner. He returned moments later, carrying three packages of Twinkies.

"You've probably heard," Rush said, "that the FBI has taken full control of this case. I haven't been brought up to speed on the exact mindset during the decision-making process. But I can assure you that the FBI will take all precautions from this point forward. Did you see what the man looked like?"

Blane dropped into his recliner, shook his head, his hands still shaking as he opened one of the Twinkies, pulled the cakes out, and threw the wrapper in the overflowing trash can beside his chair. "Too dark. He kept my drapes and door closed. Can't see a thing in there when it's that dark."

"What about his voice?"

He crammed a cake in his mouth and shook his head. "Whispered the whole time. Kind of raspy. He was white though, I'm sure of that. From the South, too."

"You mean a southern accent?"

"Yeah. He never said the 'g' on words ending with 'i-n-g.'"

Know what I mean?" A small chunk of Twinkie dropped from Blane's mouth onto his lap. He picked it up and studied it, glanced at Rush, then flicked it at the trash can. It landed on the floor.

Rush nodded. "I know you focused on remembering the message, but what about other things he might have said? Was there anything that might help us identify him?"

Blane stopped chewing, cocked his head, thought about it. "Not really. Knows what he's doing, though. I could tell that. Smart. That's why I want protection. I'm the only guy who's had direct contact with him, right?"

"The only one I know of."

Blane took another bite. "What about those lies? What's Agent Zeke gonna do about them?"

Rush said nothing. The fat man gazed off, slowly shook his head. "Thought about those lies while I was tied up. Must be important to him—the lies I mean—to risk coming here. How'd he know you didn't have a couple of agents in here? That's a big chance. So I figure he must be telling the truth for him to do that." Blane paused and looked at Rush. "Will Agent Zeke admit it? To the press?"

Rush rubbed his forehead and tried to think of what psychobabble Zeke might use to answer that question. He gave it his best shot. "An analysis of Jackson's movements will take place over the next several days," he said finally. "But let me give you a possible explanation of Jackson's motive. Simply, that this *is* a copycat shooter, just like the FBI has reported. The shooter from past years is dead, and because this copycat desperately wants credit for the entire series, he had to risk capture tonight to force Agent Bunning into dispelling the copycat notion." The fact that this lie came out sounding as convincing as it did surprised Rush.

Blane ate another Twinkie, considering Rush's words.

"Sure is persistent for a copycat." He shrugged. "Only him and the FBI know, I guess. Ain't really my deal. But I tell you one thing, if Agent Bunning *has* been lying to the press, I'd come clean with it. That Jackson boy's crazy."

"That, he is," Rush said.

The room fell silent for a moment. The smell seemed to intensify. Rush needed fresh air. "I'll have a forensics team come in and try to find any trace evidence," he said. "We'll also videotape your statement. You feel up to it?"

Blane shrugged. "It's not like I'll be sleeping any more to-night."

Rush strode to the door. "They'll be here within the hour. And Agent Bunning's on his way. Tell him everything and demand that he move you to a hotel."

Blane nodded and mopped his face. "Can I ask you something?"

"What?"

"Are you the lead detective on this? The cop target?"

Rush looked at him for a moment. "I've got things to do, Mr. Blane. You have a nice night."

At 2:20 A.M., B.J. pulled his truck over to the curb several blocks from the great detective's cul-de-sac. He should have both cameras out of the planters and be back to his truck within fifteen minutes.

He set off at a quiet trot, carrying the Pelican case that would hold his cameras, transmitters and batteries. After several minutes, he climbed a fence, passed through a backyard, then crouched through an unlocked gate into the alley. A chain-link fence enclosed the backyard of the great detective's next-door neighbor. Drapes were drawn across the back windows, but he saw a shadow moving around inside the house.

Slowly, B.J. made his way two yards to the left and cut between those houses. The great detective's driveway was empty, his house dark. The house with the planters had a Honda Civic and a Ford Explorer, as expected. He hesitated moving into the open to retrieve his equipment after having seen a shadow moving around inside the house, but he also knew he needed his stuff so he could video the shooting of the judge. And he was here. And the cul-de-sac was vacant, except for vehicles parked in each of the other driveways.

Hearing the short gasps of his own breathing, feeling his heartbeat inside his chest, he cut across the great detective's front yard, crept over to the first planter, and pulled up the bush, quietly placing it on the ground.

Then he stopped. Listened.

Locating the camera, he disconnected it from the transmitter and lifted the battery from under the soil. After placing everything into the Pelican case, he replanted the bush. He crossed the sidewalk and repeated the procedure at the second planter. He was about to click the lid shut when he heard a sound.

He froze, exposed, kneeling on the ground three feet from the end of the stoop.

The sound was a hinge squeak, followed by a click: the front door opening and closing. After a moment, two new sounds: a shoe scraping across concrete, a man clearing his throat.

Rush climbed into the passenger's seat of Chinbroski's car and slammed the door. "Get me the hell away from this pigsty."

Chinbroski dropped the car into gear and pulled away from the curb. "Either you or me," Chinbroski said somberly.

They rode in silence for a moment.

"Zeke's plan is shit." Chinbroski looked at Rush through the darkness.

"It's me, Chin. We've talked about this. I'm the lead; you're going on vacation, getting married. In fact, I want you off this thing tomorrow."

They stopped at a stop sign. "No. I've got the rest of this week and all of next. You asked me to stick with you on this. Remember? That's what I'm gonna do. That's what partners do."

Rush knew the possibility existed that Jackson didn't know which one of them was the true lead. He had to get Chinbroski off the case. But he'd have to be forced off. He'd never volunteer. Especially after being threatened in the middle of the night. Make him appear a coward. Rush didn't agree, but he knew Chinbroski.

"Okay," Rush said. "Your call."

"Right. You tell Zeke his plan is not only for shit, it's over."

Rush nodded. "It's been over for me. I'm not getting any-where near him."

Chinbroski blew out a breath. "The gear, right? Your house?"

"Yeah." Rush yawned and rubbed his eyes. "Zeke's on his way, I guess? You called?"

"While biting my tongue."

Rush grabbed his cell phone and called dispatch, told them to send a forensics team to Harold Blane's house. "Not that they'll find anything worth a damn," he said after he ended the call. "How can a person live in a rat hole like that?"

Chinbroski shrugged in the darkness. "We never scoped out the cemetery. Your mom's grave."

"Maybe tomorrow night," Rush said. He was quiet for a

moment, fatigue draining his enthusiasm. "Probably ought to go home and check for Jackson's equipment tomorrow. During daylight. Assuming he even has any."

Chinbroski slowed the vehicle and looked over. "Want me to blow it off? Back to my place?"

Rush considered it. Closed his eyes and yawned again.

"We're only a few blocks. Just make one pass and we'll see if there's anyplace Jackson could have hidden some cameras."

"Sure."

Rush read the sound of his voice. "Big waste of time?"

"Probably. But desperate people do desperate things."

"That's original. I'm desperate?"

"As hell."

"We'll just make one pass and then head home."

B.J. held his breath, frozen in a kneeling position, like a man praying in church. The equipment case wasn't locked yet. If he ran now, he'd risk losing his gear, and leaving it was not an option. He didn't want to shoot the man in the alcove because of the noise. And hand-to-hand combat in the dark wasn't an attractive option, either. Slowly, he reached around to his left hip, grabbed his hunting knife, and placed it on the ground next to his feet.

He could see brief flashes of a cigarette glow as the man swung his hand from his mouth, down to his side, then back to his mouth. He was just out of full view. B.J. slowly lifted the bush and set it in the planter. That gave him enough cover to hide his entire body, if he stayed crouched. Then, reaching over to the equipment case, he quietly, slowly, and with the utmost care, snapped shut one of the locks.

It sounded like a muffled gunshot. And the man heard it. He walked to the front of the alcove and looked into the street. A large frame, intimidating. Shaggy hair, square jaw, shoulders wide, chest thick. He came out of the alcove and took several steps toward the street, peering in all directions.

Now almost behind the man, B.J. scooted around the planter, between it and the house. The equipment case was two feet to the left of the planter toward the middle of the yard. If the man turned to his right and looked down, he'd see it for sure.

B.J. watched him drop his cigarette butt and crush it under his heel. He blew out his last drag of smoke and coughed. As he pulled a handkerchief to blow his nose, he turned to his right and looked at the great detective's house next door.

A bead of sweat tickled B.J.'s hairline as he reached around to his sheath for his knife. Empty. Then he remembered placing it at his feet before moving. Cursing silently, he peeked around the planter and saw it two feet in front of him.

The man blew his nose.

B.J. reached for his knife, gripped the handle, and swung his arm back to his side. The blade slapped against the side of the planter.

The man turned and looked straight at B.J. "Who are you?" Showing no fear, he took a step toward the planter.

B.J. gripped the hunting knife. The man looked at the equipment case and stepped forward again, towering above the planter now. "I asked who you are!" He shoved the handkerchief into a pocket, freeing both hands.

B.J. remained silent, knowing that a man, any man, couldn't be totally ready for combat while talking. He held the knife upside down, with the sharp edge of the blade pointing toward the ground, the back side of the blade against his forearm.

The man shuffled another half-step toward the planter

and reached his hands out. "I ain't asking you again, boy. What are you doing here? And what's in that case? You trying to get some pictures? I've kicked four of you bastards off this property already. Can't you sons-a-bitches leave the poor bastard alone? What the hell's your problem?"

B.J. refused to speak. He focused, decided he'd attack the next time the man opened his mouth.

"Boy, I'm gonna kick your—"

B.J. sprang and swung the knife in an upward crossing slash across the man's throat, cutting him off in mid-sentence.

The man staggered back, grabbed his throat, tried to scream. Gurgling and sucking noises filled the night air.

B.J. shoved the man backwards and hit him with a reverse swing. The knife sliced downward into his right eye, across his nose, and opened his left cheek. His spouting neck sent streams of blood in every direction.

Grabbing at his wound, the man fell onto the grass. He thrashed around, finally settled into a fetal position.

B.J. pushed the knife into the back of his neck, probed upward, and found his brain stem. The man stiffened, then went limp. The blood stopped spouting; the sucking sounds died.

The night air was cool, deathly quiet as B.J. cleaned the knife blade across the man's shirt. Then he froze as a car turned onto the street and headlights lit him up.

"What the hell!" Chinbroski said, pointing to the house next to Rush's.

Through the darkness Rush saw a figure rise from a crouched position, bend, make a swiping motion across a large mound at his feet, and stand.

"Son-of-a-bitch!" Chinbroski said, flashing on his high

beams and gunning the car forward. "That a body?"

Rush couldn't tell through the thirty yards of darkness.

"He's got a knife!" Chinbroski shouted just as Rush saw it.

"Running!" Rush caught a glimpse of a white face. "Army fatigues! South! I'll take him!" he shouted, shoving his door open, ready to bail from the car as soon as Chinbroski slowed. He grabbed his portable radio and flashlight and almost stumbled when his feet hit the pavement. "Get some units over here!" he screamed over his shoulder as the running man disappeared around a corner two houses over. "And hurry!"

B.J. cut a hard left between the first set of houses, his right foot digging for purchase.

Cops! Son-of-a-bitch! How did they get here? He couldn't tell if one of them was Stubs. He heard the screaming to get some units on the way, but didn't recognize the voice, didn't know what Stubs's voice sounded like after almost thirty years.

The handle of his knife was slick with blood and he almost dropped it rounding the corner. Slowing, he slid it back into its sheath. He approached a four-foot chain-link fence at a full run, planted his hands on the top rail, and swung both feet over in one move, hardly breaking stride.

The backyard was small, dark, weeds and tall grass, a broken swing set. A noise. To his right. Growling, coming at him. Then a dark shadow, low, moving fast.

B.J. sucked in a breath and dove headfirst over the fence near the alley just as a Rottweiler jumped, teeth bared. The dog nipped his right foot as he cleared the fence. He spun in mid-air, landed hard on his left arm, and skidded across the concrete, leaving a trail of skin from his forehead.

He rolled onto his back and felt his .380 automatic pressing hard against his spine. Dazed for a moment, he scrambled to sit up. Blood dripped into his left eye.

The dog charged the fence, teeth snapping against the wire.

A light flicked on above the back door and B.J. scrambled behind an overgrown bush. The door opened.

The fence rattled across the yard.

The dog spun and charged toward one of the cops, who had jumped into the dog's territory.

"Demon!" A man screamed from the porch.

B.J.'s left ribs ached, his left elbow throbbed. Struggling to his knees, he wiped a sleeve across his forehead. A fire of pain doubled him over. He grabbed the ground, scooted to his left, hiding more fully behind the bush. He couldn't run yet. At least the dog would keep the cop at bay.

The fence across the yard rattled again—the cop retreated to the other side.

"Demon!" the homeowner yelled again, bounding off the porch toward the dog. "Quiet!"

The cop flicked on a flashlight. "Police officer!" he shouted. "Grab your dog! Do it now!"

B.J. rubbed his elbow, leaning farther left as the cop swept the alley with his flashlight. The glow lit the edges of the cop's face. His eyes were black holes and the powerful beam washed out his body frame. B.J. couldn't tell if it was Stubs. The cop ignored the dog, only inches from him now, as well as the dog's owner, who was slowly edging closer. The cop's focus was the shadows of the yard, the alley.

"What the hell you doing out here?" the homeowner asked, grabbing Demon's collar.

"Quiet," the cop shouted over the noise of the dog. He jutted his head forward as though he'd seen something.

B.J. hid himself behind the thickest part of the bush.

Slowly he stood, shook his head to clear the cobwebs, and prepared to run.

Then the cop lit up the bush with his light.

B.J.'s truck was four blocks away. More cops were hauling ass toward him. But he wouldn't move with the cop so close, not before he knew if it was Stubs. For almost thirty years he'd fantasized about meeting him face to face, dreamed of what it would feel like to stick a knife into his gut and twist, to see the look on his face when he realized who had returned to repay an old debt.

Tonight, with a single yard separating them, he might be as close as he would ever get.

As the homeowner grabbed Demon and started dragging him off, B.J. strained to see through the darkness. He just couldn't tell.

The cop drew his pistol. "Police officer!" he shouted. "You, behind the bush, don't move!" Then the cop's partner joined him at the fence.

"I'm with you, Rush," Chinbroski said, drawing his .45. "Gotta be Jackson!" His voice broke. "Guy's dead over there. I called out the troops."

"Behind that bush in the alley," Rush said quietly as the homeowner dragged the struggling Rottweiler toward the back porch. "You stay with the victim. I'll get this guy."

"Bullshit!"

Rush didn't have time to argue. The dog was almost to the porch. "Let's go!" Rush saw movement in the alley just as he started climbing the fence.

"There he goes!" Chinbroski said, following Rush over the fence. "North. Give me your radio. I'll call it in." He grabbed the radio from Rush's back pocket and shouted their location.

"Stay with me," Rush said, sprinting through the yard. He scaled the fence and jumped into the alley.

"I'm on your ass."

B.J. ran hard, pain spearing through his ribs, elbow, and forehead. He glanced back. The two cops, each with long athletic strides, arms pumping, were closing. The light was too low to determine if one was Stubs. It didn't matter now. He had to get the hell out. The FBI task force would already be rolling, with the helicopter and dogs.

Holding his ribs, he lowered his head and sprinted as fast as he could. The chase last night had brought back that breath-snatching high. But this chase was bullshit. His ribs, elbow, and forehead were slowing him down. Damn it! Had to make it to his truck.

After 100 yards or so, a sudden thought chilled him.

His equipment.

The pelican case was still next to the planter, his fingerprints all over everything.

They'd have the prints identified within the hour, his face by noon. They wouldn't have his new identity or the name he was born with, but they'd start closing the noose.

It was what the FBI did best. It'd probably be another week or so before they had his new identity. Even less time before they figured out his birth name. With the birth name, they'd find the farmhouse.

Almost over. Glad he'd fixed the hinges on the trapdoors in the tunnel.

B.J. ran hard, saw a ninety-degree turn up ahead.

They'd have his face from the prints. Once they had his face, Stubs might know immediately. But he might not. Not after almost thirty years.

The cop's ragged breathing grew louder. They'd closed

the distance. B.J. would never win a foot race. Time to slow them down. He pulled his .380 Colt Mustang and cut right, between two houses. Fired three rounds into the air, not breaking stride.

Rush heard the shots and dove to the right, slamming into a green trash can under a carport overhang. Chinbroski rolled left and came up into a shooting position, firing two shots into the darkness ahead.

Rush aimed his .45 but saw nothing, held his fire. "Get it on the air!" he shouted to Chinbroski. His partner cranked the volume of the radio. Dispatch was sending units from all over the city.

Chinbroski started to transmit, but was cut off by a tidal wave of other police units responding to their location. "Damn it!"

"Switch to NCIC," Rush ordered, still watching the darkness ahead.

"Got it. Ida three-thirty-three!" Chinbroski shouted into the radio. "We've got shots fired in the west alley of Debbie Drive! Me and three-thirty-two. We're northbound. And tell Dispatch One to keep that damn channel clear!" He flipped back to Dispatch One and Rush heard the shots fired broadcast.

Sweat ran into Rush's eyes as he fought to control his breathing. The fleeing figure was just a shape. A three-dimensional shadow. He'd seen Jackson cut right less than thirty yards ahead. Just before the shots. Before the shots. No muzzle flash.

"Chin, that was a diversion. You see a muzzle flash?"

"Damn it. Slowing us down."

Rush headed north again. But slower, skirting the shadows, trying to distinguish the sounds ahead of him.

Chinbroski was to his left. Both had guns at the ready.

The first siren came from the north, directly ahead, distant. Rush ignored that and turned between the houses Jackson had just bisected, scanned the ground with his flashlight, and saw three shell casings glittering in the grass.

Other sirens drifted in from the west, faint but intensifying. Two dogs directly ahead, across the street, had just come alive with a fury. Then the rattle of chain link. Rush dashed into the deserted street and looked both ways.

Movement to the north, just in front of a house nearly a half-block away. The two dogs barking so furiously were directly ahead, slamming their bodies against the fence, alternating their attention between Rush and something to the north.

Jackson. Had to be. Probably tried the yard with the dogs before having to change course. Chinbroski was snapping their location into the radio just as Rush took off in a dead sprint.

B.J. left the two dogs behind, sprinting with everything he had. Two blocks to his truck. Had to make it. There, a house with no fence. He glanced back, saw the cops coming hard. He stopped, crouched, fired two rounds over their heads because one of them might be Stubs and he didn't want to kill Stubs yet.

They both dove forward, landed hard on their bellies, and fired simultaneously, five or six blasts that looked like fire spit from a dragon. B.J. recoiled. Forty-fives probably, or something large, and auto-feeding.

Time to move! He cursed himself for not bringing a bigger pistol, at being outgunned by these sons-of-bitches.

He had other guns back at the farmhouse, but they weren't as easy to conceal.

He threw himself left behind the corner of a house, heard sirens growing louder from the north. Couldn't be more than a couple of minutes away. A light came on in a window just to the right of his head. Voices, muffled, but frantic, from inside.

His ears were ringing from the gunfire. Sweat dripped into his eyes. Or maybe blood from his forehead. The ribs on his left side felt crushed. Hard to breathe.

Straight ahead was clear all the way to the alley. No fences. He bore down, churned his legs with everything he had.

Damn those cops. Why were they out here? And why in the hell wouldn't they back off? Did they *want* to get shot?

He gripped his .380, careful to keep his finger off the trigger. Didn't want to shoot himself. Just as he hit the alley, he heard a voice, low but urgent, barking orders into a radio, giving directions.

Had to reach his truck. One block. Then he'd turn on the police radio from the officer he'd shot last night. Another mistake, not having it with him.

Damn.

Cutting hard left at the alley, he sprinted across one driveway, and flew between two more houses, veering left again as he came out on the street where his truck sat waiting.

Sirens were everywhere now, alive with the challenge of pursuit. B.J. had been a cop and knew what was racing through the mind of every officer headed his way: *Is this the night I die?* Only a seasoned veteran wouldn't have that near the front of his mind, and seasoned veterans didn't work the graveyard shift. A million things were crashing around between these rookies' ears. With a veteran detective screaming directions into the radio, reporting that he's taking gunfire, the cops heading B.J.'s way would hardly be able to function.

His truck was 100 yards up, straight ahead. He'd never

reach it before the cops made the turn onto the street and had a clear shot. And they would shoot. All bets were off now. They could put fifteen rounds in his back and a grand jury wouldn't touch them. And if Stubs was one of the two and he could shoot a pistol like he used to shoot a rifle, B.J. was in trouble.

So he veered off, headed across the street, and planted himself behind a tree. Gasping, he aimed between the houses where the cops should emerge any second.

Rush scrambled to his feet as soon as he saw the darkened figure disappear between the houses. Chinbroski was up and moving, shouting into the radio, on Rush's heels.

They reached the corner of the house from which Jackson had fired and Rush skidded to a stop. He quick-peeked around the corner and saw nothing.

Chinbroski slapped him on the back. "Move!"

"Wait, damn it!" Rush whispered.

A light flicked on to their right and the front door of the house burst open, a man with a shotgun charged onto the porch. He worked the pump and shouted, "Who's out there?"

"Aw, shit," Rush said under his breath.

"Police officer!" Chinbroski said too loudly for Rush's comfort. "Back in the house! And put that damn shotgun up before you hurt yourself."

The man just stood there.

"You heard me!" Chinbroski said. "We're getting shot at out here!"

The door slammed seconds later.

"Let's go," Rush said after he was sure Jackson wasn't hiding around the corner.

At the alley, Rush looked both directions, each deserted.

He turned on his flashlight and inspected the grass between the houses straight ahead. Dew-disturbed footprints led the way.

Chinbroski gave a location update on the radio as Rush followed the trail with the beam of his light.

The truck sat fifty yards north. B.J. should be there by now. He'd thought the cops were closer. He prepared to make a run for it when he saw the flashlight beam dancing across the grass. The cops moved slowly, careful of an ambush.

The sirens were louder. He didn't know how long he'd been running, a couple of minutes, maybe three. But more cops would box him in for sure.

From behind the tree, forty yards from where the cops would soon emerge from between the houses, he'd shoot at them, then sprint to his truck. They'd drop for a moment and that'd be long enough. But B.J. only had two rounds left. And he hadn't brought another magazine.

Taking a breath, he stepped out from behind the tree and fired. Bullets ricocheted off the house. The flashlight beam went out.

Something hit Rush in the arm.

"Kill the damn light!" Chinbroski barked behind him. "You wanna get us killed?"

Rush ignored him and crawled to the corner, stuck his head around, and saw Jackson almost a hundred yards north. "He's running, come on!"

He scrambled up and tore around the corner, slipping on the grass. Jackson had stopped at a pickup with a camper top. Like the truck old man Drain had described.

"Chin, he's getting away! North on Ridgewood! Broadcast! Broadcast! Tennessee tags! Need a chopper!"

Rush pumped his arms, sprinting with everything he had. Seventy yards, sixty, fifty. The truck's engine roared to life. The back tires burned rubber and the truck shot forward.

The truck flew through a stop sign and disappeared around a turn. Rush slowed; stopped; bent over, gasping for breath, his lungs on fire.

Chinbroski caught up. He broadcasted the truck's directions while slumped on one knee, hardly able to breathe.

The sirens screamed from every direction. From the east, Rush heard the faint thumping of rotor blades. Lights were flicking on all over the neighborhood.

Rush shoved his flashlight into a back pocket and tried to holster his .45. It wouldn't go. He looked at it. Empty. The slide was locked back.

It made him laugh. Was it stress or was it funny? He glanced at Chinbroski, still on one knee. "Look, Chin," Rush said, holding up his pistol. "Look at this."

His partner looked at Rush's .45. "You shot all your rounds?"

"I guess so. What if I had caught him?"

CHAPTER THIRTEEN

The strong pair of hands locked onto B.J.'s shoulders and jerked him backwards. He dropped the rifle as someone else clamped his wrists. Stubs's retreating footsteps through the woods sent a knife of fear through him.

He was on his own. The screaming from the teepees echoed through the trees.

Flashlight beams violated the darkness and B.J. caught a glimpse of his own pants, darkened with urine.

"Got him?" a voice to his left shouted.

A grip like a steel cord pinned B.J.'s arms to his sides, lifted him up. His feet slapped against the tree stump where Stubs had seen the squirrel.

"Yeah," someone yelled into B.J.'s ear. "Grab the rifle. There. See it?"

A flashlight spotted the rifle. "Got it," said the first voice.

His captors were college kids, counselors who lived in the teepees. The last two nights B.J. had gotten to know them both.

The first voice was Steve, the camp range master who wanted to be a FBI agent. The other was a black guy, Gerald, who played Malcolm X recordings in his teepee.

Gerald squeezed B.J. so tightly he could hardly breathe. When the flashlight beam lit up his face, Steve gasped, "B.J. Cagle? What the hell?"

"Come on!" Gerald barked, spinning around, his arms still pinning B.J. against his chest. "We gotta make sure Funky sent for help. Gotta make sure an ambulance is coming." Gerald crashed through the underbrush and stepped into a field.

That's how they'd gotten there so fast. He and Stubs had only been a few feet from the edge of the woods. Less than fifty yards from the teepees.

Struggling against Gerald's grip, B.J. tried to speak, tried to scream his innocence. But it took all his effort to breathe. Gerald would kill him if he didn't loosen his grip.

Steve jogged ahead of them, lighting the way, carrying the .22 with the barrel pointing to the sky. He looked back at Gerald. "Funky'll get the bleeding stopped, but I wanna stop and check on him."

"Lucky I didn't get hit!" Gerald snapped, his hot breath on B.J.'s neck. "Lucky we was out for a smoke. Can't believe this shit!"

They pressed forward, B.J. struggling to breathe. Suddenly, as if the teepees had sprung forward from the darkness, they were there. Dozens of boys in their underwear milled around a teepee on the right. They were quiet, their hands to their mouths or covering their ears to block the screaming.

And the screaming was close, coming from the teepee in the center of the boys. Gerald veered that way, headed straight for it.

"Where you going?" Steve asked, stopping, his flashlight beam following Gerald's path. "You can't take him in there."

"The hell I can't! This little son-of-a-bitch needs to see what he did!"

The group of boys parted, all eyes on B.J.

B.J. tried to speak. The words wouldn't come. He shook his head, tears streaming down his face. He kicked wildly, frantic at what he would see inside.

Steve ran over and grabbed Gerald's arm. "Bad idea!"

Gerald stopped, spun around, and shouted, "Why?"

Steve recoiled. B.J. shook his head, desperate to speak through the pressure against his chest. They stood just outside the teepee and the noise from within sent chills racing down his spine.

"Be—because," Steve stammered. "It might be bad in there. That's nothing for a kid to see."

"This little bastard needs to see!"

Gerald adjusted his grip. B.J. sucked a huge breath. The air gave him words. "I didn't do it!" he yelled. "I didn't do it!"

Steve shined his light in B.J.'s face. "What?"

"Like hell!" Gerald squeezed B.J. again and stepped through the opening of the teepee.

Large enough to sleep eight boys with room to spare, moonlight filtered in from above, where the supporting poles were tied together. A lantern hung just under the supporting poles, casting uneven shadows. Gerald threw B.J. to the ground. He landed on his stomach and his face bounced against the dirt floor.

On the other side of the teepee, Funky sat hunched over a boy, talking quietly into his ear. The boy lay motionless on his back, arms and legs spread wide. Funky's hands were covered with blood. He pressed a rag against the boy's throat. Nothing below the boy's neck moved. Blood covered his tee shirt. It pooled underneath his neck.

"Glad you guys made it back," Funky said. "I sent one of the boys for the nurse. Gonna call an ambulance."

Gerald grabbed the flashlight out of Steve's hand and pointed it directly at the boy's injury. "See what you did?" he said to B.J., his voice hard with anger.

Funky turned toward Gerald. "This who did it?"

"I didn't do nothing!" B.J. protested.

Gerald stomped his foot near B.J.'s head, kicking dirt into his face. "Shut up! We caught you!"

B.J. flinched. "I was in the woods. But I didn't do anything!" He scrambled into a sitting position and wiped the tears from his eyes. The air was so thick and hot he could hardly breathe. The smell of the blood made bile rise in his throat.

The boy coughed and spit blood on Funky.

"Jay," Funky said quietly, "turn your head to the side and spit the blood out."

Jay's eyes were wide, his face soaked with tears. He swallowed hard and nodded slightly. "I'll try."

Steve approached Funky and put a hand on his shoulder. "Want me to take over?"

Funky shook his head. "I got it. I just can't put too much pressure on his throat." He looked up at Steve.

"Get me?"

"Yeah." Steve leaned over Jay and put a hand on his arm.

Gerald turned toward B.J. "Hope you're happy, you little bastard!"

"I didn't do nothing!" B.J. said again.

"Then who did?" Gerald asked, edging closer.

B.J. remembered his blood brother oath with Stubs. A promise to never tell on the other. But he never thought something like this would happen. He had to break the blood oath. He wouldn't take the blame—not for this.

"So?" Gerald pressed.

"Uh, a guy in my cabin: Stubs. We were hunting squirrels. Stubs thought he saw one on a stump. He shot at it. Then he heard the screaming. When he saw your flashlights, he dropped the rifle and ran. I didn't do anything! I picked up the rifle. Then you grabbed me. I swear! I didn't shoot him!"

"Squirrel hunting!" Gerald barked, shaking his head. "In the

dark? In the pitch black woods?" He looked at Steve. "Can you believe this shit?"

Steve shrugged.

"I don't believe this bullshit. This punk's trying to blame it on somebody else!"

"I am not!" B.J. shouted. "I didn't shoot! Stubs did! Go ask him!"

"All right." Gerald grabbed B.J.'s arm and jerked him to his feet. "Let's go ask him."

At that moment the flap of the tent was thrown back and the camp nurse rushed in, took a quick look around, and hurried to Funky's side. "Out!" she shouted. "Everybody out! The ambulance will be here soon and I'll take over until then. One of you go make sure the driver can find us."

B.J. felt naked when Gerald carried him back outside. A hush fell over the crowd of boys who clustered around the teepee. Gerald's grip made B.J.'s hand numb. Several of the boys turned their flashlights on B.J.

The sound of a distant siren stirred the boys. They pointed at B.J., whispering to one another. The murmur of the group grew as the siren neared.

In a renewed flash of panic, B.J. pulled hard against Gerald's grip, trying to jerk free. But Gerald held fast, snarled harshly into his ear. "You can make this hard. But you'll never forget the pain if you try."

The other camp counselors began herding the milling campers toward the bunkhouses. A few ran ahead, toward the back of the camp, where cabin 24 held Stubs—and the truth.

Struggling to keep his fear in check, B.J. thought again of the blood-brother oath, the promise they had made. But Stubs wouldn't hold B.J. to that oath now. Not with B.J. facing jail for something he didn't do. Stubs would clear it up. That's what blood brothers do.

Light seeped from the cracks in the shades over the windows in number 24, as well as from every other cabin. Two boys stood just outside the front door, one pointing at B.J. as Gerald carried him toward them. They stared at B.J. with curious expressions.

Gerald pushed through the door, dragging B.J. behind him. Every boy watched as Gerald shoved B.J. to the ground and slammed the door shut.

"Okay, who you gonna blame for this?" Gerald demanded.

The silence of the cabin closed in around him. B.J. fought back tears as he picked himself up off the floor. He felt pressure behind his eyes as he slowly looked at the other boys in the cabin. Stubs sat in the middle of his bed, his hair slick with sweat, his face red. B.J. wanted to cry out, but he held himself as he tried to make eye contact with Stubs. But Stubs wouldn't look at him; instead he watched Gerald, as Stubs slowly scooted to the edge of his bed.

"I'm waiting!" Gerald boomed, glaring at B.J.

B.J. continued to watch Stubs. And slowly, B.J. sensed, every other head in the room turned to watch him, too. Stubs's face was blank, void of emotion. Finally, Stubs looked at B.J. blankly. His eyes were dark, lacking recognition.

"Tell him," B.J. said, his voice weaker than he'd hoped.

Stubs glanced around. "Are you talking to me?"

"Tell him! Tell him what happened!"

Stubs rubbed his forehead. "What happened when? I just woke up. What's going on?"

B.J. pointed at him, his hand shaking with rage. "Tell him you shot the gun! That it was your idea! That you ran off like a coward!"

"What are you talking about?" Stubs said. "Shot what gun?"

B.J. was speechless. A flash of hatred clamped his throat shut.

"I'm talking about squirrel hunting!" he finally shouted. "You shooting the gun!" B.J. lunged forward, but Gerald grabbed him.

For an instant B.J. saw fear flicker across Stubs's face.

"I didn't shoot nobody," Stubs said, shaking his head. "I just woke up."

"You liar! You damn liar!" B.J. wrenched out of Gerald's grip, rushed to Stubs's bunk. "I'm not taking the blame for this, you son-of-a-bitch!"

Gerald grabbed at B.J., and B.J. resisted with all his strength. Gerald fell backward. B.J. rushed the upper bunk again.

Stubs jumped to the floor and squared off with B.J.

"Admit it!" B.J. screamed. "Tell him the truth!"

Gerald recovered and clamped an arm around B.J., pulling him off his feet. "Enough," he said, dragging B.J. toward the door. "Enough of this shit."

"Let me go!" B.J. fought against Gerald's grip. "He's lying! I didn't do it!"

"Shut up, you little asshole."

Gerald flung the door open, pulling B.J. behind him. B.J. twisted around and caught a last look at Stubs. He stood still, fists clenched at his sides, his eyes distant, despite the tears running down each cheek.

It was over with Zeke. As Jackson squealed away, with Chinbroski still on his knees gasping for breath, Rush knew he'd had enough.

Ignoring the squeal of tires from the police cars that screeched to a halt around them, the sirens of more approaching units, and the shouts of FBI agents as they scrambled to find something important to do, Rush and Chinbroski walked away in silence.

Rush held his police radio close to his ear, hopeful that some officer would announce that he'd found the pickup with Tennessee tags.

They moved slowly, carefully, the beam of Rush's flashlight searching the ground ahead of them, retracing the route of the foot chase. A small group of patrol officers followed, and Rush stationed one to protect evidence at each location where gunfire had been exchanged. He'd also given directions to a patrol sergeant to have officers baby-sit any witnesses until Plano detectives arrived to take written statements. He'd also ordered them not to share any information with the FBI.

Rush felt forced to fight this war on two fronts.

After several minutes, they arrived within a block of the spot where Jackson had first fired at them. Having positioned most of the small group of trailing patrolmen, the last one followed closely, head down, carefully searching the ground Rush had just inspected.

"Gonna have to give our guns to the IA boys," Chinbroski told Rush quietly, his shoulders sagging from fatigue. "Not that they did us any good tonight."

Rush could hear the distant rumbling of a growing crowd ahead of them.

"Lucky Jackson can't shoot worth a shit with a pistol," Chinbroski added.

Rush wiped sweat out of his eyes, then grabbed Chinbroski's arm, stopping him. He glanced back at the patrolman. "Hey Jimmy, hold it there a moment." The officer nodded and cut off his flashlight.

Rush maneuvered Chinbroski into the darkness and lowered his voice. "Jackson never shot at us."

Chinbroski laughed. It came out a croak. "What?"

"He didn't. The first time, we didn't see a muzzle flash because he had already turned the corner. The second time he shot quick. Bam-bam-bam. Too fast to expect to hit anything. The third time he didn't even wait until we were around the corner. Saw my flashlight beam and put a couple of rounds right in front of us."

Moonlight reflected off Chinbroski's sweaty face. He stared at Rush, processing.

Rush glanced back at the patrolman and wiped his forehead. He couldn't steady his quivering hand.

"What are you thinking?" Chinbroski asked.

Rush started to speak, but no words came. He cleared his throat, took a breath. "Jackson's gonna kill me on his own terms. Make me sweat it out."

The only sounds were car engines and distant voices from the next block over.

"On the other hand," Chinbroski said, "it's dark as hell. Jackson couldn't know for sure who was chasing him. Could've been a couple of FBI agents, for all he knew."

"We pulled up in a Plano unmarked, Chin. He's gotta at least be that smart." Rush shook his head, waved at the patrolman, and headed toward his dead neighbor's house again.

He stopped at the point where Jackson had first fired at them. "Here," Rush told the patrolman. "Guard these shell casings with your life. McBride will be around to collect them eventually."

A half-block now from his neighbor's house, a white glow hung over the rooftops and filtered through the neighborhood trees. The media in full swing. If anyone within a couple of blocks was still asleep, they wouldn't be for long.

"Okay," Chinbroski said. "I'll give you that Jackson probably knew it was Plano cops chasing him. But that don't mean he knew who."

Rush slowed and turned to his partner. "Who else would it be, Chin? A couple of juvenile detectives? Come on."

Chinbroski snorted. "What difference does it make, anyway? *So what* if he decided he didn't wanna shoot you yet?"

Rush stopped, looked hard at his partner, hoping what he

was about to say was a case of faulty logic. He didn't think it was. "Self-control, Chin. If I'm right, Jackson has a level of self-control that's beyond . . ." His voice broke then, and Rush walked away, leaving the unfinished sentence hanging in the air and his partner staring off into the darkness.

At the spot where Jackson had jumped from the yard where the dog had chased him, Rush almost missed the blood smeared across the concrete. He dropped to his knees, shining his flashlight. "I'll be." Several drops led from the smear over to the bush Jackson had hidden behind. "Has to be Jackson's," Rush said. "This stuff's recent." He looked up at Chinbroski. "You know what this means?"

"Means we still gotta catch him. But once we do, we got him by the balls."

"And we might be able to prove it's not Jackson. Has Zeke ever mentioned that they have a DNA sample from Jackson?"

"Not around me. But they should have. Hell, the bastard was arrested and charged with the rape/murder of that college kid."

"Right," Rush said. "Forgot about that. I'll call Nashville in a few hours and have them round up a sample."

"*You'll* call Nashville? Ain't you cutting somebody important out of the loop?"

"He's out of our loop, Chin. Starting right now." Rush pulled out his police radio and called for two patrol officers to meet him in the alley. He was about to double-protect the blood evidence.

"What are you gonna do, Rush? About Zeke."

Chinbroski's voice had an edge. He was either really nervous or scared shitless.

"About to step out on a limb. And I'd suggest you turn your head, so you don't see what happens when the chief saws the branch out from under me."

Rush inspected the spot where Jackson had hidden behind the bush.

"So you gonna tell me?" Chinbroski said. "Or just talk in metaphors?"

"You know that word?" Rush said, glancing up. "Metaphors?" Then he noticed a smear of blood on a leaf, head-high, assuming Jackson was a few inches below six feet.

"Heard you use it once," Chinbroski snapped. "Knock it off."

"You think Jackson was wearing gloves?" Rush asked, stepping around the bush.

"How would I know that? It was dark. Now what about Zeke?"

Rush cut off his flashlight and turned toward his partner. "Look, Chin. I'm not discussing Zeke. Don't even know what I'm going to do yet. But my investigative alliance with Mr. Bunning ends tonight."

Chinbroski said nothing.

"Besides, how can I tell the chief I went temporarily insane if I tell you about it in advance?"

Headlights from a squad car lit them up from the south as it pulled into the alley. Rush flicked his flashlight, then slapped Chinbroski on the back. "As soon as I show the uniforms these blood smears, we'll go see what gift Jackson left behind for us."

Rush's neighborhood glowed as though bathed in heavenly grace. In the thirty minutes since Chinbroski's broadcast of the foot pursuit, the press had thrown up a tent city. Truck after truck, each with its own crew, had crowded the entrance to the cul-de-sac. Rush squinted at the bright lights as he and Chinbroski crossed the yard heading toward the murder scene. A couple of Plano squad cars sat haphazardly across the entrance to the cul-de-sac, and a long yellow crime scene banner ran from the edge of one corner house, across the street, to the edge of the other. The media bunched up against the banner shouting questions at the uniforms, who stood silent at their respective squad cars.

Rush saw Plano PD Crime Scene Supervisor Randy McBride stop his van next to Chinbroski's car in front of Rush's neighbor's house. He jumped from the driver's seat and hustled around to the back of the van to retrieve his equipment. He tugged at his droopy pants, his white hair glowing like a halo in the white light.

Rush stopped near the dead man, Chinbroski behind him. Three uniformed officers stood guard around the body, shielding it from the cameras down the street. Rush didn't recognize him; maybe a relative of Brenda Swells, Rush's long-time neighbor.

No sign of Zeke Bunning.

A patrol sergeant stepped out of the dead man's front door and approached Rush. The sergeant was the only female supervisor on the night shift. Short and small-framed, Sergeant Jenny Brazos had a waist so narrow her Sam Browne was barely long enough to hold all of her equipment.

"Tell me," Rush said after Brazos stepped wide around the body and stopped in front of him.

"Name's Jeffrey Elman," Brazos said. "Here visiting Brenda, his sister. Went outside for a smoke about thirty minutes ago. Chain smoker. Night shift factory worker down in Houston. Probably wasn't sleepy. His wife, Janet, went to bed after Elman went outside. Hadn't gone to sleep yet when Brenda came screaming into the house."

Rush winced.

As though reading Rush's mind, Chinbroski said, "Maybe

I should've stayed here to make sure Brenda didn't see nothing."

Randy McBride walked up and joined the trio. Rush nodded at him, then turned back to Brazos. "What are the injuries?"

"Upward slash across the throat, a second down across the face through his right eye, and a large puncture at the base of the neck. From the looks of the blood patterns, he flopped around a little before he died."

"Neighbors?"

"So far not a thing. No one heard or saw anything until Brenda started screaming."

Rush glanced around the cul-de-sac. His neighbors were all in their yards now, uniformed officers quietly speaking to a few of them. The media horde was growing louder, still shouting questions at the uniforms.

"ME's been called," Brazos said. "Should be here any minute."

Rush looked over at the body, at a black case sitting near a large planter next to the sidewalk. "Anything else?"

Brazos looked at McBride. "Randy, I know how you are about your crime scenes, but I want to show something to the three of you. She turned and pointed. "The planters."

"The what?" McBride asked.

"The planters. On each side of the walkway. Brenda said she noticed something different about them."

"Brenda said?" Rush asked. "Brenda noticed her planters with her dead brother lying four feet away?"

"Said she heard a noise outside, some shouting. Few minutes later she opened the door, but it was quiet. She flipped on the porch light and noticed something funny about the planter on the left."

"Left when you come out of the house?" Chinbroski asked.

"Yeah. She stopped and looked at it before she saw Jeff."

Rush stepped toward the planter. McBride followed.

"And? What's funny about them?" McBride asked.

"Says the bushes have been dug up and replanted."

Stopping at the planter next to the body, Rush saw dirt sprinkled on the rim as well as on the ground around the base. The bush looked normal to him, although the soil was disturbed, loose.

Rush knew why Jackson had used the planters. He turned away and watched the media behind the tape. A bank of cameras, spread across the width of the street, each had a red eye that filtered out through the banks of white light. Recording.

He rubbed his eyes and turned back to Brazos. "Nothing else?"

"That's it."

"Great. Fine. Good job." Rush turned to McBride. "Randy? The scene's yours. But I want a look inside that black case as soon as you get the outside processed. I mean *as soon as.*"

"You bet," McBride said. He waved his arms like he was doing a backstroke. "Hey, everybody. You heard what Rush said. The scene's mine. Out! Give me some room."

Chinbroski cleared his throat, caught Rush's attention. His partner nodded toward the media mob.

Rush turned and watched all of the cameras spin on their tripods. Then a gap opened in the center like the parting of the Red Sea.

Zeke Bunning had arrived.

"Follow me," Rush told Chinbroski. "And pay attention. I need a credible witness."

Zeke ducked under the crime scene tape, flanked on each

side by a fellow FBI agent. Rush headed straight for him and held up a hand like a traffic cop, stopping several feet away.

Zeke halted a few feet inside the tape. Rush and Chinbroski maneuvered themselves directly in his path. The media cameras spun in their direction; several boom mikes hovered high above their heads.

"Hold it, Zeke," Rush commanded, still holding his hand out.

Zeke wore a suit that appeared slept in. "What do you have?" he asked, his voice thick with sleep.

"Stabbing," Rush said. "One dead. No unauthorized personnel allowed." He knew every word would soon be replayed for breakfast eaters everywhere.

Zeke's eyes narrowed as he looked over Rush's shoulder toward the body. "You jumped Jackson." He refocused on Rush. "That not right?"

"Who's to know? He got away." Rush folded his arms and squared his shoulders.

Zeke took a step to the side and started around Rush.

Rush grabbed his elbow. "Authorized personnel only."

Zeke stopped and looked down at Rush's grip. "What's going on?" he said quietly, his mouth hardly moving. "What the hell are you doing?"

"Protecting a crime scene. We have a stabbing. And unless you can break out a book showing me where the Feds have jurisdiction, I'd appreciate you and your two buddies stepping back behind the tape."

"Can you lower your voice?" Zeke forced out between clenched teeth. He jerked his arm free and stepped back. Then he moved in front of Rush, right in his face. "I heard Chinbroski screaming on the radio about chasing Jackson. Unless he's totally full of shit, you'd better step aside and let me work my case."

Rush stepped to the side just enough to position himself between Zeke and one of the other agents, just enough for a least one camera to have a clear shot of him. The crowd had fallen silent. Rush could hear cars in the distance, the faint sound of a helicopter closing on their location, the chatter of police radios.

"Copycat shooter this year. Right? Isn't that your official position? Why are you still here?"

Zeke's weary face grew tight as he locked eyes with Rush. The agent shuffled his feet and adjusted his baggy suit jacket. "You're badgering me," he said quietly. "And I have no interest in my response being regurgitated for all of America to chew on. I'd suggest you step aside and let me do *your* job."

Mutt and Jeff, the two agents flanking Zeke, took a half-step forward as though about to create a crease for Zeke to slip through.

Rush put a palm in the center of Mutt's chest. "If you take one step past me, I'll have you arrested. Murder is local jurisdiction. I have an investigation to run, a crime scene to protect." He looked at Zeke. "If I discover anything that suggests a connection to Billy Ray Jackson, I'll forward that evidence to you at my earliest convenience." He removed his hand from the agent's chest and glanced at Chinbroski. "Have I made myself clear, partner? Did you hear and understand the lawful order I just gave FBI Agent Zeke Bunning and his two sidekicks?"

"Yes, sir," Chinbroski answered, mimicking Rush's volume.

The crowd murmured and Zeke snatched a glance in their direction. Then he leaned forward and lowered his volume even more. "You're about to wade into a sizeable patch of federal quicksand. I'm going to hold out a rope for the next sixty seconds. Give great thought to grabbing hold."

Zeke crossed his arms and took a small step back.

Rush hadn't had time to consider seriously how easily he could kick Zeke off the case. He wasn't versed in the legalities, or the consequences. He couldn't prevent Zeke from working the Jackson case, but he *could* keep him out of *this* crime scene. At least for a few hours. As soon as it became evident that this murder was Jackson-related, Zeke just might throw the federal book at him.

And then what? Sit in jail while Jackson killed another Plano detective? On the flip side, if the equipment in the black case led to a serious break in the case, Zeke might be too busy catching up to worry about anything else.

Rush glanced at Chinbroski, whose forehead was wrinkled with concern. He held up a finger at Zeke, took a step back, and motioned for Chinbroski to join him a few feet away.

"Have you lost your freaking mind?" Chinbroski whispered. "The chief's already gonna have your ass for spouting off in front of all those cameras. You think he's gonna back you, after he announced that Plano PD is supporting the FBI?" Chinbroski wiped his forehead and ran his hand across the front of his shirt.

The cameras had followed Rush and Chinbroski's movement away from Zeke. Rush knew he could risk jail or let this buffoon continue leading everyone in circles. His decision didn't take long.

Rush grabbed Chinbroski's elbow and whispered, "I'd suggest you distance yourself from me."

Chinbroski tensed and Rush gripped his elbow harder. "Latch onto McBride and get his ass on AFIS if he finds a print on that equipment. Get every detective we have to report to the training room by daybreak. Burglary, Auto, Sex, Forgery, everybody. Less than three hours." Rush backed away and shoved his partner toward McBride. "Hurry. We're living on the FBI's time and they're stingy as hell."

Chinbroski stepped away, his eyes wide. Then he turned and jogged toward McBride.

Rush motioned to Zeke. All three agents walked over. Rush crowded them, positioning himself where no cameras could see his face. He didn't want any lip readers deciphering his words.

"This is the deal, Zeke. You haven't done a damn thing right since you got here. *I* thought of the newspaper angle. *You* put a couple of dickheads in charge of watching Harold Blane. *You* laid a trap for your fake witness last year, but not for a *real* one this year. Three years you've been on this case and you never considered Jackson might be videotaping. Three years!" Rush swallowed and lowered his voice. "You're not stepping one foot closer to that crime scene up there. And if you even *try* to stick me with some bullshit federal charge, I'll blow the roof right off your psychobabble house of cards. You really think you can make anything stick against me? Who'd blame me for trying to save myself from an arrogant, incompetent ass?"

Rush stepped back. "Now get out of my crime scene. Go look in your book of investigations and figure out how you're going to explain all of this to that pack of wolves standing behind you.

"Officer Johnson," Rush shouted to the nearest uniform. "Kindly escort these gentlemen outside the tape."

Rush turned and headed toward McBride. He'd taken no pleasure in what he'd just done. But street fights were rarely pretty. And this was a street fight to the death.

CHAPTER FOURTEEN

B.J. could smell his own sweat and the dried pee on his pants. He could hear his heartbeat pounding in his ears. His butt was sore from the hard wooden chair he'd been sitting in since last night. Even though the room the camp director had him locked in was set off from the main waiting area of the camp administration office, B.J. could see through a small window as each and every boy in cabin 24 was led into the director's office and grilled. The director's office was on the other side of the wall, across the room from where B.J. sat. He could hear snatches of conversation if he leaned forward a little and held his breath.

The director had been at it since after breakfast, and the last boy from his cabin was in there now. Not counting Stubs. The director must be saving the best for last, B.J. figured. Kind of a cop trick B.J. read about once. Get all the evidence, all the information, then spring it on him all at once. Make him crack.

Stubs was probably back at the cabin under guard, sweating rivers, shaking in his underpants. B.J. couldn't wait until the director sank his teeth into Stubs's pack of lies. If that stupid Gerald would've grilled Stubs back in the cabin, he would've cracked right then.

The noises of the camp increased the later it got. B.J. was hungry, needed to pee. The stain on his pants wasn't too noticeable, but he wanted to take a shower more than he ever remembered. Steve, one of the camp counselors, had stuck his head in the office earlier and told him that the director had decided to isolate him from the rest of the boys until camp was over tomorrow. Steve didn't know anything about the rifle championship match. He didn't know anything about the boy who'd been shot, either. Only that he'd been rushed to the hospital.

B.J. hated the waiting. He'd dozed in the chair sometime before sunrise, until the director had begun parading in the boys from B.J.'s cabin.

The sound of a chair scraping across a wood floor signaled the director getting up from behind his desk. A few seconds later the door to his office opened and B.J. saw the last boy leave.

Then he heard the director call for Stubs, who must've been sitting right outside the office. B.J. climbed from his chair and caught a glimpse of Stubs through the small window just as he entered the director's office. When the door slammed, B.J. crept over to the common wall to listen.

The director's voice was distinctive, a high whine that reminded B.J. of the old farmer who sometimes visited his grandfather.

"We have a situation here, young man," the director told Stubs. "I'm inclined to just call the sheriff and turn both you boys over to him."

A knot gripped B.J.'s stomach.

"But I know that whoever fired that shot didn't mean to harm Jay Harrington."

The director stopped talking. B.J. sat down on the floor and pressed his ear closer to the wall. He could barely hear. He found himself holding his breath so he wouldn't miss anything.

"The problem I'm having," the director continued from another part of the room, and closer to the wall, "is your denial."

B.J. grinned. Here it comes. The bomb is about to drop.

"That's 'cause—"

"I'm not finished," the director interrupted. "A lie is like cancer. It'll eventually eat your insides out."

He stopped talking again and B.J. heard slow, heavy steps moving away from the wall. "I've seen you around," he continued. "And right now you look like you've got a huge lie sitting right at the edge of your throat. It's making your face pale, pulling your eyes down. It's got a grip on your lower lip, making it quiver; it's squeezing so hard you can't keep your head up."

B.J. clenched his fists. It was all he could do to remain silent.

"I have reports that you sneaked out with B.J. Cagle."

The statement hung in the air as heavy as fog. B.J. heard nothing from the other room. He imagined the director standing over Stubs, hands on hips, glaring over the top of his glasses. He sensed that the next one to speak would score the first points.

"No, you don't," Stubs said, his voice calm and straightforward.

B.J. looked at the wall and started to shout his protest. Stubs had called his bluff?

Silence filled the room again. Had the director given up already?

"Ah, but I do," the director finally said, his footsteps thumping against the floor. "Three of your bunkmates saw both of you leaving the cabin. One of the counselors saw you enter the woods. And as soon as the sheriff fingerprints the rifle, we'll have enough to file charges."

B.J. was unable to move. A cold sweat made him shiver. How could his mother ever bear to visit him in jail? He said a silent prayer as tears filled his eyes.

"Bring 'em in here," Stubs said, his voice still calm. "Bring them in here so I can call them liars to their faces."

"Are you denying that you and B.J. walked out that door just after midnight?"

B.J. slumped against the wall. He knows nothing! Nothing! And now Stubs knew it. B.J. felt lightheaded, the fatigue from the night suddenly crashing down around him. Stubs had played it cool, waiting for the director to trip up. If three boys from the cabin had actually seen them sneak out, the director would have known that they'd gone out the window.

"They're liars. So is the counselor," Stubs said. "Sure, me and B.J. have been hanging around together. But I didn't sneak out and shoot no gun. He's a liar, too. A damn liar."

B.J.'s hands started trembling. He slowly stood, trying to be quiet because Stubs was still talking.

"Only reason I hung out with him all the time is 'cause the other boys laugh at him behind his back. He's a sissy, maybe even a queer. And now he's trying to get me kicked out of camp."

B.J. clamped his eyes shut and clenched his teeth so hard his jaws hurt.

"He's been telling me for three weeks that he's been dying to go hunting on the mountain. But I didn't think he'd really do it. Especially at night. That's dumber than anything I've ever heard of."

Stubs paused and B.J. heard the camp director sit down in his chair.

"He can shoot good," Stubs continued. "Better than me, probably. But that don't mean he should blame stuff on other people."

"Well—"

"I feel sorry for him," Stubs interrupted. His voice sounded funny, almost like he was about to cry. "He's, like, obsessed with shooting. I think it has something to do with his dad, who's dead. One time we almost got into a fight because he thought I insulted his dad. He's got some kind of problem. I almost came here once and reported it. Maybe he's just trying to get me kicked out of the

rifle championship 'cause he's afraid he'll lose and his dad will know it somehow."

B.J. couldn't take any more. In a fog of rage, he burst out of the little office, through the camp director's door, and hurled himself toward Stubs. He landed on the bigger boy's back, his first punch connecting solidly on the side of Stubs's face.

Stubs fell out of his chair, B.J. on top, swinging his fists with all his might. B.J. connected against the side of Stubs's nose. Stubs covered his face and B.J. was unable to penetrate with another solid punch.

B.J. had just grabbed Stubs's throat when he was jerked straight up. The director threw him across the room. B.J. hit the door and fell to the floor.

"That'll be quite enough, young man!" The director picked up the toppled chair and helped Stubs to his feet.

Stubs wiped his bleeding nose and smeared blood across his face.

"Pinch the top of your nose and tilt your head back," the director said, leading Stubs into a small bathroom that connected to the director's office.

B.J. slowly stood, legs and hands shaking, and considered running. But he couldn't. Not until this was settled.

B.J. took a step toward the bathroom door. "Stubs is a liar!" he said, his voice cracking with rage.

Water started running in the bathroom.

"Rinse your face," the director said.

"He's lying to you!" B.J. said, stepping closer. "Everything he just said is a damn lie!"

"Use a towel and press it against your nose." The director ignored B.J.; his voice was quiet, gentle. B.J. could hardly hear him over the splashing water.

"It was Stubs's idea. I tried to tell him we were heading toward the teepees, but he wouldn't listen."

The director charged out of the bathroom, his face red with anger. B.J. jumped back in surprise. The director grabbed him roughly by the arm and dragged him back to the small room where he'd spent the night. And locked him in without saying a word.

At lunchtime, B.J. was led back to cabin 24 by one of the counselors, forced to shower, and given a meal of cold bacon, eggs and biscuits. He was alone in the cabin, not unusual for this time of day. And he'd be alone until an hour before the dinner bell, when the rest of the boys would return to clean up for the evening meal.

He was told to pack. He'd spend the night alone again, and then be watched by a counselor until his mother picked him up tomorrow.

After a counselor removed his empty food tray, B.J. climbed his bunk and cried. He wished his mom would pick him up now, although he didn't want her to see him with tear streaks down his face.

His dad wouldn't have cried because he was a soldier, a hero. Even on his last day, with B.J. and his mom lying on either side of him on his hospital bed, both crying so hard that they weren't able to talk, his dad had been brave.

The memory made B.J. cry harder. He was alone. And his mom would never understand.

Later in the afternoon B.J. jerked awake to the sound of boys gathering outside his window. He rubbed his eyes and watched as most of the boys from camp filled the spectator area at the shooting range.

The rifle championship! B.J. had forgotten. A knot gripped his stomach as Stubs pushed his way through the crowd of boys and stepped onto the range. He stopped next to a boy named Tim, the boy closest to Stubs's second-place standing. They shook hands as the range master shouted for everyone to be quiet. Tim didn't have much of a chance, B.J. thought. Just as Stubs wouldn't have had much of a chance against B.J.

They would shoot thirty rounds, ten each from the prone, sitting and kneeling positions. Both right-handed shooters, the rifle slings would cut the circulation in their left arms, which would start aching long before the match was over.

After the first ten rounds, from kneeling, the range master announced that Stubs was ahead by three points. They took a short break while the range master changed targets. After the string of rounds from sitting, Stubs was up by five.

It was over. Every boy in the crowd knew it. They started drifting away, bored by the anticlimactic match. Fifteen minutes later it was over for real. Stubs won by a total of seven in front of fewer than half the boys who were there at the beginning.

B.J.'s chest tightened when the range master declared Stubs the winner and pointed to the trophy table standing next to the range house.

The table held six glittering trophies. The one in the middle was the largest, standing a full two feet, including the little man shooting a rifle on the top.

Stubs stared at the table as the range master began presenting the awards, starting with sixth place. More of the audience drifted away.

"Bastard's gonna get my trophy," B.J. said under his breath.

"And first place goes to . . ."

B.J. slammed the window shut and turned away, unwilling to listen. He flopped down on his pillow and stared at the ceiling, his throat aching. But he refused to cry again.

Then he heard chanting, faint at first, but growing with every repetition.

"B.J.! B.J.! B.J.!"

Boy's voices. From the range. B.J. scrambled to the window. Stubs held the first place trophy, but the look on his face was one of hatred. The boys who held the other trophies were standing in a *circle around Stubs chanting B.J.'s name.*

They knew Stubs didn't deserve first place.

B.J. opened the window and laughed as Stubs pushed his way through the group.

"Yes!" B.J. punched the air. "Yes! Yes! Yes!"

As Stubs walked off the range with the trophy under his arm, he looked over at B.J.'s window.

Their eyes locked. Stubs stopped, grinned and held the trophy high above his head.

The chanting stopped when Stubs shook the trophy, spun around and stalked away.

B.J. stayed at the window until every boy had drifted off. None of them looked his way. He was already forgotten. With a tremendous emptiness, B.J. stretched out across the bed once again and stared at the ceiling. The sounds of the camp became distant as most of the boys headed off to the stables for one last chance to ride horses. He wished his mother were here.

Then he thought about Stubs. What kind of person, B.J. wondered, can lie so convincingly? What kind of person discards someone else so easily, just to avoid facing the truth? Hadn't Stubs learned anything from his mother before she died?

B.J. was surprised when a tear slid onto his pillow.

"No more crying," he mumbled to himself.

He sat up and sighed, looked around the room. Most of the boys had started packing, most probably glad to return to a life of air conditioning.

Stubs's suitcase was on the end of his bed, partially open. B.J. wondered where home was for him. Stubs never talked about his home life, except to occasionally refer to his foster mom. Except for Dallas, B.J. didn't know where Stubs lived, in fact, wasn't even sure of his full name.

With a sudden thought, B.J. pulled a pencil and paper from his suitcase and climbed over to Stubs's bunk. He opened Stubs's suit-

case and quickly found the little plastic slot inside the lid with his name and address.

"So that's who you are," B.J. said under his breath as he copied the information. "Maybe some day I'll pay you a visit. Invite you to a shoot-off. As a matter of fact, you lying bastard, you can count on it."

B.J. jumped when the door to the cabin opened. The camp director walked in with a sheriff's deputy on his heels.

"B.J. Cagle," the director said, glancing at the tall deputy beside him. "Jay Harrington died in surgery this morning. This is Deputy Wilcox. He's here to take—"

"I'm here to take you in, son," the deputy interrupted. "Just climb down off that bunk, grab your things, and come with me."

B.J.'s eyes misted as he stuffed the piece of paper with Stubs's name and address in his pocket.

Five minutes later the deputy led B.J. through the camp. As the boys who saw them stopped to watch them pass, B.J. was grateful that he wasn't handcuffed. B.J. tried to act dignified, though he knew he probably wasn't fooling anybody. And certainly not Stubs, who was leaning against the side of the cafeteria, alone, with the first-place trophy at his feet and tears running down his face.

At 3:15 P.M., Rush adjusted his tie before opening the door to the chief's law library. He was fifteen minutes late and all the heads at the table turned his way as he stepped into the room. The chief and his assistant, the captain, the lieutenant, Chinbroski and Zeke Bunning.

Rush's effort to keep Zeke from Plano's latest crime scene had lasted less than an hour. That's how long it took Zeke to get an assistant director of the FBI to talk to the chief.

Despite getting his ass chewed for twenty minutes, Rush had felt vindicated. It was he who had contacted Nashville

PD and had them run the latent print that identified William Jonathan Raines. And it was Chinbroski and he who had almost captured Raines. Rush had reacted from his gut, from self-preservation, and he felt good to know his instincts were intact.

Rush hadn't spoken to Zeke since two nights ago in the street. And the FBI agent avoided his gaze now as Rush slid into the only available chair. Rush looked at the chief, but it was Zeke who started the meeting.

"We know who he is," Zeke said. "Raines's current identity."

The room remained silent. This was new information and Rush was sure that Zeke was about to extol the greatness of the FBI.

He did. Zeke broke into a monologue, a self-serving, egotistical rant about how the bureau cracked the next layer of the manhunt.

He told of a team of agents running down the motor home lead, of going to a farm outside Duck River, Tennessee, to talk with a man named Gilbert Cage, who lived on 500 acres at the end of a narrow gravel road. The house was almost a half-mile from the road, hidden inside a large grove of trees. And deserted. No animals, no people, no cars.

After they knocked on all the doors, they walked behind the house and found a big barn at the edge of the trees with big swinging doors, big enough to park a motor home. Locked tight, like the house. Behind the barn was a shooting bench with a berm 700 yards away. Pretty far for an old country boy just doing some plinking. So one of the agents walked down to the berm and dug around in the dirt for some spent bullets.

Without a warrant. Why was Zeke spilling his guts? Rush wondered. Then he knew. Rush looked at the chief, who sat staring at the table, and then at Zeke, whose face glowed like a kid who had just been handed the keys to a new car.

Plano PD was out.

Zeke was sharing information on a federal case with full knowledge that they couldn't repeat any of it. He'd pretend the FBI would've discovered all of this anyway, forgetting the fact that they wouldn't have had shit without Plano PD's help.

The monologue continued with the agents matching a fingerprint they took off the gate by the road, legally standing outside his property to lift the print. It matched Raines's on seventeen points, easily enough for a court of law. The FBI would be serving a search warrant for the entire property within the hour.

Like a mole in a moist, spring garden, B.J. had dug in. In the two-and-half days since his escape from the two cops, he had finished converting the ten acres surrounding his farmhouse into a minefield under surveillance. They knew his cop name, William Jonathan Raines, and his face was on every TV station in America. Soon they would have his birth name. With that, they'd come to the farmhouse.

In addition to all of the security he had put in place over the last few months, he'd worked nonstop over the last twenty hours and completed the rest of what had become a true fortress.

The cops would face nothing like this ever again in their careers. Using fishing line to rig trip wires, he wrapped the entire property with explosive booby traps. Canisters filled with nails, razor-sharp metal scraps, and glass were positioned in strategic locations around the outer perimeter.

Some of the traps, those simple in configuration, were decoys the cops would easily discover.

But during the few seconds their guard was down, they would trigger more elaborate traps placed within a foot of the obvious ones—a layering effect.

Still other traps he hid in the trees along the perimeter fence line, well above eye-level.

He used a chain saw to clear the trees and underbrush between the house and outer perimeter.

Inside the house he secured the windows and doors with thick lumber, caulked every opening, and plugged the chimney to make it harder to penetrate his negotiating center with tear gas. He reinforced the walls, installed motion detectors, ripped up shingles and mounted cameras in the roof, and built a video and communication control center in one of the bedrooms.

In the barn—his shooting center—he drilled several holes in each wall for gun ports.

The only entry into the house was a tunnel running from the barn to a fake shower stall in the hall bath.

Mounted in two trees on the outer perimeter were wireless, pinhole-lens cameras, each powered by twelve nine-volt batteries, wired in parallel. The battery packs, hidden inside deep holes he'd cut in the trunks of the trees with a chain saw, were designed to power the cameras for weeks. The camera receivers, inside his communication room, were hooked to television monitors, giving him eyes along the road in front of the property as well as the front gate. Six cameras covered the farmhouse property. A seventh was inside the communication room.

After two days of hard physical labor, the preparation was completed. Now B.J. spent most of his time in the communication room watching the monitors, dozing when he could, eating when he got hungry. The front-gate camera was wired into the only motion-sensor alarm he had. Any movement activated a warning inside the room. Because the farmhouse stood at the foot of a dead-end gravel road, B.J. didn't expect many false alarms.

The media assault on his Nashville PD identity was non-stop, the TV news stories endless, his picture on every channel. The FBI reported hundreds of sightings from all over the country, according to CNN, but B.J. doubted that the FBI had strayed too far from Dallas.

According to the local news, hundreds of investigators from the FBI, Texas Rangers, sheriff's departments, and local police were scouring the North Texas area for evidence of where William Raines had made his home during the Plano shooting spree.

B.J. watched a thirty-minute special chronicling the life and times of the fallen Nashville police officer. He laughed as old friends expressed disbelief that he was still alive, much less that he was the Billy Ray Jackson sniper.

His former life was ripped open, disemboweled, allowing an opportunity for the entire country to gawk. Serial-killer experts pointed to a head wound he'd received as a rookie Nashville officer as the primary cause of his monstrosity. They theorized that the injury, when combined with the constant violence of police work and the deaths of his wife and child, had sent him over the edge. Several psychiatrists actually claimed he had some kind of illness. B.J. chuckled as he considered calling those experts to testify for him at his trial.

But B.J. knew there'd be no trial.

At 3:20 P.M., the motion alarm jolted B.J. out of a light doze. A sheriff's car slowly approached the gate at the end of the driveway. B.J. leaned close to the monitor and watched as a single deputy climbed out of the squad and walked over to the gate.

The deputy rattled the chain on the gate and inspected the

heavy padlock. Then he surveyed the property, as though trying to figure out why so many trees had recently been cut at a ninety-year-old house that appeared ready to collapse any second. After a minute, he walked back to the car, opened the trunk, and returned to the gate to look at the house through a pair of binoculars. Then he scratched his head and returned to his car. But he didn't leave.

Across the hall from the communication room was a bathroom with a fake shower stall. B.J. flipped the light switch that he'd rewired to light the tunnel and carefully removed the floor of the stall. Then he climbed down the short ladder and entered the tunnel. The tunnel was eight feet below ground, but only three feet tall, which meant crawling. But it was cool despite the stifling heat outside. The smell of the rich earth brought back memories of the thousands of hours he'd spent digging over the last six years. The white Christmas lights strung together and hanging from the two-by-twelve ceiling offered enough illumination to negotiate the ninety-degree turn that marked entrance to the barn straight above him.

He came out under the motor home, inconvenient, but a necessary component for his hopeful escape. He slid the heavy sheet of steel over to one side and crawled out, careful not to slap his head against the frame of his Road King.

Hurrying up to the loft that ran the length of the south wall, B.J. picked up his rifle and peered through the scope toward the deputy's car. The officer had his driver's door open. B.J. couldn't see his face because of the reflection off the windshield.

A few minutes later a second sheriff's car arrived. A sergeant. When the first deputy climbed from his car to talk with the sergeant, B.J. immediately understood why the deputy had shown up in the first place.

"Bobby Higginson," B.J. said under his breath. "I ain't seen you since ninth grade." Higginson's hatchet face and protruding chin were unmistakable, even through a rifle scope 200 yards away. Higginson must have recognized B.J.'s Nashville PD photo playing on every TV in America. He'd been one of the few kids who had believed B.J.'s account of what happened at Camp Indian Hill. He'd been B.J.'s only friend before B.J.'s mother had moved them to Memphis just before B.J.'s fifteenth birthday.

The deputies stood talking for several minutes, the sergeant looking through Higginson's binoculars. Then the sergeant handed the binoculars back, strolled over to the gate, and rattled the chain. He started to climb the gate.

B.J. watched, fascinated. "Hold your ears, Bobby," he whispered. "And don't come any closer."

Higginson walked to the gate and leaned against it, shaking his head and pointing to the house. The sergeant stood inside the gate, his face turned toward the house while he listened to Higginson talk.

After a minute the sergeant turned and walked toward the house.

He made it ten feet.

The explosion threw him a couple of feet off the ground, ripped off his right leg, and shredded his right arm.

Higginson, hit by shrapnel of nails and glass, staggered back and fell to the ground. He dragged himself to his car and climbed in. After what seemed an eternity, the car roared into reverse and careened into the bar ditch. The car rocked back and forth, jerking forward then backward; it shook and shuddered, like a mouse struggling to free itself from a glue trap. Finally, the driver's door opened and Higginson staggered to the sergeant's car. Within seconds he'd driven the car 100 yards east, where he maneuvered it sideways across the road.

"The game is on!" B.J. shouted to the empty barn.

The room remained silent while Zeke seemed to gather his thoughts. Finally he said, "Raines, Bubba to the old-timers at Nashville PD, handled Billy Ray Jackson a couple of times. So there was a connection."

Zeke explained that the FBI had never considered Raines because he had reportedly died a couple years before the shootings started. Car wreck. Explosion. Killed five years before, when his car crashed into a gasoline tanker truck on a road outside of Murfreesboro, Tennessee. Raines and the driver of the truck were burned beyond recognition. The gasoline fire had burned so hot that even dental comparisons were impossible. They identified Raines's car by the VIN on the engine, and Raines by a finger they found fifty feet from the crash site.

They'd been interviewing cops all day, Zeke continued. Raines had been a sniper on SWAT. Ten years ago, his wife got pregnant after years of trying. She carried the baby for seven months and went into early labor. She and the baby died during childbirth. A hatred for doctors. Raines got a lawyer and sued the doctor and hospital. Told a couple people at Nashville PD that his lawyer promised him a victory for malpractice. Judge threw it out of court, adding lawyers and judges to his list.

Nashville PD didn't see a connection, nor did the FBI. The fires at the courthouses and law offices, Raines covering his tracks, all happened over a two-year period after Raines had allegedly been killed in the accident. The judge's brakes failed, his lawyer was killed in a mugging, one of the emergency room doctors was run over while jogging, and the other was killed during an apparent home burglary. No one made a connection, because they weren't all reported as homicides, and the three that were appeared random. A year or so after his wife died, Raines married a barfly from a sleazy topless joint in Nashville. After the crash, she bragged about his three-quarter-million-dollar insurance policy and how she was putting all the money in a suitcase and going to Vegas.

She never made it. She withdrew the money and headed west, and her body was found the next day in a ditch outside Little Rock. The car was found abandoned in the slums a week later. No money anywhere.

No one said anything until Zeke spoke again. "Raines isn't his birth name. We've found the courthouse where his mother changed both their names. Had the file sealed. The federal subpoena will be served tomorrow morning. We've put him in every city at the time of the shootings through credit card receipts. We've found the rental he used here. It's closing in on him."

Rush rubbed the back of his neck while waiting for the shoe to drop. With Raines's face on every newscast, on the front page of every paper, with both his vehicles about to become as famous as his face, Rush knew that the Billy Ray Jackson case had entered a new phase.

The FBI would find him. And it wouldn't take them long.

Rush regretted the missed opportunities, the trap at the cemetery that he never got to spring, his close call to catching Raines two nights before. Although grateful to be alive, being shot at had pissed him off. He considered it his case, the case of the century. For him, the case of a lifetime. Now it was over and he felt hollow.

"I'd like to thank Detectives Rush and Chinbroski," Zeke said, looking squarely at Rush for the first time.

"And I'll only say this once. My judgment regarding my attempt to ensnare Raines was based on sound profiling principles, and I stand by them. However, I respect Detective

Rush's right to object. And I can't say that he didn't strike a chord of truth in his assessment. But all that is in the past. The end is near and justice will prevail."

Zeke nodded at everyone at the table before finally locking eyes with Rush.

"So we're out?" Rush said, speaking for the first time.

"Yes," the chief said. "Unless Raines is holed up in Plano. And that seems highly unlikely."

Rush continued staring at Zeke. "Haven't you omitted a major piece of information?"

Zeke shrugged, confused.

Rush spoke slowly. "Why did Raines shoot all the homicide cops?"

"Ah, yes, of course." Zeke paused. "We don't know. A challenge? An effort to create uncertainty in the mind of the one most responsible for finding him, thereby fostering mistakes? Some ingrained hatred or jealousy? We just don't know."

Zeke pushed his chair back, preparing to leave. "We'll be searching his house within the hour. Maybe something there will enlighten us." Zeke nodded at Rush and stood. "Gentlemen, the FBI thanks you for all the effort. And despite the differences in tactics, we made a wonderful team."

Zeke's cell phone rang. He answered quickly and within seconds was red-faced, pulling out a pen, and scratching something on the outside of a file folder. The room grew silent as all eyes watched the FBI agent. Zeke listened for nearly two minutes before he spoke again.

"I've got it." More scratching on the folder. "On my way."

Zeke punched off the phone and looked directly at Rush.

"Got a man barricaded in an old farmhouse outside Trenton, Texas. You know where—"

"Fannin County," Rush said. "Straight up 75 toward

Oklahoma. Go east on Highway 121 about twenty miles."

"Okay," Zeke said, writing it down. "Sheriff's sergeant is dead. Some kind of explosion, land mine." Zeke glanced at his notes. "Deputy named Higginson recognized Raines's photo. Knew him as a kid by another name. Went to investigate the old farmhouse the kid lived in with his grandparents. We've got all our agents heading that way."

"Don't know Raines's childhood name?" Rush asked, as if it would make a difference to him.

"I'll know as soon I get up there." Zeke gathered his things and quickly shook everyone's hand.

Rush was the last to shake his hand and the only one who didn't return a pleasantry. After joining Chinbroski in the hall, Rush took his partner's arm and guided him toward the door to the back parking lot.

"About time I think about a service for Mallory," Rush said. "And you need to get to Kansas City and spend some time with Nanci."

"You're damn right. The FBI has set us free. And boredom has never looked so inviting."

Rush felt a sudden flash of relief wash over him as he realized that he had never felt so happy to be rid of a case. But just as suddenly he felt a stab of pain for Mallory. Her ashes sat waiting inside Daniel's house in McKinney, while his house sat empty of her presence. He needed some time off. Some time alone.

"Hope it's him they've got cornered," Chinbroski said. " 'Cause I ain't wanting this case back."

Rush nodded in agreement. "Did I ever tell you," he said on the way to Chinbroski's car, "that Raines looks vaguely familiar to me?"

Chinbroski stopped and looked at him. "Damn, Rush, I was just thinking the same thing."

"There's something about his face that's been bothering me for a couple of days." Rush started back toward Chinbroski's car. "I'm thinking I might have arrested him once. Maybe a DWI or something."

Chinbroski unlocked his door and popped the lock on Rush's door. "I was thinking maybe it's been in the last couple of weeks," he said. "Since this whole thing started."

"Where?"

"Don't know for sure. I'm thinking maybe he was in the Bennigan's the night we talked about the cemetery. Remember the night the pimpled kid had his hand up his girl-friend's dress?"

A cold chill passed across the back of Rush's neck. It certainly would have been possible. "How would you remember that?" Rush asked.

Chinbroski shrugged. "Don't know if I do. I just know that I've seen that face before."

Rush got in the car, leaned back in the seat, and sighed.

Chinbroski cranked the engine. "Had a dream last night," he said. "That Raines showed up at my wedding wearing a tux. Carrying a Bible in one hand and a sniper rifle in the other. Asked me, do I take Nanci as my bride? Can you believe that shit? Raines the preacher at my wedding?"

"Just thank God it's over," Rush said. "And that Raines is Zeke's problem."

B.J. timed it. It took forty-five minutes for help to arrive: three more deputies, two Texas Highway Patrol cars, and an ambulance.

One of the troopers inched toward the front gate, stared at the mangled body of the dead sergeant, then looked toward the house.

B.J. quartered the trooper's nose with the scope's cross-hairs. It was a 200-yard shot to him, and another 100 to the group of cars down the road. B.J. knew he could kill most of them now, but he waited.

The trooper's head rotated back and forth, up and down, his eyes searching. B.J. felt he could read the trooper's mind: the lawman didn't know if anyone was in the farmhouse. And maybe the explosion was caused by something else. The house certainly appeared abandoned, with no vehicles in sight. Probably itching to be a hero by dragging the dead man to safety, B.J. figured.

The trooper stared at the dead man for over a minute before finally putting his right foot on the gate. Then he started to climb.

"A hero," B.J. said out loud, placing the cross-hairs on the butt of the trooper's pistol. B.J. sighed and waited for the exact moment to fire. The trooper twisted to the right as he threw his left leg over and straddled the gate for a few seconds. B.J. had always heard that Texas troopers considered themselves invincible. The trooper pushed up and threw his right leg over the gate and landed with his back to the barn.

B.J. fired. The trooper's holster disintegrated.

The force of the shot spun the officer around and slammed him against the gate. He grabbed for his gun and found nothing there. Then he hit the dirt and covered his head.

"What a manly position," B.J. said. He worked the bolt on his rifle and put a round through the trooper's left foot.

B.J. moved the scope and watched the crowd of advancing officers. They shuffled forward, guns drawn, screaming at each other, searching for the location of the shooter.

The downed trooper pulled himself up onto the gate and swung his arms over the top. His left leg hung limp. His rescuers stopped at the gate. Three of the officers stood guard, guns sweeping toward the direction of the house and barn.

Two others grabbed the trooper and pulled him over the gate.

"Say, boys, lookin' for a little rain?" The entire group stood under the largest tree on the property. Up in that tree was the largest nail nest. B.J. took careful aim and shot the homemade detonator. The explosion rocked the tree, splitting limbs and turning leaves and small branches into mulch.

The nails, sharp metal slivers and glass ripped into the team of lawmen, penetrating their heads, shoulders, and backs. The injured trooper received the worst of it. Being carried belly-up, his face, chest, and abdomen were fully exposed.

B.J. laughed as two of the officers opened fire at their unseen assailant. They fired wildly, blindly. Struggling to keep balance, the men backed up the road, staggering like drunken sailors.

The ambulance moved toward the group, more for cover than medical assistance, B.J. figured. The group climbed through the back doors of the ambulance, which promptly reversed back up the road.

Within five minutes the lawmen had moved their outer perimeter back another 200 yards, near a bend in the road. B.J. reloaded his rifle just as several new model cars skidded to a stop near the injured lawmen.

"And the FBI has come a-callin'," B.J. said, glancing at his watch. It was straight-up 5:00, four hours until dark. Time for final preparations.

CHAPTER FIFTEEN

Just as the sun began its late afternoon descent, B.J. saw the first signs of fresh activity. Camera four, mounted in the roof at the rear of the house, picked up movement near the fence line. A rifleman was low-crawling through knee-high weeds toward a thick clump of Johnson grass. It was one of the spots B.J. would have chosen.

An explosion ripped the man apart just as he had secured himself behind the clump of grass. B.J. mourned the loss of a fine sniper rifle.

Ten minutes later, a megaphone interrupted the silence of the communication room. "This is the Texas Department of Public Safety. We have the property surrounded. Come out of the house with your hands in plain sight."

B.J. looked at the monitor from camera one. The image hadn't changed. The dead sergeant still lay ten feet inside the gate, and Higginson's squad car was still in the ditch. The road was clear all the way to the bend.

A sudden chirping confused him until he recognized the sound of his beeper. Immediately he recognized the problem. The beeper had one purpose: to alert him if someone entered his house in Duck River, Tennessee.

All of the exterior doors on his house were armed with silent sensors. Each sensor was tied into his computer, which would alert him. He grabbed the beeper off a shelf and read the message. "Front door—zone one—front door."

"So soon."

Then it went off again. "Patio door—zone four—patio door."

A third time. "Attic door—zone six—attic door."

The attic door was concealed behind a row of boxes in the closet of a room he never used. He'd almost decided not to wire that small door because the opening was little more than a crawlspace.

The fourth beep read, "Barn intrusion—zone nine—barn intrusion." The only alarm sensor in the barn led into the tool room. The tool room held all of his reloading equipment. It also had a few empty .308 casings stamped with Billy Ray Jackson's thumbprint.

The megaphone sounded again. "This is the Texas Department of Public Safety. We have the property surrounded. Please come out with your hands in the air."

B.J. thought about his trophy room in Duck River, the place where everything was kept: all the videotapes, the collection of magazines and newspaper articles, and the surveillance notes and hand-drawn maps. He hated to lose it all.

The door to the room was an old bank vault door he'd picked up at an auction four years earlier. He'd ripped the drywall off the studs and replaced it with quarter-inch steel boilerplate. The solid steel walls were welded to an identical floor and ceiling. He had cut holes for electrical outlets and air conditioning vents, and then covered the walls with drywall and wallpaper. The bank vault door was in the master bedroom closet, behind a row of men's suits he never wore.

They'd have to use a blowtorch to cut their way in. In fact, they could use the one he had in his barn.

B.J. grabbed one of his two prepaid cellular phones and punched in a number he had ready on a small sticky note.

The phone rang at the Dallas ABC affiliate and B.J. asked to speak to the news director. An impatient man came on the line a minute later.

"Newsroom."

"You know about the standoff in Fannin County?" B.J. asked.

"That's my job."

"My name's B.J. Cagle."

A pause, then, "Don't recognize the name. Cagle?"

"I'm the one in the barn up here. I'm the Billy Ray Jackson sniper."

"Right. My mother was Marilyn Monroe."

"You've got one chance to take me serious before I call Channel Five."

B.J. heard scrambling. "Okay. You're serious and I'm writing."

"A sheriff's deputy blew himself up a few hours ago. Then about five minutes ago somebody's rifleman did the same thing. Is that what your people out here are telling you?"

"They reported a second explosion. They said it's a mine-field out there."

"That's mighty complimentary. Just a little perimeter protection. But listen, the FBI might shut off my phone any minute. Do you have a video receiver in your truck outside?"

"Yes."

"Have your technician tune to 904.850. I'll be transmitting a message to the country in fifteen minutes. My farewell speech, if you will."

The man's silence was long enough to make B.J. nervous.

"You still there?" B.J. asked.

"Yes. 904.850?"

"Right. Now that you know my real name, feel free to use it. One other thing. You writing this down?"

"Every word."

"Tell the FBI to leave their Hostage Rescue Team in Washington. I'd hate to embarrass them on a national stage."

"Let me ask you about—"

B.J. punched the end button and looked at the small camera he would use to talk to Stubs. He hoped the Plano homicide cop wasn't getting too comfortable.

Back in the barn, B.J. spotted two riflemen. One was underneath Higginson's squad car still in the ditch outside the front gate. The second was 350 yards away, at the rear of the property, beside a large rock. The rock was the best position in the back. B.J. had scouted every inch of ground within a half-mile of the house and barn. Although he couldn't see a rifleman on the west side, he knew where he'd be: in the shadow of a low-hanging branch behind a hollowed-out log, 400 yards out. At 8:17 P.M., the sun would be in perfect position for B.J. to see into the shadow of the low-hanging branch. He'd confirm the rifleman at that time.

At 7:30 P.M., B.J. crawled back into the communication room to watch the continuing TV coverage of the standoff. A wide-angle helicopter shot of the media buildup showed a crowd already as big as the small city that had gathered at the Branch Davidian siege in Waco.

B.J.'s own cellular phone rang. He had wondered how long it would take the FBI to get his number. B.J. punched the send button and heard Zeke's voice on the other end.

"Time to come out."

"Well, we finally speak," B.J. said. "Didn't know you did

negotiating. Gonna cut off my power and water? Crank up the loudspeakers so I can't sleep? Maybe offer me something?"

"That's the way it usually goes."

"Only one problem with all that, Agent Bunning."

"What's that?"

"This standoff won't last that long."

B.J. punched off the phone. He had another couple of minutes before broadcast time. It'd be dark by 9:00 P.M. and he still had a battle to fight.

He turned on the video camera and the transmitter. Figuring the media would be exiled at least a mile from the farmhouse, he'd mounted a super-gain antenna on the highest point of the roof. If ABC's satellite truck had a decent receiver, they'd pick up his transmission without many problems.

He faced the camera, cleared his throat, and talked to the world.

Later, in a far corner of the barn, where the shadows were deepest, buried under old blankets, broken saddles, pieces of lumber, and piles of straw, the body of Billy Ray Jackson lay entombed in a chest freezer barely large enough to hold his 200 pounds.

B.J. tipped the freezer onto its side, grabbed the rope long since strung around the black man's neck, and pulled Jackson across the floor of the barn next to the driver's door of the motor home. Frozen in a sitting position, hands folded in his lap, eyes open, Jackson's tongue protruded slightly through a twisted grimace.

A powerful man in life, a criminal to avoid tangling with hand-to-hand, B.J. took Jackson with a home-run swing to the back of the head. Then he'd loaded Jackson into the motor home, hauled him to his barn in Duck River, and cut his throat. The wound across the front of his neck gaped as raw and jagged as the day he had died.

Now, B.J. took care to stage Jackson's body in the right manner. He opened the driver's door of the motor home, pushed Jackson against the step, and shoved a scoped rifle under his hands and across his lap.

Props on a stage.

B.J. strapped on a bulletproof vest, stuffed shooting plugs into both ears, and fired the first shot at 8:18, when the setting sun exposed the police rifleman hidden under the shadow of the low-hanging branch. B.J. had put the round somewhere in the middle of his head.

"And the war's begun."

He ran to the north wall and found another attacker behind a small pile of rocks. The camouflage fatigues they wore would have provided an adequate disguise in ordinary circumstances. B.J. knew that. But he'd spent his entire childhood running through these fields and years playing the part of the attacker. A faint, unnatural shade of brown was the only sign that someone was there at all. B.J. placed the crosshairs in the center of the brown patch and pulled the trigger. The man rolled to the side, exposing half of his right leg, motionless.

Having fired two shots, B.J. didn't expect to find the police sniper still hiding in the ditch under the deputy's car. He was right. The man had crossed the road and ducked into heavy underbrush. He was almost around the bend, more than 300 yards away, when B.J. spotted him.

"Outrun this." B.J. shot him in the back.

No riflemen, no eyes, no intelligence—for the next few minutes they'd be lost at the command post. That meant no decisions would be made. Basic SWAT theory: they wouldn't rush the house through the minefield. Any attempt to get closer than a half-mile might be fatal. Their only option would be an armored vehicle. Waco revisited.

Within minutes he heard the thump-thump-thump of large rotor blades. He jumped down to the first floor of the barn and ran to the double doors. Through the crack he saw a chopper heading in from the south. He dropped prone and took aim.

Apache. Their new eyes.

His .308 rounds would be useless, so he backed away from the doors. The helicopter circled high above in slow, wide arcs. He wasn't sure if it was legal to use a military attack chopper on a private citizen, but it didn't matter. All this would soon be over.

The barn suddenly went dark. With no windows, and with the fading sunlight barely seeping through the cracks in the walls, B.J. stood still until his eyes adjusted. He thought about cranking up the generator and turning the electricity back on, but decided against it. Didn't want the noise. Instead, he retrieved a small battery-powered black and white TV from the motor home and tuned it to ABC. They were already reporting shots fired. The FBI wasn't commenting about the intended targets of those shots. They were not, in fact, commenting at all.

B.J. cut off the TV and walked from peephole to peephole, checking his outer perimeter.

At straight-up 9:00, with daylight nearly gone, B.J. knew he couldn't wait much longer. The FBI had been there almost four hours and a National Guard post was within an hour's drive, no doubt where they got the helicopter. He didn't want tanks knocking his barn down Waco-style.

Time to press the issue, draw them in. Five hundred yards from the barn, the FBI had set up large portable lights that illuminated the road almost to the front gate. B.J. dialed his scope and started shooting. One by one the lights flickered out. He worked the bolt like a man possessed. Soon the entire perimeter fell to darkness, perfect for his night rifle.

Through the green-tinted scope, B.J. saw two men low-crawling toward the dead rifleman, who lay under the low hanging branch on the side of the barn. He shot them both in the leg.

"Cry for help," B.J. whispered.

Press the issue. Draw them in.

In back, they were attempting a rescue of the dead man near the pile of rocks. Three officers approached the body behind a ballistic shield. Stupid. No ballistic shield could withstand rifle fire.

B.J. lit it up, firing several rounds through the center. The officers scrambled and B.J. hit one somewhere near his ass.

Press the issue. Draw them in.

The low rumbling of truck engines drew his attention to the front of the barn. A dump truck loaded with sand was backing toward the front gate. An old SWAT trick. Dump trucks made great moving barricades if you didn't have an armored personnel vehicle. And backing it protected the driver.

He had pressed the issue and drawn them in.

He smiled as the final act got underway.

The truck had double rear axles and he shot the rearmost tires. The truck didn't stop, but it bogged down. Then he splintered both outside mirrors. Still coming. He couldn't tell if any officers were shielded behind the front of the truck, too dark. But the truck continued, rumbling slowly toward the front gate.

Then a second dump truck appeared in the distance. This one empty, its box open to its full height, the tailgate swinging back and forth as the truck backed toward the gate.

The heavy steel of the box protected the driver from taking shots through the back window. The tailgate protected the back tires. B.J. didn't see cops staged up behind the second truck, but he understood SWAT tactics.

They were coming.

The lead truck rumbled past the dead rifleman in the brush, past Higginson's car in the ditch, finally stopping at the gate.

B.J. watched, calculating how long before the SWAT team would be in position to assault the barn.

The lead truck drove over the gate, backed around the mangled body of the sheriff's sergeant, and headed straight down the driveway toward the house. It crossed trip wires, setting off explosions, ran over mines, setting off more explosions. With its back tires ripped to shreds, the truck continued on rims, digging deep gouges in the dirt driveway.

The second truck was gaining ground, following the exact route as the first. The first truck was clearing a path through the mine field. Smart. And now it was too dark to see the SWAT team behind the second truck.

Time.

B.J. ran over to Billy Ray Jackson's body, stuck a .45 automatic against the dead man's temple, and pulled the trigger. The impact of the bullet on Jackson's frozen skull was different than normal, not as messy. Bits of bone imbedded into the open motor home door, encircling the hole made by the bullet. Not much else.

"I told you," B.J. whispered to Jackson, "that your death would be a much publicized event. Thanks for the fingerprints."

B.J. patted Jackson on the arm, grabbed both of his sniper rifles, slid under the motor home, and crawled into the tunnel opening. He scooted the large piece of boilerplate over the tunnel opening and dropped onto the tunnel floor.

He dug a flashlight from his back pocket and flicked it on. The beam of light traveled only a few yards before being swallowed by the darkness. He found the small wire in the dirt and followed it until he reached the electronic ignition device ten yards up the tunnel.

The charges in the house were blasting caps placed next to mayonnaise jars filled with kerosene. The flames would catch quickly, enveloping the old house like a tinderbox. And the barn would go up even faster with the straw and old, weathered lumber.

B.J. dragged his rifles past the ignition box and crammed his flashlight into the dirt with the beam pointing up. He tried to remember how fast the dump trucks had been approaching the barn and figured that by now they'd still be seventy or eighty yards away. Still enough time.

Knowing that the SWAT team would assault the barn as soon as they could make a safe approach, B.J. had to get the fire going now. He didn't need some bloodthirsty cop, playing hero, entering the barn before it burned to the ground.

So he flipped the switch.

He imagined the small explosions, the whoosh of the igniting kerosene, the flames spreading throughout the old buildings. Within a couple of minutes, certainly by the time the SWAT team was ready, entering either structure would be suicide.

The wires running into the tunnel would burn away. Not completely, but enough to hide the tunnel openings. B.J. had an urge to peek into the barn. But foolish mistakes got people killed. The fires were out of his hands now, so he picked up his flashlight, grabbed hold of the two rifle slings, and began crawling toward freedom.

After only a few feet he stopped. Faintly, no more than a slight disturbance in the air, B.J. could hear the roar of a growing fire. On his hands and knees, he dropped his head to the ground, rested his forehead on the backs of his hands, and held his breath. The crackling of burning timber was unmistakable.

Then he heard gunfire. Only faint pops from this deep in the tunnel, but gunshots nonetheless. Single shots at first, and then more rapid explosions as the fires in both house and barn worked their way to the outer walls. He'd placed hundreds of bullets on the floor of both buildings, a guarantee against any brave cop who tried to be a hero and save B.J. from the flames.

B.J. began again, carefully dragging his rifles by their slings, careful to keep the barrels and scopes off the ground. The tunnel was cool and damp. He had crawled the tunnel more than two dozen times in preparation for this very situation and his best time had been twenty-two minutes.

After another fifteen yards, the outside noises faded completely. His breathing, the scraping of his back against the wooden ceiling, and the rifle butts dragging in the dirt were the only sounds.

Despite the coolness of the tunnel, B.J.'s clothes were soaked with sweat. He stopped to catch his breath after another fifty yards, lying still on his belly, wondering what was happening up top.

The end of the tunnel spilled into a dried-up creek bed that the neighbor to the north used as a dump. Rusted washing machines, bed frames, an old chest freezer, and other junk served as the perfect camouflage to the one-foot hole he would enlarge when he made his exit. He had cut the bottom out of the chest freezer and then secured the lid from the inside. Then he'd rearranged the junk around the freezer so it wouldn't slide away during thunderstorms.

He started crawling again and thought about Stubs. B.J. wasn't sure if Stubs had seen the broadcast. If not, he would soon. B.J. had scripted his words carefully to give nothing away to the FBI. But if Stubs possessed even one creative bone, he would know that the current version of B.J. Cagle was *his* creation. And that would be enough.

For now.

It took B.J. nearly an hour to reach the end of the tunnel. He was now 600 yards behind the back of the barn, at least 200 past the dead rifleman. He could hear, faintly, two helicopters circling, it seemed, in wide, sweeping arcs.

A backpack full of food and equipment lay at the end of the tunnel, as did a small pickaxe and entrenching tool.

He laid his rifles down, dropped his backpack, and stretched out, his head close to the small hole. The fresh air was comforting, even though he wouldn't get the full effect until he opened the freezer door in a few hours. Right now he needed sleep. He confirmed that the alarm on his watch was set for 4:00 A.M. and closed his eyes.

He sat in the quiet living room trying to catch up on a novel he'd started two weeks before, but never finished. The TV, tuned to CNN, sound muted, provided a distraction when his mind started to wander, a common occurrence during the last week. The words in the book failed to keep his attention for more than a couple of minutes at a time.

B.J.'s face was the constant distraction, a face he'd seen before but just couldn't place. Most disturbing was the twisting in his gut every time CNN showed his picture, as though some suppressed nightmare had materialized into the world of the living. Though he didn't suffer from nightmares, B.J.'s features seemed eerily familiar.

A flash on the TV pulled his eyes from the book. He'd kept up with the story throughout the evening by occasionally disabling the *Mute* button.

He did so now when B.J.'s face popped up on the screen. Dropping the novel onto the floor, he stood and took a step toward the TV screen showing B.J. sitting on the floor, dressed in camouflaged Army BDUs, staring into the camera, his back against a wall. The grainy picture flickered in and out as B.J. settled himself and prepared to speak.

"Good evenin'," B.J. said. *"I doubt the FBI is gonna let me talk for very long, so I'm gonna get right to the point."*

B.J. cleared his throat and grabbed a piece of paper from somewhere to his right. His southern accent was pronounced; a slight nasal twang gave his voice a Gomer Pyle sound.

Familiar, like his face.

"I ain't wantin' to be held up in here any longer than I have to," B.J. said. *"I know those boys outside don't, either. I'm not in much of a mood to make demands. In fact, don't have any. Soon as I'm through talkin', I'm gonna kill everybody I can see out there and be done with it."*

B.J. paused and wiped a hand across his nose. He glanced at the ceiling and sniffed. Then he looked back at the camera. *"One side of my brain wants to tell my story. The other . . . don't."*

On the TV a cell phone rang in the background. B.J. glanced to his left, but didn't answer. *"I ain't as bad as people think. Sure, I've taken some people from our society, I admit that. And I admit to causin' some disruption. But I had reasons. Valid, legitimate reasons. In fact, I've already seen a TV report describin' what happened to my wife and child."* He paused and cleared his throat. *"That whole thing made me crazy. Well . . . maybe not crazy in a legal sense, but I ain't worried about that, because everything's fixin' to be over with."*

B.J. paused again and stared hard at the camera. *"Only thing left to answer is why I killed the cops. Since I was a cop, maybe that'll be the hardest thing to understand."*

B.J. leaned forward, his voice strained. *"Let me retract that statement. It'll be hard for everybody but one man. That man's a cop, too. He's the reason. And 'cause I never got to finish what I started, maybe he's thinking he's lucky. But is he lucky? Maybe one day he'll find out."*

The cell phone rang a second time. B.J. ignored it again. *"I knew this cop when I was a kid. Blood brother. Thought we'd be friends for life. But I was wrong. He started this a long time ago."*

B.J. smiled, his lips stretching tightly across his teeth. *"To my old friend, I say this. I've made arrangements for after tonight, after I'm gone. You will be held accountable."*

The screen went black.

He dropped to his knees and stared in disbelief as a CNN anchor began recapping B.J.'s broadcast.

He punched the *Mute* button, his hand shaking with such force he nearly dropped the remote control. B.J., from Camp Indian Hill. Dear God.

A bead of sweat trickled down his forehead as he paced the floor in front of the TV. *I created this monster! I'm responsible for all this!*

He slumped back into his chair, his mind racing. On the TV, CNN had switched back to live reports from Trenton. They showed the burning buildings in the distance. B.J. was suspected dead; they'd reported that nearly thirty minutes before.

But he had to see for himself. It was the only way.

He walked in silence to the spare bedroom and pushed open the door. Rush was asleep, but jerked awake when the light from the hall shone onto his face.

280

"What?" Rush asked. "What's wrong?"

"I'm the cop he was after," Chinbroski said flatly. "I'm B.J.'s blood brother. He was the kid I let take the rap for a murder I committed almost thirty years ago."

CHAPTER SIXTEEN

Chinbroski clammed up until Rush agreed to accompany him to Trenton, to the burning farmhouse where B.J. Cagle was presumed dead.

Just as Rush got the car headed north, an all-news radio station reported that the FBI and state police had encircled the farmhouse and barn to ensure that Cagle hadn't escaped during the confusion of the fire.

Chinbroski clicked off the radio and looked out the window, silent.

Rush glanced at him through the darkness. His partner's face was tense. "Why are we going up there?" Rush asked finally. "What's the point?"

Chinbroski said nothing for a moment, then looked over. "I have to be sure. I want to see his body."

Rush nodded. Understandable. "Okay. Fine. Now start talking. What's going on?"

Chinbroski started slowly, his words peppered with pauses and hesitations. Then the story came easier, as the chain shackling the memory fell away. He described the immediate friendship with B.J., the fact both had lost a parent. Chinbroski told of their common goal to win the shooting

The Shooting Season

championship. Inseparable, they were, to the exclusion of all others.

Their differences were an attraction, a natural mystery through which they fed off each other's strengths to cloak their own insecurities. Chinbroski from the city, B.J. from the country; Chinbroski stout and strong, B.J. slight and weak; Chinbroski brave and daring, B.J. cowardly and timid.

Not much had changed in that regard, Rush thought as Chinbroski told the story, except on B.J.'s part. Chinbroski was still physically strong, brave, daring; but B.J. had more than compensated for having been a slight, timid little boy. And daring didn't come close to describing his incredible string of shootings.

Chinbroski continued the history of that summer at Camp Indian Hill. He told Rush of the blood-brother pact, of his insistence that they go squirrel hunting before camp broke, of firing the shot that had killed Jay Harrington, and finally, of the Judas-like betrayal of his friend.

Chinbroski hung his head as he spoke, his voice drifting in and out, rarely looking at Rush, opting instead to gaze out into the darkness. Rush asked no questions, not wanting to disrupt the revelation of a story that had probably never been told to anyone else. Chin was baring his soul, the pain evident in his voice.

The story ended as Chinbroski related how he had stolen the trophy that clearly belonged to the best shot in camp.

"I should have withdrawn from the championship match. Should have walked up to that deputy leading B.J. out of camp, given B.J. the trophy, and turned myself in." Chinbroski sighed and looked out the window for several moments. "But I didn't. I did nothing right during those fourteen hours. It's hard to believe it was even me."

Rush just drove, considering his partner's anguish. What a

God-awful thing, to think that you were responsible for creating a monster like B.J. Cagle. Of course, Chinbroski wasn't responsible for creating Cagle, but Rush knew his partner well enough to predict his current mindset.

"I've replayed all of it ten thousand times," Chinbroski said, his voice barely audible over the road noise of the car. "Me, a scared little kid, so fresh from losing my mother, afraid of losing everything else, of standing up and admitting my guilt. That just wasn't me."

Rush kept his eyes on the road, not sure if Chinbroski would continue.

When he didn't, Rush said, "You initially said you let B.J. take the rap for a murder. But that was no murder."

"Just a technical point. I pulled the trigger, the kid died, B.J. was arrested."

"And charged with what?"

"I never found out. I lost track of him until I was on my own. Hell, I didn't lose track; I was in no position to research until I was older. But just before I left for the Marine Corps, I went to Oklahoma and tried to find out what happened. His juvenile file was sealed. So I asked around and discovered that B.J. and his mom had moved to destination unknown several years earlier. This farmhouse we're heading to was abandoned. Evidently, B.J. and his mom moved when B.J.'s grandfather died." Chinbroski turned in his seat and looked at Rush. "I was gonna make it up to him. Somehow. I tried to find him."

The pleading in Chinbroski's voice chilled the back of Rush's neck. He had never heard his partner like this.

"I was wrong. I was a stupid kid who did a stupid thing. And three homicide cops died because of it."

Rush considered arguing the point, considered pointing out the obvious, but Chinbroski wasn't ready for logic yet.

"So we're going to see a body," he said instead.

"I have to confirm it myself."

Rush didn't think they'd be seeing a body until the ashes cooled enough to sift through, probably mid-morning tomorrow. He wondered if Zeke would even let them into the crime scene.

"I'm assuming you want this kept quiet," Rush said.

Chinbroski said nothing, not bothering to state the obvious, Rush figured.

"So you were a good rifle shot?" Rush asked.

The big man shrugged, mumbled something indistinguishable.

"I've never known you to enjoy rifle shooting."

Chinbroski looked at him. "Lost interest, Rush. Shit."

"Right. Stupid of me. Do you own a rifle?"

"No."

Rush slowed the car and turned east on a small Farm-to-Market road leading toward the outskirts of Trenton. The asphalt was still sticky from the heat of the day. The painted lines in the center of the road were faded. Darkness pushed in on the car.

"Why?" Chinbroski asked. "You thinking I'll need one?"

"No, no. Not at all. I know you're not a hunter, but I thought maybe, you know, rifle shooting might be a private thing for you. Just curious."

Chinbroski stared at him. After a while he grunted and turned toward his window.

The gravel road leading to the farmhouse was a busy place, but all the vehicles were heading away from the dying story. Rush drove the car at a crawl due to the dust and darkness. After several miles they reached the media contingent, still large enough to clog both sides of the road for over a quarter mile. A couple of crews were recording live shots. Probably for West Coast stations, Rush thought as he approached two sheriff's cars blocking further access.

Rush pulled to a stop and lowered his window. "Hi," he said, hanging his badge out the window. "We're the lead homicide team from Plano on the Jackson shootings. Came up to close out our cases."

The deputy inspected Rush's credentials and shined his flashlight close enough to light up Rush's face.

"So you were the lead?" the deputy asked.

"Right." Rush glanced at Chinbroski, then back at the deputy. "He and I."

"Bet you're glad this thing's over."

Rush chuckled. "Should be getting drunk, but we've gotta do this last thing." Rush pointed toward the farmhouse. "Agent Bunning up there?"

"Yes, sir. Told me not to let anybody in. But I doubt he meant you. He know you're coming?"

"We were with him when he got the call," Rush said. "I gave him directions."

Rush dropped the car into gear and put his badge away.

The deputy nodded and stepped away. "He's over by the barn."

Rush waved and edged his car forward. Both sides of the road, stretching almost a half-mile, were jammed with vehicles. There were marked units from the sheriff's department and highway patrol, but most of the cars were rentals, no doubt belonging to dozens of FBI agents.

A medical examiner's station wagon was parked near the front, as were three ambulances and a crime scene van from the state police. Rush pulled his car off to one side, careful to position it so he wouldn't block anyone in.

"Wonder how many are dead up here," Chinbroski said.

"How many B.J. took with him."

"It's over, Chin. Let's go look at this son-of-a-bitch and get the hell back to Plano."

The barn and farmhouse were still burning. Small flames danced among the wreckage, just enough to cast a red glow over the faces of those milling around. The smell was strong, a mixture of soot and burned flesh. Rush saw Zeke near the fireplace of the farmhouse and headed his way.

In the barn, the shell of the motor home, with the barn's roof in piles around it, looked like a bomb had gone off inside. No glass in the windows, tires burned off the rims, black smoke still pouring from inside. It might take weeks to sift through everything.

Zeke noticed Rush and Chinbroski heading his way and met them halfway between the house and barn.

"I was wondering if you two would show up," Zeke said.

"So this is it," Rush said. "His final resting place."

"Appears so," Zeke said. "Be awhile before we find him, though. We're not searching until everything's cooled off."

"Why not squirt it down?" Chinbroski asked. "Get his body hauled out?"

"Evidence," Zeke said. "An order straight from the director. Our arson people will be here by noon tomorrow. I put one drop of water on that fire and I'll be riding a desk in San Juan."

Waco repercussions, Rush thought. He and Chinbroski might as well leave now.

"Could he have gotten away?" Chinbroski asked.

Zeke laughed. "No. Not possible. We had two birds up. One with a spotlight, one with FLIR. Anybody running from the house would have been seen. Plus, once the fire was fully engaged, we surrounded the place. Cagle didn't survive."

Chinbroski nodded, relaxed a measure, Rush thought.

"This is a classical response of the profile we had on him. The mindset of—"

"You see Cagle on TV?" Chinbroski interrupted.

"Yes. That was me calling his cellular while he was talking. A spoken suicide note. One thing was evident: his hatred for the cop he knew as a kid." Zeke paused and looked at Rush. "That wasn't you, was it?"

"No," Rush said. "That wasn't me. But it doesn't matter now."

"Zeke!" someone called from near the edge of the barn. "Over here!"

Three men with FBI blazers stood near the ruins of the barn doors. They aimed flashlights toward the burned husk of the motor home. Rush and Chinbroski followed Zeke over and immediately saw what had caught the agent's attention. Leaning against the open driver's door were the charred remains of a body, an apparent male by the looks of the muscle structure. Only his shoulders and head were distinguishable among the burning ruins. Much of the roof had collapsed around the motor home, burying the body mid-chest. The smell of burned flesh drifted toward them.

"Is it him?" Chinbroski asked.

The skin on the corpse was as black as the roof timber lying across his lap. In addition to having no features, the face appeared to be covered with a heavy layer of soot.

"Won't know till we dig him out," Zeke said. "If it is, he was bigger than we thought. Look how wide the shoulders are. The fire didn't do much muscle damage."

Rush saw the same thing. And the head, besides being cocked at an all-too-familiar angle, looked bigger than what Rush remembered seeing the night he and Chinbroski had chased him.

"How'd the fire start?" Rush asked Zeke.

"Blasting caps and jars of some type of accelerant. Our SWAT team was within a minute of making entry into the barn when they heard simultaneous explosions and smelled what they think was kerosene." Zeke looked at Rush and pointed at the body. "The way his head is angled, it almost looks like he shot himself."

"I agree," Rush said. "I've seen a couple of dozen that looked just like that."

Rush pulled his shirt away from his sweaty chest. The July night was warm enough without standing near a fire.

Chinbroski stood transfixed, staring, as if trying to recall a distant memory that would somehow confirm that the impossibly recognizable body was indeed that of B.J. Cagle.

Rush pulled at his arm. "Come on, partner. Let's go get some sleep. We'll come back tomorrow and be here when they drag him out."

Chinbroski stared for a moment longer before turning toward Rush. "Right," he said. "Tomorrow."

They told Zeke that they'd be back by 9:00 A.M., then headed back to the car. For Chinbroski's sake, Rush hoped for the best. But a feeling deep in his gut told him that his partner would never be the same after tonight.

The chirping of his wrist watch alarm pulled B.J. out of a satisfying sleep. He came awake instantly, cut off the alarm, and listened for any other sounds. Nothing.

Four A.M. was the true witching hour. It was the deepest part of the night, the point when the human body most desperately begged for rest. Those guarding the perimeter of the barn—if, in fact, anyone *was* guarding—would be running on a quarter-tank at best.

With less than two hours before dawn, B.J. wasted no time. He flicked on his flashlight, unfolded the shovel, and started digging out, pushing dirt forward into the old freezer. Within a few minutes, he was unlocking the padlocks that had kept the lid to the freezer secure from human scavengers.

He cut off his flashlight, let his eyes adjust to the darkness of the tunnel, and pushed the freezer door open an inch at a time. The cloudless night and full moon offered no natural gloom to cloak him. But at least the gully full of junk, with its shadows and variety of dark colors, allowed him a small measure of concealment.

The FBI had replaced the lights he'd shot out earlier, and the glow from their command post illuminated the sky over his scorched barn. B.J. crawled to the front of the gully and peered over the edge. The scene was quiet, and from 600 yards, he could see no one moving about. No sound of rotor blades, no chatter of police radios, no one shouting orders: they were letting the fire burn itself out. Just as he knew they would.

He quietly crawled back into the freezer, reached into the tunnel, and removed his two rifles and his backpack. After slinging everything onto his back, he crept carefully to the narrow mouth of the gully, which led directly away from the farmhouse.

The hike to his truck would take him the better part of an hour. His route wound through woods, across fields, and over a single-lane bridge that served only three families. He didn't expect to cross paths with anyone, but he had his .45 holstered under a loose-fitting shirt in case he did.

The fact that his truck wasn't at the farmhouse would probably spark discussion between Agent Bunning and his FBI minions. Eventually, B.J. predicted, the FBI would decide that he had ditched it because its description and tag number had been broadcast steadily for nearly forty-eight hours. But had B.J. ditched it, he would have been forced to steal something to replace it. And although he had one complete set of fake IDs, including credit cards and credit history, marriage license, the death certificate of his wife, and the title to a small plot of land in rural Missouri, he didn't dare risk something so traceable as a car rental until he underwent a major appearance change.

So he was left with his truck, fitted with one of the three sets of license plates he'd stolen from a salvage yard off similar year trucks. The national media had covered the siege at the farmhouse, and consequently, law enforcement everywhere had probably stopped watching for his late-model Chevy.

B.J. jogged through a maize field belonging to the farmer who left all the junk in the gully, and within ten minutes he was over a mile from his farmhouse. He was sweating under his load but he kept his pace steady. The full moon, a hindrance when he emerged from the freezer, was welcomed now. He cleanly avoided obstacles pitting the rough terrain, ducked under low-hanging branches, and scaled the sagging barbed wire fences without tearing his pants.

He had seen no one during his run, and found his truck still covered with the same number of branches. He disabled the alarm, dragged off the branches, and loaded his equipment on the back seat.

Wiping the sweat off his forehead at a few minutes before 5:00 A.M., he cranked the engine and drove north into the night. Everything he needed to finish his battle with Stubs was in place and waiting for him at Camp Indian Hill.

Soon it would be party time. All he needed was the guest of honor.

At 9:10 the next morning, Rush and Chinbroski stepped from Rush's unmarked into eighty-five-degree heat and walked toward the ashen remains of B.J. Cagle's barn. Chinbroski had said little during the drive up, preferring instead to gaze out the window, his lips moving soundlessly.

Rush wondered how, after this, his partner could tie the knot in two weeks. Although Nanci was a fighter who'd survived a brutal rape, Rush knew her attraction to Chinbroski lay in his humor, his optimistic outlook on life.

Chinbroski faced danger with a twinkle in his eye and braggadocio in his voice. But he had fallen quiet when Cagle shot the Plano doctor a week ago. Rush wondered if somehow his partner had felt his thirty-year-old sin coming home to roost. Maybe the long-range shootings had opened a channel to Chinbroski's past.

Rush spotted Zeke huddled with five other agents near the front doors of the barn, where they had stood to inspect the burned body the night before. Four of the agents wore FBI Crime Lab coveralls, a cruel requirement given the heat.

Chinbroski stopped several feet to the side of the group and stared at the charred body still slumped against the open door of the motor home. Flies were buzzing and Rush knew that it wouldn't be long before other insects invaded.

Although thin spirals of smoke drifted skyward, no heat radiated from the ruins. Rush overheard Zeke giving specific instructions regarding the handling of the body. Zeke looked ragged, as though sleep were something he had abandoned at middle age. His pants were black to the knees, and his arms to his elbows. Black smudges covered his face and neck, a result of swiping at trickling sweat.

Rush stood quietly next to Chinbroski until Zeke finished his briefing with the crime scene team and strolled toward them.

"Ready to close your books on this case?" Zeke asked.

"More than," Rush said. "Looks like you've been searching already."

"This is from only fifteen minutes in there." Zeke looked at Rush and Chinbroski's clothing. "You're staying out here, I guess?"

"Just here to take notes," Rush said. "How soon until you ID the body?"

"I'd say several hours yet. It appears Cagle shot himself. The barrel of the gun is sticking up through the ashes near his right leg."

"Sure it's him?" Chinbroski asked.

Zeke looked at him and frowned, his streaked face sagging from fatigue. "No guarantees, but I'm confident. Facial features, fingerprints, gone. But we've got dental records coming from Cagle's dentist in Tennessee." He sighed. "Know soon enough. Why?"

Chinbroski shrugged, staring at the body. "He's been a slick S.O.B., that's all. Hate to jump the gun, then have it bite us in the ass." He looked at Zeke. "And we need medical certainty for our reports."

"You'll have it," Zeke said. "But it'll be late this evening."

Chinbroski nodded and looked at the body again.

"Rush," Zeke said, "I know we haven't talked about it, but I want you to know that I hold no ill feelings about your keeping me out of your crime scene the other night. You had a right. And given the psychology of this case, I might have done the same thing. I'll give you whatever paperwork you need to wrap this up."

Rush nodded. He didn't give a shit how Zeke felt and wished he could say so. "Thanks," he said instead. "The dental records should be enough." He gestured at the body. "Maybe the autopsy report and a few photos."

"You got it. Now if you'll excuse me, I need to clean up

and change clothes." Zeke shouted at a couple of other FBI agents and headed their way.

"It's him, Chin," Rush said quietly. "B.J. Don't let your imagina—"

Chinbroski's cell phone cut Rush off.

Chinbroski pulled it from a pocket and punched it up. Within seconds his face went white, he dropped to one knee, and placed a hand on the ground for balance.

"Stubs? Cat got your tongue?" B.J. dangled his feet off the ledge of the flat rock that overlooked the remains of Camp Indian Hill, the very rock where he and Stubs had given their blood oath. The valley was quiet and peaceful.

B.J. could hear voices in the background, but couldn't discern any words. He wished he had a video of Chinbroski's face.

"How'd you get this number?" Chinbroski finally asked without a trace of fear.

"I was a cop, remember? Talked one of your lovely CID clerks into transferring the call. Don't hang up, though. This is your only chance to save yourself."

Stubs said nothing, which irritated B.J. Stubs owed him at least a small measure of concern. Hell, a measure of respect! Then B.J. recalled how calmly Stubs had lied to the camp director. With ice in his veins as a thirteen-year-old, B.J. could only imagine Stubs's poker face after almost thirty years. A shiver of admiration raced down the back of B.J.'s neck. Chinbroski might actually be worthy quarry.

"I suppose the barn's cool enough to start digging around in there," B.J. said. "Tell Billy Ray hello for me."

Chinbroski grunted and B.J. thought he heard a catch in the cop's throat. Not a noticeable sign of fear, but unmistakable nonetheless.

"A tunnel system," Chinbroski said quietly, the words punching through the phone as though he'd held a hand near his mouth to prevent being overheard. "Ingenious."

"That's why I couldn't let the standoff become a fiasco," B.J. said. "Couldn't risk somebody like you eventually thinking of it."

"Well," Chinbroski said, his voice fluttering just a smidgen, "I'd have never thought you'd crawl into a tunnel."

When Chinbroski didn't continue, B.J. recognized the game. So he played.

"And why is that, Stubs?"

"I assumed you were still a pussy, the same little faggot who freaked out when I piled up rocks at the mouth of that cave."

B.J.'s face heated so fast he thought his ears might bleed. He started to speak but cut himself off. He would *not* fall for such a juvenile trick. He'd played it himself while he was a cop.

"Not a pussy anymore, Stubs," B.J. chuckled with effort. "But listen, I've only got fifteen minutes on this pre-paid cell. So, much as I'd love to swap insults, I ain't got the time. You got a pencil and paper handy?"

Chinbroski's muffled voice instructed someone to hand him a slip of paper.

"Your loyal partner eavesdropping? Please tell the great detective hello. And sorry about his retarded wife. Hope he doesn't miss her too badly. Should be relieved, actually. He can have a sex life again."

Several seconds of silence, then, "Ready," Chinbroski said. "You know, I'm glad dumb asses talk slow. Makes note-taking easy."

B.J.'s laugh was genuine as he climbed to his feet and began pacing the flat rock. "Nice try, Stubs."

"It's coming back to me. Manipulating you."

B.J. squeezed the phone, clamped his jaws shut, and stopped at the edge of the rock. He could see the spot where Stubs would most certainly park his car sometime within the next five hours. He would deal with Stubs's insolence then.

"Just a few items to cover," B.J. said. "First, I burned up in that fire. That's all anyone else needs to know for now. They'll figure out soon enough it ain't me. But by then you'll be up here engaged in a fight for your life."

"Up where?"

"Come now, you're not that stupid. Second, bring the weapon of your choice. Knowing, of course, what I'll be using. Third, since it appears you're joined at the hip with Rush, he can come if he wants. I would expect no less from a dedicated partner. That's all. Any questions?"

B.J. heard rustling over the phone, a light breathing. Stubs didn't speak for several seconds. Finally, "And assuming I don't come?"

"You'll never know what meal will be your last," B.J. said. "And you'll never get another chance. Once I kill you, I'll kill your partner. Then your sweet Nanci. Loved her picture in the wedding announcement, by the way. Might even get to know her once you're gone."

When Chinbroski didn't respond, B.J. continued. "I estimate a window of approximately ten hours to complete our disagreement. Any longer than that and the FBI will have determined that I didn't cook in that fire. Then Higginson, my only true friend from childhood, the deputy who found me at the farmhouse, will tell them about Camp Indian Hill."

B.J. sat down on the flat rock again and dangled his feet over the edge. "So, to make a complicated situation simple, I'm leaving these mountains at seven tonight. Either I kill you before then or I kill you when you least expect it." He paused, then chuckled. "Or, of course, you or your partner could kill me."

More rustling, more breathing. Chinbroski still said nothing.

"My fifteen minutes are nearly up," B.J. said, looking at his watch. "So listen closely to this. From my rock here, as you probably remember, I can see the entire valley. If I see one hint of anyone besides you and your partner, I'll disappear into my new identity. And you'll live every day shitting your pants at even the smallest noise."

"And my ten-hour clock has started," Chinbroski said.

"Tick, tick, tick."

"Not much time for a fight. It's a four-hour drive and I still need to pack."

B.J. laughed. "Pack. Don't insult my intelligence, Stubs. You want time to develop a plan of attack. But that's why I'm letting Rush tag along. Best do some brainstorming on the drive up."

Chinbroski sighed loudly into the phone. "I haven't shot a rifle since the Marines. Is this the kind of lopsided battle you're after?"

"Bring your trophy from Camp Indian Hill. Maybe it'll give you confidence."

B.J. punched off the phone and threw it as far as he could into the valley below.

Chinbroski looked at the phone and fumbled with the *End* button. He finally gave up, tossed the phone to Rush, and shoved his quivering hands into his pockets.

Rush turned off the phone and watched his partner walk toward their car, head down, shoulders slumped, face as white as a dead man's.

The physical shaking, the quivering lips, the strained

voice, the bloodless face: only one man could have done that to Chinbroski. None of the FBI agents seemed to notice Chinbroski with one knee on the ground, chin tucked onto his chest, staring at the ground, but Rush had maneuvered himself into a blocking position, regardless.

Now, he followed Chin over to the car. His partner opened the passenger's door, sat sideways in the seat, and wiped his sweaty brow.

"So, we're not out of the woods?" Rush asked him.

Chinbroski looked up at him and smiled thinly. "Woods. Funny you should say that. No, we're not out of the woods yet."

Rush glanced at the body still leaning against the open door of the motor home. The crime scene technicians were approaching the charred remains from two sides, slowly sifting through the wreckage.

"We need to hit the road," Chinbroski said. "We'll talk on the way." He looked at his watch and cursed. "Hurry, Rush."

The intensity of the drive back to Plano steadily increased as Chinbroski relayed the phone conversation with B.J. And a plan slowly developed in Rush's mind.

"I don't know what to do," Chinbroski said when he finished the story. "I know I have to fight. For your sake, for Nanci's. But tactically I'm at a total loss."

"How well do you know the area?"

"You mean: how much do I remember? Very little. It's been a long time. And there's no time for reconnaissance."

Chinbroski described what he could recall: the four mountain peaks that formed a bowl, at the bottom of which sat Camp Indian Hill. Parts of the rugged terrain were impassable, with thick underbrush. Only one narrow road had led into the camp, and that was nearly a mile long.

Rush glanced at his watch and calculated how much time would remain when they hit the front gate of the camp. Probably not enough.

He'd drop Chinbroski at his house, run home, grab a few things, make the most important phone call of his life, then retrieve Chinbroski.

"Rugged country," Chinbroski said, finishing his description. "An incredible advantage for him. I can just see him leading us into some wild-ass trap he's had ready for years."

An incredible advantage was an incredible understatement, Rush thought. Alone, they had no chance. Which was why the timing loomed so large.

Timing. Diversion. Luck. They'd need all that. And B.J.'s ego. If B.J. decided to shoot them as they drove into the camp, all would be lost.

But Rush didn't think the son-of-a-bitch was capable of that. He'd want to talk, to crow, for at least a little while.

At one time Chinbroski had wanted to apologize to his old friend. Whether or not he still did made no difference: Chinbroski *would* apologize. But would the words die on his lips?

CHAPTER SEVENTEEN

Rush stopped the car in a swirl of dust and shoved it into *Park* within a mile from Camp Indian Hill. Five hours left. The play clock, half gone.

Chinbroski's signs of being a basket case had dissolved the closer they got to the Ouachita Mountains. More focused now, they discussed the details of the plan; the *ifs, ands,* and *but*s of failure; the odds of winning. As each mile passed beneath them, Chinbroski had slowly reverted to his old self. Rush wondered if his partner had been expecting this battle for thirty years. Relief seemed to be settling over him.

The equipment in the back seat, mostly borrowed from a gun shop in east Plano, would give them a fighting chance.

Then again, they might be ambushed before they drove through the front gate.

As the dust settled around the car, Chinbroski pointed straight ahead. "If I recall, about a half-mile up the road takes a dip, then passes through a cutout with rock walls forty feet high on each side. A hard right a quarter mile past that, then a couple hundred yards of straight dirt road."

"You remember all that from thirty years ago?"

"No. I drove up here the summer after high school, before

I shoved off for the Marines. Retraced most of the places B.J. and I went that summer." Chinbroski looked out the side window and shook his head. "Like walking through a bad dream you've had a hundred times over."

"Okay," Rush said when Chinbroski fell silent. "You say no gate. Just an opening."

"Right. Used to be a little building where visitors would write their names. Weren't allowed to drive past that building."

"So," Rush said, "this is your game. Drive in or walk?"

Chinbroski blew out a breath and shook his head. "I've been thinking about that for the last thirty minutes. Pros and cons to each. I think B.J. would expect us to drive up."

"Why?"

"Just a feeling. He knows we're coming, so why not drive? Besides, we need the car's PA system."

"We brought a bullhorn."

"Let's just drive," Chinbroski said. "How long?"

Rush glanced at his watch. "Four hours and fifty-five minutes."

"We gotta keep him talking how long?"

"Twenty minutes, give or take."

"Then we talk him into shooting at us," Chinbroski confirmed.

"Right."

Chinbroski shook his head again. "Shit."

"My word exactly," Rush said, as he put the car into gear.

Opening all the windows, Rush drove slowly enough to prevent the road dust from drifting into the car. The forest pushed in tightly on both sides and blocked out the mid-day sun. The soft purring of the car's engine, mixed with the sound of the crunching gravel, blocked out any sounds of nature. The smell of cedar drifted in and Rush wondered if he'd

301

ever smell it again without flashbacks. Stupid thought. Flashbacks would mean he would survive today. He was suddenly a big fan of flashbacks.

He slowed the car to a creep as they approached the cutout. He scanned the cliffs towering above the road, but saw no signs of an ambush. Chinbroski sat perfectly still, staring straight ahead.

"Like waiting for a damn bomb to explode," Rush whispered.

Chinbroski said nothing as they drove through the cutout.

"Less than a half-mile?" Rush asked, once clear of the cliffs.

"Right."

Past the sharp turn, Rush saw the opening to the abandoned camp 200 yards ahead.

"Grab the radios from the back," Rush said.

Chinbroski reached around and retrieved what might prove to be the most critical pieces of equipment they had in the car.

As they approached the front gate, Chinbroski held one of the radios out of the window. With his other hand, he picked up the PA microphone and keyed it up.

"B.J.," Chinbroski said, his voice echoing through the camp. "This is Stubs. We have a radio to give you. Call me on my cell. Tell me where to leave it."

Rush stopped next to the remains of the visitor sign-in building and shut off the car. The popping of the cooling engine was the only sound he heard. Nothing from the looming forest.

"Teepees were that way," Chinbroski said, pointing left, "about two hundred yards."

Although Rush couldn't yet see the sleeping cabins, what buildings were visible at Camp Indian Hill had survived for the most part. Constructed from thick logs, their only real signs of decay were the sagging rooflines. Wild grass and weeds grew right up to the front doors of most of the structures. Rush saw the skeleton of a baseball diamond fifty yards to the right.

"Looked a lot better in its day," Chinbroski said.

Chinbroski's cell phone hadn't rung.

"What do you think?" Rush asked. "Try again?"

When Chin didn't answer, Rush looked over. His partner sat staring straight ahead, his gaze slightly raised.

"The big, flat rock," Chinbroski said. "At the top of that peak. Can't see it without optics, but I'll bet he's there."

"How far?"

"Eight hundred, maybe a thousand yards." Chinbroski turned toward Rush. "Feel just a little exposed?"

"Just a little. Try the PA again."

He did. And they waited. The phone didn't ring.

"Remember," Rush said, climbing from the car, "no weapons yet."

"Right. He wants a battle, not a massacre. Psychological tidbits, by Greg Rush."

Rush scanned the deserted camp as he made his way around the front of the car and past the sign-in building. Chinbroski followed behind.

"Look," Chinbroski said, shoving a fist past Rush's face. "On that stump outside the director's building."

Two radios. "I'll be damned," Rush said.

Chinbroski hurried past him and stopped in front of the stump.

They were small Motorolas, yellow, two-mile range. Rush had seen them for sale at electronics outlets.

"Shall we?" Rush said, picking one up and turning it on. "Hello?" he transmitted.

After several seconds of silence, Rush looked at Chinbroski and shrugged.

"Let me try." Chinbroski picked up the other one and turned it on. "Are you watching from the flat rock?" he asked, gazing skyward.

B.J. laughed over the radio. "So I should give up my position within the first five seconds?"

"Time for your monologue," Rush whispered, tapping his watch. "Just over fifteen minutes."

Chinbroski nodded and strolled out into a treeless area, in the direct line of fire from the flat rock on the mountain.

"Before we begin all this," Chinbroski transmitted, "I have some things to say."

"I thought you might," B.J. said. "And I'll let you speak before I put a bullet in your head."

Rush glanced at his watch and slowly strolled toward the car. Turning the volume up on the small radio, he clipped it to his belt and scanned the camp for any sign of B.J.

"First," Chinbroski said, "is my overdue apology for what happened here so long ago. I was a stupid, selfish, and confused kid. I know it sounds hollow now, but I mean every word. You didn't deserve what happened."

Rush reached the car and opened the back door, looking back at his partner who had found something to sit on. Rush pulled out two soft rifle cases and two backpacks. If B.J. was watching, and Rush assumed as much, he would expect them to prepare for battle.

"I tried to find you a few years later," Chinbroski continued. "But you and your mother had moved. I wanted to set things straight."

Rush carried a rifle case and backpack over to his partner. "Sound like you mean it," he whispered to Chinbroski as he leaned over and set the backpack on the ground.

Chinbroski nodded. "I tried to find out if you had been charged with Jay Harrington's death, but couldn't get into the files. I still don't know. Were you?"

The radio remained silent for more than a pregnant pause. Rush returned to the car and pulled a rifle out of the remaining case.

"No," B.J. finally said. "They didn't charge me. They put me through an interrogation the Nazis woulda been proud of, but they couldn't prove anything because I never changed my story. Pretty easy to do when you're tellin' the truth."

"I joined the Marines out of high school," Chinbroski said. "I wanted to set it all straight before I left. I figured that if you'd been charged with something, I could get a court somewhere to overturn it. I'm glad you weren't."

The rifle Rush held in his hands was one of four identical rifles for sale on consignment, having belonged to a five-time national bench-rest shooter. The champion had willed the guns to his only child, a daughter who volunteered one afternoon a week in Rush's unit.

"You don't know how happy that makes me," B.J. mocked, "that you're glad I wasn't charged. But this flimsy attempt to make me believe you didn't find us after we moved is pathetic."

Rush jerked his attention toward Chinbroski. What was this?

"What are you talking about?" Chinbroski asked.

"Let's not play games, you lyin' bastard. I've spent more than a decade tracing your movements since high school. You murdered my mother just before you shipped off to Paris Island."

The quiet of the forest closed in on Rush. He stood statue-still, desperate to hear Chinbroski's reply.

His back to Rush, Chinbroski sat slumped over, his face

lifted toward the flat rock a thousand yards away.

"Don't insult me with a denial," B.J. continued, his voice hard, "or I'll shoot you where you sit. I know about the two-month driving tour you took before basic training. How much time did you spend in Nashville: a few hours, a day, a week? Or did you just swirl into town, find my mom and me, and then stalk her long enough to run her off the road?"

Rush knew about the driving tour. Chinbroski had often said it was the best two months of his life. And he'd gone to Nashville. He'd often bragged about bumping into Conway Twitty inside a broken-down truck stop.

But this?

Chinbroski said nothing. He stood and slowly turned to face Rush. Rush couldn't read his expression. Sweat slicked his skin. Even from where Rush stood, he could see Chinbroski's hands quivering. They locked eyes. Then Chinbroski shook his head slightly and turned around to face the distant rock.

Rush stared at the back of his head trying to interpret the head shake. *No, I didn't do it? No, I did it, but can explain every-thing?* Rush knew his partner well enough to—But did he? This whole camp thing, shooting the kid. Shit! Murdered B.J.'s mother?

Chinbroski hadn't begun removing his rifle from its case.

Rush glanced at his watch. Ten minutes.

"So you don't deny it," B.J. said. "I thought not. I also know about the conspiracy surrounding the murder of my wife and son. You obviously underestimated me."

Rush had just slung the rifle across his chest when B.J.'s words stopped him again.

"Doctor Kenneth Marisell," B.J. continued. "Ob-Gyn, University of Oklahoma Medical School. Married his med-ical-school sweetheart, a Tennessee beauty who eventually became a successful eye surgeon. Doctor Kenneth followed his lovely bride to Nashville a week after they graduated."

The radio went silent and Rush found himself holding his breath.

"You recognize the name, Stubs?" the radio asked.

Chinbroski said nothing. He stared at the distant rock and simply shook his head.

"No? He was in cabin 23 that fateful summer. You beat him in the first round of the championship."

Rush's cell phone rang. He grabbed it off his belt and dropped down below the window of the open car door.

"Rush," he whispered.

"Zeke, here. You ready?"

B.J. was talking on the radio again. Rush had to hear this. "Hold on."

". . . you deny."

"Okay, yes," Chinbroski hesitated. "I think . . . I remember him."

"Of course you do. He murdered my wife. Butchered my son."

The blood coursing through Rush's head nearly prevented him from hearing Zeke yelling at him on the cell. He put the phone to his ear.

"Yes," Rush said. "We're ready. Haul ass. It's not going like I planned."

Rush punched off the phone, clipped it back on his belt, and stood.

Chinbroski still hadn't started unpacking his rifle.

Rush threw on his backpack and strode over to his partner.

Chin's radio hung limp in his hand; his face was sweat-slicked and blotchy red from staring into the sun at the mountain.

"Damn it, get ready," Rush snapped in a hissing whisper.

"We're under five minutes."

Chinbroski looked at him, his eyes almost distant.

"Do what your partner says, Stubs," B.J. transmitted. "Now a couple of questions for you, Rush. Who was on the phone? And five minutes until what?"

Rush frowned at the question. A thousand things to think of, a thousand scenarios to consider. Too damn much to prepare for in such a short amount of time. As he stared at the radio in Chinbroski's hand, he knew what B.J. had done.

Holy God, Mother of Mary. This possibility had slipped through the cracks. Just a couple of dumb asses.

Rush peered up at the distant rock.

Then B.J. spoke again. "You bastards."

A shot rang out. Chinbroski tumbled to the ground. Rush sprinted toward the nearest building and dove through the empty doorway as a second shot sounded. He landed face-first on the dirty wooden floor, then immediately rolled, holding the rifle high in the air to prevent damaging it. He scrambled to his feet and ran back to the door.

A trampled area in the high grass next to the place Chinbroski had been sitting easily gave away his location. Rush heard nothing from his partner, saw no grass moving.

A third shot, then a fourth. What was he shooting at? And from where? He couldn't determine the exact origin of the shots. Direction, but not distance.

Chinbroski still wasn't moving. Rush looked at the radio clinging to his pocket. His gut told him to smash it against the wall. But he might need it.

He glanced at his watch. Three minutes. He hoped.

After a quick search of the three-room building, being careful to avoid the windows, he found a back door already standing ajar. He crept through and circled around the end, hugging the edge. Back at the front corner of the building, he squatted and peeked just enough to check on Chinbroski. He was about to call out when he remembered the radio.

He jerked it off his belt, turned it over, slid off the battery cover, and removed the batteries.

"Chin," he whispered. "Can you hear me?"

No response.

"Take the batteries out of the radio and talk to me."

Nothing. No sound from his partner, only a hissing sound that Rush recognized immediately: a leaking radiator. B.J. had disabled their car.

Ten yards, Rush estimated, from his position to Chinbroski, ten suicidal yards.

If Chin were dead, Rush needed to find a safe hiding place and wait this whole thing out. If not, Rush needed to drag him to safety.

Rush dropped to his belly, said a quick prayer, and started a slow, careful feet-first crawl toward his partner. Although the tall grass offered concealment, it would also telegraph his advance, which was why he went feet first. Didn't want to take a head shot.

His backpack, stuffed full of tactical toys, shifted to one side and pressed against his kidneys. Rush readjusted and continued to inch his way toward Chinbroski, separating the grass with his feet, trying desperately to disturb as little as possible. After a few feet he stopped to listen for signs of life from his partner.

Still nothing.

He started moving again, gripping the rifle, sweat running into his eyes, dust filling his nostrils. A few more feet. He looked back, carefully pushed aside a large clump of grass, and saw the top of Chinbroski's head several feet away.

"Your five minutes are almost up," B.J. transmitted over

Chinbroski's radio. "Stubs, are you playing dead? Is this part of your plan?"

Still looking at the top of his partner's head, Rush whispered again. "Are you hit?"

"I don't think he is," B.J. answered. "The first two shots—"

B.J. was cut off in mid-sentence.

"Rush," Chinbroski whispered. "Sorry. Took me a minute to get the batteries out. Get your ass back behind cover."

"Don't move until I throw the smoke," Rush said. "Be just a minute."

Rush crawled back behind the corner of the building, stood, and removed three smoke grenades from his backpack.

"Get ready," he ordered Chinbroski. He pulled the pin and threw the first grenade five yards past his partner.

Dirt exploded at the edges of the rapidly expanding smoke, bullets smacking the ground. Then the report of the shots rang out. Rush suddenly knew a small thing about B.J.'s location. With the bullet arriving so far ahead of the sound, some serious distance was involved.

Chinbroski started a frantic belly crawl toward the building seconds after Rush threw the second grenade directly in front of him.

More shots. Chinbroski flattened himself in the dirt and pulled himself forward with his elbows, dragging his rifle and backpack behind him, the small radio clutched in his hand.

"Hurry!" Rush whispered, tossing the third grenade a couple of feet from the corner of the building.

In one violent lunge Chinbroski threw himself around the corner of the building at Rush's feet.

"Time," Chinbroski gasped. "How soon?"

"Any minute now," Rush answered. He pulled the AA

batteries from his pocket and put the first one in the radio. "Talk to him, Chin. And keep him talking until the Cavalry arrives. But let's do it from inside." He shoved in the second battery, handed Chinbroski the radio, and stepped past him toward the back of the building.

"We're ready, B.J.," Chinbroski said, his voice vibrating. "You about cheap shots? Shooting at us before we're ready?"

Rush stepped through the back door with Chinbroski on his heels.

"The smoke was good," B.J. said. "Ready for some real smoke? Best get your ass out of that building."

Chinbroski spun toward Rush, his eyes wide. *Explosives?* he lipped.

"Tick, tick, tick," the radio said.

"Go! Go!" Rush shouted, shoving Chinbroski toward the back door.

Chinbroski exited at a sprint, Rush nearly climbing his back. Rush followed his partner to the baseball field, then hung a left, racing straight for the largest building in sight.

B.J.'s laughter drifted from the small radio and sent a chill down Rush's neck.

Chinbroski stopped outside the front door of the large building, gasping. "Cafeteria," he said.

He turned to enter and Rush clamped a hand on his arm. "Wait," he said, wiping sweat from his eyes. "That first building might have been a freebie. Before we barge in another—"

A massive explosion from behind threw both of them against the wall of the cafeteria. Rush dropped to his knees and covered his head, his ears ringing like a train whistle. Chinbroski dropped to the ground and clamped his ears.

Dirt, debris, and wood mulch rained down on them. The ringing in Rush's ears made him dizzy as he scrambled around to the side of the building.

"Stay out and play, boys," B.J. mocked over the radio. "Hidin' in the buildings ain't allowed."

Through the dust and smoke Rush saw Chinbroski crawling on his hands and knees toward him. No rifle, no backpack.

"Your gear!" Rush shouted.

Chinbroski stopped, disappeared back around the corner, then emerged seconds later with his rifle and backpack slung over one shoulder.

Rush looked toward the flat rock on the mountain. "If he's up there," Rush said pointing, "there's no way he can see us now."

"The trees," Chinbroski agreed.

"Maybe I have cameras," the radio said.

"Shit!" Rush yelled, grabbing the radio from Chinbroski. He ripped off the back cover and flung the batteries to the ground. "We can't operate with him listening to every damn word."

"Where's our help?" Chinbroski asked, his eyes wide.

"How do I know? Zeke said any minute." Rush turned away and breathed heavily. "Know what he's doing to us, all this shooting? Playing." He took another breath, then scolded himself. They *had* to stay calm.

"Where else would he be?" Rush asked. "We don't know that the shots came from the rock."

Cordite-filled smoke drifted across the camp as Chinbroski considered Rush's question. There were hundreds of places B.J. could be, Rush thought. Thousands. They didn't have a prayer without some help.

Rush visually searched every tree and building around them, but saw no evidence of surveillance cameras. He wondered about a tunnel system.

"Any caves?" Rush asked.

Chinbroski looked at him and nodded. "At least one. Probably more."

"Can you find it?"

"While dodging bullets?"

Rush glanced at his watch. Zeke and his army should've been here by now.

"We need to do something," Rush said. "Get our radios from the car, spread out. See if we can find him. 'Cause this sure as hell isn't going like we planned."

"I'll go to the car. This is my battle. You wait here. Give me five minutes."

"Brilliant, Chin. He shoots you, then disappears forever. I'll go. As long as you're alive, he hangs around. And give me ten minutes."

Rush picked up the radio batteries. "Where's your radio?"

"Gone. Maybe blown up. I think I dropped it inside the director's building."

"Find someplace to wait. But not near any buildings."

Rush installed the batteries, clipped the radio to a pocket, then headed toward the car.

He cut across the far edge of the baseball field, just inside the weed line, duck-walking most of the way. By the time he'd made it halfway through left field, his legs were on fire.

"I hear some heavy breathing," B.J. said through the radio. "Is it Stubs or the great detective?"

Rush considered ignoring him, but then realized that his plan still hinged on B.J. being somewhere in the valley when Zeke and the rest of the Cavalry arrived. "It's Rush."

B.J. chuckled. "I really didn't expect the two of you to come alone. Although I haven't seen anyone else yet, I'm prepared for whatever you might throw at me."

B.J. sounded confident. And Rush could certainly understand why he would. The bastard was dismantling Rush's plan brick by brick.

"I don't expect you to give anything away," Rush said. "But what would you have done in our place? How would you have attacked this problem?"

B.J. laughed again. "Clever. Excellent. I have a cerebral opponent." He paused. "But to answer, knowing what I know . . . I would have fled the country and never come back."

Rush stopped at the edge of right field and poked his head above the weeds. A couple of small fires burned inside the exploded building, but nothing that caused Rush any concern. The car was still another sixty yards west. To his left was a stand of thick pine trees. Not much cover or concealment under those, but at least he could move from trunk to trunk. He low-crawled in that direction.

"Or," B.J. continued, "if I was Stubs, I'd have committed suicide. It's hopeless for him. Should've just ended it. See, there's no way to catch me, Rush, regardless of what you have up your sleeve. And if I don't get Stubs today, I'll get him later."

"Chinbroski didn't kill your mother," Rush said, pushing his way toward the stand of pines. "He didn't plot to kill your wife and child. You've twisted everything around in your mind and put Chinbroski in the middle."

"You're an authority on your partner's dark secrets?"

B.J. had spit the words into the radio.

Hardly, but Rush wouldn't admit that.

"You knew about Camp Indian Hill?" B.J. asked.

"Of course."

"You're a lying bastard."

"And I knew about how he tried to find you." Rush reached the edge of the tall grass and belly-crawled behind the closest pine tree. Then he stood. "Why don't you just admit that somewhere deep inside your head some wires got crossed and you turned into a monster."

Rush darted to the next tree.

"Did you see my TV broadcast?" B.J. asked.

"Reruns. It led in the Nielsens."

"And you've gotten a typical bullshit briefing from Agent Zeke, so you know my history—a revenge killer. After I kill Stubs, I'm through with the messy stuff. Except to stay out of jail. I'll never go to jail. But am I crazier than Stubs, who started this whole thing? At least I can justify my killings. His was for the sport of it."

Rush's cell phone rang.

"Oh, good," B.J. mocked. "An update."

Rush set the radio on the ground and covered it with pine needles. Then he sat down and pressed the top of one of his legs against it to muffle it even more.

"Rush," he said into the phone.

"Sorry for the delay," Zeke said. "Had a breakdown. We're one bird down, but still plenty strong. Any ideas?"

"He's in the valley. That's as close as I can get you. Maybe on the flat rock I told you about earlier."

"Stay alive for ten more minutes." Then Zeke punched off.

After darting past another couple of trees, Rush could see his car. But a thirty-yard clearing loomed ahead. A suicide run.

"Stubs found a cozy little hiding place," B.J. said. "In one of the few places I can't shoot him."

Rush darted a final time, behind one of the largest trees in the stand. A chunk of wood exploded near his head. The report from the shot arrived a half-second later.

"Evidently you haven't found such a spot."

Standing perfectly still, Rush held his breath and made sure his entire body was behind the tree. Then he turned sideways, cutting his profile in half, and felt better. Until his rifle flew from his hands, and the blast echoed through the valley.

"Shouldn't leave your weapon exposed," B.J. said.

The rifle landed a couple of feet away, the stock splintered. Rush sighed relief. Still operable, assuming the scope hadn't been jarred out of place.

He closed his eyes to picture his position in relation to the layout of the camp and surrounding mountain peaks. The shots were coming directly from the north. Other trees would have prevented such a shot from diagonal east or west.

"Are you calculating?" B.J. asked, reading his mind. "Do you know where I am?"

Controlling his breathing, Rush answered with as much courage as he could muster. "Trying to get a handle on it." Keep him talking, Rush thought. Help will soon be flooding these hills. "Why not use your silencer? Seems stupid not to."

"You're distance-shooting ignorance is showing, Rush. Accuracy. Besides, by the time the sound reaches you, it's little more than an echo, hell, almost a rumor. Think your rifle still works?"

"I hope so."

Rush's rifle jumped as a bullet smashed the scope and tore into the trigger assembly.

"How about now?"

Sweat dripped into Rush's eyes but he was afraid to raise his hand to wipe it away. He clenched his teeth to keep them from rattling.

"Wonder if Stubs thinks you're dead? Think he might slip out of his hole to find out?"

Rush had no way to tell Chinbroski not to. What fools

they'd been to leave their radios in the car.

Hurry, Zeke!

"Well, speak of the devil," B.J. said, humor dripping from every word. "Mr. Stubs. Come on out. Just another couple of inches."

Nothing except his .45. Rush calculated his chances of making it back to Chinbroski.

A shot rang out. Rush flinched and held his breath.

"I think my business is done," the radio announced after a moment of silence. "Detective Rush, have a nice life."

CHAPTER EIGHTEEN

As an animalistic rage swelled his throat, Rush battled back an urge to scream and charge up the mountain like a Rough Rider at San Juan Hill.

Chinbroski dead? Impossible. But when had B.J. ever missed? Tears flooded Rush's eyes while he cowered behind the tree, afraid to move. His gut churned with indecision about what to do next.

If Chinbroski were dead, he didn't need the radios any longer. In fact, he had no reason to stay at Camp Indian Hill a moment longer.

Then again, B.J. was escaping, and that was reason enough to stay.

Rush wiped his eyes and drew his .45 as a single thought took hold: B.J. had just turned himself from the hunter into the hunted. Rush would *not* allow him out of these mountains alive. He looked at his handgun and knew it wasn't enough. Rush had to find Chinbroski; he needed his partner's rifle.

He had to find his partner for another reason: confirmation. Although B.J. had been quiet for the last few minutes, Rush couldn't discount the possibility of this being a charade, an attempt to draw him out from behind the tree.

While deciding what to do next, Rush heard a sound sweeter than anything he'd ever heard before: the whirl of helicopter rotors, distant, but everywhere.

His cell phone rang.

"Rush."

"We're approaching the valley," Zeke said. "You should hear us by now."

"How many?" Rush asked.

"Six birds. Nine canines should be within a mile of the front gate." Zeke's voice sounded distant against the backdrop of the helicopters.

"How many on foot?" Rush asked. "And how close are they?"

"One hundred and four FBI, thirty-three national guard, and eight from the local sheriff's office. Grouped in threes. They've just started moving in and should have a tight outer perimeter within the next thirty minutes."

Rush sighed heavily, relief washing over him. The plan was to put a fuel tanker a few miles away and rotate the helicopters after the first couple of hours, fueling them during the pilots' rest periods. As the first chopper became visible in the distance, Rush looked at the radio clipped to his pocket and wondered if B.J. was still listening.

"I'm high over the flat rock now," Zeke said into the phone. "Looks like there's something there. I've got agents escorting some bloodhounds up there from the back side of the mountain. Also, we found B.J.'s truck about six miles from here. I put a team on it in case he slips through."

Rush told Zeke about the explosion, that he suspected B.J. had activated the bomb via remote control. He also mentioned the possibility of cameras, listening devices, booby traps, and tunnels. "He's had years to prepare," Rush said. "The search needs to be thorough, but done carefully." He didn't mention Chinbroski, couldn't bear to. He'd check that out himself.

"He won't slip through," Zeke said. "Every bird has infrared and half the dogs are bloodhounds. We're setting up an infrastructure for the long haul. We'll search until we find him."

He sounds confident, Rush thought. Just like he did at the beginning of this mess.

"We'll hook up later," Rush said. "Good luck up there."

Rush punched off the phone, grabbed the radio, and keyed it up. "If you're still listening, you bastard, pay attention. I'm coming!"

He took the batteries out, tossed the radio to the ground at his feet, and smashed it with his heel.

The sky was full of helicopters now, and Rush could hear the baying of the approaching dogs. He stayed behind the tree until he saw a small army approach the camp from the same direction he and Chinbroski had, nearly forty-five minutes before.

Feeling the time was right, Rush darted from tree to tree until he came to the edge of the stand of pines. But instead of crawling across the outfields of the old baseball diamond, he sprinted directly down the middle, dodging this way and that in case B.J. was still perched somewhere, watching.

Shortly, he was back at the front door of the old cafeteria. Chinbroski was nowhere to be seen. He stepped around the corner where he'd last seen his partner and saw nothing that would have served as a hiding place.

Rush was at a disadvantage because he didn't know the layout of the camp. He'd told his partner not to hide in any of the buildings. The question was how far he would have strayed, knowing Rush would return with the radios.

He could hear the baying dogs being spread out in a

straight line across the front of the camp. They'd do a line search straight down the center and then repeat the process side to side. He wanted to find Chinbroski before the dogs did.

To Rush's left were the remains of the director's building. Behind him, the baseball field. To the right sat a small building and the old swimming pool, enclosed by a rusted, eight-foot chainlink fence.

The swimming pool! Rush sprinted there and immediately saw a spot where the fence had been pulled up. He dove to the ground, scrambled under the fence, and ran to the edge of the concrete hole.

Chinbroski crouched near the shallow end, rifle ready, the left side of his face covered with blood. Eyes wide and jaw set, he spun toward Rush, raised his rifle, then cursed. "Damn it, Rush!" he whispered. "Ever think of announcing yourself?"

Rush nearly collapsed in relief.

"And I'd get your ass down here if I was you."

Rush dropped into the pool and pointed to Chinbroski's face. A gouge ran from his temple to the back of his head.

"Grazed me," Chinbroski said. "The son-of-a-bitch." He pointed to a pockmark just under the lip of the pool. "Bullet went in there."

Filled with relief, Rush inspected the bullet hole and looked toward the mountain with the flat rock.

"Already did that," Chinbroski said. "Could've shot from almost anywhere up there. I didn't hear shit. Not that it would've helped."

As the helicopters made swooping arcs above them, as the dogs slowly approached from their rear, Rush relayed being pinned down behind the tree. "I thought you'd bought it."

Chinbroski lightly felt the groove across the side of his

head. "So he *does* miss. He'll really be pissed when he finds out."

"Yeah? Let him. He'll never get out of this valley."

Rush slung Chinbroski's rifle. "We've got to clear out while the dogs search the valley. Let's go."

They climbed the steps at the shallow end and headed for the hole under the fence. The line of searchers was almost upon them. Rush waved to the nearest canine handler and pulled up on the fabric of the fence until the hole was twice as big. Chinbroski crawled under.

"If you were trapped in this valley, where would you hide?" Rush asked as he slid under the fence.

Chinbroski helped pull Rush to a standing position. "You think he'll hide, not run?"

Rush shrugged. "Can't see him fighting it out. And if he can't escape, he'd hide, right?"

Chinbroski shrugged. "Or eat his gun."

"But if he hid . . ." Rush headed toward the cafeteria building.

Chinbroski shuffled along beside. "A cave, maybe. But that'd be the first place we'd look. Maybe he's got another tunnel. Or some hole dug in the side of one of the mountains. Shit, where couldn't he hide?"

Rush nodded. "Hey, they found his truck," he said after a moment. "Got a team waiting for him." He stopped and looked at his partner. "How about under one of these buildings? Some kind of bunker."

They stopped near the back of the cafeteria. Rush looked for anything that might indicate explosives, but knew he wasn't qualified to recognize anything but the most obvious device.

"Could he be gone by now?" Chinbroski asked. "Think that's possible?"

"With this crafty bastard? Yes, it's possible." Rush stepped away from the building. "Let's stay clear of any buildings. He could still be watching."

Rush headed toward their disabled car.

"I'm not leaving these mountains until I see his dead body," Chinbroski said, "or I kill him."

Rush stopped and studied his partner.

"No matter how long it takes," Chinbroski continued.

"Nanci will—"

"The wedding's off until I tell her it ain't. And I called her just before I attempted to crawl out of that pool to check on you. She won't see me again until this is over."

Rush frowned.

"I've got nine weeks of vacation saved. I'll use every hour if I have to. If he's in this valley, I'll starve him out."

"Sounds like that crease on your head did wonders for your judgment." Rush started walking again.

"I ain't kidding, Rush. If he's gonna kill me, he's gonna do it up here, not when I'm sitting in a restaurant with Nanci three years from now. And she understands that."

Rush couldn't blame him for taking this stance. It was nice to see his fire had returned. "How's your head?"

"Better than I thought. Hurts like hell, but I can function."

They walked in silence for a moment. "There's one other option," Rush said. "One tactic we could use against B.J."

"What?"

"He thinks you're dead. Said his job was finished. We could let him continue to believe that."

"And?"

Rush chose his words carefully. "Create a Plano PD version of witness protection. If we don't catch him, I mean."

Chinbroski stared at him as they walked, his brow furrowed, evidently processing the full extent of what Rush had suggested.

"You talking about faking my death? Changing my ID? Moving?"

"Might work," Rush said.

Chinbroski snorted. "I got a shot in the head, Rush. At least I've got an excuse for making stupid suggestions like that."

"What's stupid? If he's already out of this valley, we'll never see him again. I'll bet his new ID is so complete the neighbors already know him. Give him a few months and he'll look nothing like he does now. The only way you'll breathe easy is if he continues to think you're dead."

They both shielded their faces as a helicopter made a low pass and threw dirt in their direction.

After the noise died down, Chinbroski said, "You talking about a funeral and everything?"

"We could pull it off," Rush said. "We could get the ME to do the death certificate. Have a small, closed-casket service."

Chinbroski rubbed the back of his neck, his face hard in concentration. Rush let him chew on it for a few moments. They approached Rush's car from the front. Antifreeze soaked the ground under the radiator.

"Why don't you think it over?" Rush said. "We'll monitor how the search is going between now and tomorrow morning. If we don't find him by then, you can call Nanci." Rush placed a hand on his partner's shoulder. "You could even pick a name that isn't Polish."

His partner smiled. But it was a tight smile, and his eyes were distant. Then he seemed to focus and looked straight at Rush.

"Okay, I thought it over. Not only no, but hell, no. I appreciate you wanting to help and everything, but the whole idea is crap. I ain't about to let that sick bastard make me change my name."

Sudden shouting caused both of them to spin around. One of the dogs yelped, then screamed; a pain-filled, agonizing scream. The commotion came from the center of camp. Several other searchers ran in that direction.

Rush and Chinbroski sprinted that way as a gunshot ended the dog's cries.

In a small clearing next to a broken-down playground Rush found a group of men standing around a coffin-sized pit. The men were silent, staring into the hole. Rush pushed his way through the crowd and peered inside. One of the bloodhounds lay at the bottom impaled by four poles sharpened to needle points. The spikes had pierced the dog's stomach, neck, chest, and one back leg. A gaping hole in the dog's head was from the mercy killing.

An older man wearing denim overalls had dropped into the hole and laid the dog's head on his knees.

"What kind of sick bastard . . ." somebody mumbled softly. No one replied, allowing the dog handler to mourn silently.

"I'd like to say something," Rush said loudly. "I'm Detective Greg Rush from Plano PD. I'm the one who called Agent Bunning and told him to arrange this search party. I don't know how much you've been told, so I apologize if I'm about to cover old ground."

Rush slowly backed away, forcing everyone's attention away from the hole. "You all know who we're after: B.J. Cagle. He's had years to prepare these mountains for battle. This . . . unfortunate incident is an example of his preparation. He's somewhere in these mountains. I'm convinced of that. But this manhunt might be the most dangerous thing you'll ever do. If one of your dogs tries to lead you inside one of the buildings, don't go until it's been checked. Zeke brought his entire team with him from Cagle's old hideout in Texas. That includes three bureau bomb techs. They'll start clearing the buildings soon."

Rush made eye contact with several of the men. "Cagle got away once when we thought we had him trapped. He *will not* be taken alive. And it's too late to change any traps he's set in this valley. Go slow, be careful. I don't want to lose anybody out here."

Rush turned away and headed back toward his car. Chinbroski followed without saying anything.

Rush's phone rang.

He punched it up. "Rush."

"Zeke here. Two of our bloodhounds have a scent," he said, with no helicopter noise in the background.

"Where?"

"The flat rock you told me about. We airlifted a team of dogs halfway up the back side. You and Chinbroski want to come up?"

"Yes."

"I figured. Should be a chopper setting down behind your car in a couple of minutes."

Rush looked skyward and saw one heading straight for him. "See you in a minute," he said to Zeke before punching off.

He turned to Chinbroski. "They've got a scent. Near the flat rock."

Chinbroski adjusted the .45 on his hip, and looked straight at him. "Let's go catch this bastard."

The helicopter took off like a rocket, circled high above the camp, and headed north toward the rock. From the air

Rush could see just how overgrown the camp had become. Chinbroski pointed out the field where the teepees once stood, the tree line where he'd taken the shot that eventually killed Jay Harrington, and the remains of the shooting range.

Over the headset, Chinbroski told Rush about the research he'd done on the camp, prior to joining the Marines. Word of the shooting had spread like wildfire, and even though the camp banned rifles the next year, attendance dropped steadily until the camp finally closed a short three years later.

More burden to bear, Rush thought, as the chopper swung around to the back side of the far mountain. He kills a kid, ruins another kid's life, turning him into America's most wanted, then bankrupts a family enterprise.

They rode in silence the rest of the way. The pilot brought them around and set one skid down on a washed-out gully two-thirds of the way up. None of the mountains were towering, and they would pale in comparison to the Rockies, but Rush dreaded the climb regardless.

An FBI agent wearing jungle fatigues led them up the steep slope. They followed the dry gully until it disappeared in the trees near the top. The agent led them left, through a stand of small cedars, then up a steep patch of basketball-sized rocks.

Zeke met them just as the ground flattened at the top. Chinbroski bent over at the waist for a breather as Rush shook Zeke's hand.

"Sorry we couldn't drop you in closer," Zeke said. "But the dog handler was afraid of blowing the scent around." Zeke looked at Chinbroski and his eyes went wide.

"He's lucky," Rush said, anticipating Zeke's question. "Cagle thinks he's dead. We hope."

"Enough about me," Chinbroski said. "What do we have up here?"

"Follow me." Zeke turned and pushed through some thick underbrush into a small clearing. Two bloodhounds sat panting off to the right. An overall-clad handler, dressed much like the man who'd lost his dog in the pit, stood behind them, both leashes clutched tightly in his hands. Rush nodded and stopped behind Zeke as he pointed straight ahead.

"The infamous flat rock," Zeke said.

Sitting directly in the center of the rock was a small pile of clothes and a pair of shoes. The clothing, army fatigues, appeared thrown there haphazardly, and included dirty socks, a tee shirt, and underwear.

"No question the best vantage point in the entire area," Zeke continued. "After Jed, here, let his dogs sniff the source material, they immediately alerted on the pile of clothes."

Rush's stomach clenched. This was strange, had the appearance of being careless, but thus far B.J. hadn't been careless. These clothes meant something and Rush doubted he'd know what until it was too late.

"How come the dogs are just sitting there?" Chinbroski asked, his face tight with concern. "You shouldn't have shut them down just to wait for us."

"Didn't do that at all," Jed, the handler, said, in a thick southern drawl. He gave a command to his dogs, then strolled over.

Grizzled is how Rush would describe him. Tobacco stains on his chin, a three-day beard, unkempt graying hair, and boots worn through to his socks.

"Lost the scent," Jed continued. "Needed to wait twenty or thirty minutes, anyhow. So it didn't make no difference."

"How does waiting help the scent?" Rush asked.

Jed turned away and unleashed a stream of brown spit into the weeds. "Needs to settle," he said, wiping his chin. "Left a scent pool on the rock, but once he moved, went airborne. Had to wait."

"He said a person's scent is like a mist," Zeke said. "It pools on the ground when a person is stationary for a period of time. But once they're on the move, it floats around awhile before it settles."

"Wind could blow it," Jed added. "Not much up here today, so that's good. But you gotta be careful and read the wind."

Rush glanced at Chinbroski, who wore a blank expression. Fresh blood had seeped from his gash.

"He means that the wind could blow a scent across a field and trap it against a row of hedges before it finally settles," Zeke explained. "The dogs would track the scent along the hedges, even though the suspect never actually ran there. So you have to read the wind and then try to anticipate exactly what's what. That's why the chopper didn't drop you off up here."

"Should be 'bout ready now," Jed said. "If you boys will just stand back, we'll get to it."

Rush turned and noticed a few other FBI agents standing several yards behind them. Chinbroski moved back some, Rush and Zeke followed suit.

"On command!" Jed yelled at the dogs. They both came alive. Jed pulled a small zip-lock baggie from a pocket, opened it, and waved it under the noses of both dogs.

"Where did you get the source sample?" Rush asked Zeke.

"From Cagle's house in Tennessee. Had it flown out at the beginning of the standoff at the farmhouse. In case we needed it then."

Rush nodded as the dogs practically jerked Jed across the

clearing to the pile of clothes. From the clothes they started circling, making wider and wider arcs until they both finally turned in circles at the edge of the rock and sat down.

Jed put his hands on his hips, led the dogs back near the tree line, and gave them an aggressive rubdown.

Chinbroski looked at Rush and shrugged. A cold chill raced down Rush's spine.

"On command!" Jed shouted again. And again the dogs jumped to attention. This time Jed guided the dogs along the tree line of the small clearing, and then through the trees, slowly circling behind and around all the officers. The dogs sniffed the air primarily, but occasionally dropped their noses to the ground.

Rush's gut twisted tighter with every passing minute.

Finally, Jed gave up, parked the dogs, and strolled over. "Nothing. Only scent is them clothes."

"Shit," Chinbroski mumbled under his breath.

Was B.J. ever up here? Rush wondered. "Does it matter how old the clothes are?" he asked Jed. "Could he have left them up here a couple of days ago?"

"Hell, could've left them up here a year ago, long as the scent didn't get washed out." Jed spit again.

Zeke faced Rush and Chinbroski.

"Chemical suit?" Rush asked. "Is that what you're thinking?"

Zeke nodded. "That'd be my guess. Can get them about anywhere. And he had to know we'd bring dogs." He paused and looked at Chinbroski, who had paled. "This doesn't mean anything," he attempted to say with conviction. "We still have everything sealed off." He waved one of the other agents over, took the man's radio, and gave it to Rush. "Here, never got a chance to give you one of these. I'm going air-borne again. Want a ride back down?"

Rush gazed out over the valley, glanced at the pile of clothes, and sighed. Was it possible for an army of law enforcement officers to be in over their heads against one man?

Not only possible. Probable.

By the time the sun dropped below the horizon, the search team had formed a ring around the valley as tight as a hangman's noose. Rush had to admit that Zeke had done a masterful job of arranging his resources.

Zeke's command post was a large military tent erected just outside the cliffs overlooking the road entering Camp Indian Hill. With a large topographical map of the valley and surrounding mountains, he charted forward progress like a field general in the midst of war.

The helicopters were rotating, keeping four of the six in the air at all times. The pilots, armed with FLIR units, could clearly see the warm bodies of each searcher against the cooler temperature of the ground. An FBI agent in each chopper marked smaller topographical maps, then relayed the information to Zeke.

Several other piles of clothes were found, and each discovery threw Rush into a deeper depression. The bloodhounds were tiring, and as the shadows drew deeper, became more easily distracted. Once the clothes were removed, an effort to clear the valley of B.J.'s scent, the dogs detected nothing.

The searchers themselves, grouped in threes, were instructed to stop all movement once full darkness came. They slept in shifts, one at a time, while the other two kept guard. With their locations marked on the map, the choppers would investigate any movement on the ground.

Rush and Chinbroski received permission from their chief to assist in the search until all efforts were exhausted.

Chinbroski got sixteen stitches down the side of his head and planted himself in the corner of the command tent, helping Zeke plot the progress of the search. Because Chinbroski knew the camp and surrounding valley better than any other searcher, Zeke adopted him as his right-hand man.

The night passed uneventfully. No movement except the grid search rotation of the helicopters. Rush, Zeke, and Chinbroski slept in snatches, jerking awake at every crackle of the radio.

The second day the search took on a different attitude. The excitement of pursuit had waned, replaced by determination tainted with doubt. Chinbroski fell silent as he watched the circle on the map, representing the as-yet unsecured area, close in on itself.

Zeke's patience thinned as each update produced nothing new. The camp itself was secured mid-afternoon on day two. Five other spike-filled pits were discovered, seven other explosive devices, but no video cameras or listening equipment. B.J.'s shooting perch from the previous day had not been determined, and by the time the sun dropped below the horizon on the second night, Zeke looked ready to throw his hands up in desperation.

Reinforcements arrived the morning of day three, replacing not only the searchers, but also those who shuttled food and water. The area around the command center was a tent city, with dozens of various sizes and shapes covering both sides of the gravel road. The media contingent was kept a half-mile back, at the mouth of the road leading to camp.

By late afternoon, with replacements in position, Zeke declared the entire valley secured. He looked at Rush and Chinbroski, shrugged his shoulders, and sat down on a stool next to the map table.

"So you're telling us," Chinbroski said, "that he's not in this valley? That every inch has been searched? Every creek bed, every cave, every trench and depression on that map?"

Rush stood next to his partner. Chinbroski's face had become a ragged collection of lines and creases. The dark spots under his eyes were as large as silver dollars and his voice grated like a rusty gate.

Zeke waved his hand over the map and looked hard at Chinbroski. "You've been here the entire time. I've marked the three caves they found, penciled in the progress as it was made. I'm not declaring the search is over, I'm just telling you the valley appears secure for right now."

Chinbroski was frustrated, Rush knew, and rightfully so. They both knew the bloodhounds hadn't hit on a scent in nearly forty-eight hours, knew that B.J.'s truck was still under surveillance, knew that every building had been inspected for a tunnel system.

"We're flying in a team of FBI search specialists to double-check my work," Zeke continued. "Even though I've been on the phone with them every step of the way."

Chinbroski glared at the map, moved his lips silently, and worked both fists as though preparing for a fight. "So what now?" he finally asked.

"Now we start over, except this time from the center out. The replacements will do most of the searching while we double our perimeter strength with the men who've been here from the beginning." Zeke looked at Rush and nodded toward the map. "Anything to add?"

"I can't imagine what." Rush shrugged and glanced at his partner.

"I can't believe he can just disappear like a damn ghost," Chinbroski said after a long silence. He turned to Rush. "I mean, how in the hell did he do it?"

Rush shook his head. Chinbroski had asked that question at least a hundred times over the last three days.

"There was a gap between Cagle shooting you and us getting the perimeter locked down," Zeke said as he stared at the map. He tapped a spot with his pencil, then looked at Chinbroski. "Although I once considered the odds practically nonexistent, he could have slipped through."

His first admission of failure, Rush thought. He'd wondered how long it would take Zeke to admit the obvious. Rush had suspected B.J. had escaped the moment he saw the pile of clothes on the rock. Then, when the dogs found several more piles spread out through the valley, he fully understood the ramifications: diversion. B.J. had planted obstacles with the intent of tying up the dogs. He knew they would key on the first scent offered.

"So cut the bullshit," Chinbroski said to Zeke. "You think he's gone?"

Zeke stared at the map, his face hanging loose with fatigue. He lifted his eyes to Chinbroski and nodded.

"Yes. I think he's gone. The radio mistake cost us. He knew we were coming. Made him shoot early."

Zeke's criticism of Rush's mistake bore no hint of resentment. They had discussed what happened and could do nothing about it now.

Chinbroski walked to the door of the tent and gazed out. Rush could see the activity outside, agents washing up, eating, napping under shade trees. The thumping of rotor blades in the distance reminded Rush that Cagle's escape was not being taken for granted despite his and Zeke's suspicions.

"You've been talking about walking the valley yourself for the last couple of days," Zeke said to Chinbroski. "If you're not satisfied with the search—"

"Come on, Zeke," Chinbroski snapped. He turned toward

the agent and shook his head. "What am I gonna do that ain't already been done?"

Zeke shrugged. "I agree. But since you've seemed intent on going up—"

He shook his head again and rubbed his forehead. "I just can't believe he walked out of here under our noses. Damn it!"

Rush walked over and put a hand on his shoulder. "Let's give it a rest." He turned to Zeke. "We'll be in our tent if anything breaks."

Rush led his partner to the tent they were sharing. Chinbroski said nothing, apparently content to stare at the ground. Although tempted the last three days, Rush had avoided asking Chinbroski about B.J.'s accusations of masterminding the plot to murder everyone in B.J.'s family.

He couldn't think of a tactful way to broach the issue without appearing to take stock in the accusations. So rather than insult his best friend, he'd decided to allow Chinbroski to mention B.J.'s demented ramblings. But he hadn't.

Chinbroski pushed back the flap of their tent, stepped inside, and sat down on one of two stools. Rush took the other. His partner's eyes looked vacant, haunted, as he stared at the ground at Rush's feet.

"I'm quitting the department," Chinbroski said after some time.

This bomb left Rush speechless. Finally, he started to object, but Chinbroski's glare silenced him.

"Nanci and I are getting out."

"I really don't think—"

Again Chinbroski cut him off. "Can I really be sure—" He paused and blew out a breath. With a shaky hand he wiped a bead of sweat from his forehead. "Cagle will know he didn't kill me. Hell, Rush, for all we know, the son-of-a-bitch is already making plans. Would you hang around?"

The pleading in Chinbroski's voice made Rush's throat tighten. In all honesty, Rush couldn't discount the possibility that B.J. had wounded Chinbroski on purpose, knowing he had a foolproof way to escape the mountains, thus throwing Chinbroski into the middle of a psychological mind game lasting years.

Since B.J.'s entire purpose for killing detectives in the other cities was to ensnare Chinbroski in an emotional nightmare, this might be one last effort to drive him over the edge before finally killing him. Rush could almost understand B.J.'s motivation for such a tactic: to fill the void left by the chase, the intrigue, the challenge of matching wits with America's brightest law-enforcement officials.

Rush couldn't honestly answer Chinbroski's question. Men do desperate things to stay alive.

"Like I said three days ago," Chinbroski continued, "I won't fake my death. But I will hide, change my name, whatever it takes to have a normal life with Nanci. I'm not going back to Plano."

I'd probably do the same thing, Rush thought. The thought of B.J. Cagle loose in society made his skin tingle.

"Going to Nanci's mother's lake house," Chinbroski continued. "Outside Kansas City. At least for a few days. We'll pick a place from there. She said she'd have all my stuff packed and shipped. Will you help her, if she needs it?"

"You don't have to ask that." Rush sighed and shook his head. "I can't believe this." He considered this departure in plans. It made sense. Assuming B.J. had indeed escaped, he would eventually hunt for Chinbroski. But that still left Nanci's past.

"Wouldn't you expect Cagle to try and find you through Nanci? You think staying at her mother's lake house is wise?"

"It'll only be for a few days. Just to gather our thoughts. She can do her computer software stuff from anywhere. He'll never find us after that, believe me. Matter of fact, I might actually use him tracking Nanci's background to my advantage. Get my drift?"

"You mean wait for him to show someplace?" Rush asked. "Like her mother's lake house? Nice thought, to lay a trap. But what if he waits five years? Ten? Fifteen?" Rush shook his head. "A man who can disappear into thin air like he has is not going to walk into some trap. And he has to know that the longer he waits, the less likely you'd have something waiting for him."

Chinbroski nodded, looked away, then finally stretched out on the floor of the tent. They were silent until the sun dipped below the horizon.

The FBI search and rescue experts showed on day four and confirmed that everything that could have been done had been. The valley, searched again and again over the next two days, produced nothing new as the effort slowly thinned in manpower and resources. The dogs left first, then three of the six choppers. Nearly half of the FBI agents were sent back to their regular duties, as were all but one rotating deputy from the local sheriff's office. Once the media saw the exodus, they broke camp even faster.

On the morning of day seven, Zeke terminated the search. It took most of that day to break everything down and clear out. Chinbroski had remained faithful to the cause. Despite Rush's insistence, Chinbroski rebuffed suggestions of leaving, claiming dedication to duty. He refused to leave while others searched to his benefit.

Rush suspected another motivation: fear. For as soon as Chinbroski set foot out of the mountains, his old life was done, over, and the hiding would begin in earnest.

Four hours of sunlight remained when Zeke's helicopter left Rush and Chinbroski standing alone just outside the front gate of Camp Indian Hill. The remnants of the searching army lay scattered about the grounds, yet Rush suspected that nature would soon overtake all evidence that anyone had been here at all.

With their gear already stowed inside Rush's repaired city vehicle, Rush turned to his partner and slapped him on the back. "You ready to get the hell out of here? I'm so sick of tents and fast food I can hardly think straight."

"I'm finally ready," Chinbroski said, staring at the mountain peak, home to the flat rock. "Been ready for the last couple of days." He looked over at Rush. "But leaving ain't what I'm talking about."

Walking over to Rush's car, Chinbroski opened the front passenger's door and pulled out the topographical map Zeke had used to track the progress of the search. He then laid it out on the hood of the car.

"What are you ready for?"

"A hike of these mountains." Chinbroski didn't look at Rush, he studied the map.

"You've gotta be kidding me. I've hiked these mountains ten times and asked if you wanted to go every time."

"Wasn't ready then. Now I am."

"Why?"

Chinbroski turned and looked hard at Rush. "Because now everybody else is gone and it's quiet enough to think."

"About what?"

"How he got away."

Rush rolled his eyes and snorted. "You're a lunatic."

"Yeah, I am. Maybe that will help."

"With what?"

"Damn it, Rush. I . . . just want—"

"How will it help, Chin?"

"I don't know. Okay? I don't know." He rolled up the map. "Maybe I'll see something that nobody else noticed. Maybe he left something for me."

Rush looked away for a moment and rubbed his forehead. Time for a reality check. "You don't want to leave, because you know the minute you take one step into the real world you'll be officially admitting defeat. You can't stand the fact that some punk kid you used to know is smarter than you. Well guess what, partner? He's smarter than me, too. And Zeke. Hell, the son-of-a-bitch is smarter than the whole FBI. Let it go. You can prance around in those woods for the next ten years and you still won't know shit about how he escaped."

Chinbroski stood motionless, his jaws working. Rush stared at him and finally shook his head and turned away when his partner refused to comment.

"Go back to Plano," Chinbroski finally said. "I don't care." He spun on his heels, slapped the map against his leg, and walked into Camp Indian Hill with a purpose Rush just couldn't grasp.

Their hike began with a tedious, winding escapade through the camp. After an hour Rush began to wonder if his partner had begun to teeter on the brink of madness. During this series of double-backs, sudden changes in direction, and pauses that sometimes lasted minutes, Chinbroski said nothing. He would occasionally lift his head as if searching his memory for some specific detail, yet not once did he utter a word.

Rush followed at a distance and made as little noise as possible.

Once they left the camp site and entered the woods, Chinbroski's route seemed to become more certain. He fell into even strides and rarely seemed hesitant with his directions. Over the next two hours he stopped several times, unrolled the map, and made a mark with a pencil. Still he said nothing, and Rush continued to grant his wish for enough silence to think.

Halfway up the northern peak, home of the flat rock, Chinbroski suddenly stopped. He looked around, studied the map, tapped it with his pencil, then stared at a spot against the rocky cliff ten yards to his right.

He slowly turned in a complete circle before studying the same spot again for several moments.

Rush leaned against a tree and rubbed the tops of his legs. A mosquito buzzed near his left ear.

Chinbroski looked at the map again and, for the first time in nearly three hours, spoke. "Right over there is where the dogs found one of the piles of clothes. If I'm reading this map right."

Rush nodded. "And . . ."

"And something's missing."

The expression on Chinbroski's face made the hair on Rush's arms stand up.

"What? What's missing?"

"A cave." He pointed at the rocky wall of the mountain. "It ain't on the map, but neither were the other three caves the searchers found. I asked Zeke about that, you know— would small caves show up on a topographical map. He checked with the state and they said they probably wouldn't."

Rush wasn't getting it. "So how—"

"I was in that cave, Rush. And there's absolutely no doubt that I'm at the right spot. It's the same cave where I played a joke on B.J. Stacked rocks against the opening while he was inside. Scared the shit out of him."

Chinbroski looked at him, his eyes wide. "Now it's gone."

And suddenly Rush got it.

CHAPTER NINETEEN

Rush stepped behind the tree he'd been leaning against and peered around the edge toward the rocky cliff. "You're absolutely sure?" he whispered.

Chinbroski had retreated even farther away, choosing to crouch behind a large boulder to Rush's right. "Yes," Chinbroski whispered back. "Of all the places in these woods, B.J. and me passed by here the most. Must've walked by here dozens of times."

Rush considered that piece of information for a moment. "That's good news for you, then."

"Why?"

"Because Cagle thinks he killed you. He'd have never wounded you on purpose and risked having you participate in the search. For this very reason."

Chinbroski said nothing.

This area of the mountain was as rugged as any spot in the entire valley. Rush, Zeke, and several other searchers had stood at this very spot after the searchers discovered the pile of clothes.

"So he put the clothes at all the other locations to mask this spot," Rush said. "If he entered the cave somewhere near here, the scent would be explained away by the presence of the clothes." He shook his head. "He's a bright son-of-a-bitch."

"Think he knows we're out here?"

Rush had already given that some thought. "No. Here's why. First, the FBI did a frequency search of the entire area. Remember Zeke talking about that? No wireless transmitters, no microwave stuff, nothing. Second, if Cagle knew he might have to spend weeks in there, he wouldn't risk planting microphones anywhere outside the cave for fear of them being found."

"Right," Chinbroski added. "His goal was to make us think he got out. If we found anything outside the cave, we'd only look closer."

"Exactly. But I'll bet he's *receiving* signals."

It must have taken a moment for Chinbroski to catch Rush's meaning. "You're talking radio or TV," he finally said. "He's gonna wait until the media says the search has been called off."

"Right," Rush said. "And if I were him, I'd get out quick after it's over."

"Why?"

" 'Cause he was a cop. That's when we're most vulnerable, and he'll know it."

Chinbroski's silence prompted Rush to explain further. "It's human nature, Chin. How many cops stop searching a suspect once they find a weapon, never figuring there'd be another one? We constantly let our guard down. B.J. knows that everyone out here left tired, homesick, and dejected. At this very moment we're exposing our underbelly. Our guard is down. And he'll take advantage."

With only an hour of sunlight left, Rush knew they'd be at a serious disadvantage shortly.

"Any other way into that cave?" Rush asked.

"Don't know. We never explored the damn thing 'cause B.J. wouldn't go in after my little prank."

So, Rush thought, there's no way to know how far back it goes. He had another thought. "Chin, you say Zeke marked three caves on that map?"

"Yeah."

"How close are they?"

The map rattled as Chinbroski checked. "Two on the other side of the valley. The third about eighty yards, around the back side of this mountain."

"So it's possible B.J. already had this entrance blocked off, entered from the other cave, and created a cave-in somewhere in the center to lock himself in."

"Wouldn't he cut off his air supply?" Chinbroski asked, reading Rush's mind.

"Maybe not. If there's a large cavern, he might survive weeks. But to hell with all that," Rush said. "We're wasting daylight. The question is where he'll come out. What do you think?"

Chinbroski rattled the map as he considered. Deep shadows now draped the woods. The rock wall in front of them appeared impenetrable. A whippoorwill cried somewhere behind them.

"If he made a cave-in," Chinbroski said, "wouldn't he just dig himself out?"

"If I knew that, I'd send you home and just ambush the bastard."

"You're wanting us to split up," Chinbroski said. "One stay here, one take the cave?"

"You have a better idea? Maybe call Zeke and his boys back?"

"I ain't even gonna honor that with a response."

"I hoped you wouldn't," Rush said. "Listen, we need some of our stuff from the car. You wanna go?"

"Could you find your way back, if you go?"

Rush thought about that. "Probably."

"I'll go. Then I'll take the cave because that's where he'll probably come out."

Payback time. If Chinbroski hadn't wanted the cave, Rush would have been worried.

"I'll be back before dark," Chinbroski said, stepping out from behind his rock. "If you see him, empty your magazine."

It took Chinbroski less than forty minutes to make the trek to and from the car. He carried the rifle B.J. hadn't destroyed, both backpacks, and ballistic vests. The sun had disappeared behind the mountains and darkness would overtake them within the next twenty minutes.

"Your radio and extra batteries are in the backpack," Chinbroski said, setting Rush's pack at his feet. "Not much food or water, but enough to last until tomorrow evening."

"The night vision goggles in here?"

"Yeah. And the electronic earmuffs." Chinbroski looked skyward and shook his head. "I need to haul ass to that cave before it gets too dark. You pick a spot yet?"

Rush had. Down the hill about fifteen yards, behind a rock outcrop. He pointed it out. "Use your radio earpiece and neck mike, in case we need to whisper to each other. Sure you don't want to call Zeke?"

"Cagle wanted us up here alone, right? Well, the bastard got his wish. Except this time the table is turned. No, we ain't calling Zeke."

As Chinbroski geared up, Rush carried his backpack to his rock outcropping. "You keeping the rifle?" he asked his partner.

345

"Yep. You broke yours. Besides, it's ambush time. And it's my turn. Soon as he steps foot out of that cave, he's history."

Rush strapped on his vest, clipped the radio to his belt, adjusted his earpiece and neck mike, then conducted a radio check with Chinbroski.

"You need to walk with me over to the cave," Chinbroski said. "So you can view the body once it's all over."

"Right. You mean so I can pull your ass out of the fire." Rush covered his backpack with dried leaves, then walked over to join his partner. "Let's go."

Chinbroski led the way. They hiked sideways across the face of the mountain. Chinbroski stopped twice and held the map up to the dying sunlight. Rush spotted a deer path down below them that led in same direction and pointed it out. Chinbroski put the map away and dropped down onto the path.

They hiked for another few yards when Chinbroski suddenly stopped and pointed through the trees on his left. Not more than ten yards away, nearly hidden under the deep shadows of a cliff, the cave opening was a jagged hole less than four feet wide. A thick tangle of brush guarded the entrance, further obscuring the opening. Directly above the mouth of the cave there was a flat granite platform large enough to stretch out on.

Chinbroski inspected the area in the fading sunlight and seemed to come to a decision. "I'll wait up there," he whispered, pointing to the rock above the cave. "And when he comes out, I'll rip his head off and shit down his neck." He stalked over to the cave, quietly placed his gear on the platform, and climbed up, careful to make no noise.

Rush turned on his radio, motioned for Chinbroski to do

the same, and whispered back, "I'll double-click you when I'm in position."

Chinbroski gave a thumbs-up, and Rush turned back.

He found his way back to his perch without difficulty. His eyes had fully adjusted to the darkness of the woods. He estimated that he could reach Chinbroski in under two minutes if need be.

He wondered if Chinbroski would hear any digging noises drifting from the cave during the night. If B.J. had entombed himself at one end of the cave, and if he eventually dug himself out, it made more sense to come out on Chinbroski's side, where he could work in absolute blackness, and where, once he did surface, he could do so without disturbing the natural landscape. That exit would also allow him to be ready to fight if confronted.

To come out on Rush's side would be a more dangerous and difficult proposition. B.J. would be forced to remove the dirt and rock used to hide the mouth of the cave. Not only would that be loud, it would also disturb the appearance of the mountain and leave him vulnerable to attack.

So all logic pointed toward Chinbroski making first contact. That is why Rush found himself on edge. That crafty son-of-a-bitch *never* did what they expected.

As Rush settled back against the boulder, making sure he could see the wall of the cliff where B.J. might exit, he noticed the night sounds slowly intensifying. With all the sounds magnified by his electronic earmuffs, the crickets, the hoot owl in the distance, and the two whippoorwills, who alternated the same tune, all seemed closer than they really were. Off to his right, leaves rustled momentarily before the noise resumed down the mountain.

Rush double-clicked his radio and got a return click a moment later. Chinbroski wouldn't talk on the radio unless he had to. Both believed that unnecessary radio traffic could get you killed. And tonight it was doubly true. Neither could pay attention to their surroundings if distracted by needless banter, and their voices, even a whisper, might give away their element of surprise.

Rush couldn't help wonder if B.J. already knew they were here. The bastard had thought of every possible contingency for capture, and to think he might be caught by a couple of detectives sitting on their asses stretched Rush's imagination. He also wondered if Chinbroski was mistaken about the location of a cave entrance he hadn't seen in almost thirty years. Everything depended, assuming B.J. was in fact hiding inside this mountain, on how strongly B.J. believed he had killed Chinbroski.

Then Rush wondered something else: how B.J. had gotten into his hiding place. The cave entrance Chinbroski believed once existed appeared as though it had never been there. The rocks imbedded in the dirt and the weeds growing against the rocky wall, were signs that B.J. had covered it up years ago. If he had, it stood to reason that he would've prepared an entrance point similarly disguised. Could he have created a cave-in during the small amount of time between shooting Chinbroski and the searchers finding the cave? Rush didn't know. But what he did know was that he and Chinbroski wouldn't last for much longer than a day or two out in these woods.

Rush didn't realize he had fallen asleep until he jerked awake. Disoriented momentarily, he held his breath and froze. Then he heard the noise that had evidently awakened him. The scratching noise, somewhere in front of him, sounded like the blade of a knife against wood.

The whippoorwills had fallen silent, the crickets, likewise.

Rush leaned forward, turned up the volume on his electronic earmuffs, and cocked his right ear toward the noise. More than just scratching, a thumping sound preceded each scrape. And the sound seemed to be rising, floating toward the sky.

He couldn't determine the distance, although it seemed close. He removed his microphone-enhanced earmuffs to get a better gauge of the noise. Still in front of him, still rising. And the sound seemed muffled now, obscured in some way.

Sitting perfectly still, scarcely breathing, Rush searched the darkness in front of him but saw nothing that didn't belong. As quietly as possible, he strapped on his night vision goggles. But the green world now in front of him offered no clue as to the origin of the sounds.

Metal scraping against wood. Rush was certain of the sound. The thumping noise sounded hollow, as though coming from a large tube. The tops of the tree branches rustled in the mild breeze, and the scraping continued.

Then an unnatural movement caught his eye. Twenty yards directly in front of him, a large, dead tree vibrated in rhythm with the thumping. The top of the tree was no more than twenty feet above the ground and narrowed slightly at the top. There were no branches and the top was jagged, as though once struck by lightning, causing the top half to rip away.

The bastard was climbing out the center of a hollow tree! Rush sat mesmerized as the tree vibrated more violently the closer B.J. got to the top. He quietly drew his .45 and rested it on his lap. To make any noise now and risk scaring B.J. back into the cave might prove disastrous. Rush wanted no part of having to follow him down his hollow log into God knows what waited beneath the earth.

Rush held his breath as a hand gripped the top of the tree

and the top of a head appeared. When B.J.'s entire head cleared the tree, Rush saw that B.J. was wearing night vision goggles, too.

The rock outcrop hid some of Rush's body, but not enough. As B.J. inspected the terrain beneath him, Rush quietly slid behind full cover.

But he made some noise. Rush's foot kicked a pile of leaves just before snapping a small stick.

And the woods became as still as a cemetery. Nothing from B.J.'s tree; no rustling noises, no scrapes, no breathing. Cagle didn't know what he'd just heard, Rush knew. He'd been looking away, then probably snapped his head around at the breaking twig. But Rush had been hidden by then, he was sure of it.

Twin beads of sweat trickled down the bridge of Rush's nose. He didn't dare breathe or adjust his feet or move in any way. Not until B.J. resumed climbing out of the tree. His hands quivered. Can't screw this up. Can't let him get away.

A hundred thoughts crowded Rush's mind, most prevalent of which was to simply jump out and kill this bastard. For Mallory. He wanted to. More than anything else in the world, he wanted to. And who would blame him? Rush would *never* encounter a more ruthless son-of-a-bitch than B.J. Cagle. And certainly none better prepared. America's most wanted criminal was less than twenty yards away. He swallowed hard at the prospect of failure. Murder. It'd be so easy.

But could he kill Cagle and sleep at night? Legally, that wasn't an issue at all. But murder was a tricky thing. To do it right, one needed some quality preparation time. And standing out in the woods behind a rock with ninety-nine other things crammed inside your head didn't qualify as quality preparation time. Forensics, ballistics, trace evidence, witnesses, any or all could spell doom.

They could hide B.J.'s body in the cave, Rush knew. But could they guarantee it'd never be found? Zeke knew that Rush and Chinbroski were the last to leave this valley.

Zeke. That was the biggest reason of all *not* to kill B.J. Rush wanted nothing more than to deliver the FBI's most wanted criminal to the FBI's most arrogant agent. Despite Rush and Zeke's recent truce, Rush remembered how quickly Zeke had locked Plano PD out of the investigation once B.J. had barricaded himself inside his barn.

"I did in three weeks what you couldn't do in three years," is what Rush would tell him.

The drops of sweat dripped off the end of Rush's nose.

And he waited, marveling at B.J.'s patience. It must have been a full five minutes before Rush finally heard several seconds of rustling and then the familiar sound of metal against wood. When the rhythm of B.J.'s descent indicated he was well on his way to planting his feet on the ground, Rush slowly leaned sideways and got a clear look. Like a telephone lineman, the bastard wore leg braces with side spikes and a large leather belt around his waist that encircled the tree. He had a rifle strapped to his back and a pistol on his hip. His head was in constant motion, scanning the forest around him.

Rush waited until B.J. was halfway down before he made his move. Needing to notify Chinbroski, Rush pushed the transmit button on his radio, jumped out from behind his rock, and pointed his .45 at B.J.

"Police officer! Keep your hands where I can see them!" Rush released the transmit button, and gripped his pistol with both hands as he advanced.

B.J. spun his head around and froze, both hands on the leather belt.

Rush stopped ten yards from the tree. "If you move, and I mean one sliver, I'll empty this .45 into your ass and dump

351

your body back into your hole."

"Well, I'll be," B.J. said after a moment, a slight grin forming at the edges of his mouth. "Detective Rush. How could I ever forget that voice?"

They must have both heard Chinbroski crashing through the woods at the same time.

B.J. cocked his head in that direction and grinned even wider. "I missed Stubs, didn't I? Was it a clean miss or a graze? 'Cause I saw him fall, saw blood on the side of the pool." He looked back at Rush. "I'll be damned, first time for everything, I guess. He's the only one who would've known that I hid the entrance to the cave."

Rush pushed his transmit button. "Take your time, Chin, I have him covered."

Chinbroski's approach grew louder. "Don't kill him until I get there," Rush heard through his radio earpiece.

"So I'm caught," B.J. said. "Doomed for a dungeon. You think that'd be better than death?"

"Your choice, asshole. I don't give a shit either way." Rush considered removing his night vision goggles because he was having trouble picking up the front sight of his .45. But it'd probably get him killed.

"On the other hand, my trial would rival O.J.'s in media coverage. I'm quite popular." B.J. adjusted his hands, moving them toward the tree.

"Another minute," Chinbroski transmitted, as his frantic crashing through the woods grew louder.

"I assume it's just the two of you," B.J. said. "I saw on the news that Zeke-The-FBI-Man had called everything off."

"Easier to cover up your murder that way," Rush said. "I'm gonna let Chinbroski decide."

Though brief, Rush saw a flicker of emotion wrinkle B.J.'s brow. If Zeke's profile was correct, and B.J. had the mental makeup of an assassin, the prospect of death might be an acceptable conclusion. That meant he'd try to shoot his way out. Rush swallowed hard.

Chinbroski suddenly burst through some underbrush and stopped on the other side of B.J.'s tree. His night vision goggles hanging around his neck, rifle strapped to his back, .45 clutched in both hands, he wiped his forehead against the sleeve of his shirt and looked up. "You gotta be shitting me."

"Stubs, Stubs, Stubs. I can't believe I missed. Looks like you win again."

B.J.'s voice, his mannerisms, were so calm that Rush wondered if the bastard might have something else up his sleeve. Rush adjusted the grip of his pistol and glanced at his partner.

Chinbroski began moving toward Rush, his gun trained on B.J.

"Are you going to take me into custody, Stubs? Or murder me and hide my body? If you do, you couldn't tell anyone and I'll never be seen again. That would add to my national mystique, balloon my hero status. I'll be forever known as the man who outsmarted them all." He laughed then, an arrogant cackle that sent a chill down Rush's neck.

Chinbroski took a step forward. "How about this, dick head? I shoot you in the spine right above your shoulders and you can suck your meals through a straw for the rest of your life."

B.J.'s cackle faded into the silence of the woods.

"I want you to slowly remove your night vision goggles and drop them," Rush said. "Chin, if he makes any kind of funny movements, light him up."

"Count on it."

Lifting both hands from his leather belt, B.J. carefully removed the night vision and let it drop.

"Now the rifle," Rush commanded. "Don't touch the

weapon, handle it by the strap."

"You want me to drop my masterpiece?" B.J. asked with a note of incredibility. "You can't be serious."

"Drop it now!" Chinbroski screamed.

B.J. held up both hands. "Hey, man, calm down." He slipped the rifle sling over his head and dangled the weapon as low as he could, before dropping it to the base of the tree.

"Now your pistol," Rush said. "Reach around with your left hand, grab it by the grip, and toss it overboard."

B.J. complied.

Chinbroski ran over to the base of the tree and retrieved the weapons. Then he walked over and stood next to Rush.

"It's your call," Rush told him. "Dead or alive?"

"Might as well kill me, too," B.J. said. "It'd give you the complete set."

Chinbroski snorted. "I didn't do anything to your family. Why do you think that?"

"Because it's true. You tapped our phone for years, opened our mail, searched our house while we slept."

"I did all this *before* killing your mother?"

"And more. I could never prove it, but I know. I suspected it for years, all through high school. My mother didn't believe me. Sent me to a doctor, some prick who told her I was delusional."

"He pegged it," Chinbroski said.

"But I saw you!" B.J. shouted, his voice echoing through the woods.

Chinbroski glanced at Rush. "What in the hell are you talking about? You saw me where?"

"Inside my house. My junior year of high school. You jumped out of my bedroom window in the middle of the night. I woke up and saw you!"

"You're a lunatic! And what happened here all those years

ago didn't make you that way."

"You ruined my life," B.J. said in a near-whisper. "It all started here. And it'll end here. It's what I planned for. To kill you here."

"Yeah? Well you had your chance. And now it's over."

B.J. repositioned himself and grimaced. "This belt is cutting the shit out of my back. Can I come down now, or are you gonna make me stay up here all night?"

Rush glanced at his partner.

"Come down," Chinbroski said. "Slowly. As soon as your feet hit the ground, lock your fingers on top of your head."

B.J. leaned forward, maneuvered the belt down, and one foot at a time slapped his spiked shoes into the tree, each foot lower than the next.

Rush and Chinbroski moved closer to the tree, both still aiming their .45's. Their distance was less than five yards from B.J. when his feet hit the ground and he did the unimaginable.

Fast as a blur, B.J. planted his feet, leaned into the tree, and spun around to the opposite side, disappearing behind the three-foot trunk. Rush went left, Chinbroski right. Just as Rush caught a glimpse of him, an explosion threw Rush onto his back.

The deafening roar and blinding flash came from in front of the tree, Rush and Chinbroski's side. Percussion grenade, flash-bang, diversionary device. Same thing SWAT cops used after kicking in a door.

Rush was blind. The flash had flared Rush's night vision goggles. He ripped them off. Better, but still almost blind, nothing but shadows.

Gunshots. From two guns. Close. Chinbroski yelled, grunted. More gunshots. Fighting to see, knowing he needed to move, Rush rolled left, putting the tree between him and where he suspected B.J. to be.

Movement, more gunshots, muzzle flash directly ahead. Rush took aim, but couldn't see his target. Was it B.J.? Couldn't shoot his partner.

Chinbroski yelled out again, in pain, several feet to Rush's right.

Shoot the shadow directly ahead! But he couldn't see it now. Rush screamed. The shadow moved. More muzzle flashes. Dirt exploded around Rush's feet. He scrambled to get into firing position.

Chinbroski cursed and fired. B.J. spun around and fired back.

Rush caught enough movement to get a target. He fired until his gun went dry. A body slapped against the tree and collapsed. Rush rolled, slammed a new magazine into his gun, climbed to his feet, and waited for his eyes to adjust.

Only Chinbroski was moving. He moaned and sat up, gripping his left shoulder. Rush stepped out from behind the tree, kicked away the gun that lay near B.J.'s feet, then handcuffed his limp body. The only wound Rush noticed was a hole in the center of B.J.'s forehead. He quickly inspected the back of his head. No exit wound; the bullet had lodged. He'd put a bullet in his brain, like he'd promised Mallory.

"He dead?" Chinbroski asked.

"No. You okay?"

"I'll live."

Rush grabbed B.J.'s handcuffs with both hands. Then his whole body shook from the adrenaline dump. "I swear to you, Chin. I ain't letting go of this son-of-a-bitch until he's behind bars."

Chinbroski climbed to his feet and slapped Rush on the

back. "Do me a favor, partner. Don't."

It was nearly a month before all the moons aligned sufficiently and Rush and Chinbroski made the trip to the federal prison in Ft. Worth, Texas. In addition to the paperwork surrounding the capture and subsequent shooting of B.J. Cagle, Chinbroski had gotten married and honeymooned. And after a quiet ceremony in his living room for Mallory, with only Daniel present to mourn with him, Rush took a two-week sabbatical on a beach in Florida, during which time B.J. underwent brain surgery at taxpayers' expense.

Housed in the prison infirmary, reports were that B.J.'s brain had about as much life as the tree he'd climbed out of just before being shot. But, like B.J.'s alleged death at the farmhouse, Chinbroski insisted on seeing his nemesis with his own eyes.

Zeke had cleared the visit with prison authorities the previous afternoon, and within minutes of parking, they found themselves whisked through the labyrinth of hallways and taken straight to B.J.'s small hospital cell.

A report Zeke faxed to Rush earlier that morning explained in layman's terms the extent of B.J.'s injury. In short, B.J. would never again be able to connect outside stimuli with a coherent internal thought. Mush. Melting ice cream. A fate worse than death? Rush hadn't yet decided.

When a guard opened the door to B.J.'s cell, they found him sitting in a chair next to the bed.

"Well, I'll be damned," Chinbroski said. "Looks almost normal."

B.J. was dressed in prison garb and white slip-ons, hair combed, cleanly shaven. An angry scar from the bullet wound in the middle of his forehead was still pink and puffy. Hands folded on his lap, B.J.'s eyes were dull, as though someone had turned off a light switch inside his head. Zeke had told Rush that physical therapists would work with B.J. daily to prevent muscle atrophy.

"So he can eat?" Chinbroski asked.

Rush nodded. "He can chew and swallow, sip from a straw. Zeke believes it's some ingrained survival function. See, he can blink, too."

Chinbroski walked over and knelt in front of B.J.'s chair, waved a hand in front of his face. "Know what this reminds me of?" he said, looking back at Rush.

"What?"

"Reminds me of when he used to shoot."

Rush frowned. "What do you mean?"

"He used to get in a bubble before he took a shot. Somehow, he went to a place inside his head and blocked everything out. I used to tell him that if I jumped on his back while he was shooting, he'd never know." Chinbroski turned back to B.J. and waved a hand in front of his face again.

After a moment he climbed to his feet. "So he'll be transferred soon?" he asked Rush. "That what Zeke said?"

"Yeah. Another week or two. A facility for the criminally insane. This place isn't set up for long-term care."

Chinbroski nodded. "So he'll never stand trial."

"No."

"Think he feels pain? Think if I walked over and kicked him in the nuts, he'd flinch or something?"

Rush rolled his eyes and said nothing.

"Maybe they'll do some more brain surgery on him. Experiment. Make him a lab rat." Chinbroski chuckled.

"Yeah, what if it worked?" Rush asked. "And he came back a different man? Remembered nothing? And a jury let him off?"

The smile died on Chinbroski's face. "Don't talk shit like that."

"Then let's just leave him like he is. I don't want some doctor trying to fix him."

They both fell silent. Rush looked at the frail man in the chair, hands folded so politely in his lap, and could hardly believe that he'd been the source of the deepest terror Rush had ever felt. Just the memory made the hair on his arms stand up.

Chinbroski laughed, a sudden burst.

"What?" Rush said.

"Just had a weird thought, is all." He laughed again and looked at Rush. "Just wondered if B.J. is in his special place right now." He tapped his temple. "Up here. You know, just faking all this."

"Huh," Rush said, looking from Chinbroski to B.J. "I'd say that'd be impossible."

It was then that Rush thought he saw a flicker in B.J.'s eyes.

ABOUT THE AUTHOR

Steve Copling has over twenty-five years in law enforcement and corporate security. He currently serves as a police lieutenant at the Plano, Texas police department. His sixteen years of investigative experience include stints in the Narcotics Unit, juvenile and property crimes, Internal Affairs, and five years in the corporate field. He has been a rifle instructor for seventeen years and served for several years as a marksman in the Tactical Unit.

Steve lives in a small north Texas town with his wife of twenty-eight years, has three wonderful sons, and one beautiful grandson.